# PRAISE FOR LAURA SPINELLA

## PRAISE FOR *GHOST GIFTS*

"An engaging writing voice, realistic characters, and a compelling mystery make this a must-read! Aubrey and Levi are compelling and likable, both individually and as a team, and the way their stories intersect increases the appeal. Just the right blend of emotion and humor combine with captivating suspense for a paranormal mystery that is sure to delight fans. The flashbacks heighten the tension and deepen the poignancy, and the romantic angle has a great slow-burn passion."

—*RT Book Reviews* (4.5 stars)

"A wild adventure of a mystery, brimming with layers, secrets, and more than one person who should feel guilty . . . Paranormal mystery/romance fans will find a gem of a story in Laura Spinella's *Ghost Gifts*."

—*Fresh Fiction*

"*Ghost Gifts* transcends labels like 'murder mystery' or 'love story' or 'ghost tale,' giving readers a masterful plot that weaves effortlessly between past and present, sharply pivoting whenever you think you've put your finger on it. The characters and setting come to life so vividly that you'll forget you're reading a book. Laura Spinella's *Ghost Gifts* is an absolute treasure."

—David Ellis, #1 *New York Times* bestselling author

# PRAISE FOR *FORETOLD*

## AMAZON EDITORS' PICK, A BEST BOOK OF THE MONTH

"Laura Spinella has created a captivating heroine in Aubrey Ellis. Be prepared to believe in her psychic gift. *Foretold* bridges suspense and romance, making an intricate journey between the past and present. Unexpected twists from the dead kept me reading late into the night. I loved it."

—Kendra Elliot, *Wall Street Journal* bestselling author

"In the highly anticipated sequel to her bestselling *Ghost Gifts*, Laura Spinella entrances the reader with another suspenseful tale full of mystery and secrets. *Foretold* artfully weaves the past and present, bound together by otherworldly 'gifts' that, in various forms, often come at a grave price. A fast-paced read with a jaw-dropping twist that I never saw coming."

—Kristina McMorris, *New York Times* bestselling author, *The Edge of Lost*

# PRAISE FOR *ECHO MOON*

"Enthralling and imaginative, where the past intertwines with the present, Spinella masterfully delivers in the third and final installment of her Ghost Gift trilogy. *Echo Moon* is filled with suspense, mystery, and romance, and kept me turning the pages and on my toes until the very end, an ending I didn't see coming. I love unexpected twists! Fans, new and old, as *Echo Moon* can easily stand on its own, will devour Peter St John's story. I sure did."

—Kerry Lonsdale, Amazon Charts and *Wall Street Journal* bestselling author

"A powerful love story in its own right, *Echo Moon* offers a stunning and deeply satisfying conclusion to the Ghost Gifts trilogy. Every thread in the series effortlessly weaves together; every question you didn't realize needed asking, is answered. As Pete St John, now an acclaimed war photojournalist, runs from both his lives—in 1917 and the present—Laura Spinella, who creates gloriously complex, tortured heroes, also proves herself to be a master of historical fiction. My advice? Cancel your weekend plans and read *Ghost Gifts*, *Foretold*, and *Echo Moon* back-to-back."

—Barbara Claypole White, bestselling author of *The Perfect Son* and *The Promise Between Us*

"I highly recommend *Echo Moon* for readers of historical, contemporary and paranormal romance. Spinella is a masterful writer who weaves all these elements together into a story full of plot twists and memorable characters."

—Debbie Herbert, author of *Charmed and Dangerous*

## PRAISE FOR *UNSTRUNG*

"In Spinella's wrenching tale of love and loss, one woman must come to terms with her past and the decisions that have shaped her life. Spinella has filled her incredibly emotional novel with multifaceted characters, and nothing is as simple as it seems in this true page-turner."

—*Publishers Weekly* (starred review)

"Every character is a work in progress, which makes this tale extremely realistic."

—*RT Book Reviews*

# ECHO
# MOON

# ALSO BY LAURA SPINELLA

## Ghost Gifts Novels

*Ghost Gifts*
*Foretold*

## Other Titles

*Unstrung*
*Perfect Timing*
*Beautiful Disaster*

# Writing as L.J. Wilson

# Clairmont Series Novels

*Ruby Ink*
*The Mission*

# ECHO MOON

## LAURA SPINELLA

Published by Montlake Romance, Seattle

www.apub.com

Amazon, the Amazon logo, and Montlake Romance are trademarks of Amazon.com, Inc., or its affiliates.

ISBN-13: 9781503901131
ISBN-10: 1503901130

Cover design by Jason Blackburn

Cover photography by Chrissy Wiley

Printed in the United States of America

Dock, Foot of Gillette Avenue.                    Bayport, L. I.

*When I spent two weeks on this beach,*
*I didn't think of you then. E M*

*If Paris is France,*
*then Coney Island,*
*between June and September,*
*is the World.*

*—George C. Tilyou*

*Author's note: The Elephantine Colossus burned down in 1896. I've chosen to re-create and let stand this Coney Island attraction for the purposes of this story.*

*To Karin Gillespie, critique partner extraordinaire.
I am grateful for your fortitude, friendship, and faith,
sticking it out novel after novel. Thank you for sharing
your literary sixth sense, for cheering me on, for always
telling me what works, and more importantly, for
telling me what doesn't. For forever making me laugh
and lending me your invaluable easygoing nature.*

## ACT I, SCENE I
## BROOKLYN, NEW YORK
## 1917

"Silence! The spirit world demands silence!" Oscar Bodette pressed his hand to the air as if placing a finger to the lips of each audience member. They obeyed. "If the Amazing Miss Moon is to connect with a world beyond this one, she will require your cooperation." Mystified hums surged. "Please! I beg of you, in hopes that Miss Moon can reach to the stars and what's beyond!"

Oscar arched his arm like a rainbow, another gesture Esmerelda knew from behind her closed eyes. She sat perched on a throne as bejeweled as the gown she wore, which flowed like the heavens around her. From a catatonic state, she pulled erect. On her head, she balanced a Louis XV crown fashioned of paste gems and trailing beads. Esmerelda opened her eyes and stared like a china doll into the hushed audience. Her strawberry-blonde hair fell in a wavy cascade, enhancing her bewitching pose. It was a good-size crowd, at least twenty deep. Oscar pivoted fast, his arm a divining rod aimed at the chosen man. "You, sir!"

"Me?" A well-dressed patron stepped forward.

"No. Not you." The divining rod became a fan, Oscar waving him off. "Miss Moon sees that gentleman! The departed loved one connected to his soul." He wagged his finger passionately. "Behind you."

"You mean me?" a different man said.

"Yes!" Esmerelda announced. She placed her hands, as if casting a spell, over a glass globe. "The spirit of your beloved wife greets you from beyond the grave. She beckons to me now." Speaking in a monotone voice, Esmerelda lurched about as if this spirit might be making a bodily invasion. "Anna." She was loud and exact, her small brow scrunching.

"Good heavens. That's right!" the man cried.

"Of course it is, sir," Oscar said. "Miss Moon is never wrong. Come forward." The man, who walked with a pronounced limp, made his way onto the stage, helped by two men who appeared from the wings. "Miss Moon, what is your message for . . . ?"

"Thomas," Esmerelda said.

"Good heavens! That's right too." Thomas dotted himself with the sign of the cross.

"Naturally, sir. The Amazing Miss Moon is communicating with your dead wife, who would surely know your name." Oscar looked to Esmerelda. "And what is Anna's message for young Thomas?"

"Anna says . . . she says . . ." Her tone strained to a climax and she stared into the ball. "She says she misses you a great deal, and she hopes the children are fine."

"Fine as they can be without their beloved mama." Thomas removed his cap from his head and covered his heart with it. "Does Anna say anything else?"

"Why, yes. She does." Esmerelda sat taller and turned her crowned head smoothly, her gaze tracking Thomas. "Anna says you will forever miss her, but that you'll live a long life. That you should take the children and move to your mother's in Minnesota."

"I've been thinking I should do that! Did Anna really say I should?"

"It's a certainty," Oscar said. "How else would the Amazing Miss Moon know your family hails from Minnesota?" Noises of agreement rose from the crowd. "Miss Moon, does she bring forward other insights from beyond heaven's gate?"

"Only that Thomas shouldn't be too hard on young Edgar. The lad merely misses his departed mother. A switch for not bringing in firewood is too much."

The man looked sheepishly at the floor.

"Anna, she . . . wait!" Esmerelda cupped her hand to her ear. "She grows fainter. Thomas's dear wife tells me that he's endured enough hardship. Good fortune is also in his future." Esmerelda announced the last part with renewed fervor. "Anna promises it." The filled hall whooped into a frenzied roar, clapping and cheering. Esmerelda slumped back in the chair. "That is all. She is gone."

Oscar removed his straw boater hat and held it out. Thomas dropped in a silver coin. "Why, thank you, friend," Oscar said, his expression tinted with surprise. "The price of admission was enough, but tokens of gratitude are most appreciated."

The same men who had appeared from the wings assisted the limping Thomas down from the stage. "Who is next?" Oscar boomed. He pointed. "Madam. Miss Moon and her otherworldly gifts, they seek you out!"

The woman drew a handkerchief to her mouth; the man beside her steadied an arm. Oscar touched fingertips to his forehead as if willing forward information. "I believe Miss Moon sees . . . she sees . . ."

Esmerelda had fallen into another trance. She opened her eyes to see Oscar twist toward her, his own eyes shut tight. "I see a child. A daughter," she said.

Oscar shook his head in a terse stroke, mouthing "sister."

"No, wait . . ." Esmerelda fluttered her fingers as if they danced with the spirit world. She basked in a dramatic pause. "It's a sister. Sally's younger sister."

"That's right," Oscar said in a low voice.

"You know my name—and my Tilly! You see my sweet Tilly?" As the woman from the audience confirmed the spirit, earthly utterances of astonishment rose.

"Yes," Esmerelda said. "I'm also seeing . . ." She rolled her eyes high, lids fluttering like snapped roller shades. "Parents."

"But just our mother."

"That's right," Esmerelda quickly agreed.

"She went to heaven on the Spanish flu last winter."

"As did your sister, Tilly." The odds were overwhelming, and Esmerelda went with them. It had been her own mother's fate. Sally sobbed into her husband's tweed jacket. Her other hand remained gripped over her abdomen. "Your mother, she always called your sister by her Christian name, Matilda."

"Well, Mother was Jewish."

Esmerelda traded a panicked glance with Oscar.

"Although, Tilly was named after my aunt on my father's side," Sally said. "They're from Kansas—and Lutherans."

"Correct!" Esmerelda exclaimed. "And so it's your sister's Christian name I'm hearing."

"What else?" The woman's desperate tone tugged on Esmerelda's heart.

"She, um . . . she says she loves you a great deal and . . ." Esmerelda homed in on the woman's hand, still clutching her stomach. She drilled two fingers to her temple and cocked her head. "Tilly says she'd be so pleased if you named the forthcoming child for her."

"How do you know . . . ?"

Esmerelda smiled and Oscar threw her a searing glare. The woman's hand moved from her stomach and pressed against her wet cheek.

"I haven't even told Wallace yet. I wanted to wait longer, until . . ."

"You're not serious?" Wallace's accidental timing was impeccable. Stunned murmurs traveled the hall. Oscar cleared his throat, instructing the couple to come forward. They made their way onto the stage, and the man looked at Esmerelda with godly awe. "We thought sure Sally couldn't do it. She's lost so many babies. So this one will make it?

You're telling us that?" They were stage left now, their anxious faces so close and real.

"I . . . saying for certain, it's, well . . ."

"But the sign out front. It says that's what you do—speak to those who have passed and tell the future." Wallace pointed to the spot where Thomas had stood. "You and your crystal ball knew to tell that other fellow to go to Minnesota."

"She did indeed." Oscar approached the couple, his large hand resting firmly on the man's shoulder. "Naturally, the child will come to term. A sure blessing." He turned to Esmerelda, who exhaled and eased back on her throne. "Have the sister . . . and mother figures retreated, Miss Moon?"

"They have," she insisted.

Oscar took a step back, bowing low with his hat extended. Wallace dug deep into his pocket and placed a few coins in the hat. His stunned expression clung to Esmerelda, who hadn't recovered enough to slip into another trance. "Thank you. Thank you so much, Miss Moon. You've no idea what it means to Sally and me. After all this time—a child."

"Yes . . . yes . . ." Oscar shooed the couple offstage. The same two men appeared, escorting them back to the audience. "That, my friends, was merely a sampling—sweet and tempting as your mother's peach pie. It's a small offering of the Amazing Miss Moon's psychic gifts when combined with her powerful gazing ball, discovered in Machu Picchu, left by the ancient Incas." Oscar cupped a hand to his ear. "I believe she may sense another soul connecting. Is it for you, sir?" He pointed with authority at a man. "Or you, madam?"

"She's the devil and they need to know it!" A woman's voice cut through Albee's dim hall. "If the girl possesses that power, it's Satan whispering in her ear!"

"Where are the doormen? Where is your ticket, madam? This is a paid performance."

"Never mind my ticket. My Ernie come by here the other night. Then he came home talkin' gibberish. Said he wanted to speak to his daddy, that he was comin' back till she"—the woman stabbed a finger in Esmerelda's direction—"digs up my dead Henry." Esmerelda wriggled her nose at the thought. The woman was halfway up the aisle, commanding the crowd like a preacher. "Nothin' changes death—'specially no she-devil! Don't matter how much gold you wrap her up in or rouge you paint on her face."

Esmerelda clutched at her low-cut bodice with one hand and touched her painted cheek with her other.

"There's no gettin' back to someone you loved and lost. Not through no phantasm." The interloper thrust a worn Bible into the air. "Deuteronomy, 18:11: Anyone who practices divination or tells fortunes or interprets omens, or a sorcerer or a charmer or a medium . . . whoever inquires of the dead is an abomination to the Lord! It's scripture!" Clamor rose, patrons sounding more concerned about evil and less awed by foretold futures.

"It's a free country, ma'am." Oscar stayed steady. "No one forced these good people to gather."

"So said the serpent. 'Tis the way of temptation, sir." Her voice boomed, rivaling Oscar's. "Recognize what you're doing!" She spun in a circle, pointing. "If that girl sees your dead loved ones, listening puts your soul in the devil's hand. Says it right here!" She thrust her Bible upward. Esmerelda's gaze followed, wary of a hail of brimstone.

"Pull the curtain!" Oscar was caught in the velvet fabric, and his large frame floundered like a weighty ghost under a bedsheet. The ruckus grew as patrons demanded refunds, perhaps absolution. Making his way to the other side of the curtain, Oscar barked directions at his troupe. "Could be worse. She could have called us swindlers."

Bill, and his true gimpy leg, hustled past Oscar, laughing. "Thank goodness she sided with the Lord instead of the truth." Bill portrayed the widower Thomas nightly, after he and Barney gathered personal tidbits from marks in the crowd. Sally had been the first of a half dozen intended recipients of messages from beyond.

"Let's get the hell out of here," Oscar said. "Barney, Jimmie, grab the chair and load it on the wagon. Don't drop the ball! If we lose either, there goes half the act!" The two men all but dumped Esmerelda from the chair. She and the crown spilled forward. Esmerelda caught the headwear but tripped on the gown, which was several sizes too big. She'd inherited the costume and *gift* from Marlena the Mystic. Marlena had abandoned Oscar Bodette's Traveling Extravaganza to run off with a contortionist from Istanbul.

Minutes later, they were all packed in the wagon and doing double time, galloping across the Brooklyn Bridge. The horses, Go and Fish, were sweaty and snorting by the time Oscar slowed their pace, coming into Lower Manhattan. From there, the team clip-clopped up the city avenues. After a while, they came to a stop, and Esmerelda peeked through a hole in the canvas-covered wagon. They were parked at the rear of Hupp's Supper Club & Hotel.

She sighed. This was the grind of a traveling life—the show *would* go on. Oscar worked them hard but protected them well. He was the anchor, if not the security in life. Like much of Esmerelda's world, this was one of many facts she never imagined two short years earlier.

She closed one eye and spied Hupp's sign again. Still, she wasn't sure Oscar could do a thing to save her from Benjamin Hupp's attentions. She was being silly, of course, and scoffed at her folly. *As if any girl should require saving from an heir to a fortune . . .* Yet something about Benjamin left her stomach in an uneasy flutter.

Esmerelda rested back on her heels and opened a small crate. A china doll lay on top. Marigold was one of the few threads that had trailed her from a life in New England to one in New York. She'd outgrown the doll ages ago but hugged it anyway, the gold lamé fabric crunching between the two of them.

She looked at Marigold and imagined the doll's aqua glass eyes could see fortunes, old and new. Esmerelda brushed at her own beaded gown. She glanced at the crown balanced upon a broom handle, the gazing ball nested in a box of straw. Bells chimed from blocks away, the Church of the Resurrection. Before they faded, Esmerelda said a prayer and made a wish. She wanted it to be true, that these props and possessions, maybe even mystics, had the power to predict all that was to come.

# CHAPTER
# ONE

*Present Day*
*Surrey, Massachusetts*

Peter St John thought a lot about murder. To say it was an obsession wouldn't be far from the truth. Church bells from Our Lady of the Redeemer sounded. The bells confirmed, if not forewarned, that Pete was home. The car idled, the back-seat window rolled down. Homestead Road was quiet. Almost midnight and the neighborhood was dark—unaware. Images of bloodied bodies and violent deaths crowded Pete's mind. They slowed him down.

The Uber driver gave an anxious look back, silently asking his passenger to get out or provide a different destination. After two years away and now two days of travel—Mumbai to Surrey—Pete wasn't sure he could follow through. His homecoming plans had been easier to execute when mentally walking himself through each step, on planes and in airports. He sighed. It was time to man up. He prompted himself: *Get out of the car. Go into the house. Just do it.*

"I'm good. Thanks for the lift."

He blindly tipped the driver, vaguely hearing, "Holy crap. Thanks, man," as he exited the vehicle. His duffel bag thunked onto the sidewalk as Pete looked at the house. An upstairs light turned on and the element of surprise was lost.

"Move, Soldier," he said to no one. Pete picked up the duffel bag and swallowed down a slight surge of vomit. *You promised. They're waiting. This is inevitable.*

It was all true.

So were a host of less pleasant realities. Pete closed his eyes and grappled for courage—the way he approached everyday war zones. Going home required something else. Something more. A power Pete didn't possess. He rubbed two fingers across his brow, his lungs filling with the kind of breath that said the front walk held a trip wire. It did. The ironies of Pete's life were a land mine.

His past had begun with spirits that visited Pete as a small boy— inside this house, in his own bedroom. While a younger Pete struggled with his psychic abilities, there was normalcy in knowing his mother lived with a similar gift. This was an inherited thing, like being left-handed, the same as his father. But Pete's psychic abilities also provided a portal. They allowed him to access a life he'd lived a hundred years ago as a decorated soldier in the Great War. His role in that war was information he knew; he recognized blood and valor.

When Pete was twelve, these anomalies changed and a beautiful girl invaded his other life—*Esme.* She unearthed emotions impossible for a boy to process, unfair and unrelenting. He loved her—intense feelings that he'd never experienced as an adult in his present-day life. And while Pete was destined to relive violent Great War battles, it was only a single scene that he relived with Esme—the night he killed her.

For the past six years, Pete had tamped down that life and portal by diving into modern-day war zones, employing his more grounded gifts as a photojournalist. But now he was home, at his father's insistence, because of his mother's mysterious malady. Home, where the past was guaranteed to rear up again. Guaranteed because his mother, Aubrey Ellis, lived in this house too. A place where her presence and energy exacerbated Pete's former life and every inch of hell connected to it.

◆ ◆ ◆

At first, the conversation was soothing, and Pete was drawn into or distracted by familiarity. Aubrey and Levi were like any parents who missed their son, and Pete couldn't deny missing them. The back-and-forth exchange was appropriate for an adult child returning home: *"How were your flights, son?" "Have you played much golf lately, Pa?" "You look great, Pete—older, maybe a little older." "I grabbed some English chocolate in Heathrow. It's in my duffel bag." "The* Times *ran one of your photos just yesterday. We saved it . . ."*

But with the late hour, his mother was quick to tire. Levi was scheduled to film a segment of *Ink on Air*, his newsmagazine program, the next afternoon. They would talk more in the morning. His parents went upstairs, and Pete remained in the living room. "I'll be up soon." He stalled by saying something about homecoming adrenaline, jet lag, or the effects of a midnight cup of coffee. The excuse didn't matter.

Alone, Pete wandered the house like a ghost, visiting his old war models in the basement and taking an inventory of each room, the things that had changed. Things that hadn't changed kept him from going to bed. Around two in the morning, he stood in the living room and stared at his duffel bag. Based on the tip he'd offered, Pete guessed the same Uber driver would be willing to fetch him and take him to the nearest hotel. But hell, he'd already seen his mother, absorbed her otherworldly energy. Whatever the rest of the night brought, he doubted location would make a difference.

He was right.

It was closer to four o'clock than three when Pete succumbed to sleep. Closer to that world than this one as he drifted restlessly, the past orbiting until it snagged on the present. From there the dark night spiraled, not into a dream, but into a frighteningly real place—the same way it had for the past sixteen years.

*Pete teetered on a precipice, then he lost the fight. Time devoured him, quick as a blink, clear as a gunshot. The early twentieth century surrounded him. The noise from the gun was deafening, and the air grew acrid. The weapon was heavy in his hand, though his aim had been steady. Through the puff of smoke, he witnessed Esme's last breath. Shock filled her face. She stared at him, threaded fingers clutching her belly, blood spilling out. She fell limp. Chivalry said to catch her, even if you'd killed her. He dropped the pistol and gripped her lifeless frame. Aghast, he let go, and she hit the floor harder than he meant, even for what was now a dead girl.*

*His heart pounded, more thunderous than artillery shelling in Belleau Wood. This scene was less bloody, twice as alarming. Pete's gaze rose, searching for God's forgiveness or a spider-hole exit. But he remained in the room, in this place. He stood across from the dresser mirror, where his stark eyes stared back. The eyes of a murderer now. Different than the eyes of a battle-field warrior—a hero. The shelling in his chest continued. From the corner of his eye, he glanced left at a window.*

*Think. He needed to think. What came next? No wagon would be by to gather the dead en masse. Dispose of the body. Hurriedly, he scooped her up. Beads from the costume detached, plinking, rolling, sparkling. Compared to her, the beads displayed a startling burst of life, scattering across hardwood. The mirror continued to witness the scene: in his arms lay a fallen swan, Esme's dress and her limbs resting at lovely flowing angles, the snowy dress ruined by a growing splotch of blood. Objects were present: china doll in a chair, clothesline fashioned from bedpost to hook, English hunting scene above the mantel. The tail of a black cat flicked from beneath the bed. "I'm sorry," he whispered. He couldn't tell tears from sweat, shock from fear— right from wrong. He only knew he had to get the hell out of there. As if she weighed no more than that swan, with her dead body in his arms, he charged for the door.*

Then it ended, and the whirlpool churned the opposite way.

"Jesus Christ!" The prayer or the plea left Pete's mouth as he jolted upright, his fingers strangling a pillow in his boyhood bedroom. He couldn't get air in or out in his present-day life. Layers of guilt tangled like the bedsheet, and perspiration saturated everything. The smell of gunfire still filled his nose, the taste of fear redolent. No dead body was present, and this amazed him.

His bedroom door burst open. "You're okay, Pete!" Levi pounded to his bedside, Aubrey steps behind. Pete hadn't forgotten the concerned look on Pa's face, the shamed expression episodes like this brought to his mother's. "Just breathe."

At the ages of three, seven, and even ten, his father's commanding voice had brought comfort. It could anchor Pete to the here and now, rescue him. At twenty-eight, it no longer punctured the surface of this particular hell.

"I can't . . . I gotta go." Pete lurched from the bed and scrabbled for the pants he'd discarded earlier. "I mean, I can breathe. I can't be here. I'm sorry."

"Pete, please," his mother said. "Don't do this. Stay. At least for a few hours. The sun's just coming up."

Pete's fervor slowed as hinting dawn glimmered. He looked at his mother and her eerie eyes—Ellis family eyes. "It's better if I go."

"We've missed you so much," Aubrey said. "I . . . I need more than the hour from last night."

Pete's wide-eyed stare moved between his mother's tense face and his duffel bag. He panicked, the way a killer might, and dove for the canvas bag, his camera gear. Levi was right there, gripping his shoulders.

His father had always been a brave son of a bitch, willing to put himself between Pete and his other life. But eventually the tables turned—first, a lanky sixteen-year-old Pete coming at him—unaware of what he was doing—then at nineteen and stronger, finally stronger than his father. When Pete had broken his father's nose after one of his near-nightly visits to his past, he'd known it was time to go. Faced with what he'd physically done to his father—even if it was all accidental—Pete couldn't begin to process the danger of turning on his mother.

Years removed from those episodes, grown man faced grown man. But it was Pete's eyes that glassed over, a lump jammed in his throat. He backed up, his mind askew from the dizzying effects of his homecoming. Ricocheting from that life into this one was never a smooth transition. He reached for the wall. Solid plaster was cool to the touch, and he tried to steady himself. With his other hand, Pete dragged his fingers through his hair. Sweat and flesh and fear made for a slick, ropey knot of human being. He suspected that committed mental patients presented more rationally.

His father's grip eased. "Are you okay?"

*Well, fuck, no.* But what else could he ask; what could Pete say in reply? "Yeah. I'll be all right."

"You're sure?"

Pete hesitated, then nodded.

"Then for your mother . . . please. A few hours."

Family obligation influenced him, and Pete lowered his arm, grunting a noise of agreement. He plucked the cotton button-down shirt, the one he'd been wearing for three days, from the bedpost. He tugged it on, offering his mother a feeble smile. "What the hell, right? I'm up now anyway."

"I'll, um . . . I can make pancakes. I still have that pure maple syrup you like, from last time. Does syrup go bad?"

His father shook his head but looked more like he was guarding against the prospect of his son bolting. He wasn't wrong.

At the door, Aubrey said, "I understand it's hard to be here, Pete. With me, but . . ." She pointed lamely to the beaten bed. "I'm grateful, so happy you came home."

Pete only sighed as she left.

Levi waited until the stairs squeaked, telling them she'd reached the bottom step. "You know I understand how you both feel. I'm not unsympathetic, Pete, but—"

"But this time it's not just about me, my demons. I saw it last night, how tired she looks. Thin. You don't have anything new to tell me? Anything you didn't want to say in front of her?"

"No. Your mother continues to baffle medical experts. We've no diagnosis for her symptoms—her fatigue, numbness, muscle weakness, bouts of dizziness. But it's a catch-22. For every medical test that comes back normal . . ."

"It makes you think the underlying cause is ethereal." Levi nodded at a conclusion that could only be drawn in the privacy of the Ellis–St John home. "You know, Pa, I hope it doesn't work both ways. I hope my being here doesn't make her worse. Did you consider that?"

"Actually, I did. But what was I supposed to do? Tell her that on top of an illness we can't identify or treat, her only son is off-limits too?"

"I suppose you have a point." Pete sat in a chair and pulled on a dirty sock.

"We'll take things an hour at a time if we have to. For now, let's go with you being the best medicine. I'll see you downstairs." Levi headed for the door.

"Pa?"

He turned back.

"Despite everything, I'd stay a year, do the time . . ." Pete gestured to the violent jumble of sheets. "If it helped her, I'd do it."

Levi looked at the bed and Pete as if he might see past the sodden sheets and his son's pounding heart. "I understand how hard this is for you. I'm sorry I can't do more. I'm sorry—"

Pete held up a hand, controlling what he could in this life. He wouldn't watch the man who'd been the anchor in his mother's life—and his—falter. "Listen, I've got some great shots to show you from Yemen. Managed to get myself a ride along with a SEAL team."

Levi latched on to the segue. "No kidding? I saw your photos from Kandahar in the *Washington Post*."

"Yeah. I heard CNN used them too."

"Impressive. Your mother, she's got quite a scrapbook to show you. Maybe spend a little time telling her about your travels. Not everyone on the block has a photojournalist son embedded in hostile territories."

"Or one who lives with the dead and his past." He raised a brow and pulled on his other sock.

"Yeah. Well. We try to lay off that part at barbecues and cocktail parties."

Sweat lessened and the rigid knot that was Pete's entire being eased slightly. "Maybe I should grab a shower before coming downstairs."

Levi brushed a hand across his nose. "Not a bad idea. I'll hit the laundry room, put your wash in."

"Right. With Mom . . . with me, I was distracted. I wasn't thinking how I smell like six countries in three days."

"Get some shorts from my room." Levi picked up the duffel bag. "And make that more like eight countries in two days—hot ones."

Pete's serious tone returned. "I'm sorry, Pa." Levi turned at the door. "Sorry that the best I can offer is to make her happy by doing my stinky laundry . . . or making pancakes."

Levi nodded his salt-and-pepper head, pushing his glasses upward. The lines on his face were also evident. Pete knew he'd put most of them there. "When it comes to her son . . . laundry, making breakfast, is what makes her, both of us, happy." He left the bedroom, toting the duffel bag.

Pete removed the socks he'd just put on and stood. He reached for the bedpost, shakier than he'd let on to Levi. While Pete couldn't control his visits to the past, he also couldn't contain the reentry. He wished those events could be perceived as nothing more than a bad dream. He squeezed tight to the bedpost. Then he held his hand out before him— the one that shook yet could make a formidable fist. The same hand that had pulled the trigger of a gun. He sighed. The least he could do was work on presenting as a "normal son" in this life. He snickered while heading toward the hall. "Normal" was a trick he'd never mastered.

# CHAPTER TWO

Inside the bathroom, Pete stripped down and tossed the last of his dirty clothes into the laundry chute. Levi grumbled, "Thanks . . ." from below. The metal-lined shaft was a lighter memory. If you happened to be standing in the laundry room near the chute, you'd take a direct hit to the head from whatever came flying down. Years ago, the way boys might, Pete and Dylan Higley sent a watermelon rushing down. It would have been better if their projectile had gotten stuck. Dislodging the watermelon would have pissed off his father's orderly nature, but not as much as ten pounds of splattered fruit all over the laundry room floor.

The memory relaxed Pete. He took a head-clearing breath and turned on the shower. But before getting in, he made the mistake of looking in the full-length mirror. *Carnage.* It was the only word that made sense. His sinewy frame was a war zone, having nothing to do with the ones he'd visited in the past six years. He stepped closer and absorbed the naked inventory: Adam's apple, clavicle, biceps, the narrowing *V* of his pelvic area, muscular quads. The body parts itemized basic anatomy, but these things were not what Pete's eye observed.

He scanned scars he could not explain—some he'd had since he was a boy. Pete ran his fingers over a knot of flesh beneath his rib cage, to the right of his navel. The knot had mysteriously turned up two or three years ago. Common sense said to have the protrusion checked out. But it'd taken hard-core bravery for Pete to go as far as the radiology department at a hospital in Mumbai to explain it. On a previous trip, he'd gotten into a deep conversation with a Dr. Mayon Kapoor. He was a hybrid Hindu who believed in mysticism as much as he did modern medicine. Because of this, Pete had confided his past—the one that occurred during World War I. He was comfortable with Dr. Kapoor diagnosing the internal knot, whatever it turned out to be. The scan revealed Pete's most-feared assumption—nothing modern medicine might treat. Dr. Kapoor was fascinated, concluding that the knot was internal scarring, the by-product of a crude operation.

"And you're sure you didn't suffer an injury in one of the many war zones you travel?" Dr. Kapoor had asked. "Perhaps an infection set in, a fever struck, and you simply don't remember. It is possible."

Pete assured him this wasn't the case. "A war zone, maybe—just not from this life."

Dr. Kapoor, a serious student of re-embodiment, hadn't argued.

Pete's stare lingered on his tattered body. He ran his fingers over the fleshy souvenir from another life. He pressed his hand to the mirror's cool glass and drew closer, doing the same with his forehead. He closed his eyes and his heart picked up pace. *Touch.* As if another person had come into the bathroom, he felt a touch. Soft fingers laced around Pete's chest, and a tickle of hair brushed the back of his shoulder. The urge to turn and kiss someone was potent.

Pete didn't move, head and hand pressed to the mirror, like he might fall into it and pass through to the life he so often relived. A woman's lips pressed to his back. He responded physically to the invitation. His breathing grew heavier, the mood intensifying, emotions more vivid than they'd been in recent years. Since the last time he'd been inside this house. *Fuck.* This never happened when he was conscious, present in this life. Yet, Pete smiled. He longed for Esme the way you might want air in a sealed tomb.

Along with the torturous memory she produced came feelings Pete wanted to sink into, grab on to. *Relive.* They were wildly powerful. He squeezed his eyes tighter, concentrated harder. It was rare for Pete to encourage these feelings; he couldn't help himself. The fragile moment grew more surreal. Then the unprecedented occurred. Esme spoke. He heard her voice. He'd never heard her voice before. It presented the way he might channel an ordinary apparition in his twenty-first-century life.

*"If Paris is France . . ."*

Soft lips grazed his ear, a delicate brush. Smell proved to be the greatest trigger. It was Esme's skin, infused with a sweet layer of gardenia. Scents penetrating from another time. Then it all vanished—her voice, her presence, the passion so desperately attached to a dead woman. From a shaky state of arousal, Pete opened his eyes. Nothing stared back but a stressed-out Peter St John—a person who straddled this life and one he wanted more. How did that even make sense? Why the hell would he want a life where his single memory of the woman he loved was of killing her?

Pete squeezed his hand tight and slammed it into the glass. Tiny chips of mirror sprinkled onto the tiled floor. He withdrew his fist from the spiderweb crack; red laced through the glass. Blood dripped from his fist. He backed up, surveying his handiwork. "Great. Now I can explain that on top of everything else I can't." Defeated, he turned to the claw-foot tub, ripping at the curtain and stepping into the steam.

◆ ◆ ◆

Aubrey's breakfast subterfuge wasn't lost on Pete—a presentation of normal. The table was set on the outside deck, which included a calming view of the nature preserve behind their house. Going outside did help, but the July heat wave only ended up highlighting Pete's discomfort.

Last night, as he stepped from Boston's busy Logan airport, sticky air adhered like a gas mask. He'd arrived during those rare New England days when everyone wondered why they didn't have central air and the daytime swelter glued itself to the night.

His mother came outside carrying a plate of pancakes that would be the envy of any IHOP. The table tried to keep up the *"welcome home"* theme, dressed in a clean white cloth, the vintage 1950s plates he recognized, and a mason jar holding fresh cut flowers. "Looks great, Mom. Thank you." He sat and forced down a sip of orange juice.

"What happened to your hand?"

Pete brushed his fingers over the gauze wrapped around his right palm. "I, um . . ."

His father had come out the French doors, answering with a question. "Did you get dizzy in the bathroom, Pete? Maybe the mirror broke your fall." Apparently he'd been upstairs before coming outside, and Pete knew enough to expand on the timely fib.

"Uh, yeah." He grabbed his fork and speared two pancakes. "Sorry. I wasn't as steady as I thought. The mirror didn't fare so well. I'll replace it before I go."

"I don't care about the mirror." It wasn't heat, but hazy waves of worry, that circled his mother. "You're okay? There's no glass in your hand or anything?"

"I'm fine, Mom. It wasn't more than a scratch."

She continued to stare at the layered gauze, blood-soaked enough to insist that wasn't true. Pete busied himself with food, ignoring the roil of his stomach.

"Tell me how you're feeling." Pete said this as his father passed behind his mother, squeezing her shoulders. The nod he and Levi exchanged acknowledged the slight lie they'd just told.

"Same-ish. You're here. Whatever ails me, it's not what I want to spend time talking about."

"If you say so." He smiled at his mother and glanced at Levi.

As his father noted earlier, batteries of tests had eliminated autoimmune disorders and blood disorders, arthritis and thyroid conditions. Thankfully, the tests also ruled out anything worse. Like the lump in Pete's stomach, it appeared his mother's ailment was not anything traditional medicine could treat.

He inhaled humid air. The night was over and he was booked on a flight to Iceland that evening. He'd get through the day. Pete dug into the pancakes and aimed for cheerier conversation. "Nevertheless, you look good, Mom. Pretty."

"You're both horrible liars." She busied herself by dunking a tea bag. "Tell me about your last assignment. Cities surrounding Damascus, right?"

"Didn't pan out. Flagler's lead fizzled," Pete said, referring to the managing editor at PressCorp. "There was an incident near Aleppo—northern Syria. But the rebel insurgence didn't last. In the airport, I ran into a marine sergeant I rode along with on an Afghan border checkpoint op. He invited me to spend a few days south of Kandahar. I got some good images."

"And from Afghanistan?" Levi said, sounding impressed, maybe a little envious.

"It was only a matter of time until things heated up in Syria again." Pete hesitated with his next thought. "So staying on that side of the world seemed reasonable. After that I bummed a seat on a medical aid flight to Mumbai."

"Mumbai?" Aubrey perked up.

"Yeah. Just a short trip. Barely two days."

She was quiet, sipping her tea. Then she pounced. "So you know I'm going to ask. Did you see Dr. Kapoor?"

Pete poked at the pancake and then the sausage, which he did not think he could get down. He fought another swell of nausea. He thought of lying about his trip to India. But one more lie and, really, what would be the point of having shown up?

"Yeah. I did," Pete said. "Dr. Kapoor and I, we had dinner before my flight back to the Middle East."

His mother opened her mouth and shut it, a tight-lipped smile and deep breath speaking for her.

"Let's cut to the chase," Pete said. "Yes. Dr. Kapoor brought up past life regression therapy. And no. I'm not going to do it." His mother remained silent, and Pete thought that was going to be it. She returned to her breakfast. But then her fork hit her plate, hard enough that Pete was amazed she didn't crack the atomic-design dinnerware.

"I don't understand why. After all these years, everything you've endured, why you wouldn't take the chance. After everything you've told us about Dr. Kapoor. You like him . . . you trust him."

"Aubrey," Levi said, from what had been a rather quiet position.

"Do I like that he doesn't think I'm insane?" Pete said. "Of course. Do I want to be his ultimate lab rat? Not so much. Dr. Kapoor's experience with past life regression is fascinating. But I believe it's also bound to the ordinary." Aubrey's expression didn't relax and Pete launched into his usual defenses. "Dr. Kapoor has used it on patients driven by a theory about their own experiences. People of his faith who have a deep interest in the subject." Pete pointed the tines of his fork at himself. "*Not* someone like me. An unknown entity that not only is acutely aware of a past life, but—oh, by the way—possesses the added novelty of being able to chat with the dead. No thanks."

His mother's voice hit the pitch of old arguments. "But if it can find you answers, close the gaps in your life, I can't understand why you wouldn't—"

"Because I don't want to know. There are too many questions that scare the shit out of me." He dropped his fork like Aubrey had. "Face it, Mom. Your war correspondent son, traveler to the most violent places in this world, is nothing but a coward."

"Pete, don't say things like—"

"Aubrey." His father spoke firmly. "We've been through this a million times. Pete doesn't want to pursue any past life regression." Levi reached for the syrup but didn't pick it up, looking soberly at his wife instead. "Let's not spend the next few hours haunting him with it. Okay?"

*Fitting choice of words, Pa . . .* Pete closed his eyes, the conversation yanking him back about fifteen years. He and his mother could relate on communication with the dead, but Aubrey could not grasp her son's reluctance to seek insights to his other life. Ongoing disagreements had taken a toll on their family. His mother had wanted normal for herself, for them. But with their son, she and Levi had only doubled down on the incomprehensible. Getting out of his parents' everyday lives was the wisest thing Pete had done.

Pete rose abruptly from the wrought iron table, signaling that the discussion was over. But he walked away with his coffee cup in hand, a tacit sign that he wouldn't bolt. Standing at the deck rail, he stared into the preserve. Heated rays of sunlight sizzled like flaming arrows past his head and into high weeds. The old tire swing still hung from a lumbering oak, and the air was rich with the boyhood scents of home. Pete imagined this to be the same for everyone: the sights and smells, the aura of youth—one small thing he had in common with a larger populace. He tried to find solace in it.

Instead, a voice came at him. The same voice that had woven its way into the privacy of the bathroom—nearly stepped into the shower with him—burrowed into his thoughts. Esme spoke again. *"If Paris is France, then Coney Island, between June and September, is the World . . ."*

Then she was gone. Pete stifled a gasp. His mother could spot a ghostly presence like a snowy owl spying its prey. His brow knit tight and Pete studied his surroundings. The only visual was his childhood stomping grounds, but in place of the smell of home was the faint scent of gardenias. His heart thumped faster and a prickle of sweat stood out on his neck. Pete swiped at it, hoping mundane heat would take the blame. Fortunately, his mother did take his father's advice. She'd moved on, saying something about grace—maybe that Pete should find some, along with compassion for his long-suffering parents.

She was right, even if she'd said nothing of the kind. Feeling like a shitty son, Pete fixated on a family of rabbits poised at the edge of their burrow. Ears flicked, a twig snapped, and they vanished. "Everybody in . . . right down the rabbit hole." He slung his arm outward, coffee from his cup spraying the lawn. Words about grace filtered back into his ears.

"So I texted Grace back," Aubrey went on, "and she said that would be fine."

Hearing his ex-girlfriend's name, Pete whipped toward his mother. "What?"

Levi leaned back in his chair, mumbling, "I told you not to do it." He sipped coffee, his squinty stare set on the preserve.

"I only thought it serendipitous that there was a text from Grace this morning. She wanted to know if she could drop by a book she borrowed. It's not like we talk regularly, but we are friendly, Pete."

He sighed, wondering how fast he could get on a flight to anywhere—Somalia, the Sudan, Afghanistan . . . Newark.

He was overreacting. The news wasn't as unwanted as it was unexpected. Pete had plenty of positive memories when it came to Grace Hathaway. He understood why his mother wanted to label her "Saving Grace." From the time they'd met at Brown—his father's alma mater—until Pete had dropped out and left the country, Grace had represented the most sedate years of his life. Part of it, Pete was sure, involved removing himself from his mother's energy. But a piece of it had been Grace.

He'd loved her in a distracting way, like a comforting movie you'd watch again and again. Among Grace's most winning traits was her ability to accept Pete's peculiarities. She grasped his psychic gift and other life with the same ease as agreeing that his left foot was a half size larger than his right. The relationship worked until it didn't, until Pete broke Grace's heart on a rainy March morning.

He'd called saying he had something to tell her, ask her. Afterward, he realized, if only from the disappointment on her face, that she'd anticipated words about lifelong commitments and a question involving a ring. Instead, Pete wanted to tell Grace he was leaving Brown, leaving Surrey—by default, leaving her. What he wanted was a ride to the airport. He squeezed his eyes shut at the memory, at one of many Pete St John social shortcomings.

But it was all old news. After a period of noncommunication, surefooted Grace resurfaced. She insisted their romance had been based on friendship, and she couldn't see letting that go to waste. Not when Pete could surely use a friend now and again. If she was fine with it, he couldn't disagree. They resumed a cordial relationship, mostly text messages. Months ago, Grace called to tell Pete she'd gotten engaged. He was happy for her, but it wasn't as if he planned on attending the wedding. He certainly hadn't considered seeing Grace on his short jaunt home. Yet there he stood, twenty minutes later, answering the front door.

# CHAPTER THREE

Pete swung the door wide. Grace stood before him holding a paperback novel, a violinist pictured on the cover. The book looked like something Grace would read. She'd changed little, if at all. Pretty. Wavy brown hair, shorter maybe, and indigo eyes—sharp, always emotion filled. Upbeat. In charge. They'd only been twenty-one at the height of their relationship. It had also been a point in Pete's life when he hadn't minded someone else doing the navigating.

An accidental reunion in Italy was Pete's last vivid Grace memory. He'd been taken aback to run into her on the plaza in front of St Mark's Basilica, to end up with her in his hotel room shower. Grace had viewed their tryst as passion reignited. Pete had thought it was more about convenient sex. The miscue reminded him why things never quite worked. In truth, a variety of enablers had breathed life into a relationship that continued long past its expiration date. He'd been there for Grace through her parents' shitty divorce. He'd supported her career goals, which spun like a compass unable to locate magnetic north. The same wonky compass had landed them both in Italy more than two years ago. Pete hadn't seen her since.

Grace casually said hello and walked past him into the living room. "Great to see you, Grace. This is a nice surprise."

"Is it?" she said coolly.

"Sure." He pointed to the sofa and she sat, Pete plopping down on the other end. "Like my mother said, it was serendipitous that you texted her."

"I texted Aubrey?"

"Yeah." He gestured to the novel. "She told me you wanted to return a book."

She frowned. "Uh, no. Your mother texted me, asking if she could *borrow* a book. I ran into her a few weeks ago at Trader Joe's. We talked for a bit. I know she loves to read, so I mentioned . . ." She sighed. "We've been duped."

"And not very cleverly." He glanced toward the stairs. "I'll talk to her. She could do better if aiming for a ruse. Sorry."

Grace relaxed into the sofa. "No harm done."

"She means well. But this is a reach, especially with your engagement and all."

"Right. That." Grace's frame tightened. "When I saw Aubrey, I told her the engagement was off. I was making conversation. It seemed relevant."

"Oh, makes more sense now. Not about your engagement—just my mother's meddling."

"She adores her son. She wants to see him happy. Don't fault her for that."

"I don't. I'd love to see me happy too, it's just—" He paused. "So you're *not* getting married. What happened with . . . sorry, I don't remember his—"

"Andy."

"Did you realize Andy didn't meet the Grace standard?" He paused again. "A high bar with good reason, of course."

"No. Nothing so flattering. He kind of broke it off." She looked down at her folded hands. "Said he wasn't ready."

Pete inched back. "What an ass. How blind could he be?"

Grace's count-on-it smile went crooked. "I don't know, Pete. You tell me."

"Sorry." He cleared his throat—miscues. "My exit from your life was for your own good. Unless he can say the same . . ." Pete shut up. Andy's sins would have to be indictable to put him in Pete's league. "I'm sorry," he repeated.

"Mmm. Had I told you this when it happened, I'd be halfway through a box of Kleenex by now. As it is, I've returned the bread warmer and steak knives, without plunging one through him. If you know anyone looking to 'say yes to the dress,' mine is for sale on Craigslist."

She shrugged, and Pete was quietly glad things had never progressed that far between them.

"Andy," she went on, "was good enough to eat the country club deposit. Clearly, I'll live."

She put the book on the coffee table and her gaze stayed with it. But seconds later, in pure Grace fashion, she supplied her own *"chin up"* advice. "Maybe the third time will be the charm, right?"

"Like I said, it's a deservedly high bar. Obviously, old Andy didn't meet it. As for me, a lifetime of you having to walk that bar like a tightrope . . . it would have been ridiculously unfair."

Grace knotted and unknotted her hands. "That's nice of you. To put it that way."

"What other way is there to put it?"

She eyeballed Pete. "That you were never in love with me the way you were . . ." She snatched up the paperback, rhythmically thrumming its pages. "So tell me how you've been. How are your . . . *lives*?"

"About the same. Fewer episodes involving Esme when I'm not around my mother, or the energy she brings to a space." Pete moved his hand in a sweeping motion. "There are still the war stories I visit."

"In real time or in your sleep?"

"Both. I'm sorry for the world that my day job exists. But as long as it does, it keeps my mind exhausted. So I continue to live with bouts of visitant chaos—"

"Followed by flashes of brilliance."

Pete crinkled his brow at her claim.

"I'm not so cool that I won't admit to following your work. Your photos are incredible, Pete. So is your nerve, to be able to get that up close to the things you do—war, oppression, catastrophe . . . death."

He thought for a moment. "Situations like that, they don't strike me like they do other people. They should. They don't."

"You're not moved by what you witness? That doesn't sound like you."

"It's hard to articulate. More like I've seen it all before. Not that a person ever gets used to conflict or tragedy. It's more like the benefit of a learning curve. I'm witnessing, for the hundredth time, what everyone around me is experiencing for the first."

"Still, it's quite—"

"Don't say 'brave,' Grace. It's not bravery. I'm searching for numbness by way of twenty-first-century wars. Time spent in places like Syria, northern Africa, Afghanistan, it's a résumé footnote: *war zone coping skills.* A never-ending thirst for diversions."

"Your perspective is different. I get that. It doesn't diminish what you're doing." A scrapbook lay on the coffee table. "Is Aubrey keeping a page-turning account?"

Pete shrugged.

"Mind if I have a look?"

He repeated the gesture, and Grace pulled the large scrapbook onto her lap.

One page in and Pete realized he'd never looked at his work from this angle: an artistic presentation of mayhem. Something only his mother would arrange, maybe the Whitney Museum. The distinguished

New York venue had contacted him about an exhibition of his work. Pete had never returned the calls or e-mails. He didn't want that kind of attention. Each photo—war-torn regions, a terrorist attack in Paris, an avalanche in Italy—was an individual moment of heartbreak and terror, all captured through his eye. It was another anomaly that had taken root in his youth.

When Pete's fascination with basement war models had worn out, about the time he turned fifteen, he'd picked up a camera. It was an old, first-of-its-generation digital model that belonged to his father. Photography had provided a crafty diversion, a counterweight to his past life visits and his psychic woes. When his photography progressed to images that told a story, Pete realized how it also busied his mind. At first, Aubrey and Levi were encouraging. But hope turned on his parents when Pete left to photograph real wars.

His twenty-second birthday was marked by a fierce argument between Pete and his parents. He blew out candles and announced that he was leaving home, leaving Brown. Not to study abroad, but to pursue something more precarious than his own life.

*"I don't know how we stop him, Aubrey," his father had said. "He's of age. He's not asking us for anything, not even a ride to the airport. He's a brilliant photographer, a solid writer. Yes, it's dangerous, but is it really any more dangerous than the lives he's been living? And who knows, maybe it will help Pete find answers about his past life that we can't give him . . ."*

Six years later, Pete didn't have any better answers, but he had a noteworthy career. It was a surprising coup for a guy who spent much of this life just trying to get through it.

"The *Surrey City Press* ran this one." Grace pointed to a photo of an Afghan village ravaged by the Taliban. "Of course, that was after the *New York Times* ran it, right?"

Pete didn't reply. The photo depicted a lone girl moments after a bomb blast. She held a doll whose face was equally smeared in blood, their dresses tattered and soiled. Pete touched the photo. He could still hear the voices. He'd taken a burst of photos before calling the girl to his side. Less than thirty seconds later, another blast went off where she'd stood. He'd had no hearing in his left ear for weeks.

After the photo, after the explosions, Pete had spoken to the girl. In a language he did not understand, by way of an intense spirit, he conveyed words that caused the girl's dark eyes to startle so much her bloody face became secondary. In broken English, she'd offered back the message "Mama says: *'I love you, my little one. Papa and I will miss you so much. Tell the man with the camera to take you to the Red Cross. In Saghar, they will find Navi. My sister, she will come for you.'*"

It wasn't the first time something like this had occurred, and Pete gathered up the blood-streaked girl, carrying her a mile to the Red Cross station. As he left her, Pete heard, *"Rahmat . . . rahmat . . ."* While he didn't understand the words, he understood gratitude, how much a mother only wanted her child to be safe.

Grace marveled at the photos and Pete smiled humbly. There was satisfaction in facilitating awareness; it was good work. In addition to the scrapbook, on the staircase of the St John home was a wall of photos—a parental homage. His parents and Grace knew a little about the messages he ferried, the lives he'd altered for the living. But Pete was also leery of his brilliant photographs. How would the world perceive the photographer if it knew the truth? Would he still be brilliant, or just brilliantly flawed?

As Grace continued to flip through the book, Pete rubbed his gauze-covered hand over three days of stubble. He moved his gaze between the pictures in the album and the ones on the fireplace mantel. One photo in particular caught his eye: his maternal grandfather, Peter Ellis. His namesake, his mind-sake. Pete knew how the world would see him: a madman, just like his grandfather.

"What are these?" Grace pointed, drawing his attention back to the scrapbook.

The images had changed. Instead of violence and desperation, gentle pools of serenity overtook the pages. "Oh, geez. I almost forgot about those."

"They're beautiful. So different."

Pete tipped his head at the postcard-size images. After a bitch of a tour through the pirate-plagued east coast of Africa, he'd retreated to London, awaiting his next assignment. The city was too noisy, filled with too many people.

A guy on the train mentioned Walberswick, a rural respite a few hours north. The place sounded like heaven to Pete, and he took off in that direction. The beach hut he rented had no running water, no electricity, and a squeaky cot—an upgrade from some of the places he'd spent recent nights. While creature comforts were in short supply, what he did find in the hut were paints and small canvases. Outside the hut, Pete also found astonishingly tranquil views. He'd never painted before, or at least not since grade school. In Walberswick, the weary traveler from two lives discovered a new way to relax his mind.

Pete had stood by the River Blyth, indulging in quiet and painting small landscapes—the bumpy beach, tufts of grass, the sky, and waterfowl. The local color. Then he decided to photograph the images he'd painted, delving into elaborate post-processing techniques while drinking tea and eating scones in a nearby café. He painstakingly adjusted the color temperature, exposure, contrast, and clarity, toyed with hues and saturation—luminosity. Various filters resulted in a vintage look. He'd laughed at the finished products, thinking the canned filters on Instagram couldn't have produced better iterations. Ultimately, Pete thought the final products were pretty, if not pretty useless. Not sure what else to do with photographed paintings, he packed up his art projects and sent them to his mother. He thought she might like to have something born out of the softer, gentler side of her son.

Pete smiled, recalling those transient days in Walberswick. "They're nothing," he said. "Painting them was a distraction from . . . well, present-day battlefields and the ones not so present. I was messing around. Paints, the camera—de-stressing."

"Pete, we dated for almost three years, lived together for part of it. I never knew you could paint."

He absorbed the scenes and spoke wistfully: "Neither did I."

Grace brushed her slender fingers over the images. "You haven't really said, how is your past life? Are you coping?"

He flexed the bandaged hand. "I was doing okay until I got to . . . *here*." He looked around the craftsman—the place representative of his mother, all her energy. "The house is so connected to her, sometimes I think it knows I'm here."

"Like the Amityville horror, it knows you're here?"

"No. Nothing so over-the-top. At least not B-movie-grade terror." Explanation was cumbersome, even with Grace. "When inanimate objects take on a vibe, they're often connected to a person. That makes me pay attention. Generally, it means there's a spiritual entity bonding the physical world to an ethereal one."

"Something like your mother's ghost gifts."

"Something like that. Because I've lived my whole life in this house, my surroundings never stuck out. Not until I left."

"I'm not sure I'm following. I thought being around your mother was the trigger."

"It is. For sure my mother's psychic gift exacerbates mine. After twenty-plus years . . ." Pete gingerly flexed his bandaged hand. "That's a definite conclusion." He took in the tangible elements that defined the circa-1900 home: stone fireplace, antique millwork, buffed hardwoods. "The house plays a part because I associate it with her, probably because she's lived here for so long."

"Interesting. Even so, have you ever looked into the house, its history?"

"No. But it's like every other old house on this street. I know my mother bought it with her first husband."

"Whoa . . . *first husband*? Now this is really getting interesting."

"Not so much. My mom was briefly married to somebody else before Pa. They bought the house together. From what I know, her first husband spent about a dozen nights here before the marriage went south."

"What a fascinating tidbit. What was his name?"

"Whose name?"

"Her first husband."

"Oscar." The "O" name dropped from Pete's mouth without thinking. "No . . . that wasn't it." He shook his head. "Why do you want to know?"

"I'll look up the sale in town records—curiosity." Grace's job, working for the town of Surrey, gave her access to all sorts of records. It was great if you wanted a parking ticket to disappear; otherwise Grace could sometimes come off as a busybody.

"Don't."

"Don't what?"

"Look it up. I don't think of this house as belonging to anyone but them, our house. Even if being here is never the mother-and-son reunion we'd like."

She closed the scrapbook. "Forget I said anything."

"It's forgotten." He glanced at his watch. "As it is, this family reunion is on a timer. I'm on a flight to Iceland tonight."

Grace gently touched the cover of the scrapbook. "And from there you can continue to what, run from this life . . . and that one?"

"Here we go. If you wanted to partake in the usual past life regression theory-slash-argument, you should have showed up for breakfast."

"I was only thinking of your mother. It's hard for you, Pete, no one denies that." She paused; he waited. Old habit. "But it's just as hard on Aubrey. My gosh." She flailed a hand at the paperback. "She can't have a conversation in a grocery store about you without tearing up."

"Thanks, Grace. I'm well aware of the happiness I don't bring to my mother's life. It's been part of the package deal pretty much since I arrived." He held up a hand to her incoming remark. "I also get that all anyone wants to do is help. Aside from encouraging past life regression experiments, an idea that couldn't appeal to me less, I'm not sure anyone can."

"Okay, but surely you'd like to find some resolution."

"How?" he said. "And to what end? Everybody's so hot on the idea of forcing those memories to the surface. Why? What's in it for me but discovering my motive, learning how I ultimately got rid of Esme's body? No matter how much you and my parents claim to understand, you're hearing a story. What you don't grasp is that my past life is as real to me as this one."

"Fair enough. But I wouldn't want answers at this point. I'd need them." She folded her arms, her gaze searing him. "If it were me—"

"Well, it's not." Pete returned the hot stare. "Are you sure you and my mother didn't have a full-on strategy session at Trader Joe's?" He sank farther into the sofa cushion. "I have a normal life, Grace. Maybe not by your standards or theirs." Pete pointed to a room permeated with his parents' lives. "Why can't all of you let it go? It's not like I'm living on the streets, consumed by hallucinations—which is how most medical professionals would define my experiences. I've done all right for a guy who's got one foot in this life and a trench foot in another."

She ducked back. "What did you say?"

"About what?"

"Trench foot."

"Nothing." Palpable agitation swirled around her; Pete stood. "I was making a point. You misunderstood. Look, thanks for stopping by, even if it was based on my mother's lame attempt at rekindling romance. But I think we both agree, we're not a thing. We haven't been for a long time."

"You're right." Grace stood as well. "Had I still felt that way about you, I would have never agreed to marry anyone else. Regardless of how it worked out—or didn't."

He backed up a step, feeling shitty all over again for having done the dumping between the two of them. "Grace, that came out—"

"You know what else, Pete?" Her tone was clear code for *"don't answer that."* "If I never said so, I should have thanked you for not letting me spend my life chasing after yours, dodging your . . . *outbursts*."

"At least you realize how unfair it would have been, saddling your life with the . . . *insanity* that's mine." He rarely said the word aloud, but Pete needed to emphasize that his choices had been in Grace's best interest.

"No. You were the one hyperfocused on that. And I'm not saying it wouldn't have been difficult. I'm not even saying I would have been happy. You've zero capacity to make anyone happy, least of all yourself." He sobered further at the cutting remark. "The reason I'm glad you broke things off is because I hate the idea of having almost spent my life with a man who, at best, is in love with a ghost."

## Act I, Scene II
## New York City
## 1917

"Everybody out!" Oscar shouted. "If you want to eat this week, we've got some making up to do." Gas lanterns lit the alley sign for Hupp's Supper Club & Hotel.

"You're not serious, Oscar?" Esmerelda put the doll aside. It was an awkward climb from the back of the buckboard to the front, and a gold lamé gown didn't help. Barney, Bill, and Jimmie moved in the opposite direction. Cora sat like a lump of earth, poking her fingers through a crate that held a cat. Esmerelda hovered behind Oscar, who sat at the reins. "After what happened at Albee's? You expect me to sing, to go on?"

He twisted toward her. "I might not, Miss Moon, if we'd collected the door from Percy. But you know how it works. Acts don't get their cut until the crowd's cleared out, satisfied customers."

"But that wasn't our fault."

"Very astute, girl, but Percy doesn't give a shite about why he had to make refunds." He fished into his pocket, coming up with their meager tips, most of which was the nickel he'd given Bill prior to showtime. "Look at the bright side. For Hupp, you only have to open your mouth to sing. It's got to be easier than making contact with the dead." While it was true—singing being Esmerelda's God-given gift—she didn't budge from Oscar's whisker-filled ear. He aimed a glance at her. "Listen, it's thanks to you Mr. Hupp's agreed to put in most of our acts. But we've talked about this. You've got to play nice, Esmerelda. It's your singing he's after."

"It's not what he's after, Oscar."

"Has the rich rascal been anything but a gentleman?"

Esmerelda shrank back into the wagon. That much she couldn't argue. Since Benjamin Hupp had discovered Esmerelda at Luna Park, he'd been mesmerized. After only two Coney Island visits, he'd offered Esmerelda late billing at Hupp's Manhattan establishment. Oscar had parlayed the invitation to include Barney and Bill's soft shoe, and Jimmie's playlet oration. In the cutthroat world of vaudeville, slots at the supper club were a coup, and she couldn't deny them the chance.

Since then, onstage and off, Esmerelda felt as if she were putting on a performance. Naturally, none of this mattered one iota to Oscar, who was going on about Cora. She was the other girl in Oscar Bodette's Traveling Extravaganza—a juggler—and by default Esmerelda's friend. "So you see the potential," Oscar said. "Hupp's even mentioned putting Cora in on speculation."

"And she comes away with fifty cents," Esmerelda countered. "It won't make or break us."

Oscar looked over his shoulder. "That's assuming she doesn't drop a cup, saucer, or the cat."

Cora poked out her head, narrow face and ears like wings peeking around Esmerelda's gold-covered frame. "I beg your pardon, Oscar, but I've only dropped two cups and a saucer in the past month, and Licorice not once." In her arm was a long-haired black cat. "His claws are like razors. I'm mindful, believe me."

"Then I'd do well to install razors on your china cups, Miss Cora, if that's what it takes to keep me from replacing them." He looked harder over his shoulder at both girls. "The two of you don't look a lick alike, but posed like that, I could pass you off for a Siamese twin act. Do you have any idea what folks pay for that sort of sight?"

Esmerelda pushed on Cora's shoulder, forcing her inside. "Back to the point, Oscar. You can't expect me to sing after—"

"I know what you're doing, Esmerelda. You're not so easily shaken by an ornery crowd. You want to avoid Hupp." He paused. "You're a smart girl. Smarter than most." Oscar glanced into the dark hole where Cora had gone. "I've no idea why you're being such a fool about this. Hupp's put you at third billing. Do you know what that means?"

A screen door slapped open and a young man appeared in the alley. "It means my father will see to it that she's handsomely rewarded for her efforts tonight! I'm sure of it."

"Just what I was gettin' to," Oscar mumbled.

Benjamin beamed at Esmerelda. While only her head was visible, she felt exposed. "And naturally, I will be enchanted to hear her sing." His voice was deep and well educated; no one would argue he was anything less than dashing. Benjamin looked like money might. As if his parents' wealth could purchase fine features. In one hand, he held a champagne bottle, in the other, a glass.

He placed the glass on a stack of crates and approached the wagon. He wore boots in the summer heat, and she was surprised to see him slog through dishwater mud in the fine footwear. Benjamin reached up and shook her keeper's hand. Oscar's arm crossed in front of Esmerelda. She wanted it to be a symbolic shield, but his silence was the more obvious cue.

"Benjamin," she said brightly. "How lovely to see you." She made no effort to move out of the wagon. "If I am performing, I need to change my dress." She waved her arm, the gold sleeve swaying and glinting off lantern lights.

He stepped back. "My heavens, you've come dressed as an angel!"

"That's a damned perceptive conclusion, Mr. Hupp." Oscar said this, and Esmerelda shoved her elbow into his wide back. Benjamin was unaware of their medium act, which wouldn't be suitable for Hupp's upscale revue.

"Miss Moon . . ." Benjamin appeared to suck in all the alley air. "She clears my mind, and strangely enough, at the same time I only have eyes for her. She is a rare prize, indeed."

Esmerelda inched back, feeling like a trophy in her gold gown.

He pointed the champagne bottle at her. "Come down here and let me see you in your angel gown!" He granted Oscar a grin. "Tell me, did you finally purchase her a proper frock in which to perform? Because—"

"No," she answered. "It's from a show we did earlier. I don't think it's right for the supper club. The gown is a bit big, gaudy, and—"

"And perfect on you, I'm sure. But I did notice you were shy on costuming. I asked our stage mistress to gather a few things from which you can choose." He smiled wider and wagged a finger at her. "Keep any you like, Esmerelda. But I most certainly want to see you in that one."

"You'll still be wantin' the rest of my troupe?" Oscar said.

Benjamin's gaze clung to Esmerelda. He blinked and retreated a step, as if a large wagon, sweating horses, and the rest of Oscar's menagerie had just appeared in front of him. "Yes . . . yes, of course. You drive a hard bargain, Mr. Bodette. But yes, your entire group, as long as Esmerelda sings." His gaze returned to hers. "My father may be so impressed he'll want to steal her as a permanent featured performer."

Oscar grunted. "So long as her agent gets his share, we could likely work something out."

"Oscar," Esmerelda hissed in his ear, "I'm not a prize heifer, available to the highest bidder."

Benjamin swung the bottle toward the back entrance. "All of you, come in. Mrs. Downey will escort you to the dressing rooms. Esmerelda, I'll see you and that gown inside." He pivoted, gracefully plucking his glass from the crates and raising it in her direction before disappearing into the club.

The others followed, leaving Oscar bent over his horses and Esmerelda breathing down his neck. "So you've nothing more to say."

He peered over his sweaty team. "Do Mr. Hupp the courtesy of singing on key, would ya? The young man is more anxious than usual." She stuck her tongue out at the back of his head, and Oscar pointed to the rear entrance. "Now get moving." He turned. "This is just another act, Esmerelda."

"Really? I suppose it's fine as long as Benjamin Hupp hasn't taken a shine to you."

"If he'd had, I'd be pushing Barney or Bill on him—they'd be his type. As it is, so what? So the son of a filthy rich man is smitten." Oscar pointed to a city she could smell, the poor and rank tenement dwellings blocks away. The things other girls did to get paid. "Play along and we all get fed."

"At what cost to me, Oscar?" She ducked back into the wagon.

"The high price of singin' in one of Manhattan's finest halls." He shook his head. "Lordy, girl. It bothered you less to do the devil's bidding little more than an hour ago, at least according to one woman."

"I chose to do the devil's bidding!" Esmerelda squeezed her eyes shut and murmured, "Saints, forgive me." When she opened them, Marigold stared back. She closed the doll's paper-weight eyes and shouted at the wagon's opening, "You know what I meant, Oscar!" He laughed at her upset. Esmerelda reached for one of the two black dresses she owned, the wool stockings that also hung over a hook.

"No you don't." Oscar glanced back. "Young Hupp wants to see the gown. Wear it."

"But it's not a singing gown. It's a costume—and a gaudy one at that."

"It's a prop, Esmerelda. One your current employer would like to see. Let's not disappoint him, eh? You're still well to the right of respectable."

"Oh, for . . ." She threw one black dress to the side and reached for a rag.

"The rouge stays too. Without it, you're pale as one of your would-be ghosts. A little color will lend some drama when hitting those high notes in 'Love Will Find a Way.'"

"You want me to sing that?" She pointed at the upscale club. "With Benjamin Hupp watching?"

"No, I want you to sing 'The Star-Spangled Banner.'" Oscar's voice turned gruffer; he was done negotiating. "Seems a girl who's got me between herself and those streets can't be too choosy. And he's not asking a thing that isn't proper. Now leave the gown and the rouge. We're done. If these horses don't get some water, we'll be carrying your throne on our backs."

In a small act of defiance, Esmerelda grabbed one of Cora's ribbons and gathered her long hair into a topsy-turvy knot. Taking another, she belted the gown to rein in its angel-like angles. Esmerelda collected the heavy skirt and lowered herself out of the wagon's rear. She came around to stand by a snorting Go, avoiding Oscar's watchful eye. "I'll see you inside."

"I'll be watching." He looked past the horses and back at Esmerelda. "Did you learn that new song yet, 'Over There'? I paid two cents to get you the sheet music."

"Yes. But I don't care for it. Crowds want to hear ballads, or popular songs like 'Old Kentucky Home' and 'Spanish Dance.' I don't understand why you want me to learn that one."

"I'm stayin' ahead is all. Songs like 'Over There' is a sign of times to come." Oscar didn't clarify and slapped the reins, grunting a forward motion noise at Go and Fish.

They pulled away and Esmerelda sighed. Oscar Bodette was her employer, not her friend like Cora. Nor was he a man like her father—useless. Mercifully, he wasn't anything like her brother-in-law, Lowell—Hazel's husband and the man at the core of Esmerelda's very circumstance.

Yet, most of what Oscar did ensured survival, the hard-to-find security in a vaudevillian life. Despite this evening's squabble, she trusted him. Oscar might not wear kindness on his sleeve, but he was a good man. It was the first thing she gauged: the margin between a good and evil man.

# Act I, Scene III

Esmerelda bit down on a thumbnail and stared at the back entrance to the supper club. Oscar was right; she was being a fool—and a selfish one, at that. She headed for the door. At the same time, a pack of young men rolled around the corner on a wave of intoxication. She'd seen enough liquor to spot a drunk—several, in this case. The rowdy male voices skewered her attention; they weren't from this part of the city. The gown rustled as she held the heavy bottom bunched above her knees and hurried for the door. The largest boy was quicker, darting in her path, grasping her arm.

"What have we here, boys?" He was muscular, with shoulders wider than the hall's alley entrance. "A pretty slip of a thing." His gaze drew down her as he threw his cigarette into the mud. "Dressed for a date with a prince, are you?"

"So definitely not you," she said, and the other boys laughed. He smelled like her father and felt as threatening as Lowell. Esmerelda tugged her arm, but his grip was stronger. It tightened. He was a heavy breather, reeking like a vat of whiskey and intention. Esmerelda kept a cool head. "Let go of me. I'm performing here tonight. Mr. Benjamin Hupp will be looking for me straightaway."

One young man elbowed another. "Mr. Benjamin Hupp. Do you hear that?" This time they laughed at her. "She's a quick liar."

"Give her some credit," another boy said. "Hupp's as close to a prince as you'll find around here."

The boy holding on to her tightened his grip and his expression went flat. "I thought we'd struck out in this part of town—uppity, snooty cunts. But at least we've found where they keep the sure ones."

"And finer looking than the average strumpet." The second boy stepped in, and his dirty fingers skimmed the neckline of the gown. "'Course, I never had one dress for the occasion."

"I told you," she said through gritted teeth, "I'm working here."

"That I believe." The boy holding on to her leered, sniffing her hair. "I'd also bet that sort of *work* isn't something Hupp's likes to advertise."

"Won't find it on the bill, for sure," said the fourth boy.

"I'm a singer," Esmerelda insisted.

"You're alone," said her captor. "But that'll work, since your trade is obvious and we've got no money. Surely you won't mind passin' the tin for free."

The second boy took hold of her other arm and the first one grabbed at her breasts. She felt gold beads and his fingers bruise her skin. When she tried to scream, the largest boy covered her mouth with his hand. He shoved her hard against the brick exterior. Esmerelda was pinned there, and her eyes moved right and left, seeing only a narrow alley of mud.

"And to think, a belly full of whiskey was all we thought tonight's invite would get us." He shuffled his hand under the heavy fabric. She wore no proper corset, too restricting for a fast costume change. His hand eagerly groped her bare thigh. "Keepin' the whores out back, there's a rich businessman's scheme for you."

A boy with a sudden anxious look grinned. "Keeps the rooms cleaner, I bet."

Esmerelda mentally begged for Benjamin's presence. She'd be screaming for him if she could. Then she recalled part of the reason Oscar had earned the mark of protector. She employed a hard thrust of her knee—something Oscar had made her practice before playing rowdier venues. Her captor cried out like a kicked dog. He let go of Esmerelda and stumbled back. Then he came forward even faster, striking her across the face.

"You fucking bitch." He had her by the hair, his fingers winding through it and the ribbon. "And here I thought we'd be nice and say thank you after taking a turn."

"What the . . . Archie, Ralph, what the hell are you doing?" A voice drew their attention, and they turned, a collective twisting of heads from a salivating pack.

The boy's hold was fierce, and Esmerelda felt as if her head were impaled on a pike. She could only see from the corner of her eye. But fast as the boys had seized her, they let go. She scraped her body farther down the wall, knees buckling, beads popping as she went. With a clearer look, she saw two more boys. One rushed forward.

"You stupid, drunk bastards. I let you come all the way uptown, and this is what you do?"

"We was just messin' with her, Phin. No harm done."

Esmerelda heaved heavy breaths, her gaze darting between boys.

"I think she'd beg to differ." The two newcomers were outnumbered and outsized, but clearly the one who spoke had a hold over them. A silent boy with long braided hair stood by his side, though his mouth gaped, his expression fairly appalled. "Just get the fuck out of here before the local dick catches the lot of you." They scattered like pigeons from a coop.

Esmerelda's head drooped and she caught her breath. When she looked up, the boy who'd done the talking was coming closer. "Follow them, Hassan," he said. "Make sure they get on the trolley, get the hell out of here." He now spoke in a language Esmerelda could not place. The boy with braids grunted a reply. But he obeyed too, vanishing into the dark from which they'd all come.

It was a standoff. Maybe this boy wanted what his friends did, but just for himself. She sized him up. He was tall but reedy, not nearly as bulky as the largest boy. Untangling her gaze from his, she looked to her left. The door was steps away. *Wait. What was she thinking?* "Benjamin!" Esmerelda screamed in her loudest stage voice. The boy lunged, placing his hand right where Ralph's or Archie's had been.

"What the hell are you doing? I just saved you from a gang of boys with ideas that'd make nuns faint! Even if it's how you earn your livin' . . ." With one hand gripped over her mouth, his other settled firm on her waist. "Nobody deserves that."

Esmerelda blinked. *Nobody did.* She hadn't expected to find them in agreement. Pressed tight to him, she felt his heart pound. Perhaps it was fear that Benjamin would come to her rescue. She imagined the resources at the young heir's disposal—club overseers, surely the police. But the swell of patron noise said Benjamin wasn't within earshot.

He broke the stalemate. "If I take my hand away, you'll be quiet?"

She nodded. Yet it could be he thought being raped by one man, instead of a mob, was a favor. She could assure him it was not. He removed his palm, but in the same motion braced his other arm above her knees.

"And we won't be havin' none of that either. I don't want anything from you—particularly a kick to the groin."

Esmerelda brushed the back of her hand through the hot tears on her cheeks. "I told them I'm working here tonight."

He backed up, a fair sign that his presence wasn't a threat. "And I'd think a girl like you had learned a trick or two of your trade. You don't go offering services to four drunk idiots in an alley." He thumbed over his shoulder. "Actually, I'm surprised." His strange eyes, blue sea melding with gray sky, perused the gown. "I didn't know Hupp's . . . *menu* went dicier than Blue Point Oysters and French champagne."

"What is it you think I'm doing here, working here as?" She willed herself forward, in the moment as in life. The boy backpedaled.

Maybe he wasn't quite a boy. She was unsure.

He stopped and boldly leaned in, whispering, "No offense, but there's only so many trades that call for a getup like that one. And the Hupps do own both buildings." He pointed to the hotel under construction next door.

"I'm a singer. I'm performing here tonight."

"In that? Sorry—but I've seen Hupp's revue. I sometimes photograph his guests and talent." The way he said it, clearly it included bragging rights. In the mud, she spied a weighty canvas bag. "People like to be seen here. Or at least they did." He shook his head. "I've never known a singer to come dressed like a . . . well, a . . ."

"A what?"

He hitched up his breath. "A prostitute, if you're gonna make me say it."

She wasn't about to be accused twice in one night. Esmerelda came at him swinging, scratching, wishing she'd hung on to Licorice and his razor claws. "You're all filthy, stupid boys! I'm the third-billed act. I'm Esmerelda Moon!" she said as if this should mean something to him.

He ducked and darted; he was quick, and now he was laughing. Managing to get behind her, he fastened his arm around her waist and the gold gown. "You are feisty, Esmer . . ." He tried again. "Esm . . . *Miss Moon*. I'll give you that!" She thrashed about, but it was futile. "So we're back to this. If I let go, will you quit trying to remove my body parts?"

She didn't reply, though she'd stopped flailing. Gingerly, like she might be made of ribbon candy, he let go. Esmerelda turned. At least she'd altered the look on his face: smug to wary.

She looked down—the bottom of the gown was covered in mud. Oscar would not be pleased. Esmerelda looked back at her more immediate problem. "I'm with Oscar Bodette's Traveling Extravaganza. We had a show earlier, over the bridge in Brooklyn. The gown . . . it goes with a different act. I, um . . . it's more theatrical than singing."

"What's more theatrical than singing on a stage?"

"It's different. Certain venues and crowds lend themselves to more creative acts."

"You mean like juggling . . . doing a jig, acrobatics?" He smiled. It caught her eye. He had pretty teeth and a full set. "I can't see doing none of it dressed like that."

In an attempt to convince him, she blurted out the truth. "It's a soothsayer act."

"Soothsayer?" He tugged the cap from his head and ruffled his fingers through his dark hair. "Like a mind reader?"

She felt a blush rise over the rouge on her cheeks. "Yes. I speak to the dead, or I have on Tuesdays and Saturdays at Albee's in Brooklyn. New Faces in Queens before that." His expression remained muddled. "It's one of a dozen acts we do. Like you said, dancing a jig, dramatic readings, and such." She rolled her eyes. "For a person photographing a fancy club, you're more naïve than Cora."

"Who's—" He stopped, his stare still examining. "Never mind her name. Tell me yours again."

"Esmerelda . . . Moon." She pointed to the one overhead.

"Esme."

"What?"

"Less of a mouthful. Suits you."

"Suits me? You don't even know me." Esmerelda brushed at the gown. It felt like an effort to straighten her dignity—currently covered in gold, rouge, and mud. Herself having been taken for a common trollop.

"Maybe not," he said. "But at least I'm making an effort, and not with much help from you. So you truly don't speak to the dead? And you're not a . . . well, a woman whose living might be assumed from her wardrobe?"

Esmerelda folded her arms, the wide sleeves drooping, beads dangling. "Aren't you as quick as Wall Street ticker tape." She raised an arm in the direction Oscar had gone. "People will jump at any chance to visit with their departed loved ones." She glanced at the ground. "Or so I've learned."

"If only that could be." He squinted at her. "But you don't like doing it."

"How do you know that?"

"Because everything about you changed when you said it—like if you had a choice, you'd rather not be a soothsayer."

She thought it a queer statement, like anyone sat around mulling over the option of being a soothsayer. "I'm not . . ." She looked at the mud. Then her head bobbed back up. "It might not be the most honorable job, but I prefer it to being a common . . ." Esmerelda was unsure how she'd become the focus of the discussion. "What's wrong with your friends, anyway? If you want to speak of dishonorable behavior."

"Ah, they're just Hell's Kitchen riffraff. More like a gang than mates. They'd been asking to tag along to this part of town. And they did think you were . . ."

Esmerelda's jaw slacked.

"I'm not defending them." He hoisted an arm in the direction they'd gone. "But all the boys are a little drunk and dizzy, yet tight in the mind these days."

"Why's that?"

"Everyone's got the call. Ralph's going next week. We're all going eventually."

"Going where?" Esmerelda stepped back, thinking he meant the influenza that had taken so many, Sally's sister, Tilly; and Esmerelda's own mother. "You're not sick, are you?"

"No. Nothing you might live from."

She blinked, never having heard it put that way before.

"The war, Esme. We're all being called sooner or later. They're making an army out of us boys—even Mr. Benjamin Hupp. Surely you see a newspaper now and again, hear talk in your travels."

Esmerelda shook her head, far preferring a book when she could get her hands on one.

"You don't know about the *Lusitania*? German subs are sinking ships every day, coming closer to this side of the ocean."

Of course she knew about the luxury liner sinking, but she didn't know about other boats.

"Krauts have already taken Belgium, they're working on France. Mr. Wilson has no choice. We're already in a war over there."

"'Over There.'" The song clicked. Esmerelda's fingers caught around the hair ribbon, which came undone. She felt stupid and at a loss. "I didn't know."

"I guess lots of women don't."

"What's that supposed to mean?"

"Nothing." He paused, shoving his hands into his pockets. "Most women don't like to talk of war or know about it. It's men who'll do all the fightin'."

"It's men who have all the power and rule. Seems you'll be doing nothing but lying in the bed you've made for yourselves." She looked in the direction the drunk idiots had gone.

"I see your point."

She looked back with surprise.

"Anyway, none of it is an excuse, but add some whiskey to the fact and rash behavior won't be far behind. You . . . you're all right, then?"

She nodded and hoisted the loose shoulder of the gown into place. Other than having the wits scared out of her, she was fine.

"So you're really singing on Hupp's stage tonight?"

She'd nearly forgotten. "Not if I don't get inside." But Esmerelda didn't move. In the spotlight of a gas lamp, he bedazzled her—no regalia needed. Wavy dark hair and eyes like an incoming storm. But it was more than what Oscar would call "stage presence." An itch of familiarity invaded her—like Esmerelda had known him all her short life. "You . . . you've never been to New England, have you?"

"New England?"

"Massachusetts."

He shook his head.

"Well, um . . . thank you, Mr. . . . ?"

"Seaborn. Phineas Seaborn. But Phin to my friends."

"Thank you for your assistance . . . Phin," she said carefully. "If it weren't for you, I might have ended up like Desdemona."

"Desdemona?"

"She was murdered."

"Was she?" He stared as if Esmerelda had been an eyewitness.

"Onstage. I might not know newspapers, but I know a little Shakespeare. It's a popular dramatic scene. Jimmie and I have played it a few times." Esmerelda shrugged softly. "Desdemona is murdered by her jealous lover."

"Then it's even better I turned up when I did. We wouldn't have wanted it to come to that."

Esmerelda's shoes had sunk into mud, but it was their twined gazes that held her still. "It is indeed."

The two were bound to silence, maybe time. The moment felt wavy, like the rings from a rock skipped over a pond. The buzz inside Hupp's club echoed, not steps away, but from an entire world away. Even odder, the young man replied in kind.

"This is a curious thing for a fellow to say, a stranger to think— standing in an alley, talking to a girl I didn't know this morning." He came closer, and Esmerelda only felt . . . *safe*. "Know that if I could prevent it, I'd never let harm come to you, Esme. Not in a hundred years. I promise you that."

# CHAPTER
# FOUR

*Surrey, Massachusetts*
*Present Day*

Aubrey sat on the bed, a journal open on a lap desk. Word by word, voices rose from the living room. The ones she wrote slowed. Eavesdropping wasn't intentional, but as Grace's soft tone hardened, then Pete's boomed, it couldn't be helped. Aubrey tapped the pen against the bound notebook. She bit down on her lip and cringed. The people who could comprehend Pete's circumstances were a short list, and Grace Hathaway happened to be on it. Aubrey's earlier text was meant as a nudge toward a friendly reunion, nothing more. She continued to listen, her gaze weaving over the other items on the bed: a fabric-covered cardboard box and a laptop, some papers she'd printed out earlier.

The front door slammed, and Pete came up the stairs and into his parents' bedroom. "You shouldn't have invited her here, Mom."

"I just thought—"

"You thought what? Grace would pop in after everything that's happened, and we'd say, 'Gosh, aren't we two crazy idiots? Guess Mom knew best. Marry me, darling.'"

She tossed the journal aside and offered Pete a deadpan look. "No. I thought you'd at least take her to lunch before declaring your undying love."

"This isn't one of your 1940s, cue-the-romantic-music classics. I don't get the girl or the happy-ever-after ending."

"Not with that doomed attitude, you won't."

"My attitude is a reasonable reaction to 'Here, Pete! Say hi to the alive-and-well girl whose heart you broke, in addition to a full-on visit with one you loved and—'"

"Don't say it."

"Why? Is there an alternative interpretation?" He turned for the hall.

Having witnessed twenty-plus years of unyielding visits to his past, Aubrey didn't doubt what Pete experienced—that he'd killed a beautiful girl named Esme. Of course, what she heard now spilled over into more of an in-the-moment rant.

"Pete, I'm sorry." Her plea was loud and placating enough for him to turn back. "I didn't think . . . or I thought too fast. I wasn't going for the 'big picture,'" she said, air quoting her words. "I only thought it wouldn't be the worst thing if you and Grace reconnected on some level. I get that you were better friends than anything else."

Pete heaved a sigh, tapping his knuckles on the door molding. "Look, the only way happily ever after works out is if Esme's ghost turns up, forgives me, and we end up in a remake, *The Ghost and Mr. Muir.*"

"Esme's ghost?" He'd never broached the subject—ghosts and Esme were two different talking points. "Why would you say that?"

"Say what?"

"*Esme's ghost.* Your other life has nothing to do with spectral encounters. It's two divided worlds, and your father and I have always viewed it as a huge part of your frustration. Has something changed?"

And now he looked ambivalent. "Maybe."

"Maybe?" Aubrey scrambled off the bed, faster than she'd moved in months. But when your child—even an adult one—stood near fire, reaction was instinct. "Esme. You encountered her spirit?"

Pete held up the gauze-covered hand. "I wasn't that unsteady in the bathroom. I was shocked, frustration expounded tenfold." His Adam's apple bobbed. "I'm not sure what it was—a woman's voice, a presence. It's never happened before, nothing like that, nothing so *connected* to her."

"And you what, decided that not telling your father or me was the way to go?"

"I was trying to figure it out. As you know, the threshold for 'never happened before' is damn high in this house."

He wasn't wrong. Pete's knowledge of Esme was the vision he relived. Years ago, he'd concluded the reason he never encountered her spirit was anger. Who'd visit the person responsible for their death? Unless, perhaps, it was to haunt them. "Was her presence surrounded by anger? Is that how you cut your hand?"

"No. Not hardly." He stared at his bandaged palm. "I'm just foggy about what I'm dealing with in terms of a specter."

"But you're positive it was an apparition?" The look Pete offered, it was as if Aubrey asked if the sky was blue. "Sorry. Dumb question. But what makes you say the ghost was Esme?"

"A feeling." He was quicker with this reply, which, while vague, told Aubrey something. Only a specter connected directly to you could elicit emotion, intense personal feelings of love or loss. She knew this from encountering thousands of specters that belonged to other people, and one that belonged to her—Zeke Dublin.

"She, uh . . . she spoke to me."

"Did she?"

"Yes. After all these years, it was very enlightening. She said, *'If Paris is France . . .'*"

"'If Paris is France'?"

"Yeah. In the bathroom. Then when we were at breakfast."

"You heard her a second time?"

"Yes. Outside, on the deck. Esme said, *'If Paris is France, then Coney Island, between June and September, is the World.'* Then she vanished."

Aubrey sat on the edge of the bed and Pete plopped down next to her.

"For years I've imagined all the hellish things Esme might say if I encountered her—on this side of life or the next." He sighed, and Aubrey listened. "Last year, I was pinned in a bunker in Mosel, a hundred yards away from a bomb blast that took out three blocks and dozens of people. I was positive I wasn't getting out of that day alive."

"Pete! You never said a word to us."

"The point is I did what any person does in a situation like that. I thought of the people I loved. I thought of you and Pa."

Aubrey smiled small. "You thought of Esme."

"I did. Insane as that would sound to anyone beyond these walls." Pete's gaze moved around the bedroom. "But in that bloody ditch, I'd never been more ready, more prepared to face her."

His words made Aubrey's heart ache, that her son was so bold about death in the present, fearing his other life more. "I can't imagine how terrifying it was, from every perspective."

"In the bunker, with body parts landing on me, explosions coming closer, I envisioned Esme's wrath. But even then, all I could think of was how much I loved her. When I walked away from the bunker unscathed, I paused in the middle of what was still dangerous real estate. Then I hustled the hell out of there. If only for a split second, I dreaded this life more than that one." Pete rubbed the thumb of one hand over the bloodied gauze on the other. "All that, and yet I remain too terrified to seek any real answers. How's that hitting on your crazy meter?"

"You could have called. We could have talked it through."

"To what end?"

It was Aubrey's turn to sigh; she was well aware of how long they'd wandered the maze of Pete's mind.

"Then after all these years," he said, "today, in my own bathroom, in my own house, Esme does more than turn up dead in my other life. She's present in this one. And what do I get from her? Not confrontational words or a specter on the attack. Nothing that might make sense." He laughed, which sent a chill up Aubrey's spine. "I get a riddle about Paris and Coney Island." Pete stood, slapping his hands against his sides. "Teaser text. It's about the only thing I've never considered."

"It might have sounded cryptic in a twenty-first-century moment, but maybe you're miss—" Aubrey cocked her head; the phrase was familiar. "'If Paris is France' . . . wait. Esme didn't say that."

"Oh, she did. Believe me. Along with putting a bullet in her, those words are also now burned in my memory. Maybe we should start a second scrapbook."

"Just hang on a second." Aubrey pulled her laptop toward her, typing furiously. "There!" She pointed to the screen. "'If Paris is France, then Coney Island, between June and September, is the World.'"

"What are you . . . ?" He leaned in, staring at the results.

"Esme didn't say it. Well, not originally. George Tilyou did." Aubrey quickly read through one Google result. "Tilyou was the entrepreneur who built Steeplechase Park, and eventually Coney Island. He coined the phrase."

"Around World War I?"

"Late nineteenth century. But it stuck, enough to index more than a million Google entries."

"Huh. I never heard it before this morning." He glanced at his mother. "Why would she say that to me?"

"A better question is what does it mean between the two of you? After all this time, all these years, if Esme is making herself known, there must be a reason."

"And what are the chances of that being good news versus bad?"

Aubrey started to reply. She wanted to reassure her son. She ran her hand over her pockmarked arm. That and the scar on her chin were compliments of evil specters. Aubrey couldn't promise Pete what had happened that morning was a positive thing. But she did as any good mother would and offered the most supportive answer possible. "Why don't we keep an open mind? Not make assumptions."

Pete looked at his watch. "Well, in a few hours, it won't matter. I'll be on a flight to Iceland."

"You can't be serious. After this?" Aubrey pointed to the laptop screen as if it contained a computer-generated image of the mysterious Esme.

"Whatever it was, whatever it might be . . . I'm still in the 'I'd prefer not to know' camp. Let it go."

She closed out the Google search. "So no Esme, and no Grace."

"Mom, you know how difficult it is to fit normal inside my life—or lives. I've accepted the fact that what you have with Pa is not in the plan for me."

"Don't say that, Pete. You don't know."

"Yeah. I do. I know what I felt for Grace was special. I also know it's not anything close to what I feel . . . *felt* for . . ." And the thought hung there like it had for years—impossible to fit into the context of rational thinking.

"Her." Aubrey provided this as if Esme were the girl Pete had loved and lost last year, instead of in another life.

"Did it ever occur to you that my existence in this life is punishment for the last one? Maybe this morning was a reminder. In case I thought I was beating the odds by living on the edge of death."

Aubrey was too short on energy to offer a meaningful reply. Pete's take on life was difficult to argue. She had so few facts and none that could be used in his defense—a World War I medal bearing his initials. Blood tests from years ago that showed traces of coal, part of an absurd trial tetanus vaccine, as well as antibodies to a strain of influenza eradicated a century before. His role in the Great War was common knowledge by the time Pete was twelve. All of it came before Esme, his horrific and methodical reliving of having killed her. Pete's telling was so vivid it often felt like a weighty secret Aubrey harbored about her son.

"Okay. You win," she said. "I respect your right not to pursue answers." Aubrey went about busywork: closing her journal, tidying the items inside the box on her bed, shuffling loose pages into a stack.

"Wait. What's that?" Pete cocked his chin in her direction.

"The box?" She pointed to the most obvious item.

"No. The papers."

Aubrey reached for a single sheet of white paper, which included a color photo of a house that had belonged to her grandmother Charley. "A newer piece of my past. Kind of ties in with what I've been working on. It's an e-mail from a law firm in New Mexico. It seems Charley owned a property, a house on the east end of Long Island."

"Long Island?" There was an uptick in Pete's tone. "That's a few worlds away from Albuquerque, New Mexico."

"It's part of the reason it took so long for the legalities to play out. Charley owned a house with Truman Heinz." She furrowed her brow. "And/or Oscar Bodette."

"Oscar?"

"Yes, Oscar. The details are unclear. Apparently, after they both passed, the deed transferred to Charley. But it was never properly recorded. For some reason, she never updated her will to reflect it. When her estate was settled . . . what? Ten years ago?"

"About that. A day shy of her hundredth birthday."

Aubrey smiled at the woman and her longevity. For a time, she'd clung to a sweet fantasy that part of her grandmother's gift had been eternal life. On the eve of her birthday, she'd passed peacefully in her sleep. Upon learning of her grandmother's death, Aubrey had held back a sea of tears, remarking, "Charley kept insisting she didn't want any one-hundredth birthday fuss. I suppose she got her way."

She cleared her throat and returned to the paper. "With no one inquiring about the house, it sat for years. Charley could be secretive, and the house doesn't surprise me all that much. If I remember . . ." Aubrey had to think hard for tidbits about Charley's surplus of husbands. "Truman's carnie roots were Midwest. At some point he hooked up with Oscar. Eventually, it became the Heinz-Bodette troupe."

"When did all this occur?"

"Oh, gosh. Which part? I think the modern-day troupe came into existence around World War II. You know that Charley was married to both men—Oscar, twice."

He shook his head. "No, I didn't. How did that happen?"

"If I have the story straight, Charley and Oscar divorced amicably. He was a good bit older than her or Truman, who she married next. When Truman passed unexpectedly, freak Ferris wheel accident," she said, recalling distant details, "Oscar turned back up, and they rekindled their May-December romance."

"You're kidding." That much got a smile out of him. "Tell me more."

"Charley always told me she loved both men equally and they drove her equally mad. Anyway . . ." Aubrey picked up another paper, this one bearing a law firm letterhead. "Fast-forward several decades. That's where the attorney chain letters come in. Seems the property was declared abandoned by Suffolk County and sold at auction. With one last title search, lawyers finally connected the house to Charley and subsequently me." She squinted at the fuzzy image of a small wooden structure surrounded by woods. "Maybe it's the era, but the house looks kind of rugged. Not the sort of place Charley would have liked to spend her off months. But the attorney's point, if I'm understanding all the legal mumbo jumbo . . ." She picked yet another paper brimming with text. "Is that the sale can't proceed until I sign off—if that's what I want to do."

"So just a yes-or-no question?"

"Not quite. The attorneys go on to say the house is jam-packed with memorabilia. Sounds like troupe members used it for storage or a respite in the off season. I do vaguely recall talk of a 'house back east.'

I remember Charley offering use of a house to Zeke Dublin and his sister now and again."

Pete stared at the photo. "Bungalow. It looks more like a bungalow."

She hadn't thought about it. "Okay, bungalow." From beneath a stack of legal papers, Aubrey produced a map of Long Island. "Whatever sort of house, it's located right on the North Fork, a town called East Marion. If I want to sell, I have to arrange to dispose of the contents or come get them, which I don't have the energy to deal with right now."

"You could call one of those estate companies, have them toss most of it, sell anything of value."

"How would I know what's of value unless somebody sees it? And what kind of value? Monetary or a memory? Could be both." She stared at the facsimile photo. "Maybe it's filled with the fame and fortune the Heinz-Bodette troupe never realized."

"More like mayhem and mysticism."

"Possibly." She held a different paper out to Pete. "This is a rough manifest of its contents. The place sounds like a living Heinz-Bodette archive." She poked at the map. "I googled the directions. If you take the New London ferry, it's not far."

"Send Pa."

"I would, but you know his *Ink on Air* schedule. He's busy with the newsmagazine." Aubrey eased back into the pillow. "Unless maybe you're intrigued enough to—"

"Love to help, Mom. But as noted, I'm booked on an Icelandair flight." Pete grinned at his mother, the same rare but genuine expression that belonged to Levi. "We have some time right now. Want to tell me what else you're working on?"

She poked at the journal. "It does, in part, tie back to the information from the lawyers." She pointed to the paper still in Pete's hand. "Your father's been encouraging me to write another book. But I can't even settle on fact or fiction. He suggested I be my own *ghostwriter*, chronicle my early years with the carnival. He thinks it would be cathartic and a page-turner."

"He's probably right."

"Maybe. But can you even answer the question, would it be labeled fact or fiction?"

"So you invent an entirely fresh genre. I'd read it."

Aubrey nudged at the fabric-covered box. Pete looked between it and the old leather-clad letterbox, which sat on the dresser.

"Is that box like your father's, full of future predictions?"

"Nothing so fascinating. I only bought the box a few weeks ago at HomeGoods. I thought it was pretty." She removed the lid. "Inside are small things that belonged to Charley. I wanted them somewhere prettier than a plastic bin."

They were both quiet. In her younger years, Charley had been the reassuring constant in Aubrey's life, the person compelling her "dear girl" to make a life for herself regardless of ghosts and unknowns. Aubrey always wondered if she'd done enough to be that person for Pete.

She looked at the bandage around his hand, something like the force field her son kept around his heart. Covered, closed off. Her handsome, troubled, exquisitely gifted son. For better for worse, a complex Ellis–St John combo.

"You were saying, Mom? All this might play into a book idea?"

"It's barely an idea." Aubrey closed the lid. "Never mind about it. Maybe we could just have lunch downtown or go for a walk."

His smile emerged again, so like Levi's it gave Aubrey hope. Maybe the toughness ingrained in the father had been passed on to his son.

"Are you going to offer to buy me an ice cream cone too?"

She supposed every mother was susceptible—the urge to baby her adult child. "Fine. We'll look through the box." She shrugged. "It's nothing terribly mysterious. Charley kept a few journals throughout her life." She plucked one from the box, opening it randomly. "Look, she even mentions the Long Island house." She pointed to the paper

Pete still held, which read something like one of Aubrey's old real estate listing sheets. She grazed her fingers over Charley's handwriting. "She goes on about her dreams—the living connected to the dead. I suppose writing was an outlet for them. She mentions my father now and again, which is interesting." Aubrey pursed her lips. "Like all diaries, clearly these were never meant to be read."

"Why do you say that?"

"Because in this one"—she held up a different green-leather-covered diary—"she goes into stunning detail about her Niagara Falls honeymoon trip with Truman."

"Oh, we can so skip that part."

"That's what I did, but not before I got to . . ." Aubrey's face warmed.

Pete changed the subject as his free hand dove past hers and into the box. "Hey, this isn't Charley's. It's yours. It's a ghost gift." He sat up taller on the bed, holding a vintage postcard.

Aubrey didn't do more than glance at a ghost gift that had been part of her larger collection for years. "You know, I had both this box and my ghost gifts out not long ago—just trying to see if anything connected. I must have put it in with Charley's things accidentally." She looked Pete's way as her son's gaze moved across the old card. "You've seen it before, Pete. It's just a ghost gift I've never been able to place."

Aubrey knew the image like the cover of a treasured book: a watercolor scene that showed off a millpond bay and a long wooden pier, a gazebo poised at its end. A faded postmark noted New York, NY, June 1918. This alone had labeled it a ghost gift in Aubrey's mind—a postmark, yet no address. No sender, no recipient. No mess—"Wait. How is that . . . ?" She reached for Pete's arm and drew the card closer. "That is unbelievably weird."

"Mom, when you say 'unbelievably weird,' it freaks me out a little. What?"

"I must be mistaken. I've had this card for . . . well, it seems like forever. I don't even recall when or where it turned up. It always had a postmark." She turned it over, showing Pete the stamped date. He turned it back. On the front were preprinted words: "Dock, Foot of Gillette Avenue. Bayport, LI." Aubrey blinked at cursive handwriting that filled the bottom edge. "It's never had a handwritten message. You don't remember?"

Pete shook his head. "I know the postcard. I couldn't have told you what it said." His gaze shot to his mother's. "Or didn't say." He read from the card, *"When I spent two weeks on this beach, I didn't dream of you then. E.M."*

Aubrey blinked at her altered ghost gift. "I swear. This card has always been blank." She ran her fingertips over feminine cursive that did not look fresh, but as aged and worn as the postcard.

Pete drew a breath that expanded like a flame drawing air, enough to spark a fire. "Esme." He didn't simply speak her name; it was more like a force that welled up from deep within.

"Esme? What about her?"

"The initials. The E."

Aubrey shook her head at his conclusion. Even she had her limits with ghostly interpretation versus wishful thinking. "Pete, the *E* could stand for anything . . . Ellen, Elizabeth . . . even a man, Edward, Evan. And as far as I know, you're unaware of Esme's last name." With a paper object now in either hand, Pete jolted up from the bed. Aubrey thought it was the way people moved when they saw a ghost. "Let's borrow a little Levi logic here. After what you experienced this morning, you don't think it's possible that you're projecting?"

"Possible." He looked at his mother. "If it weren't for one thing."

"What's that?"

His gaze detached from the card and ticked around the room.

Aubrey knew the look, what her son was experiencing. "What do you hear?"

"Her." He looked at his mother. "For a third time. Esme. She says, *It's me."*

# CHAPTER
# FIVE

Pete validating the postcard, making a connection to Esme, was enough to get Aubrey up off the bed. "Esme. You just heard her again, clear as I'm hearing you? You're sure?"

"You're seriously going to ask me that? And according to you, the postcard never bore a message before today."

"You've got me there." Aubrey glanced down at the card. "But you think the card means what? You believe the girl who's haunted your visions, your . . ." Levi and Aubrey had been vigilant about not using the word "dream" to describe Pete's visitant episodes. "You think your other life connects to an old postcard that I've been carting around for decades?"

"It's suddenly not just any postcard, Mom. Not even your everyday ghost gift. You said it yourself, you've wondered for years what it meant, why you have it. Maybe Esme's the reason."

Aubrey wasn't entirely sure she wanted to further ideas about Esme. As it was, she'd never told Pete about the blue star, the ghost gift she'd recorded herself. It'd been her own prognostication, taking a message from a girl named Esmerelda. In the back of her mind, Aubrey had always known Esmerelda and Esme were one and the same.

When Aubrey was five, the ghostly girl had told her to draw a house with a red roof bordered by the sea. That she should keep the paper safe until she needed it. Aubrey's father, Pete's grandfather, had made certain that happened. Years later, the information on the paper star had saved her son's life, leading Aubrey, Levi, and the authorities to Pete.

He'd been taken, held hostage in a scheme to cash in on her father's ghost gifts, his foretellings. To keep Pete quiet, his captors had pumped the drug propofol into him. While her son had recovered from the physical effects of the anesthetic, the drug had also proved to be a mental trigger. It widened Pete's access to another life, inviting in Esme and the strong emotions of being in love with her, the clear visual of having killed her.

But as years went on, Aubrey had come to question Esmerelda's motives. Did she want Pete alive so she could spend this life tormenting him? For many reasons, Aubrey was both grateful to and skeptical of the mysterious Esme.

"I'll go you one better," Pete said. "There's something else." He dropped the vintage postcard and legal papers onto the bed and darted from the bedroom. "Hang on a second." His feet thundered down the stairs like they hadn't for years. But the sound stopped halfway. Seconds later, he came back up. In Pete's hand was a framed collage Aubrey had put together. They were small paintings he'd sent home some time ago. He laid the framed collection on the bed and placed the vintage postcard beside it. "Do you see any similarities between your ghost gift and the pictures I painted?"

The postcard could be described as both a photograph and a watercolor painting—she'd never been able to decide, the skill applied was that unique. It was uncanny, the sameness between the pictures Pete had produced and the postcard that was most certainly a ghost gift.

"Pete, if you touch the postcard, do you feel anything, maybe heat?"

Cautiously, with his gauze-wrapped hand, he picked up the postcard. "No," he said, shaking his head. "But is it that surprising? Messages from the other side, they've always been more . . . in my face." These were facts Aubrey knew. While her gift had reliable subtleties, Pete's was wired differently, sometimes producing these telltale signs, more often showing up like a chatty stranger on a street. He dropped the postcard on the bed and picked up the legal correspondence again. "Uh, Mom . . . does it have to be heat?"

"No. Not always. Sometimes it's a—"

"Vibration," they said simultaneously.

At present, Aubrey's bed held an unlikely collection of her life. Things that would not normally intersect. She imagined the cumulative energy it could produce. "Pete . . ." She thought for a second, then dove. "I know you're totally against any past life regression therapy." Aubrey held her hand up to his incoming objection. "But there was a time in my life where I had to find a way to take control. Our gifts, they may differ." She held out her pockmarked arm. "As hard and deliberate as taking charge was, in the end, I was so much happier."

"But a lot of that took Pa. You've said it yourself."

"That's not untrue. And I'm also not saying Grace is your Levi. So let's get that out of the way. But you do trust her. She does seem able to grasp—"

"A phenomenon that most clock-punching and even think tank minds would label absurd?"

Aubrey went around it. "Grace has a great capacity to think outside the box—at least your box. Give her credit for that."

"Your point being?"

"Instincts and experience." She eyeballed her son. "Which I wouldn't be so quick to dismiss. Given the convergence of physical elements"—Aubrey pointed to the bed, the paper he held—"in addition to your sudden presence, it seems to me that it demands a call to action. You'd be foolish to ignore it."

"And?" He crossed his arms.

"And what?"

"We've been doing this awhile. I know there's more."

"I believe everything that's happened since you arrived home, especially hearing Esme's voice, is a bread crumb trail. I've been deciphering ghost gifts most of my life." She studied the bed harder, folded her arms. "What more do you want in terms of an enticement or temptation? This is as strong a merging of evidence as I've ever seen."

"Okay, but it still doesn't—"

"Pete. If you're waiting for them to skywrite it, if you want them to tell you it all turns out just fine . . . we don't live in that world, do we?"

He didn't agree verbally but didn't argue either.

"Take Grace and go to Long Island. See if this *bungalow* . . ." She squinted at a structure that looked more like a shack. "The objects inside, combined with these, and your admitted ghostly nudge, offer any insight to your life."

"Past, present, or future? Could you be more specific?"

"I'm afraid my clairvoyant edge won't help you here. The best I can do is motherly advice."

Pete scanned the pieces of Ellis family history with a sober stare.

"Listen to me when I tell you it won't stop, Pete. The dead haven't anything better to do. They'll only come at you harder. You can't run forever. All I'm suggesting is—"

"I get it." He backed up several steps. "I hear you. And if it weren't for a sweet assignment that includes a hot springs sauna waiting for me at the end of this Reykjavík trip, I might consider it. As it is, my immediate calendar is full." He dropped the papers he held onto the bed. "Sorry, Mom. Even an ethereal shove from Esme isn't enough. It won't make me chase that ghost."

This was where her ability to grasp Pete's point of view dead-ended, and she could only speculate. If you believed you'd killed the love of your life, would you want to face that ghost?

Yet Pete's gaze stayed with the clues and keepsakes on the bed, and he offered dryly, "I can't poke a stick into that cage. I'm not that brave."

"No. Of course not." Aubrey looked toward the window that over-looked the nature preserve. "Not when it's so much handier to keep running into war zones. That's a great cover, Pete. Sorry if I don't see the everyday dangers you face as a fair trade."

"Okay, we're not having this discussion again."

Sometimes he sounded so much like Levi, Aubrey could only narrow her eyes at the most rigid aspects of her husband reproduced in another human being.

"It's a moot point for a thousand reasons. No matter how you're interpreting this . . . *stuff*—" Pete's phone rang and he looked at it. "It's Flagler. I have to take this." He answered. "Hang on a sec, Austin." Pete hit "Silent" on his phone. "My future had been foretold, okay? It's set for Iceland, not Long Island. It's my choice." He clicked back to the call.

Aubrey turned away, stumped by the dangerous, endless path her son continued to cycle through. Hearing Pete's tone, she listened harder.

"A what? A volcano?" He glanced at Aubrey. "You're not serious."

Motherly instinct leaped, but Aubrey bit her tongue—almost literally. He was a grown man, even if his life involved many unknowns. Instead, she merely continued to eavesdrop.

"They anticipate a closed airport for how long? All right. But what about that piece we were considering in the Congo? There's always action . . . yeah. Leslie Winger, she's a great photographer and a good writer. I can see how you wouldn't want two correspondents in such a hazardous region. Why don't we look into . . ." Pete continued to listen to his PressCorp editor, who doled out assignments. "Say that again." He nodded deeply. "One Direction." He paused, his jaw slacking. "No . . . yeah. I've heard of them. It's more about what I do, Austin. Or more to the point, what I don't do."

Aubrey could hear Austin Flagler's wooing tone offering information that was clearly irritating her son.

"Right. I'm sure a surprise reunion album debuting in Times Square will rock the world. At the very least cause serious gridlock." He held the phone at arm's length, hissing at his mother. "Do you believe this?" Pete rolled his eyes and pressed the phone back to his ear. "You're serious? That's what you want me to cover?" The aggravated look on Pete's face deepened. "Did I do something to piss you off?" He laughed, but there was nothing funny about it. "Yep. I'm sure plenty of photogs from the pool would be rabid for the chance. It's just not *my* kind of assignment, and . . ." An audible rebuttal cut him off. "Yeah. I'll think about it. But if you don't hear from me, feel free to scalp my press pass." He ended the call, tossed his phone onto the bed, and thrust his hands to his waist. "You heard."

"Kind of hard not to. Why did Flagler want you?"

"He thought someone unfazed by fame would do a better job of capturing the human side of the event. Plus, I'm already here. Stateside."

"Seems reasonable."

"Are you kidding? I covered Middle East conflict, radical Islam, oppressed nations, and erratic dictators. The occasional natural disaster. I don't photograph boy bands."

"Oh my. Someone inherited his father's unyielding attit . . . *ethic*."

"Is there something wrong with choosing serious work over frivolous assignments?"

"Or maybe it's about a lull in your life compared to the distraction and adrenaline you count on in a war zone."

"That's your interpretation."

"I'm entitled to my opinion." Then Aubrey backed down. "So. You're not flying into a volcano?" Pete moved his head tersely. "Do you mind if I consider that good news?"

"Reykjanes erupted last night. According to Flagler, it continues to blow. That will produce some great images, but the smoke and ash have halted Icelandic flights. Otherwise, the greater universe is a little sedate at the moment."

"If you ask me and the universe, Pete, there's one more prod. Obviously, you have no intention of taking the boy band assignment."

She picked up the paper from the attorney. "But I'm also guessing that hanging around this house for any length of time is not on your greatest desires short list."

"No offense." He attempted to flex his bandaged hand. "I tend to fare better in actual war zones."

"Then either way, your schedule is oddly free, making you all but homeless and available to check out a property on the east end of Long Island. If nothing else, it would help me out." In what she might describe as incensed silence, Pete gathered his courage. She was also sure this mind-set was far different from the one that allowed her son to descend on war-torn regions. *Interesting,* Aubrey thought: at the heart of bravery was the thing that scared a person most.

Pete's breath shuddered, his bandaged hand scraping across his forehead. "Okay. I'll do it. I'll go to Long Island. What's the worst thing that could happen?"

Aubrey shrugged, but she also clasped her left forearm with her right hand, feeling the deep divots—bite marks left by an enraged specter. Evil's calling card. Instant buyer's remorse took hold. She almost said, *"Stop . . . wait. Let's rethink this."* He'd resisted for so long, and Pete's sudden agreement caught her off guard.

"Pete." She looked at her son—an adult who'd navigated danger that most people observed from the safety of the nightly news. No. If he was going to have a life in the present that didn't include war zones, maybe doing this would unearth a path. "Just be careful," she said. "Be very careful."

# CHAPTER
# SIX

In the middle of the Long Island Sound, pearly haze gave way to glistening seas. For now, it was clear sailing. Pete and Grace had started out that morning after he spent the night on the Hathaways' living room sofa. Once Grace accepted his apology and agreed to the trip, she'd said, "It's late. You're exhausted. You'll sleep better here than . . ."

"In the same house as my mother?"

Grace hadn't replied, but Pete came back from brushing his teeth to find the sofa made up like a bed in a four-star hotel.

The two sat on the ferry's upper deck, where the open sea breeze tangled Grace's hair. "Sun is bright." She captured and recaptured locks that were generally never out of place, tucking them behind her ears. "I'd forgotten how windy the ferry is."

"We can go inside," Pete said. She shook her head, saying it was fine. "Grace, if I didn't say thanks for . . ."

"You did. When I agreed to come along. Then on the drive down 95. Again, when you bought me a drink and yourself a second."

"And I'd forgotten they had bars on the ferries. Just the same . . ."

"Pete, listen. I'm not reading into your invitation to tag along. If nothing else, I came for Aubrey's sake." Grace crossed her legs, swinging one in an agitated thrust.

At times, Pete had trouble reading people, their emotions tripping him up. But he didn't think he'd said or done anything to irritate Grace. Not today, anyway. In fact, it was the Grace-ism he'd relied on most— her ability not to be put off by his occasional obtuse nature.

"If you want the truth"—she shimmied ice around a plastic cup— "your invitation was perfect timing. My mother and I had a good tiff yesterday."

"Why's that?"

"Seems she wasn't thrilled about informing eighty-nine friends and relatives that they could cancel their plans for the second weekend in September." Grace concentrated on the circling gulls who'd hitched a ride.

"Oh, I didn't realize . . ."

"The wedding had been so close?"

"Uh, yeah."

Grace downed more of her drink. "Personally, I thought the phone calls were less humiliating than her daughter being literally left at the altar. As it is, I still haven't canceled the honeymoon." She smirked at him. "Italy, curiously enough."

And now Pete guessed they were recalling the same shower scene. He puffed his cheeks and blew out neutral advice. "Did you buy the trip insurance? Or maybe you could go with a friend . . . a girlfriend?" The second he clarified, Pete knew it was a mistake.

"Seriously. No worries. I didn't pencil you in."

"I didn't mean it that way. I was trying to offer realistic advice, be a good listener."

She rolled her eyes. "Please. You're only listening by default. If your mother hadn't texted . . . well, it's not like you planned on calling while you were in town." He didn't reply; she prodded. "Well? Am I right?"

And this was also Grace—a crapshoot as to which response was the right one. Pete chose silence. She sipped her drink, and the two sat that way for a time.

"Think what you want," he finally said, "but I am sorry about your engagement. I'm also offering. Do you want to talk about what happened with Andy?" He was grateful to recall her ex-fiancé's name. "Your life?"

She turned her head sharply. "No. Not really."

Crapshoot.

Grace finished her drink and crunched down so hard on an ice cube, Pete felt sorry for it. "Unless," she said, "you have a solid opinion on the bottom-line offer I should accept for a never-worn Vera Wang trunk show original, pearl bodice, Italian tulle fit-and-flare wedding gown." She glanced at her phone, which had been gripped in her other hand since they'd boarded. "A woman from Haverhill messaged. She offered me $100 for the damn thing."

Pete trod carefully with additional guidance. "Well, what did you pay for it?"

"Five grand."

"Do you want me to get you another drink?"

An hour later they were on the outskirts of East Marion. Before leaving Surrey, Pete had taken the *Wikipedia* tour. His mother's map wasn't enough. He needed to know what they were driving into. East Marion's history was as old as the island's, though towns to the west and Orient, where the ferry was located, appeared to have higher real estate appeal. He supposed the sale of his great-grandmother's house was an indication that the area had caught up with the times.

The immediate scenery remained understated—no fancy shops or restaurants within miles. His phone's GPS guided him, Grace, and his mother's Audi Q5 down roads that turned rural. With each passing mile, the pattern—newer million-dollar properties next door to old farmhouses and 1960s ranches—also faded. When the GPS instructed him to "Turn left onto Rabbit Lane," Pete glanced at Grace. "Rabbit Lane . . . rabbit hole . . ."

"Stop," Grace said. "Back up."

He hit the brakes. "What?"

She twisted in her seat. "There's a mailbox." Pete threw the car into reverse and backed up about a hundred feet. Tangled in briars was a rusted, fallen mailbox. Even less noticeable were the remnants of a dirt driveway.

Pete snatched the attorney letter from the visor. "One eighty-three." He squinted at a gapped one and three, still visible on the mailbox. He smiled at Grace. "We're home, dear." Pete turned down the driveway, the luxury vehicle absorbing bumps and deep divots.

Before Pete and Grace left Surrey, Aubrey had contacted the New Mexico attorney. Supposedly, that lawyer had arranged for her New York counterpart, who represented the buyers, to meet them there. The SUV rolled to a halt, and Pete gave closer inspection to a dark brown, cedar-sided structure. Ivy trailed over it, foundation to rooftop, and Pete thought maybe the vine was the only thing holding the house together. "How much did my mother say the house went for at auction?"

"Close to $400,000."

"For that?" He pointed. "Is there buried treasure under it? I can't even imagine the land being worth . . ." He didn't finish the thought as another vehicle pulled up, a swirl of dust encircling them.

Car doors opened and closed, and a middle-aged man, dressed in a suit, hurriedly met Pete halfway. He extended a hand. Pete shook it, and the man identified himself as the real estate advocate, emphasizing "on the New York end." "I believe you've been in touch with your New Mexico counsel."

"Well, my mother's lawyer person. I don't know that you'd call her 'counsel.' She was really my great-grandmother's estate attorney, and—"

"Gotcha. I know how these things go. The sudden boon of an unknown inheritance. And Long Island real estate being what it is, I appreciate your mother's interest. *Savvy.*" He spoke as quickly as he walked, fishing a key from his pocket. "Let me state up front, my clients thought this was a done deal at auction. They won't be bullied." Pete furrowed his brow at the man's twenty-first-century demeanor, so at odds with the skeleton key in his hand.

"Hey, listen. My mother—"

Grace lightly slapped Pete's arm. "I believe, for the most part, Miss Ellis—Pete's mom—is more interested in the contents of the house than the house itself."

"Amicable. That's where they all start." He jiggled the key into a rusted hole.

The lock didn't turn easily, and Pete muttered, "Maybe if you huff and you puff enough, you could blow . . ." Grace shot him a warning glance.

But the lock turned and the door opened. "After you," the lawyer said. He followed Grace and Pete, yammering the entire way. Pete took in the musty room and sun-dappled surroundings. Stuff. There was stuff everywhere, too much for the eye to tally. The pent-up heat was oppressive, a lasso around its new occupants. Pete dragged a hand around his damp neck. A slight wave of nausea pushed in between his lungs and stomach. Things shifted in his brain, and the buzz of the lawyer merged with a thunderstorm of incoming spirits. Pete tried to focus on the grounded world in front of him.

"So to be perfectly clear," the lawyer went on, "while my clients understand the unanticipated complexities of having located the technical rightful owner—"

Pete swung around, unable to negotiate the unearthly noises colliding with the live lecture. "Could you please shut the fuck up?"

Grace, who'd already staked a path to a wall of bookcases, offered a disapproving glance.

"What?" Pete shrugged at her. "I said 'please.'"

"I see I've made my point." The lawyer headed for the door. "I have calls to return. I'll be outside. As documented, the execution of the sale is entirely your mother's call. But I see how this will go. As it is, additional gold seekers are already en route."

"What does that mean?" Pete said.

"On the drive out, my assistant called. Seems a relative of one of the owners of this . . . *stuff* was informed of its existence. Naturally, they want to lay claim." He looked around the hodgepodge room. "My guess is the whole matter will end up in a lengthy court battle—P.T. Barnum versus the Ripley brothers." The door squeaked as if in protest to the deluge of traffic, and he exited.

Pete swiped at a bead of sweat on his upper lip. "What a jerk. I should tell my mother to keep the damn shack just to piss him off."

Grace moved past the bookcases to a window at the rear of the house and tugged on it. It opened with a creaky grind, humid summer and imprisoned air mixing. "True." She brushed dust from her hands. "But I don't know if he was that far off. This place is . . . *weird*."

Between an anxious spirit populace, the mouthy lawyer, and his queasy gut, Pete hadn't defined anything beyond random clutter. He concentrated harder. *Clutter?* It looked more like an episode of *Hoarders*. Although, as he took a turn around, there was a theme. Carnival—circa twentieth century. Getting a breath in or out was suddenly a challenge.

Grace was right there, plucking a bottle of water from her shoulder tote. "Here. You okay?"

"Yeah." He took the water from her. "Thanks." After a few sips, Pete mentally inventoried the room. He guessed the space could double as a warehouse for props and product. An entire corner was dedicated to carnie magic—black hats and a coatrack where silk scarves, fake rabbits, and springs dangled. Mirrored boxes in assorted shapes filled the space. A large table was the showstopper. Pete examined the blood-covered saw jutting from its middle and the waist down portion of a woman's figure supine on top. Grace turned in the same direction and gasped. In spite of his malaise, Pete laughed.

The entire room was a combo house of horrors slash funhouse. Junk. Mostly it looked like junk—the stuff of a bygone era. Circuses were all but extinct, and traveling carnivals had dwindled since his mother's heyday.

A lone carousel horse stood out, propped against a bearskin rug tacked to the wall. Pete approached the horse cautiously, the way he'd move through an alley in Peshawar. He felt off balance, but maybe that was the missing weight of his backpack, camera gear. A spear of light sliced through the rear window and his thoughts.

Visually, the sunlight connected to the gold metal rod impaling the horse. Through the rays, dust swirled, the feel of a whole merry-go-round moving with him. He reached to balance himself, a tremble to his fingers as he touched the horse. It was a startling creature with the wide-eyed look of fear that rode with every carousel beast. As a boy, Pete had imagined horses like this were angry fairytale creatures, just wanting to be freed. This particular steed sneered, its painted teeth and mane marred with deep chips—as if it'd been to battle. Ghostly voices quieted, replaced by a distant crank of carousel music. In his mind, the horse, maybe the whole room, wavered. The scent of gardenias filled his nose. *"If Paris is France . . ."* He stumbled back.

"Pete?"

He turned, almost surprised to find Grace smiling strangely. "The half lady didn't spook you, but an old carousel horse does?"

"I heard something. A voice."

Her balled hands landed on her hips. "And it's a Friday. Tell me something that doesn't happen regularly."

"It belongs . . . to her."

"Her."

He nodded. "Esme."

Grace's expression flipped from blasé to surprised. "Oh. Have you . . . I mean, I'm well aware of Esme in your past, but I didn't know she'd moved on to communicating. When did this start?"

"Yesterday morning. Not long after I came back from . . . you know. The usual." He said this in reference to a murderous scene Grace knew about, grateful he didn't have to repeat the grisly details. "Just now. She said, *'If Paris is France* . . .'"

"'If Paris is France' . . . ?" Grace's trivia-filled brain took over. "Hey, that's part of a saying, the guy who invented Coney Island. 'If Paris—'"

He held up a hand. "I know. Esme said it yesterday too. My mother figured out its origin. I just have no clue what it has to do with . . ."

"You and Esme?"

"More or less." He glanced at the horse. "After all these years, I hadn't anticipated a riddle being the icebreaker."

"Huh." She came closer to the horse. "What do you make of it? Did she say anything else? Anything to do with . . ."

"Me killing her?"

Grace offered a small shrug.

Pete stared into the eyes of the carousel horse, as if waiting for it to clarify. "Oddly, she didn't mention it. Or anything of substance." Quick as a hiccup, in his mind's eye, he saw Esme sitting upon the horse, her strawberry-blonde hair moving with the breeze. Pete drew in a low, deep breath but said nothing to Grace. "Like I told you, things have unraveled differently with this trip home." He also hadn't mentioned the postcard from yesterday. Pete was too unsure how it factored in and didn't want to invite random speculation.

But the house on Rabbit Lane, there was no speculation here. It was plain unsettling beyond its common spirit population. Pete's hint of nausea turned into a surge of panic. "You know, I don't see anything here that would be of significance to my mother. Nothing that connects to Charley. I say we came, we saw, we get the hell out."

He abruptly pivoted. Sawhorses and a saddle seemed to have galloped into his path. Shorter breaths pumped in and out of Pete, his mouth went dry, and any hint of spit evaporated. It was as if he'd crashed into a memory. The coffee-colored English saddle sat center, showing off a two-tone seat. Vintage leather through and through. Pete brought his hand forward, approaching it with more apprehension than he had the carousel horse. This object had been saddled to a live animal, one he saw in his head—a glorious black horse, at least seventeen hands. A draft horse. *His horse . . .*

Pete touched the pommel, knee roll, and stirrup leather, which showed obvious wear. His fingers hooked around the shiny but nicked stirrup iron. Equally curious, while everything in the room was covered in dust, the saddle was pristine. Its leather looked as if it had been massaged with mink oil that morning. *What the fuck is mink oil?*

Pete moved his hand over the saddle as if he were petting a horse. As he did this, the vibration connected to yesterday's paperwork, or even the postcard, didn't emerge. This feeling was more intrinsic, deep-seated. A burst of tiny electric pulses stuttered through Pete, a dotted-line connection to another life. He let go, backed up, and the sensation vanished.

"Pete? What's with the saddle? You look more startled than after your go-round with the carousel pony."

"I know these things. The saddle. It was mine. It sat on a draft horse . . . traveler."

"You don't ride. As far as I know, your interest in horses doesn't go beyond watching the Kentucky Derby."

"No. I've always known I rode a horse . . . back then, during the war." Pete's breathing labored, sweat rolling. "That was his name. *Traveller*. He wore that saddle." Pete pressed a closed fist to his mouth. Smells of a rotting war invaded, the whinny of a horse in agony. He backed up farther, hearing his mother's warning to be careful. But Pete also recalled her urging—that this house, these things, could lead to answers he'd spent more time avoiding than seeking. "There's a lot more here than a house full of memorabilia, Grace. It's like the things here connect to a whole other life."

# Act II, Scene I
## Brooklyn, New York
### 1917

Esmerelda listened as Oscar bargained and Henry Erlanger spoke. "'If Paris is France, Coney Island, between June and September, is the World.'" Mr. Erlanger went on, poking his walking stick through heavy July air, noting Luna Park's forthcoming Whip ride and the entrance to an under-construction subway rail. "George Tilyou said it best. And soon crowds will flood in from all five boroughs. After that, no one will have any need for Paris. Let the Krauts have it, I say."

His eyes were set so close Esmerelda thought he could be his own one-eyed act. He looked between her and Cora, and Esmerelda had to bite down on her lip to keep from laughing.

"Your girl on the left," he said. "I'll give her this weekend's shows, matinees too." He tapped his cane on Cora's shoulder. "I haven't any use for a juggler. They're a dime a dozen—unless they're midgets or can breathe fire while they juggle." He sniffed, checking his pocket watch before reverting his attention to Oscar.

Esmerelda drew an unsettled breath. She wasn't a fan of Luna Park's human or animal exploitations, the things that, to her amazement, drew the largest crowds.

"If that's your best off—" Oscar began.

"Mr. Erlanger," Esmerelda said, "I take it you've not seen Cora juggle while I sing 'Circus Days in Dixie.' It, um . . . it makes for the most unusual performance." She swiped at the line of sweat on her neck, which underscored her lie. "Your patrons will be wowed."

Henry Erlanger, Luna Park's talent manager, stood dumbfounded. It was as if Esmerelda were a sack of flour or a swine that had suddenly taken to speech. "And since when do sideshow acts do their own negotiating?" he asked. "Particularly females."

Oscar shot her a wary look. "The girl's mouthy, afraid it's the price I pay for her singin'. Even so, she's worth—"

"And you might be pleased to know," Esmerelda interrupted again, "guests at Hupp's Supper Club have been mesmerized." Cora laced her fingers tighter to Esmerelda's, tugging. Esmerelda held steady. If Cora went another weekend without work . . . well, she preferred not to test Oscar's good graces. "Cora here, she juggles beside me while I sing, even during 'The Star-Spangled Banner.'" Oscar widened his fair eyes and craned his neck forward as she embellished. "Clearly, we're not midgets or the elephants who roam your grounds." She gestured to one of several beasts that mingled with Luna Park crowds. "But we are an amazing act."

"A singer paired with a juggler? Maybe over at the Elephantine Colossus, dressed in your knickers, but on a main stage?" The narrow pinch of his eyes made him look like an hourglass set on its side.

Luna Park's talent manager plucked at his watch again, grunting at time, at them. "She . . . *they* go on at eight. I'll pay twenty cents an hour more. And they'd better be good!" He pivoted and pointed his walking stick at two men hanging a sign, stepping toward them. "No . . . no! Higher! And more to the right."

Oscar folded his bulky arms. "Juggles while you sing, does she? To 'The Star-Spangled Banner,' no less."

Esmerelda's hand now squeezed tight to Cora's. "We'll figure something out. It'll be fine, Oscar."

"Only if you two turn into those Siamese twins by showtime. With Cora glued to you, juggling cups and saucers and a cat while you sing might make sense."

"If we can make people believe we talk to the dead, why can't we get them to think singing and juggling is another sort of act?"

"Because I didn't think of it!" He unfolded his arms and hooked his thumbs into his vest pockets. "Besides, you'll run into a mixed crowd at Luna Park. Savvier than the mutts we get at Albee's or the Vitascope." He looked around the massive forest of plaster towers, endless minarets that dazzled in the dark and fascinated in light of day. "Even so, listening to a fine singer while watching a juggler, who ever heard of such a thing?"

"At least Cora has a paying job for two days. Can't you look at it like that?"

"Stay out of trouble until showtime." It was as close to an agreement as the girls would get from Oscar. "And don't be late or you'll both be lookin' for new representation."

With their fingers still tangled, the girls nodded.

"I've got an appointment at the Elephantine." He dug into his pocket and handed Esmerelda two nickels. "Here." He walked away, his lumbering frame and derby hat vanishing into sun-soaked crowds.

"What do you suppose his appointment is?" Cora looked to Esmerelda. "Do you think he's going to find an act to replace me?"

"Replace . . ." Naïveté rivaled Cora's juggling skills. "Um, no. Oscar's not going to the Elephant Hotel for that. Not unless he plans to completely alter the *talent* he represents." Cora's smile dimmed and Esmerelda touched her fingertips to her head. "It's got nothing to do with . . ." She let the thought go. "Maybe you and Licorice, the cups and saucers, should practice a few rounds."

"Not a bad idea." Cora pushed up the sleeve of her dress to reveal a scab that traveled from her elbow to her wrist. "Last show we worked, Licorice got me good." She looked at Esmerelda. "We'd be better off finding us a husband or two. Might be some quarrels, but surely fewer scratches."

"Thank you very much," Esmerelda said, "but if I have to be under a man's thumb, I prefer it be Oscar's." She glanced in the direction of the Elephant Hotel—its pink elephant shape on the outside, its dodgy goings-on inside. She'd heard enough talk about the wares men went there to buy.

"Why would you say such a thing?" Cora went on. "What girl doesn't want a husband?"

"This one." Esmerelda thumbed at her chest. "With Oscar, I don't have to bake him a pie or do his mending or . . ." She glanced again at Luna Park's most unique attraction. "Nothing but sing to keep in his good favor."

"You have a point. And it's good to know your shortcomings." In reply, Esmerelda shot her a look. "Well, based on your pie baking or mending skills, find me one man who'd want you as a wife. I've had to darn your stockings myself." She folded her limber arms. "'Course, you're also about as obedient to Oscar as you are a Sunday church service."

"So I imagine it's myself I'll count on to keep me from the streets."

"And they say I'm the silly girl. What is it you want from life, Esmerelda, if not a husband?"

She straightened her spine. "I'm not sure." It was a short but true answer. "And I didn't say I'd *never* want a husband. As you've kindly noted, I'm not sure what I'd have to offer one." And beneath Esmerelda's true answer was a far deeper shortcoming than Cora could guess.

"Sounds to me more like an excuse to be overly picky. Girls who look like you . . ." Cora spoke, and Esmerelda's glance dipped to the pounded dirt path. When it came to their appearances, both girls were wise to connotations. The ones that made Esmerelda feel like an object and Cora feel something worse. "Most pretty girls have a husband by now."

"Oh, like that should be the reason for anything. And a marriage bargain should be about more than maid's work and someone to pay for your dinner. Certainly not for the sake of . . . well, things a fellow will go to the Elephant Hotel for. Marriage should be about being together because . . ." Esmerelda couldn't find the exact words. "Because being apart isn't an option."

"Like the Siamese twins Oscar's been wishin' for?"

She sighed at Cora. "Never mind."

"Then explain your indifference to Mr. Hupp. Seems to me you don't care much for the wooing type either." She narrowed her eyes at Esmerelda. "I haven't missed something, have I? You're not like Barney and Bill, are you?"

"Barney and Bill—" She hadn't imagined Cora had picked up on such a thing. Esmerelda had been stunned herself when Barney and Bill's relationship became evident. This occurred after she accidentally pulled back a daybed curtain in a rooming house where the troupe stayed last winter. Since then, she chose to say nothing. Vaudevillians boasted a wide berth for the uncommon, and Esmerelda had settled on silence as her policy.

Esmerelda rolled her eyes at her friend's remark. "No, Cora. I don't fancy you. But I wouldn't mind having what I see between Barney and Bill." Cora's brow knotted so tight Esmerelda thought it might twist inside out. "Marriage should be about what you feel. Not an exchange of goods and services, not even an amicable one." She paused, thinking, if not rambling. "The 'till death do us part' words. It shouldn't signal an end, but the thing a body might fight against, even after it's left this world."

Cora widened her eyes. "Is that truly what you think, or are those words from a dramatic scene Oscar has you practicing? Something like *Hamlet* or a song from Misters Gilbert and Sullivan?"

"It's what I think, after what I've seen. Why do it at all, if that's not how you feel?"

"To avoid being a spinster, I'd think." Cora's mousy faux bob swayed as she shook her head. "Esmerelda, you confuse me more than arithmetic. Fight beyond 'Death do us part.' Practicality may have something to say about that." She laughed. "Or has the Amazing Miss Moon seen life beyond this one?" Cora arced her scabbed arm past Esmerelda, mimicking Oscar's onstage antics.

Esmerelda's face warmed. "I'll not be teased by you, Cora. I'm entitled to my thoughts, even if it includes death not being the end to a love story."

"Love story?" Cora's fisted hands settled onto her hips. "Listen to you. Sensible Esmerelda Moon spoutin' on like she's one of the Brontë girls. Life doesn't work like that. Love certainly doesn't. It's why people pay a nickel to see it on stage."

"You don't know," Esmerelda said. "There could be something other than what we see and what we pretend."

"And they call me a ninny. Keep your head in those clouds and all you'll end up with is the last scene from *Romeo and Juliet.*"

A man's voice interrupted. "Do they sing in that show? I would love to hear Esmerelda's version." The girls turned to find Benjamin Hupp. He removed his derby hat, taking a deep bow. "Ladies. Warm afternoon, isn't it?"

Cora giggled, which had been her breadth of conversation around Benjamin. Since June, he'd become a fixture in Esmerelda's staged life. Cora finally managed a sentence. "Mr. Hupp. We were just speaking about you."

"Were you?" He looked pleased, smiling at Esmerelda.

"We didn't know you'd be here today," Cora said.

"Didn't we?" Esmerelda would have been more surprised if Benjamin hadn't turned up near the venue in which she was scheduled to perform. Since she'd started singing at Hupp's Supper Club, Benjamin had sat regularly in both audiences, turning up backstage, alternating flowers with candy. He'd also insisted Esmerelda stay in the hotel above the club. The room had its own bath, a perk that admittedly caught Esmerelda's eye. It was divine opulence compared to the

Flatlands, where Oscar and the rest of the troupe camped in Brooklyn. Logistically, since she was a fixture on the supper club's billing, the hotel room made sense. But Esmerelda had also been quick enough to invite Cora to bunk with her.

Not long into her hotel stay, Benjamin showed up at her door with champagne in hand—a prop as permanent as the deep dimples in his cheeks. He'd blinked at the clothesline she and Cora had fashioned from a bedpost to a wall hook, stockings dripping from it. His square jaw turned oval as Benjamin spied Licorice on the moonlit sill and Cora, who'd lit a fire, reheating a bit of pigeon leftovers.

He'd stumbled through his next thoughts. "The room. I hadn't considered . . . I didn't think you'd invite . . ." Esmerelda had smiled sweetly. He'd gulped, his gaze moving over her and the cluttered space. "I, um . . . I trust you'll both be comfortable here."

"We will. Thank you again, Benjamin. I do hope the show was *everything* you were expecting."

While Esmerelda's move had been strategic, she thought innocence remained her best ally. She'd performed flawlessly. There were no other terms to her contract with Hupp's Supper Club. She owed him nothing.

Benjamin and Cora traded words about the weather, and Esmerelda's stare drifted. On the far edge of Luna Park stood Phin. Her heart thumped, her brain uncertain if it should believe her eyes. He was a good distance away, throngs of people causing him to vanish and reappear like the rabbit in a magic act. Esmerelda's insides jumped every time she caught a glimpse of him. He struggled along, his own balancing act, which included an easel, tin box, and, so it seemed, ample determination. "Now what do you suppose he's . . . ?"

"Esmerelda?"

Her gaze flicked back, her ear catching on Cora's tone. "Are you going to answer Mr. Hupp, or have you gone into one of your trances?"

"Her what?" Benjamin smiled at her like always, as if he'd bit into a peppermint petit four from the supper club's dessert tray—so sweet it left you woozy.

"Nothing," Esmerelda said. "A different act we perform."

"Sounds fascinating. Right now, I was asking if you"—he hesitated, breathing deep at Cora—"and Miss Cora would like to get a lemonade. They serve it on ice, a booth just a little farther down. Quite refreshing."

"Lemonade. On ice." Esmerelda strained her neck, as if looking for the booth. Phin and his curious belongings turned for the sea. "That sounds . . . lemony—and tempting." Esmerelda squinted toward the edge of Luna Park and back at Benjamin. "But we can't."

"Can't?" Benjamin repeated.

"No. Cora and I are performing a new act in Mr. Erlanger's main event." She pointed to one of the larger plaster-front halls. "He just agreed to it. We need to practice."

"But Esmerelda," Cora said, "it's not for—"

"Really," she said loudly. "If Cora and I don't work out the particulars, we might find ourselves out on the street." Cora shut up, clearly taking Esmerelda at her word.

"Esmerelda." Benjamin studied her. "If you thought it through, worrying about things like accommodations never need cross your mind again." He leaned on his walking stick, which sported a silver eagle knob.

"Interesting. Cora and I were speaking on that very subject."

"Were you?" His deep dimples reemerged. "This is what I'm saying. If a girl were wise, and the carousel's brass ring were within reach, she should grab at it. The perks might be quite unimaginable."

"And like I was explaining to Cora"—Esmerelda's glance cut back to Benjamin—"it's neither perks nor free rides that turn my head." She looked toward the ocean, which she heard but could not see. A vision swamped her—one where Phin and his easel were swept out to sea. She moved without thinking, thrusting Oscar's nickels into Cora's hand. "Buy your own lemonade. I have something to see to, then I'll meet you at the wagon."

"Esmerelda." Benjamin grasped her arm. "It's only . . . well, might I buy you dinner after tonight's performance? Perhaps we could spend a little time . . ." He glanced at Cora. "Alone."

His grip didn't ease, and it seemed only agreement would end the conversation. "If you wish." He released her arm. "Right now, I have to go."

# Act II, Scene II

Esmerelda moved like the needle of a sewing machine through the fabric of people on the beach. Bodies and sand mixed with rows of bathhouses, where street apparel was traded for rented woolen bathing costumes. Other beachgoers carried large umbrellas, warding off a sultry sun. Gulls circled and squawked over the scene.

Phin was easy to spot: the only man with an easel. He was safe at the shoreline. The sea hadn't swallowed him. Esmerelda stopped. This was girlish folly that even Cora would have the sense to avoid. But Esmerelda damned the notion and trudged forward, sweating in her heavy skirt and long-sleeved blouse. She didn't get far before her boots filled with sand. Bending, she undid the laces, all the while looking between Phin and her footwear. Boldly, in public, Esmerelda rolled down her stockings and slipped them off. The sand was blazing hot and she moved faster.

Her intention wasn't to speak to him, but to observe Phin from a distance. The crowds had a say in that, and a serpentine stitch mechanically wove her toward him. Burning sand cooled as it met the surf, and her pace slowed. Between the human noise and ocean, a person would have to shout to be heard. Esmerelda didn't speak, acutely aware that Phin knew she was there.

The back of the canvas faced her, and the easel was dug into drier sand. His belongings sat a few precarious inches from the waves. Esmerelda scrunched her toes into the muddy shore. Twice now, mud had been their meeting point. She almost said this aloud before realizing the daftness. More poetic words occurred to her. "'If Paris is France, then Coney Island, between June and September, is the World.'"

He didn't look up. "If I were in Paris, I'd do well to trade this canvas for a steely saber. That's if I wanted to live." The thought left Esmerelda at an unusual loss for words. "Once September is gone," he went on, "the world may be at Paris's door." He squinted at her. "Is this some kind of political rant?"

Esmerelda shook her head, uncertain how she'd traded poetry for war. "I thought maybe I'd see you again, back at Hupp's."

He remained engrossed in his canvas. "The *Tribune* has me busy with less glamorous tasks. My stint at the supper club was only me filling in for the regular photographer. Turns out, he lived and—"

"Was he in the war?"

"Charlie Carlisle?" Phin grinned at his canvas. "Hardly. He survived the influenza."

"Oh. Well, that's good." She was quiet for a moment. "Dying's an ugly business." She cleared her throat at the equally gloomy remark. "What is it you do if you're not taking photographs at the supper club?"

"It's a big city, Esme. An even bigger world. War rallies are near every day. Those are the photos they want for the evening edition." He shrugged his shoulders. "Photo taking, it's the work I prefer at the *Tribune*. But that aspiration is like painting. A fellow can wow them, but he can't make his way."

Passersby bumped Esmerelda's arm, their glances caught on Phin's painting. People pointed at the canvas, commenting. Esmerelda assumed he was painting the scene, perhaps one with a grand ocean liner, like the *Lusitania*, in the foreground.

One woman stopped and gripped her husband's arm. "I've never seen anything so exquisite. So . . . surreal." When Phin didn't acknowledge the compliment, the woman looked at the back of his head with irritation. Then she looked at Esmerelda as if she were somehow tied to his ill manners. "Ask him, George. Ask the young man if you can buy it for me." George obliged, offering two dollars. But Phin declined, saying, over his shoulder, that the painting wasn't for sale.

This stunned Esmerelda. From Oscar to Benjamin, she couldn't imagine a man unwilling to profit from inventory. The couple went on, and Phin finally spoke, if only to the canvas. "I do have occasional takers, but not enough. To be truthful, I wish they'd all drown, or at least leave me be. Those were the second gawkers today, never mind the ones from last week. And then it was barely a painting."

"So why come here," she asked, "if the crowds and noise are disturbing? If it's peace you want, silence you crave. Wouldn't a stretch of beach toward Long Island be easy enough to find, offer the same view?"

"Easy enough to find." His brush stopped moving. He hauled in a breath, his blue-gray eyes meeting hers. "I don't know about the same view."

Esmerelda lingered in his meaning, as if sweat weren't streaming down every part of her body. Phin looked comfortable enough—barefooted, pant legs rolled up, his shirt half-unbuttoned. Men could get away with so much. She'd only been thinking this, though it appeared otherwise when he caught her gaze, locked on his open shirt. "I imagine," Esmerelda said, fumbling to recover, "if your intent was to find me, the crowd might present the same difficulty as me not being present at all."

"But at least, on this beach, I had a chance." He aimed the paint-filled brush bristles at her and grinned. "Seems I succeeded."

"I suppose you have."

He reengaged with his painting, which disappointed her. But Phin's concentration was worth watching, deep as the ocean beside them. Moments later, Esmerelda shook her head as if he'd induced an Amazing Miss Moon trance. "I'm confused. Even if you've sought me out, it seems I'm only interrupting. I'll leave you to your painting." She shuffled back, letting her skirt fall, the edge soaking up the tide.

"I had to think about it." She pivoted as he spoke. "Seeing you again. I was the guy in the muddy alley with the lowlife hoi polloi. I left you in Benjamin Hupp's care, if not his good graces."

"The club has treated me well." Esmerelda dug her toes into the cool silt. "I'm employed by Hupp's revue, not Mr. Benjamin Hupp personally."

"And they're not one in the same?" He tilted his head at the canvas, but the point of this small gesture didn't appear to be his work. "If that's how you need to see it."

"Is that so? I don't suppose there's any chance the club, or even Mr. Hupp, employs me for my singing ability. My talent?"

"Anything's possible. I was only thinking what's more probable."

"You stupid boy!"

He blinked at her blunt remark. Finally, he was more rapt by her than his painting.

"That's twice you've insulted me beyond all reason," she said.

"And clearly I get as good as I give. That's twice you've fitted me with a dunce cap."

"First you assume I'm a common trollop—"

"I explained that error in my favor."

"And now I come all the way down here in this heat"—she plucked at her soaked blouse—"to offer a friendly hello. In return, it takes you all of a few sentences—while you rudely pay more attention to a painting you won't even sell—to imply that my employment by Mr. Hupp is nothing more than a ruse to . . ." With her boots clutched in her arm, Esmerelda tugged on a stocking she'd stuffed inside. She leaned closer and lowered her voice. "A means to getting under my skirt." She turned, kicking up sand as she went.

He yelled after her, "Is there a chance I'm wrong? Is it not what he wants?"

Esmerelda halted her forward motion, widening her eyes at the beach stretched before her. She thought about gathering a fist of sand, nailing him square in the face, maybe ruining his not-for-sale painting. He was beyond ignorant. Phin would rather go hungry than part with a painting. It should tell her something. But Esmerelda had to give in to the source of her anger. It wasn't him, but the controlling nature of men. She turned back. "For your information, I'm a worthy songstress. Benjamin Hupp is lucky to have me perform in his supper club!"

"And what other sort of luck is he hoping for?" He looked between his painting and the sea. "I'm not saying that isn't true, about your singing. It's one reason I wanted to find you. I was curious how far Hupp would go to woo you if you sang like an alley cat."

"So here's your answer—not that you're entitled to one. Not that I care what you think." Esmerelda dropped her boots, lest she whack him upside the head with the black pointed toe. She took a salt-covered breath, overpowering seagulls and sea-goers, and burst into the verse of "In the Sweet Long Ago."

If his painting commanded compliments, her singing drew looks of amazement. The outdoor acoustics were difficult, and Esmerelda heard her voice waft upward to the bird-filled heaven. But when beachgoers applauded, she assumed she was on key. One man tossed a penny in her boot as he passed by. She'd meant for it to be a private performance— maybe in the same way Phin viewed his painting. People went on their way and Phin stared. "Does it answer your first question?"

"You're a talented songstress, Esme. I could listen to that all day." She was briefly vindicated. "'Course, it does little to answer my second curiosity."

He was bold, and a desire to know more about Phin Seaborn grew: What drove him to the beach, to his question, to this moment? She firmed up her chin. "Benjamin Hupp has only seen my stockings to the point where they've hung on the wash line Cora and I put up. I've no sway over his motivation, but I've earned my keep by sheer talent—for singing," she quickly added.

His grin seemed to go wider than the paintbrush he held. "And I believe it makes you a clever thinker, Esme."

She shrugged, finding herself attached to the nickname, or the way he said it—belonging as opposed to possession.

"Not many girls would be quick enough to put a roommate between herself and Hupp's intentions. Well done."

"It was more common sense than clever, but think what you like."

He put down the brush and wove his fingers through his wind-whipped hair. "Most any girl would have given in to a peek at her stockings, if the invitation came from Hupp." Phin held up his hand. "And I'm not saying that to get my ears boxed. But what girl turns down one of the richest heirs in all of New York City?"

Until he said it, Esmerelda supposed she'd been avoiding the obviousness—Benjamin Hupp's pursuit. She ignored the dinner invitation she'd agreed to; it'd only been the quickest route to Phin. "He hasn't asked anything, other than for me to sing." The slight fib caused Esmerelda to stare at her muddy toes. "And now I believe I've answered your query," she said, looking back up, "for whatever reason you need to know."

Phin touched the wooden handle of the brush but didn't pick it up. "Fair enough. So can I ask why is it you've come down here to see me?" He nodded. "Oh, that's right. You only wanted to say hello. Point out the similarities between Paris and Coney Island, which I'm still giving some thought to, so thank you for that." He shuffled his glance between the painting and her. "Was that all?"

Esmerelda opened her mouth, a salty sea breeze rushing in. How was it he managed to keep the upper hand, and why didn't she mind nearly as much as she professed? The truth skipped through her head. *Well, I was standing over there—funnily enough, talking with Benjamin Hupp. I saw you. I had this foolish fear the sea might swallow you whole. It only seemed natural I brush off an ardent suitor (because you're completely right) and lie to Cora, giving her my nickels, so I could wander down here and* . . . "I was curious to know what you're painting."

She stepped boldly alongside of him and faced the canvas. Esmerelda brushed her fingertips over her mouth. "Oh my . . ."

"As you realized, it was a needle in a haystack that you'd turn up. Maybe more like one gold bead on that gown. But I will say, I believe I've perfected the brushstroke, mirrored the sheen." A swallow dipped through his throat. "While I can't say why, I knew I'd find you here. I know how that sounds."

"Maybe not as odd as you think," she whispered.

"You've been etched in my mind, Esme—since that muddy alley. Since I left you at the door of opportunity."

She continued to stare at his painting. The one with which he wouldn't part.

"Once I started this painting . . . well, it became more about what I saw in my head than anything I could call mine." From his pocket, Phin produced a single gold bead. It'd come from the gown Esmerelda wore the night they met. "If this was all I'd ever have of you, I thought it best I capture the memory."

"It's . . . *magic*." Her fingertips reached toward the canvas. On it was an exquisitely painted mermaid. Its fishtail imitating the gold-beaded gown, the sea sparkling off it like a trail of fallen stars. The mermaid's eyes were cast downward, a melancholy mien. And the mermaid's face, it was the reflection that belonged to Esme.

# CHAPTER
# SEVEN

*Long Island*
*Present Day*

*Rabbits. Rabbits on Homestead Road . . . Rabbit Lane . . . rabbit hole . . .*
They hopped and tangled in Pete's head. He'd wanted to leave the East
Marion bungalow. A lack of desire to return to Surrey kept him from
escaping. It didn't matter. Grace insisted they stay, at least a bit longer.
She had a point. The contents of this house, these rooms, came disturbingly close to the contents of Pete's head. The carousel horse and saddle
resonated. Yet upon closer inspection of the pristine English saddle, the
intrinsic vibe faltered.

"Look there. That part, the skirt," he said to Grace.

"The what?"

"The small flap of leather. It's called a skirt." Pete poked a finger at
the sawhorses. "If you owned a saddle like that, your initials would be
branded into the leather."

"And you know that how?"

"The same way I know anything else. It's just . . . *there.*" Pete wanted
to say, *"Because I lived it."* But Grace knew the drill, the ever-shifting

pieces of his lives. It was like living in a mudslide. Grace peeled up the flap, and Pete fought a sense of foreboding. "Well?" Musty smells wafted up his nose, seeped into his mind. He shored up his shoulders, predicting the first solid evidence of his past life that he'd seen since he was twelve and the World War I medal bearing his initials turned up.

"Well, you're half right. There are initials, but they're not yours."

Less intimidated, he approached the saddle. "Then whose initials are they?"

Grace bent up the flap as far as the stiff leather would allow. "O.B., whoever that is."

Pete didn't offer a reply, and they took a break from the interior, long enough to tell the city lawyer he could leave. They'd be in touch. While the attorney's clients wouldn't be bullied, neither would Pete.

The man retreated to his Mercedes, dust and pebbles sputtering in his wake.

"So tell me," Grace said. "Do you want to get in your mother's car, tear out of here just as fast?"

Standing in the driveway, Pete took in the armor-like safety of the Q5 and the rickety, far less secure structure behind them. He aimed at the middle. "There's a building in the back."

Grace took a few steps to her left. "Huh. So there is."

A weather-beaten barn sat to the rear, the trees almost camouflage. They made their way to it, and Pete slid aside the door's primitive wood bolt—good enough to keep out animals, which he guessed were the only expected intruders. Inside, creases of daylight cut through wood-slatted walls, revealing a dirt floor, old hay, and a massive tarp-covered object. "I don't know why I was betting on empty," he said.

Pete's queasiness had subsided and he felt strangely connected to this forgotten space. He didn't hesitate, yanking at the fabric. It barely budged. "This is canvas," he said, getting a better feel for the dusty gray material.

"I'll go you one better." Grace ran her fingertips over it. "I think they're giant tents."

"I think you're right." It took both of them to free the first of two heavy cloths, which eventually tumbled toward them. At first, it was nothing but an unraveling of dirt and dead bugs, Grace squealing and darting as a spider landed on her arm. As she inspected herself for other insects, Pete faced the front end of an old truck. A very old truck.

The visual was obvious, but Pete was more drawn to the redolent odor of the canvas. After a few anxious breaths, he felt like he stood in two places—an old barn in East Marion and an even older life. Pete backpedaled from both, standing flat against the wall's raw boards. He clamped a hand down on his sweaty head, squeezing his fingers through a mat of thick hair. Just touching his head—hair so like his father's—made him think of Levi, and Pete wished he were there. He looked into Grace's questioning face. "It's the canvas. The smell."

"It reminds you of something?"

"Yeah. Something like a cattle-prod poke at the past." He was unable to connect it to more, and despite the unnerving ambiance, Pete remained present in the barn with Grace. "I've seen this truck before."

"This truck?" she said as if there might be an alternative. She pointed to the second canvas, which still covered most of the vehicle.

Pete reapproached and pressed his hands to the canvas, closing his eyes. "I can prove it."

He turned his back to the truck. "You look." He pulled the second canvas back like a curtain, revealing more of the truck's side. Dust rose up around him, a puff of magician magic. "On the door. It says 'Oscar Bodette's Traveling Extravaganza.' Doesn't it?"

Grace stepped back. Her expression was confirmation, and he could see her struggle for logical explanations. "Well, wait. Didn't you tell me a story or two about your great-grandmother and her carnival life?" She pointed at the truck's door, which Pete still didn't look at. "Is it possible you saw all this as a little kid and you're just recalling . . ."

He shook his head. "My everyday childhood, that's crystal clear. I've never been here, to East Marion or this house. The writing is yellow, isn't it? Yellow cursive outlined in red."

Grace's jaw slacked. Unusual, he thought, for her to be speechless. Pete finally allowed himself visual confirmation. She trailed her fingertips over the words he'd described, bending and squinting to make out the more faded embellishment. The red was more vivid in Pete's mind. Here it was mostly chipped away.

Pete nodded, affirming things he knew. The vintage truck had a flatbed frame, raised metal sides, and an arched, open metal covering. While it was old, the truck would have been considered a relic by the 1940s. Definitely pre–World War II.

"Oscar Bodette." Grace drew her fingers away from the faded but legible paint. "Why is that name vaguely familiar?"

"He was my great-grandmother's second husband and also her fourth, if I have the story right." Grace blinked at him. "Oscar Bodette founded the carnival troupe—or at least what would become the Heinz-Bodette troupe." Pete drew in musty air and exhaled an unsteady breath. "This 'Traveling Extravaganza' . . ." He gestured vaguely. "It must have come before the carnival of my mother and great-grandmother's era. That's the part of the story I know, the carnival where my mother grew up, Charley's history. It's where you heard the name Oscar Bodette."

"Okay, but as far as I know, you've never associated your other life with facts from this one. Your mother's, or even your great-grandmother's past." In the sticky air of the barn, Grace rubbed her hands over her folded arms. "What is it you think we've found, Pete?"

"You're right. I never connected my own family history to my past life. I've never even considered it. But with the things inside the house, this truck—" He stared at the vehicle as if it might hold the secrets to the universe. Well, at least his universe.

"The saddle," Grace said. "O.B. It belonged to Oscar Bodette."

"No, Grace. The saddle belonged to me."

"Pete, be reasonable. You can't deny the initials branded into that leather. Maybe you were only projecting about the saddle belonging to you."

"The saddle was mine!" His words were fitful, like a child grabbing for the thing he wanted. Pete raked his hand through his hair. "Or it belonged to whoever I was." He realized how he sounded. Surreal, wobbling on a sliver of rationality. "Sorry. I'm sorry. I didn't mean to snap."

She waved him off and turned around the dank space. The truck looked to be the barn's single clue.

"I'm more confused than when we got here—or more than usual," Pete said. "For me, that's saying something."

"Okay. Well, I don't think staring at an old truck is going to help. Why don't we go back inside the house, take one more look around, and then check into the motel?" Grace pulled her phone from her pocket, poking at the device. "It's only a few miles from here. Oceanfront," she said. "It should be nice. Maybe the sea air will help, a walk on the beach."

But Pete wasn't listening, his head crowded with voices and visions that didn't connect to Grace. They didn't connect to the time in which he stood. He moved away from her and closer to the truck. A myriad of vocal rumblings persisted, but he couldn't single any one out. It was more like the noise you might hear in a packed open-air space. The beach. He pictured a crowded beach. Instinctively, Pete's fingers locked around the metal door handle, and a wave of yesteryear assaulted him. His heart pounded like the muscle wanted to leap from his chest and into another being, another time. The physical lure was wildly intense and felt more real than the ground beneath his feet. For a moment, for the first time in Pete's life, *there* felt more accessible than here.

Grace's voice snapped him back. "Pete!"

He turned abruptly but didn't let go of the truck's door handle. "What?" He blinked at her.

"Did you hear me?"

He shook his head. Sweat moved in tributaries down his spine, across his back. He glanced at his dirty, damp hand and released the handle. The frustrated look on Grace's face grounded him.

"I said, someone else just pulled up the driveway."

The confluence of events exasperated him—those in his head and the ones playing out in front of him. Regardless, Pete followed obediently as Grace strode toward the house. But as he walked, he kept glancing over his shoulder. It was the first time Pete ever wanted to hurl himself at his other life rather than run from it. He tried to think like Levi, assemble a rational perspective and align facts. It all kept slipping from his grasp. With a last look back, Pete tripped over a fallen branch, and staying on his feet became the objective.

It didn't last long.

*Oscar Bodette?* What the fuck did he have to do with Pete's other life or Esme? The only information he knew was vague stories Charley had told—ones he honestly hadn't paid much attention to. There was the small anecdote his mother had conveyed, Charley's scorecard of marriages. But that was recent history compared to Pete's past life. A man in his eighties. Aubrey had said the second time Charley married Oscar, he was in his eighties. That alone was decades ago. Pete did the rough math, guessing the carnie mogul was around during the World War I era.

Instead of looking over his shoulder, he turned in a full circle. It was more than he could get his head around—the idea that Esme might connect to the physical world in which he now stood. Yet as he and Grace closed in on the bungalow, it seemed a given. Pete's past life and this one had found a point of convergence.

# CHAPTER
# EIGHT

At the edge of the driveway, Pete stopped moving and rubbed dirty fingers across his eyes. The disturbances radiating from the barn faded, though his heart continued to pound. He found himself planted firmly in the present day—a place where, ordinarily, a lackadaisical state of mind could get him killed. But it was Pete's lifelong fears that charged back in, and he wanted nothing more than to get away from Rabbit Lane and rush into the nearest war zone.

A beat-up compact car thwarted his escape. He stared at the vehicle, which elicited no more vibe than a pain-in-the-ass roadblock. The door to the house was ajar and an obvious shuffling about could be heard. "This is probably more action than that house has seen in forty years," Pete said, walking past Grace, who was now the more hesitant of the two.

Inside the house, near one of the many bookcases, a girl was crouched on the floor. She was scavenging through shelves as if foraging for food. Possessed or possessions? It appeared to be a toss-up as to which thing drove her. She looked up, glancing about like this was a hotel lobby, Pete and Grace being guests invading her claimed space. "Oh. Hi." She crouched into a tighter ball and examined a low shelf.

"Hi?" Pete said. "Uh, what are you doing?"

"Looking for a photo album."

Pete thumbed over his shoulder. "There's a Walgreens about six miles back. They might sell them."

She rocked back on her heels. The heat of the room, or her hot pursuit, left her face as red as her hair. A thick braid was pulled over one shoulder, wisps of it sticking up and out as if trying to break free. She wore jeans and a white shirt with sleeves that puffed like snowballs. Perspiration trickled down her cleavage, vanishing into the cotton fabric and tiny buttons that trailed the front. Pete was sure it was only the oddity of the sight that made him notice.

"Don't be ridiculous."

He did a double take, thinking she was calling him out on his mental excuse for staring.

"I don't want a new photo album. I'm looking for an old one."

Grace shrugged and whispered, "Sorry. A brick shy falls entirely into your wheelhouse."

"Thanks," he muttered. "Um, do you mind telling me who you are, since this is my . . . well, my mother's house."

She sprang to her feet, the books gathered in her lap clunking to the floor. "Oh! Oh my God!" Her reaction was so acute it felt as if she'd stabbed him with her exclamation. "You're Pete."

Pete couldn't place it, but he'd heard her say the last part once before. "I am. But I still don't have a clue who—"

The girl's pink lips smacked shut, though her hazel gaze wound up and down him. He felt ogled, a curious object she'd unearthed. She squeezed her eyes shut and shook her head. "You, uh . . . you don't remember me. Not at all?" Her speech was hybrid, a hint of British intonation, but definitely stateside. It made her even harder to place. "I'm Ailish. Montague."

When he didn't react, her awe deflated. She lowered herself back onto the floor, rejoining dust and chaos. His initial impression was *runaway teenager*—but not quite. She looked slightly older than that. Pete thought of Monte Carlo and the Bay of Kotor, the Great Blue Hole in Belize, exotic locations where he'd earned pit stops and might have run into someone like her. Nope. No gingies with pearl-white skin, a smattering of freckles, jumped to mind.

"Your mother called mine." Her stare softened, a more timid glance moving between the books and Pete.

His brain slingshot to Surrey and some girl he might have insulted or ditched in the eleventh grade. The odds were good enough. He glanced at Grace. No. The girl he'd hurt, the one destined to carry that acute memory, stood beside him.

"My mother is Nora. Nora Montague."

The girl. *What was her name . . . Ailish?* She smiled. Pete reeled, if only internally.

"Dublin. Maybe that much rings a bell?"

Because locations, often bells, drove all of Pete's memories, he pictured lush, rolling pastures of green, a castle with a bell tower. But he realized he'd never been to Ireland. Then his brain connected the word *Dublin* to a person. "Oh, right. Zeke Dublin. You're his daughter."

"Niece. I'm Zeke's niece." Her tone was irritated, as if he should have her family tree memorized. The girl returned to pillaging the bookcase, though her mad hunt had eased. "My uncle didn't have any children. He never married. He died." She stood again. She took in the surrounding mess—which she'd managed to make worse—then bull's-eyed Pete. "He was murdered."

The claim triggered facts, but they had nothing to do with a homicide. Pete's most concrete memory of Zeke Dublin was purely spectral. "Right. Your mother . . . your uncle, they traveled with the carnival when my mother was a girl. Zeke Dublin, he—"

"He was in love with your mother. Always. At least that's the story Mum tells."

Pete shook his head at her insistent delivery—like how could he be unaware of such a tender memory? In Pete's mind, only one man fit such a mold. Although he did recall a rough patch between his parents. Pete was twelve or so and strongly resembled his mother in terms of the gifts he possessed. Of course, he was far more like his father when it came to personality: pure stubbornness. Interesting how DNA could be set in bone.

At the time, he and his father had moved out of the house on Homestead Road. It was an unpleasant period, Pete experimenting with control and the depth of his gift. In the end, a physical change of address hadn't helped much. That was where Zeke Dublin came in.

Zeke was Pete's first visual manifestation of a specter. He cleared his throat, guessing a mention of that ghostly encounter would not facilitate this conversation. "Right. I remember hearing something like that about your uncle. But it still doesn't explain what it is you're doing. The attorney who was here said someone else would be coming by, but—"

"But he didn't mention me specifically." She sank back onto the floor. "Maybe your mother told you I'd be coming. Or you just knew."

"No to both. My mother didn't say anything about . . ." Pete pulled his phone from his pocket. Several unread texts scrolled past.

Spoke with Nora Montague, Zeke Dublin's sister. Daughter already in NYC. May come to house to look for photo album. Be nice.

So much for pleasantries. "You came all the way from the city to look for a photo album?"

She bobbed like a cork, treading from one bookcase to the next. "How do you know I came out from the city?"

He held up his phone. "Missed texts."

She cocked her head at him. "Mums will always catch up with you."

"Sorry . . . but are you from here or England? I'm hearing—"

"That's my dad's influence. He's a Brit. I spent a good bit of time with my granny. She lives in the UK. North of London."

Rambling, Pete decided, appeared to be her first language.

"Or the inflection, maybe it's just a habit of my trade."

"Your trade?"

"I'm an actress."

Pete hid a smirk at what sounded like a grandiose claim.

"I can offer up a dozen different dialects on cue. Sometimes that one sticks." She stood again and books carelessly thudded onto the floor. The girl dipped into a dramatic curtsy, her hand billowing before her in a subject-like gesture, speaking in a fast, full-on upper-crust English accent. "Emerald Ailish Montague, holder of dual citizenship and four odd jobs located in Her Majesty's former lands, Manhattan to Coney Island."

The mention of Coney Island slammed into his ears, and Pete breathed deep.

"One does what one must while on a quest for fame, fortune, and expensive dramatic instruction, courtesy of Kimball's exclusive and renowned studio for thespians, Midtown location." Pete and Grace traded a look. She continued, slipping into a dialect more befitting Eliza Doolittle. "And if ya blokes won't let me finish me business, find this bloody picture book, I'll miss this evenin's audition, one that Kimball's fancies as a fine fit for me." But she paused, her gaze, which seemed devoid of other characters, clinging to Pete. "Four spectacular solo bars in a Hoboken revival of *Cats*." And quick as she'd been transformed, the redheaded American actress, possessor of dual citizenship, returned. "I need to find this photo album."

"Maybe we could help," Grace said. "What sort of photo album are you looking for?"

"One that belonged to my uncle . . . my mother. Mum said she lost track of it during their carnival days. It's all she had of her family, her parents. She and my uncle spent some off season time in this house. My mother lives in Nevada, so with me in New York . . ." She looked up at the two of them. "Can you piece the rest together?"

"Yeah. I think I've got it," Pete said. "Your grandparents, did they also travel with the carnival?"

She eyed him, as if again her past should be obvious. "No. My grandparents were murdered too. Apparently it runs in the family."

Pete wasn't sure whether or not to believe her—although the moment she acknowledged grandparents, voices seeped into his head. Other sounds followed. The girl continued to stare, like she'd forgotten about the photo album. She'd been fiddling with the elastic at the end of her braid, and the stretchy tie slipped off. Instead of putting it back on, she pushed it over her hand and onto her wrist.

It was Grace who reacted, murmuring a sympathetic, "That's awful. I'm so sorry." Ailish's sad story also thrust Grace into aid-worker mode. "Really, maybe it'd be faster . . . better, if we helped you look."

Grace stepped forward and Pete grabbed at her arm. The sound of the grandparents didn't abate, violent noises connected to their demise. The only positive here was that the specters he heard were linked solidly to Ailish, not the bungalow or him. Gunfire pelted his brain, glimpses of violent deaths. Pete tasted blood. It was a strong contrast to the girl's quirky demeanor. Clearly, her remark about their deaths hadn't been a wiseass comment. Pete's angst increased and the urge to leave clobbered him. "No. We have to go."

Grace pointed to Ailish, whose fingers had shuffled through the braid, undoing it. It left her hair looking like a foxtail lying over her shoulder. The girl drew a breath like she might say something more, but only bit on her lower lip and returned to her task.

"But shouldn't we . . . ?" Grace shut up; the look on Pete's face was enough to override Ailish's mission or sad tale. "I guess we're not staying. We, uh . . . we need to check into our hotel."

"I've only come for the photo album. That's all—apparently." A gulp rolled through her throat, and Pete got the distinct impression she was lying. "I'll go as soon as I find it." She stood, heading across the room to more bookcases and cluttered shelves.

On her way, she hesitated at the saddle. It was as if it had galloped into her path, just as it had Pete's. She moved her fingers across the coffee-colored object. "Pretty." She looked at the two of them. "Don't worry. I won't steal anything, and I really need to get back to the city. Your mother knows where mine lives."

The buzz in Pete's head overwhelmed him, a collision of sounds. The heat in the room swelled and a fresh wave of nausea pulsed. The girl's glance fluttered cagily in his direction. Pete didn't hear Esme, but he did recall her words: *If Paris is France, then Coney Island, between June and September, is the World.* The smell of gardenia cut through the musty bungalow, enough to make him hold his breath. It didn't matter; it didn't help. Smells attached to psychic phenomena came from the inside.

He breathed, although his sense of hearing took the next hit. Pete heard bird wings—as if they fluttered furiously behind glass. And even more so than in the barn, he wanted to get out of the house. "Listen," he said hurriedly, "lock up when you're done. Key's in the door. Just leave it behind the bush on the left. Can you do that?"

She moved away from the saddle and the flutter of wings stopped. "I'm fairly certain I can lock a door."

"Good. Grace, do you have the car keys?"

"Uh, no. You drove."

"Right." Grace turned for the exit. Zeke's niece stood between the saddle and bookcases. Her stare stayed with him as he headed for the door. "I, um . . . I hope you find what you're looking for."

The late-afternoon sun filtered past a dirty window, and Ailish Montague was caught in a singular beam. "Don't we all?" She'd swung toward another bookcase, her long hair following a split second behind. Hues of pink and orange moved in slow motion, as if Pete had closed his eyes while staring into the sun. And for all his lives, in the here places and the there places Peter St John had encountered, he knew this action—the rushing wave of a girl's hair—was a clear memory.

# CHAPTER NINE

The Sound View Lodge wasn't about amenities. Pete only noticed this much because Grace had done nothing but fill his ears between the car, front desk, and breezy catwalk that bordered the beachfront rooms. "It is the height of the season," she said. "I was lucky to get this room. Last-minute cancellation."

She fiddled with a key and Pete turned to the beachy vista. She was right. The place was all about location, the sound roaring only feet away. Pearly puffs of gray clouds rolled out to the horizon, diving like Neptune's spear into a whitecap sea.

"Here. Let me try." Pete basically manhandled the key into a corroded lock, and the door popped open. "There. Can we just go in?"

Grace huffed at him, and they dragged their belongings inside a musty room that looked like it'd fallen out of the 1970s. Even the television was old-style, a fat, square box mounted to a post.

"Jesus. You seriously *are* paying for location."

"I said I was sorry. If you want, we can try down the road, though everything in a sixty-mile radius is privately owned and booked for months." Grace continued to poke at her phone, acting like Grace—a never-ending Google search, anticipating your next question, a click away from the right answer.

"It's fine. The room is an upgrade from where I spent most nights in recent history. Let it go, would—" The most troublesome thing in the room caught his eye: one double bed.

Grace looked up from her phone, and the device smacked into her thigh. "Oh. When the desk clerk said 'double,' I just assumed he meant two double . . ."

Pete assumed *"no big deal"* was the best course of action and dropped his duffel bag onto the bed. "We're grown-ups, Grace. If I recall, there were plenty of nights we just *slept* together in a bed."

She didn't move from her frozen pose. "And plenty we didn't."

He suspected Grace viewed a double bed in a dumpy motel room as equal to the draw of a Venice suite. Pete attempted reverse psychology. "Just out of curiosity. Ol', um . . ."

"Andy," she supplied, rolling her eyes.

"Andy. How were . . . I mean, it's a ridiculously personal question, but how was that part of your . . ."

She folded her arms. "Adequate." She hesitated. "He had other . . . *strengths*."

Perfect.

"So he enjoyed long walks on the beach, reading the same book, and . . . hell, what was the other thing?" The remark earned another eye roll from Grace.

"He liked planning a date now and again, sending flowers for no reason, cuddling by a fire. Making me feel . . . *special*."

"And aside from those . . ." Pete scrunched his brow. "Hey, that's four things." She shrugged. "So aside from my *many* shortcomings, I assume Andy also didn't carry ten times the baggage that could fit in that duffel bag." Pete pointed to his. "He didn't wake up at night, terrorized, on a return trip from another life. More to the point, I assume he never accidentally whacked you in the face, resulting in a black eye that had to be ever-so-carefully explained—"

"Two days before my sister's wedding."

"Right. Two days before her wedding." He offered a sober look at the bed, the tight space. "Maybe we should think about that, Grace. You, alone here with me." Pete didn't trust himself, why should she?

"Pete, that part doesn't concern . . ." Her thought trailed off. "I managed to stay ahead of outbursts, any reentry into this life. Unless things are worse . . ."

"They're not any better."

"I can manage."

"Can you?" The reminder of having physically hurt Grace, even unintentionally, caused Pete to take a step back. "The back seat of the Audi is roomy. I'll sleep in the car."

"You will not either. You're exhausted and I'm still pretty quick on my feet." She paused. "So, um . . . how often are you finding yourself . . . ?"

"Beating the shit out of whatever is in my path?"

She shrugged vaguely.

"It's part of the reason I live for my job. My mind is so war-weary, outbursts are infrequent, at least compared to when my mother and I are in the same house."

"Well, we left her three states behind. We'll be fine." As if demonstrating her resolve, Grace lobbed her suitcase onto the bed. She proceeded to open it, fishing out three separate cosmetics bags. "You insist your job helps. But do you ever consider the downside of that mentality?"

"Meaning?"

She slipped her hand beneath a stack of perfectly folded, layered clothes, placing them on the bed. Then she eyeballed him. "That you're using modern-day wars to dodge the aftereffects of the violence you faced in another life. It's a curious trade." She headed to the bathroom, saying before she went inside, "If it were me, I'd wonder how long I could play that game before something blew up in my face."

While Grace put on a brave front and seemed prepared to dive back into her role of putting his needs first, Pete wasn't as sure about the arrangement. He was younger when they cohabitated, too immature and screwed up to do anything but accept her willingness to put up with him. He left the room after Grace yelled from a running shower that the motel connected to a restaurant. Did Pete want to get something to eat? It was a standard Grace protocol: anything to keep the peace.

Pete declined her suggestion. He wasn't hungry; he needed to clear his head, collect his thoughts—or maybe drown them. It could be Grace had a point. Instead of food, he bought a few bottles of beer from a cooler they kept at the front desk and made his way down to the beach. Grace's observation and a larger point continued to gnaw at Pete. He'd done enough reading, observed enough soldiers in this life and his last to grasp PTSD. He opened a beer and guzzled a mouthful.

Pete focused on repetitive, rolling waves. It'd been some time since he'd stood on a beach in this part of the world. He did have good memories from a Connecticut beach—Rocky Neck. It was straight across the sound, a place that connected to his father's youth. Levi and his half-brother, Brody, spent time there when they were boys, and his father enjoyed furthering the family tradition. Pete was certain Rocky Neck was one of a few places where Levi experienced only fond recollections of the brother he'd lost so long ago.

When Pete was a teenager, he'd gone there on his own, positive a ghostly lifeguard's presence wasn't far away. He liked to think he heard Brody's voice, though it never carried the clarity of a true specter. So more often than not, Pete labeled it wishful thinking: *"Hang in there, Pete. I'm watching . . . wherever you are . . ."* At times, he'd answered, even if it wasn't real. Even if all he truly heard were waves and all he saw was the horizon.

It was nearly dusk on this beach. The clouds had cleared and Pete built himself a small fire. A few yards away, a girl sat on a beach towel, the way he noticed girls did: one leg stretched out, her other leg bent at the knee, arms splayed wide behind her. She'd been sneaking peeks in his direction. When the waning sun made sunbathing a moot point, she gathered her things and strolled toward him.

Really, a guy alone on a beach at dusk, throwing back beers? The small blaze in front of him should have read like a signal fire: *"Be smart, keep moving."* For a moment, Pete imagined something even darker . . . what if he hit the same trigger that drove him to Esme's murder—PTSD or plain crazy—dragging that persona into this life?

The girl, oblivious to Pete's demons, posed in front of him, propping sunglasses on her head. She was pretty—very pretty, blonde, a belly ring piercing the navel on her ironing-board stomach. She smiled, white teeth that gleamed even in the near dark.

"I see you like dominant women. I'm all for that."

"What?" He twisted the top off a second beer.

"Women who make the first move." She shifted her tanned, toned shoulders.

Her voice matched the rest of her, a slathering of sex on the beach. For a split second, Pete considered that route out of his funk—meaningless sex with a girl whose name he might learn afterward. It held potential for erasing his mood.

She popped that bubble by saying, "I'm Simone."

When the girl kept talking, a man's voice intruded. It pounded at the back of Pete's brain. Forceful, demanding, authoritative. "For real?" Pete took another sip of beer. He peered up at her and the fading gray sky. "I swear I wasn't going to touch her."

"What?" Simone shuffled backward through the sand.

"Nothing." He sipped more beer. Apparently, she perceived alcohol intake as an invite. She reclaimed the step and sank onto her knees, half an inch shy of spilling out of her tiny bikini top. Pete glanced, but in truth couldn't have been less interested.

"Listen," she said, "do you want to . . ."

Grace's voice rose from the direction of the motel, calling Pete's name. She slogged through the sand, spying the girl and the obvious. Grace picked up speed. In her arms was a cardboard carton, food smells wafting over sea air. She moved past the girl, flashing a smile at her.

"Oh, honey," she said to Pete, who almost spit the mouthful of beer. "I'm glad you found someone to keep you company while I nursed the twins to sleep. Mom is staying with them now so we can have our private clambake on the beach." She held up the carton, brimming with fried fish and french fries, planting herself between Pete and the girl. "He's the world's best dad." Grace batted her eyes at Simone. "Like he tells the congregation every Sunday, fatherhood was Jesus's way of making him the man he wanted to be."

The girl stood. "Right . . . of course." She looked between the two of them, Pete still listening to the male voice connected to Simone. "Your husband was just going on about that . . . well, your kids," Simone said.

"Was he?" Grace replied. And now Pete was having a hard time focusing on the voice while suppressing laughter. There were things about Grace he did so admire. "Did he talk more about Sophia or little Jackson? They're a handful!"

Simone shot a coaxing *"let me save your ass"* glance in Pete's direction. "Oh, definitely little Jackson."

"Is that right, sweetie?" she said to Pete. "Now, we've talked about playing favorites with the kids." Grace leaned, bumping his arm in some gesture of marital solidarity, and continued in a bubbly tone that didn't belong to her. "Well, if you don't mind, the pastor and I don't get much alone time. Pete's so busy with his calling."

"Right, his calling. I, uh . . ." Simone turned for the motel. To Pete's surprise, she spun back around. "You know, maybe this was divine intervention. It just so happens I'm an out-of-work nanny. Kind of stuck here for the rest of the summer. My last gig, it didn't work out. You wouldn't be in need of . . . *help*?" She raised a brow in Pete's direction, her fingers fiddling with the belly ring.

Grace started to reply, and Pete held up his hand. "Thanks." He was done with the amusement. "We're all set. MIL is the best. Travels everywhere with us. Nice meeting you, Simone."

She shrugged one bikini-strapped shoulder and turned for the motel.

"Damn it," he hissed. The voice wouldn't relent. "Wait." Simone turned back, her toothy smile directed at Pete's supposed wife and the mother of his twins. "Your father."

"What about him?" Her smile and teeth vanished.

"He has a message."

"Message?" Her expression grew befuddled. "My father's been dead for three years."

"Yeah. Part of my calling—an ability to communicate between here and . . ." Pete turned his head toward the vast sound. "Do you want to hear what he has to say or not?"

"I'm not sure what you . . ." Air sucked into her toned, tan frame. "You're kidding, right?"

"Not about this part," he said dully. "Isaiah—"

"How do you know his name?"

Pete smiled. "Names are the least of it, but an interesting question. They never really tell me . . ." He glanced at Grace. "It's just there, with them. Also happens to be one of my favorite books in the Bible." He said this part more soberly, and Grace widened her eyes at the remark. "Your father admits you had a . . . *contentious* relationship." Pete slipped in one word to take the place of the more combative adjectives being thrust at him. Clearly, father-daughter battles had been a staple of their relationship. "Just like when he was alive, he only wants good things for you. He said he's sorry he never got that across . . ." Pete listened harder as the voice softened. "Isaiah . . . *Ike* says it's why he left the box of Sweethearts candy that afternoon. It was a peace offering, but it turned out to be his message."

"Message?"

"He's not sure you got it. Not yet."

"Sweethearts . . . candy?"

Pete nodded, the visual so clear, the pink-and-red box sitting on her white dresser.

"How could you possibly know . . ." She tilted her blonde head at him. "The candy was there when we came home from the hospital that night. My dad, it was very sudden, a heart attack. I always wondered about the candy."

"You're right to wonder. He left them on your dresser before going to work." Pete watched a sand castle being claimed by the sea. "People don't see the trigger. What prompts them to do something they ordinarily wouldn't. At the time, your dad didn't know it was his last day . . . *here*." He gathered a handful of sand and let it slide through his fingers. "The candy . . . the sentiment, turned out to be his message." He listened harder. "Something about you being his sweetheart."

"This isn't possible . . ." Her tone lost any hint of a come-on. "When I was little, when things were good, he used to say that to me."

"So that's his message. The heart. Don't be so fast to give yours away—to strangers on a beach . . . or maybe . . ." Pete cleared his throat. "The last dad whose kids you were supposed to be taking care of. Ike says it's not about him being right or wrong anymore. But he doesn't want you to make a mistake you can't recover from."

Night had claimed the dusky sky, and Pete guessed he appeared a freakish vision lit by a flame. As anticipated, the girl didn't respond, pressing painted fingernails to her lips. She only kicked up sand as she bolted for the motel. Pete called after her, "'So is my word that goes out from my mouth: It will not return to me empty, but will accomplish what I desire . . .'" Simone kept running and Pete remained largely unimpressed with his ability to deliver positive messages of closure.

"Did Isaiah say that too?" Grace asked.

"In a way. It's Isaiah, chapter 55, verse 11." He stretched his long arms back and planted them in the sand. "Seemed a shame to waste the shot of religion, especially after you so perfectly set the stage."

"Been studying the Bible, have you? I've never known you to be much for Bible-based religion."

With the girl gone, as well as her father, Pete settled into the surrounding noises—the wallop and whoosh of ocean waves, the crackle of the fire he'd built, the grounding sound of Grace's voice. "About a year ago, I spent some time in South Africa. A colony of Jesuit priests was doing missionary work in Mozambique. Food aid mostly. PressCorp sent me on an extended shoot. I spent serious time with one priest in particular. We clicked. I was curious if traditional religion held any answers for me."

"Did it?"

He hesitated, downing more of the beer. It was a complicated answer—enough so that he'd studied religion under the priest's tutelage. Pete had even considered remaining in their lair, gifts and burdens hidden among a cloistered, dedicated life. "It made me feel . . . *safe*. The concept of faith and a deity being ultimately responsible for whatever *gifts* I have." He leaned forward and stretched his hands to the flame, close enough to remind Pete of his humanness. "The knowledge eased some burden. But my true struggles never left me." He balled his hands tight, drawing them away from the flames. "I prayed for an answer, definitely absolution from my past. Well, you know . . . my other past." He paused, struck again by the notion of the ways violence invaded this life. "None of it came to fruition." Pete hummed under his breath, looking in the direction the girl had run. "Hell, maybe Simone will benefit. What ails her might be cured by a good come-to-Jesus meeting." He smiled at Grace. "Not so much for me."

"It's interesting you made the attempt. Fascinating that you befriended a Jesuit priest."

"He was a good guy—loved backgammon. The priest gave me advice not necessarily rooted in religion, which is what you'd expect." Pete quietly stared into the fire.

"Are you going to tell me what he advised?"

"He felt confident my answers are out there." He pointed a finger at the now-black but not silent sea. "However, the priest also insisted peace could only be achieved by faith in the journey I'm resisting."

"Profound." Firelight couldn't mask the crinkle of Grace's brow.

"Or incredibly cryptic."

"Did you share the specifics of your life, you know . . . ?"

"My looming questions? Speaking to the dead, haunted by another life, and having murdered one woman in it? No. Those facts went beyond the boundaries of our association. But the priest also didn't seem to need to know."

"Huh. I stand by 'profound.'"

"He did make me think. And I do wonder about the journey, if I'll ever be brave enough to take it. Will I even know when it begins?" He picked up his beer but put it down, too consumed by the thought to be interested in alcohol. "I keep in touch with him. Definitely not the kind of person you meet every day."

"So then, you and a Jesuit priest had something huge in common."

Pete sighed, reaching for a fried shrimp. "I suppose we did."

# CHAPTER
# TEN

After going back to the room, Pete sat in a chair as Grace reacquainted him with her nightly ritual. It involved three different kinds of face wash followed by brushing, flossing, and gargling to the tune of Beyoncé's "Single Ladies"—or at least that's what he heard. Pete leaned farther into an upholstered chair that smelled of a dirty vacuum and wet bathing suits.

He delayed getting into bed with a little help from the Gideon society. After his talk with Grace, Pete was drawn to the motel-room Bible. He concentrated on passages, feeling Grace's stare as she finally drifted off—long, consuming blinks. Pete wondered if his association with violent behavior was affecting her differently, several years removed from their youth.

He dozed briefly, startling himself with a gasp and looking into the glare of giant red clock numbers: 2:11. He pulled himself forward in the chair, scrubbing his hands over his face. Grace rolled over, saying Andy's name, and Pete cleared his throat at what suddenly seemed like his awkward presence.

Moments later he snatched up the car keys, thinking he could grab a few hours' sleep in the Audi. By the time he got to the parking lot, he was wide awake. Minutes later, Pete was on a westward journey, heading down Sound Avenue. Since returning from the bungalow on Rabbit Lane, he'd suppressed any connection, trying to pass it off as "the house his mother had inherited." The property was more than that, but he hadn't wanted to discuss it with Grace. He didn't mean it in a negative way. It simply didn't have anything to do with her. The car's headlights cut through sea air that had turned misty, the rural road growing thick with a low-hanging fog.

Pete missed the bungalow on his first pass, like yesterday, and he backed up, turning down its driveway. He squinted at opaque air, surprised to see the Montague girl's jalopy of a car still in the driveway. He thrust the Audi into park and cut the engine before hurrying into the house, using the flashlight on his phone. His first thought was perhaps she'd scaled one of the taller bookcases and toppled the thing over on herself. Maybe it was her drama lessons, but she seemed like the type— to end up in the crosshairs of a tragic fate.

Eeriness lit his surroundings with the hair-raising vibe of a good horror flick. The beam highlighted the magic act and heaps of other junk, the creepy carousel horse, and the leather saddle mounted on sawhorses. It was all stunningly quiet, and for a second Pete forgot his mission. It was as stuffy and as unsettling as hours earlier. He shook his head and focused. Where the hell was Ailish Montague? All of the bookcases were upright. There was nothing in the kitchen but what they'd previously noted: a half dozen mason jars, cobwebs, and dirt. Nothing appeared to be in any more disarray than when he and Grace left. There were two small bedrooms that he hadn't gone into earlier.

Pete entered the first bedroom and was surprised not to find Ailish asleep on an old mattress propped up on rusted springs. He guessed she might have tired and fallen asleep before locating her prized family photo album. Alone with a beam of light, Pete went into the second bedroom. Aside from a couple of metal racks jammed with costumes and scattered boxes, the main item was a large rolltop desk. He navigated past the cartons and crap, the fusty odors. Ailish appeared to have ransacked every other storage area in the house, but she'd obviously missed this. He looked back at the door. *And she what, vanished into thin air? Decided to take a middle-of-the-night walk in the woods?*

Good citizenship, perhaps the decency his parents instilled, almost won out. He nearly left the desk to continue his search for the girl, but Pete erred on the side of reason. Most likely the car she'd showed up in wouldn't start, and a friend—nearby or from the city—had come to retrieve her. He'd look more thoroughly in a minute. The urge to explore the desk wasn't a ghostly nudge—he knew that feeling. This was more like fate whispering, drawing him closer. The tight wooden rolltop fought him, though Pete won the wrestling match. "Jackpot," he said to no one when it opened.

Under the top was a line of photo albums. They appeared meticulously stored, as opposed to everything else in the house. He sat in an old-time accountant's chair, its high back creaking worse than any ghost he'd ever encountered, the leather seat split down the middle. The photo albums would be a vintage sight anywhere. With smartphones and computers—based on Pete's own job—he considered stuff like this passé. Yet these items were preserved, and the word "treasured" slipped into his head. He plucked out the album on the far right. It had a padded floral fabric cover, sticky pages that were deteriorating and yellowed. Opening it, Pete knew he'd found the thing for which the girl had come searching.

The album began with family photos, people who did resemble Ailish. Most appeared to be taken in a city apartment building. On the pages were little handwritten notes, maybe to remind the keeper of the photo album who these people were, what they meant to one another. In neat cursive, it said: "Zeke's 10th birthday. L-R: Zeke, Louis Cavatello, Richie Green, Tommy McPhee, and Nora." The photo verified facts, including where Ailish Montague got her coaxing smile—clearly from her uncle Zeke. The trait was identical, and something

Pete recalled, staring at the living half of his long-ago encounter with a spectral entity. The angry noises from earlier erupted again—gunfire and bloody deaths. Pete connected the horror to these people. "She did say murder ran in the family."

For a guy who regularly encountered the dead, the razor chill that traveled down Pete's spine was unexpected. He glanced into the darkness behind him. The cryptic setting, the disturbing thought of homicide, it was enough to rattle even a seasoned ghost whisperer. He returned to the photo album. The pages told a story he supposed the girl would like to know, at the very least be glad to claim for her mother. But then the photos abruptly stopped, as if the family ceased to exist. "I guess it's a logical aftereffect of murder," he said to himself. The pattern of photos and thoughtful captions ended after August fifteenth, Nora's eleventh birthday. He turned a blank page, then another. Jammed into the crease was a handful of random photos.

His breath caught as he flipped through the stack. Many included pictures of his mother and Zeke Dublin. In some photos, she looked to be in her early teens, college age in others. He noticed that in each image, as his mother got older, Zeke got closer—his arm tight around her in the last one. Well, she'd never claimed his father had been her only date in life. In fact, until he mentioned it to Grace, Pete had all but forgotten a first husband, his existence so inconsequential. But this guy, in these photos, clearly he meant a great deal to his mother.

He smiled at Aubrey's younger face, unable to recall too many photos from her youth. Pete's eyes were so like hers, their only mirroring physical feature. In nearly every picture, he also saw the orbs floating through the surrounding space. Spiritual dots. It was how he'd come to think of them, having seen so many in his own family photos. Orbs often posed with Pete and his mother. He also understood the expression on her face: someone faking normal, assaulted by sounds, voices, tastes, and sightings that only she encountered. *Or combated . . .*

He closed the photo album and leaned back in the chair. The line between gift and burden was an exhausting tightrope. The two of them—and his grandfather, he guessed—forced to inch across, a lifelong high-wire act. Pete rubbed his fingers over his eyes, which reminded him that it was the middle of the night. Enough. Where the heck was the girl? He'd found the photo album; he wanted to return it to its rightful owner. He still had no good reason for having driven there in the first place, and Pete suddenly felt exhausted—like maybe sleep wasn't the worst idea.

He stood. As he reached for the Dublin photo collection, the light on his phone shone on a different album. This one was on the far left, much older. The kind with a leather cover and string laced through the binding to hold its pages together. He couldn't say how or why, but a sense of bravery fell over him as he tugged it from the row. He opened it, and tiny paper triangles scattered, black-and-white photos falling too. Pete sat again, trying to retrieve the mess of pictures that had slipped silently into dark corners. He glanced at the ones left in front of him. There was no order, no careful notation—nothing like what Zeke Dublin's mother had preserved.

In fact, it wasn't until Pete's hand made contact that a vibration took hold. They looked like carnie pictures, but even older. From the clothing—knickers, boater hats, and flapper-style dresses—he placed the era: early twentieth century. One large man wore a raccoon coat. "Shit. That coat had must have put a dent in the procyonid population." He widened his eyes. The truck. It appeared in several of the photos. It also looked brand-new, the man in the raccoon coat standing by it, the paint fresh and revealing. *Oscar Bodette's Traveling Extravaganza.* "Oscar. I'll be a son of a . . ." Pete was positive this younger man was his great-grandmother's husband, whatever the number.

There was a mix of people as the photos went on, all from the early 1920s. Two men posed tight as one, almost an embrace. Pete raised his brow at the close-knit imagery and period setting. "Huh . . . ," he murmured, tipping his head at the photos.

People varied, with some onstage, though one outdoor venue repeated. It caught his eye. It looked like an entire faux city made of plaster, buildings, rides, even elephants wandering in the background. A lighted sign identified it as Luna Park. There was a single photo of a young girl, her expression dull, her wide ears a distraction. The photo was marked 1916. Pete flipped through the images again. "So, Oscar, was this your entire troupe? I hope their talent exceeded their photogenic appeal."

Pete turned the black paper page, so dry and fragile. But the tiny triangles held tight to a single larger photo. He stopped dead. Out of pure instinct, part terror, Pete plucked the photo from its paper grip. The woman in the picture took his breath away, branded him. So did the photo. "Son of a bitch!" He dropped it—same as he had Esme's dead body. Touching the photo was akin to plunging his fingers into his beach fire. Pete looked at his upturned hand under the beam of light. Bloody blisters rose on three fingertips and his thumb. He shook his hand and repeated the swear words like an angry incantation.

A pencil sat in a desk cubby, and he grabbed it with his other hand. The photo had landed in a darker corner, and Pete used the eraser end to pull it closer. A strange light sparkled over the image. The aberration gave him a jolt; it was like the tiniest of orbs floating downward. Pete rolled back the chair until it collided with boxes. The Levi part of his brain said, *"It's dust. Years of dust, caught in the light."* But it wasn't. "Shit. Holy . . . shit."

He'd never observed anything like this, the sight of orbs floating outward from a photograph and the girl pictured in it. The two things tantalized his senses and ground into his mind. *Pleasure and pain.* The woman was posed like a true vaudevillian, lying on a chaise in a satin gown, her hair done up like she'd just come from makeup and wardrobe. In one arm was a long-stemmed spray of roses. Of course, Pete had never seen her in any way, other than with a horrified expression, seconds before her death.

He struggled with the beautiful image, trying to turn the dead into the living. On the corner of the photo was an embossed studio signature, "Royal Photography, NYC"—commonplace for the era. Yet, for Pete, the composition was as telling as DNA. He studied the photo, how the geometry of leading lines subtly guided his perspective across the image. Any viewer's eye would be drawn to hers—a natural human response. But you had to know how to finesse the subject, separating amateurs from professionals from artists. The photographer made certain the eye accelerated as it traveled the curvature of her body: shoulders, bust, and hips, gliding and swooping out of the frame. Her fair hair spread against the dark chaise, surely a deliberately chosen prop. And the flowers, set to the right, broke up the negative space, never hindering sight lines. The camera lens, perhaps that was the most telling, the way it captured visual tension. Shadows created a sense of intrigue, while her facial expression was both light and grim, giving a sense of hidden troubles.

He knew this photographer's eye.

The pencil rattled in his hand. Pete managed to get the tip beneath the photo and flip it over. Written across the back were words that underscored his lifelong knowledge; they made a haunting vision true, reading: "Esmerelda Moon, one year, five months before her death. August 1917."

A feeling of malaise enveloped the room, seeping through the floorboards and onto the leather chair. It traveled up his pant leg and scaled his spine like tiny spikes. Knowledge sank hard into his gut. It crushed his heart. *Moon.* E.M.—Esmerelda Moon, her whole name, written in Pete's handwriting. He'd know his work anywhere—even from a hundred years ago. Pete flipped the photo once more and said the name he'd been avoiding since his past had begun to seep like a stain onto his present: *"Esme . . ."*

# CHAPTER
# ELEVEN

Pete sat frozen in the desk chair. He felt the heavy hit of heart to chest. "And I do what with any of it?" He raked his uninjured hand over his pant leg, a nervous, guilt-filled motion. While Pete or a good psychiatrist might explain the war medal, saddle, and truck, seeing his handwriting on the back of the photo read like a confession. The penmanship was unmistakable—the oddly pretty, left-handed cursive so like his father's.

Twisted curiosity made him turn one more page. It revealed the depth of his depravity. Another searing burn might have been a concern, but the images negated personal safety. Lying loose in the album was a strip of photos—all were of Esme. Head shots. Various poses. The execution of these photos was far more clinical, though Pete still recognized his work. He also knew the film processing technique, which was obsolete. "Wet plate photography," he said, words populating his head. The photos seemed to offer documentation of a damn good beating, or so the back said—"Esme. Just to show. January 1919." The strip of photos also bore his handwriting.

Each picture accentuated a different injury: bruised cheek, blackened eye, swollen lip, marks around Esme's neck. Vomit raced up his throat, and he pinned his fist to his mouth. Pete thrust his blistered hand forward and stared at it. A weapon.

He couldn't get air into his lungs. The images were fantastic proof, a memento of how he'd viciously abused the woman he loved. Was this how men who committed such acts felt? Remorse after the rage, a fucking coward who knew it was a deplorable act, yet would still claim . . . *love* for the women they'd battered? He wanted to know, because these were the emotions winding through Pete—disgust at himself and profound affection for her.

One clean, intentional gunshot, aimed at Esme. Pete had lived with that fact for so long it was possible he'd grown numb to it. Biting hard into his lip, he tasted blood. His lungs burned from a lack of breath, and his scorched fingers felt the same. Tears blinded him. Through them, Pete examined the bloody blisters, rubbing his raw fingers against the edge of his palm. The pain was exquisite.

He dropped the photos and retreated. Pete had lived on an edge for the past sixteen years, and he didn't know what sliver of sanity was left to hang on to. His T-shirt clung to his body, a sweaty footnote of his state of mind. Outside the house, he leaned and pressed his hands to his pant legs. A growl of pain emanated from his gut. He held out his trembling hand and blood dripped off his palm. A fresh surge of vomit charged up his throat, and Pete gave in to it, heaving into the overgrown shrubs.

He lived with the knowledge of having taken lives on a battlefield, most vividly in a place called Belleau Wood. They were tightly mixed with other memories of the Great War. The idea that he was defending freedom, keeping himself from getting killed in the waves of gruesome slaughter, offered rationale. But the haunting visual of having killed Esme, it was the obstacle he couldn't clear, dragging her murder along like a chain that linked his past life to this one.

Pete staggered away and looked back at the house. Then he squinted upward into a foggy moon.

*Moon. Esmerelda Moon—*

Her name echoed in his head and Pete shuddered at the surreal photos. Disjointed thoughts mounted, and he considered modern-day escape routes—quick fixes for avoiding his past. A sports magazine had contacted him a while back, something about shooting a surfing competition in Australia. He'd taken a hard pass. But if he reconsidered, by tomorrow or the next day, he'd be thousands of miles from here and from her. From those damning photographs.

Pete backpedaled into the Audi, his shins making contact with the front bumper. He stared at the dark outline of the house. If he backed up a few feet more—or better yet, drove away—he wouldn't see it at all. His mind hit the one-eighty mark; it won, screaming at him to get the hell out of there. Fine. He continued to choose to run.

Pete turned for the driver's-side door, keys in hand. He dropped them, his gaze catching on the beat-up car that belonged to the girl. "Fuck. The girl." What the hell happened to her? Pete hit the flashlight on his phone again. Two percent battery. He tossed the phone through the Audi's open window, onto the seat, and started for her car. Light caught in his peripheral vision. The barn.

A glow radiated through its rotted slatted sides. The fog felt as if it had weight—an ability to push or pull, like a strong wind. Pete had the sensation of moving uphill, fighting gravity. It was like being forced into a fun house and the trappings of the dark unknown. He wiped his fingers over his eyes. His imagination was getting the best of him. Fucked-up people could spook themselves, maybe more so than normal ones. He continued uphill on what he knew was a flat plane of yard. He looked back. The mist devoured objects. Pete couldn't see his car or the girl's; he couldn't make out the house. But he was right about the light in the barn. Sliding over the wood plank, he dragged the weighty door over weedy grass. A lit lantern hung from one of the many hooks built into the truck's metal awning.

Pete moved farther inside and called out Ailish's name. There was no one. Climbing onto the truck's running board, he lifted up the lantern, which he assumed Ailish had lit. Maybe someone had come for her after the July sun had set. He moved the lantern to a wall hook.

Straw crunched beneath his sneakers. The barn siding could pass for kindling. The whole place would go up like . . . well, like a decaying old barn, filled with dry straw. Pete flirted with a sure way out. Drop the lantern. Done. He closed his eyes and struggled for composure—not the mind-fucking mess that was driving him. Concern for the girl's safety shoved him center. "Guess I should be grateful 'total prick' didn't carry over from one life to another."

There was a shift in what was present: the barn and the time in which he stood. Pete listened, his ears assaulted by tinny, old-time carnie music. They were the same sounds he'd heard yesterday inside the house. They grew louder. Dizziness swamped him, the sensation of being thrown onto a spinning carousel. The barn reeled underfoot, and Pete reached for the truck's door to steady himself. Mentally, he dug hard into the here and now: maybe the girl had fallen asleep inside the truck. He slid the heavy metal door open. The interior was empty.

There was no accounting for what Pete did next. He climbed inside the truck and settled onto the seat. He'd sat here before. Pete ran his fingers over the smooth leather seat and stared at the antiquated dash, an undersize steering wheel, and a few large gauges, lots of pedals. None were the gas. That was controlled by a lever on the steering column. How the hell did he know that? But like the parts of the saddle and wet plate photography, it was all there in his head—like a file he simply needed to click on. He ignored unsettling fears and pained validation, the shower of sweat that ran down him—a stomach that couldn't be in a greater knot. Then Pete smiled at the antiquated mechanics. "It's not possible." He mashed his foot into the tiny starter button on the floorboard. The engine did not hesitate—age, the elements, and time having no effect. Without thinking, Pete knew where to find the truck lights. Without hesitating, he imagined a different route of escape and drove forward.

# Act III, Scene I
## New York City
## 1917

Phin was the rare seashell on Coney Island's shore—not native to New York City. For Esmerelda, and almost everyone she knew, life was about survival. Phin was motivated by living, or at least, this was her impression. It was all born from a single afternoon of talk on the beach, followed by a walk through Luna Park. At the carousel, Esmerelda had sat atop a fierce faced pony impaled on doom, the creature destined to go round and round. Phin stood at her side, patting the horse's mane as if it might respond to his touch. "Seems to me," Phin said, "this horse's ill expression is all about being trapped. I think he wants to be free." The notions—about choice, about touch—dizzied Esmerelda a bit.

Later, they walked through paths of minarets, stopping at Royal Photography, where the Manhattan business rented a summer booth. Patrons from the upscale hotels farther down the shore would pay good money for holiday photos. Phin knew the photographer on duty—an English fellow who had little use for American "nobility." For free, he let Phin use the camera and costumes. Esmerelda was flattered to be his subject, and Phin chose a lavish gown with a train and tight pearl bodice from a rack. Then he handed her the prop of faux red roses. "The idea," he said, "is to make one's St. Louis cronies believe this is how everyone in New York dresses and lives." Painstakingly, he posed Esmerelda on a velvet chaise and spent a good bit of time fiddling with the equipment.

He snapped a few photos, assuring Esmerelda he'd seen precisely the Esme he wanted to preserve.

Phin's sensibilities fascinated her, everything from his interest in art to the deep emotions he saddled to a carousel horse. In Esmerelda's experience, men—even showmen—were only interested in art, and women, and time in terms of profit. While Phin was clearly a hard worker, money was not the focus of his ambition.

A week passed after Luna Park. Phin didn't show up at Hupp's Supper Club to take photographs, nor did he appear like a ghost in the alleyway. Instead, an older man who smelled of Barbasol and shoe polish stood with a camera in Hupp's lobby.

Esmerelda asked about Phin and the man snapped at her. "This is my beat, missy. Damn influenza kept me out for weeks." He coughed into a handkerchief and swiped at his nose. Positive she couldn't catch the flu, Esmerelda stood firm. "Charlie Carlisle might have lost his job to death." He thumbed at his chest, clearly indicating he was Mr. Carlisle. "I ain't losin' it to street scruff." When she tried to ask another question, he cut her off. "What do you want with Seaborn anyway? They'll ship him overseas before long. Let 'em, I say. Let every younger man go before they come for me."

After this, Esmerelda wondered if the government's new army had sent Phin to Europe—soldiers were leaving in what now seemed like a sea flooded with boys and men. She and Cora had seen them at the docks. She overheard a man explain how first the men spent weeks training before they departed. "Our boys will be ready," the man bragged. "Krauts won't know what hit 'em."

"Training to kill another person," Esmerelda said to Cora. "Can you imagine such a thing?"

Cora shrugged at the ship of new soldiers, packed like cattle and cheering as the steamer was led from the harbor. "And they seem right pleased about it too."

Thinking about Phin on a boat like that put Esmerelda's insides on rough seas. Would he really be plunked aboard a ship, moved about on a battlefield like a pawn on a chessboard? Had he left without so much as a goodbye? She knew little about Phin, other than that he was a fine painter and photographer. She'd been amazed by the photo he'd taken at Luna Park, never envisioning herself as the songstress he imagined through a camera lens. Since he'd said it, Esmerelda often considered the idea of setting carousel horses free—even if it wasn't possible. She was riveted, wondering if life could be more than a play for your next meal.

What she could not fathom was Phin setting out on a journey where the objective was to take another man's life. Although, she suspected he could fend for himself, if only from the hooligans that chased his shadow. Indeed, everywhere around her, war was the mind-set of men, which also included an ever-present Benjamin Hupp. When she was listening—whether it was at the dinner Benjamin invited her to or the stroll he insisted on—he'd brag about his number coming up. Esmerelda wished him no harm, but she also did wonder when that might be.

During her tête-à-têtes with Benjamin, Esmerelda did her best to stay engaged. He was her employer; she owed him respect. Regardless, she often found herself apologizing, remarking, "Sorry. I missed that. What did you say?" He'd prattle on about his mother's docent activities at the Metropolitan Museum of Art or his father's latest business conquest. He sometimes talked about Ingrid, an immigrant girl from Germany that the Hupp family had sponsored. His talk led Esmerelda to believe that Benjamin was rather fond of her. She wanted to ask if he fancied Ingrid like a sweetheart, but bringing up love interests felt counterintuitive. What if he said no?

A week became ten days, and Esmerelda verged on hopelessness. Then Phin turned up in the alley behind Hupp's. She'd come outside to breathe smoke-free air, to get away from everything inside the supper club. She was surprised but quickly steadied by Phin's blue-gray gaze, which appeared as unlikely as the rest of him—wavy, dark hair and his lissome frame, which caught her glance.

Phin explained that his work had doubled at the *Tribune*, with able-bodied men dwindling fast. He'd been farmed out to oversee distribution—a plum assignment, perhaps, if your last one hadn't involved photographing one of Manhattan's most popular venues. The *Tribune* had him going from the four a.m. edition through the afternoon paper, and back to the four, which started at two a.m. In between, Phin photographed rallies and the rising taste for conflict abroad. If war was bad for heartbeats, it certainly caused the newspaper business to thrive.

That night, and during others that followed, Esmerelda would slip away. She and Phin would go on their own walks. The sooty city was never entirely quiet, but this was fine. The heavy night air and streets that didn't empty became their canvas. In the chatter of these excursions, Phin remained mum about his life beyond the *Tribune*, beyond her. And it wasn't as if Esmerelda was shy about asking. But when she pressed, Phin only turned the question back on her. "So, Esme, you've worked your way up to second billing at Hupp's. Oscar must be pleased." Then he'd stop walking and ask, "And Benjamin Hupp, how pleased is he?"

She guessed cat-and-mouse conversation was the way of courtship—girls engaging but keeping a suitor at arm's length. But Esmerelda had no desire for games. A foreboding sense of time running out wouldn't allow it. "I've told you, Phin. Benjamin's my employer, perhaps friendlier than some. I don't see it any other way." Then she would insist, "And neither does he."

In response, Phin made no mention of further defining a courtship. He never took Esmerelda's hand when they walked, always bidding her a good night at the edge of the alleyway. Behind her were the late-night sounds of Hupp's Supper Club, endless rumblings of well-to-do gaiety—which, when sozzled enough, sounded no different from working-class drunks.

On these nights, Phin would slip silently into the darkness, taking with him all the things Esmerelda wanted to embrace. He generally left alone, but sometimes Hassan would show up. During one walk, Phin had explained that Hassan was a Choctaw Indian, expressly imported by the United States Army. Each week, Hassan reported to a Lower Manhattan army post, and each time the post would tell Hassan to come back in seven days. In the meantime, they did nothing to support him, not providing food or shelter. If he tried to leave, he'd be considered a deserter. According to Phin, Hassan was turned away from most every attempt at employment. "It's curious if you think about it. It's his land. For a Native American, most people treat him worse than the Negroes and the Chinese."

The pattern between Phin and herself frustrated Esmerelda, as did the attentions of a man she did not want. Phin left her mystified, the way you'd wonder what came after the stars in a night sky—something beyond her reach. And Esmerelda wasn't the only person curious about Phineas Seaborn. Everyone in Oscar's troupe had an opinion. Cora said he and his gang of thugs ranked lower than the dubious trade at the Elephant Hotel. Apparently, Cora had figured this much out, aware of what an Elephant Hotel "appointment" entailed.

Nightly, after returning to the hotel room at Hupp's, Cora doled advice out like penny candy. "And they say I'm the ninny. You might be takin' a long gaze in that looking glass." She'd stab a finger in the direction of the dresser mirror while unwinding Esmerelda's plaited bun. And because Cora gripped one end like a rope, Esmerelda had no choice but to keep still and listen. "If Mr. Benjamin Hupp learns you fancy that boy, he'll drop you and your act like hot manure from Go and Fish." By then Cora had unraveled the braid, picking harshly with a comb at a nasty knot. "You'll have lost a job and the best chance that will ever come your way." She'd yanked hard on a last tangle, and

Esmerelda had yelped. "Got it!" Cora said, holding up a sizable chunk of Esmerelda's hair. Then she eyed their reflections. "Even a stupid girl like me can tell that future."

The future did come and go, another week's worth. Cora's concerns began to wane when Phin didn't appear in the alleyway or near the fruit vendor on Stillwell Ave. He'd surprised Esmerelda there one Sunday with a shiny apple in hand. One he'd readily admitted to stealing. Phin wasn't in the audience in Luna Park's venue, where she continued to perform on Saturday afternoons. She walked the beach at Coney Island and spent a nickel's worth of pennies riding the fierce white horse, scanning the summer crowds. Phin was nowhere.

On the second Saturday evening, the troupe was packing up the wagon. Oscar and the men—Bill, Barney, and Jimmie—would head to the Flatlands. Along with other traveling acts, vagrants, even families with no roofs over their heads, the Brooklyn open land was home through the summer months. If you could stand the mosquitoes, it was better than the city rats. The girls would return to the hotel at the supper club. Cora was locking Licorice in his crate and Esmerelda was doing a poor job of filling canteens from a public spigot. Oscar's booming voice startled her. She thumped a wet, icy-cold hand to her chest. "For the love of God, Oscar, I'm right here. There's no need to shout."

"I want to make sure I have your attention."

She made eye contact.

"Especially after the way you daydreamed through this afternoon's performance. Two patrons walked out." He held up as many thick fingers. "You're not beyond my governorship, Esmerelda Moon. Keep that in mind."

She said nothing and returned to her task.

"You and Cora may be used to your running-water tub and that fine bed you've been sleeping in. But you're still part of this troupe." He looked at the puddle surrounding her shoes. "The rest of us would appreciate enough water to keep from shriveling up in the heat."

She'd been peering down the dusky sidewalk. "I'm sorry, Oscar." She turned to the spigot and focused on water going into the canteens. "I'll have them ready in a jiff."

He sighed and came closer, his broad back meeting with the brick of the building. "Listen to me, Esmerelda."

The seriousness with which he spoke caused her to abandon the canteens. She stood straight and Oscar shut off the spigot. She glanced over her shoulder. The troupe was deep into negotiations with a competing ensemble, trading food for blankets and whiskey. The activity and chill reminded Esmerelda that soon it would be fall. The air would turn icy. Her contract with Hupp's would come to an end.

"Let me ask you something." Through a bright moon, Oscar arced his arm wide. "What is it you want, girl? To be a singer like Fritzi Scheff or Mary Garden, first billing wherever you went? Your name top on a marquee?"

She was confused by his questions. Sloppy disinterest in a task, a distracted performance—it was enough to earn an earful from Oscar. She frowned, shrugging. "Wouldn't any singer?"

"Not necessarily. Some just prefer it, like Cora's juggling. It's a way to avoid an even harder life, less appealing work. But there are plenty of singers, Esmerelda, far less talented than you. They want nothing more than to be that person. First on the marquee, an act too big for my kit and caboodle of traveling wares."

"I've never thought about it."

"And I've never asked for a reason. You could do better than me." She blinked at Oscar's bluntness. "Eh, I don't feel badly about it." He spit a wad of tobacco into the street. "Any agent would do the same to keep his talent. But after your stint at Hupp's and the talk I've heard, you could have that. A different sort of life, one several grades up from Albee's. A whole other world compared to Coney Island."

"You mean leave you . . . Cora, the troupe? What a silly thought." She reached for the spigot and canteens. Oscar's huge hand halted hers.

"You need to think beyond today and common Brooklyn stages, even the lighted city that's Luna Park. And if you're of the mind that you owe me something, then I'm saying you owe me nothing."

It was the queerest talk she'd ever heard from Oscar. "After the way you plucked me out of that mess in Saratoga? Making that idiot saloon owner pay me what he owed me?" Bawdy laughter floated over from the performers and she glanced at the ruckus. "Oscar, I'm alive and I'm well because of you. That's a debt."

"If it was, it isn't anymore. You're not beholden to me, Esmerelda. But you need to decide what it is you do want to be beholden to. If you don't make a choice, fate will do it for you." The laughter stopped as noise of a skirmish rose.

"You'll take no less than a pint of whiskey, Barney," Bill said. "God knows you'll drink most of it yourself!" For as much as Bill and Barney were together, they could also end up in fisticuffs. Oscar walked toward the growing scuffle.

She stared at his lumbering moon-washed frame. At sixteen, Esmerelda had been an easy mark. If it hadn't been for Oscar, she had a fair idea what her fate would have been. She'd arrived in Saratoga already broken, having fled from her own family—her father, a drunk, and her sister, clueless. Esmerelda was working as a singer in a grimy pub near the racetrack for kitchen scraps and the promise of two dollars a week. A second payday came, and the owner only offered Esmerelda another excuse. Oscar stepped in, aiding a hungry and near-hysterical girl. She was awestruck by the swift execution of Oscar's will. He returned from a back room with her money and a tin pail filled with a real dinner. Oscar said to get her things and meet him out front.

Once curbside, he handed Esmerelda the pail and two dollars, half the money owed. At first she was livid, then intrigued when Oscar said, "Agents, girl. They get fifty percent of your earnings. If I'm yours, that much is mine. Do we have a deal?"

Since then, Oscar Bodette had defined himself as many things: representative, companion, mentor, and protector. Her Fagin, at times. He played this role now, neatly settling the argument, naturally in his troupe's favor. With tempers calmed, Oscar returned to Esmerelda's frozen pose. She smiled. He didn't, repeating his earlier question. "So what is it you want, Esmerelda? I need to know."

"Why do you suddenly need to know?"

"Because there's a storm coming."

She looked up at the glow of a giant moon, the sweeping gown of black sky trimmed in stars.

"Not that sort of storm. Don't be as daft as Cora."

She sobered and stood straighter.

"A collision of circumstance that will end in a lot of American blood." He bent down and picked up a small American flag, a casualty from a march held earlier that day.

A year ago, people were flat-out against getting involved in the war in Europe. Sentiment had changed. A growing wave of support carried through the air and bellowed from podium speeches. America needed to protect itself, and that meant helping the French escape the Germans.

"Two swirling storms, if I'm right," Oscar said, spearing her attention. "The first has to do with a great war and Mr. Wilson's growing army."

"I know. I've seen. Cora and I went to the pier one Sunday."

"Good. Then let me add to what you've witnessed. Most soldiers won't come back."

She knotted her brow, having thought of men being sent to fight the enemy. Esmerelda hadn't considered American men and boys dying, not really.

"In that kind of situation," Oscar said, "people make impulsive choices. Heading into hell and glory, they'll want hope and promise waiting for them, should they make it back."

She wasn't sure she followed. Oscar twirled the flag until its colors spun like a pinwheel's.

"I don't want you making choices because of a war." The way Oscar looked at her, it sent a prickle up the black buttons on the back of Esmerelda's dress. "I got a taste of it . . . *war*. Siege on Santiago, San Juan Hill."

"You were in the Spanish-American War?"

He looked surprised. "I forget, Esmerelda. Not only do you sing better than most, you've got a hardworking mind." He tapped the flag to her forehead, and a great flash of Oscar's rare smile followed. "My point is this: I've drawn a sword in a small war, killed the enemy."

Esmerelda reconsidered Oscar, another facet of a complex man.

"It's spit in that ocean"—he pointed east, the direction of the beach—"compared to the one we've entered."

"I still don't see—"

"Collision of circumstance," he said, repeating the phrase. "A few days ago, Benjamin Hupp came to me. The seasons are about to change, more than trading food for whiskey and blankets. Hupp offered to get you billing at the Palace—entire winter, if that's what you want."

She backed up a step. "The Palace?" It was the grandest of all New York stages, an unrealistic venue for Oscar's Traveling Extravaganza. In winter months, troupes like theirs headed south to steadier work and reliable outdoor accommodations.

"He has that sort of . . . *power*, Esmerelda. But also know, Hupp is a hard read. And I'm good at reading most types."

"Oscar, a moment ago you were talking about war. What in the world does that have to do with Benjamin Hupp and me singing at the Palace?"

"More than you think. Like I said, with war comes fast choices, and not just ones about taking the life standing opposed." He inched into the circular light of a streetlamp. "What concerns me about Hupp is I don't know what truly makes him tick. He pays regular and without argument. He's acted like the gentleman he's supposed to be." Oscar hesitated.

"What is it you're not saying?"

"Things I have no proof of, just a story I heard. And mind you, people will tell stories about folks they envy. This one went that Hupp took a shine to a comely German girl—a housemaid of sorts. She was beholden to the Hupps for her sponsorship."

"Ingrid."

Oscar raised a bushy brow. "So you know of her?"

"Benjamin mentions her now and again." She shrugged. "He speaks fondly of her. Never says an unkind word."

"The story goes that the girl went back to Germany."

"So?"

"So I find it strange that a girl makes her way to the States in search of a new life. Then she leaves to return to war-torn Europe. What kind of sense does it make?"

"Perhaps she had family she needed to take care of."

"Actually, I heard it was a suitor who'd asked her to come home."

"There's your answer." Esmerelda smiled at him. "What's strange about that? If she was unhappy, maybe Benjamin was only being generous. You see how generous he's been toward me."

"Yes. I do." He rubbed a hand around the back of his neck, pursed his full mouth. "'Course I hadn't thought of it that way. It could very well be." He bumped a finger under Esmerelda's chin. "But think about this, Esmerelda. You're a pretty girl with a voice that'd make a songbird turn pea green. You're also one of us. Well, at least you are now."

"I like being one of you."

"Where you came from, I've always supposed it looks nothing like this."

She'd underestimated him. Esmerelda assumed Oscar had never considered her life prior to their paths crossing in Saratoga. Oscar was many things, but confessor wasn't one of them. Esmerelda might have told him about the lovely house she'd left and the good education she'd known—a high school graduate. But then she'd have to explain why she'd severed such a life. It was too humiliating.

"Vaudevillians," Oscar was saying, "we live differently. Keep that in mind when it comes to Hupp. They'll pay decent money to enjoy our talents. Most wouldn't stand on the same street corner. Am I making sense?"

She nodded.

"We're like the blacks and the gypsies, people with thick accents and empty pockets. People who live in the tenements or worse, Hell's Kitchen. We don't mix with Hupp or his lot. Not beyond the German maids they hire, or the fellow who shovels the shit in their horse stalls."

"Yes, but I've never given Benjamin the idea—"

Oscar held up his hand and she quieted. "You've not dismissed him, though. You've not walked out on his offer to sing or declined a fine hotel room with a water closet."

"Why would I do that? It's business, Oscar. That was the agreement."

"And I'm telling you the time for living under that assumption has passed—war will heighten a man's willingness to grab for what he wants. All I'm sayin'—and God help me, it's not because I favor the other riffraff that's got an eye for you—"

"Don't talk about Phin like that! You don't know him."

"My point, exactly. I've said disparaging things about Benjamin Hupp while we're standing here. You've not come to his defense, not beyond his kind words about another pretty girl. When Hupp comes to you with the Palace offer, be sure what you're willing to trade for it." He headed for his troupe, saying over his shoulder, "It's not just business."

Esmerelda turned to the spigot and canteens; she twisted back toward Oscar. His caveat rang in her head, though it was a nickname she heard: *"Esme . . ."* It wasn't Phin's voice, but a heavy Native American drawl.

"Hassan?" she called out. A figure stepped into the streetlamp's glow. "What are you doing here?"

"I come to find you. Phin said not to, last week . . . even last night. But I don't think he'll be here tomorrow, so I thought I should do it."

"What do you mean he won't be here tomorrow?" She thought of the draft and Oscar's talk of bloody war. "Is that why I haven't seen him in more than a week?" She dropped the canteen. "Don't tell me he's already left to join the army!"

Hassan shook his head. "No . . . no war yet for us—not yet. But Phin, he won't make it to a war."

"Why is that?"

"Because I think he's going to die tonight."

# Act III, Scene II

She gripped Hassan's arm and said, "Take me to Phin. Now." Esmerelda left Stillwell Avenue so quickly Oscar had no chance to object, nor Cora to ask where she was going.

With the slickness of a magician, Hassan snuck them onto a trolley car. Then another, after they crossed the Brooklyn Bridge. He moved her through avenues that turned to dirt. As they burrowed farther into the streets, the city Esmerelda knew vanished. The people changed. A common mix of classes petered off to one—something beyond destitute. Dwellings grew seedier, and metal sheathing served as shelters. From those, moans and vile smells rivaled the combination of despair and open sewers. The ground beneath her feet was slippery, and every so often a hand would thrust upward, grabbing at her skirt. It might have been hell, but she guessed this was just Hell's Kitchen. Esmerelda's breath rattled, strained and fearful. Hassan's arm clamped around hers, pulling and shouting Indian words that did not sound like any foreign language she knew.

This New York City made Flatland squatters look like guests in fine accommodations. She and Hassan scooted past a doorway where a man, framed by the moon, stood with his trousers around his ankles. Pinched between him and the building was a woman who screamed.

"Hassan, shouldn't we—" Horrified, Esmerelda gawked until she tripped. She fell flat onto the slimy street.

Hassan gathered her up, and she faced forward, dabbing at a bloody scrape to her chin. A man lay motionless to her left, his pockets being picked, his shoes ripped from his feet. Hassan tightened his hand around Esmerelda's, pulling her along. "If he doesn't die, Phin will kill me." It was the clearest English she'd ever heard from him.

"Why is that?"

They stopped. Hassan turned, his black eyes glistening. "For bringing you here." He tugged again, turning them down a narrow passageway darker than the night.

All Esmerelda's common sense had dropped to her feet. She knew this because they'd quit moving. What did she really know about Phin, other than two conflicting points: he could paint and he ran with a raping gang of hoodlums. The things in between were unknowns. Their association had been fanciful meetings on busy uptown streets, moments twinkling in Luna Park lights. Her heart pounded in her ears, outside her chest. "Wait."

"But he's right here. We have a room in the back of the butcher shop."

"The butcher shop?" Her trembling fingers moved across her forehead. *Splendid . . . a place equipped with knives . . .* But the streets they'd passed through, Esmerelda would be a fool to go back alone. One step into the alley and Hassan was invisible. Only touch said he was there. "You haven't told me. Why is he dying? Is Phin injured? Did he get hurt in this place?"

"No. Phin, he's too quick, too much of a fighter for these gutter rats. This is sickness. I've seen it in my tribe. It can take you, even someone like Phin."

Esmerelda didn't need to hear any more. She damned the little she knew and moved forward.

◆ ◆ ◆

Mortality . . . the word filled Esmerelda's mind as she entered a constricted room, dank as it was disturbing. Two oil lanterns cast light, enhanced by the moon. On a cot lay Phin—although she knew this only because Hassan had told her as much. His tall frame was balled up in a knot of sweat. He shook so hard the cot moved like it sat on an earthquake. He opened an eye as the door closed, Hassan sliding a slat of wood across it.

"Good," Hassan said. "You're not dead yet."

Esmerelda's skirt swished as she turned sharply toward Hassan's chilling claim.

"He was too weak to lock the door. You see now other things that could get to him before we did."

"Influenza." Esmerelda moved toward Phin, though it was only a few feet that separated him from the door.

"Don't," he said hoarsely, managing to hold up a shaking hand. "Hassan . . . if I live, I'm going to fucking kill you. I told you not to . . ." A sputtering cough ended his threat.

"No. Hassan was right to come find me." Esmerelda tossed her shawl onto the other cot. A fast glance inventoried the space: a tiny potbelly stove, dirt floor, wooden table, and in the corner, paints and an easel. "I can't catch it, the influenza." Phin's white, sweaty face looked doubtfully into hers. Hassan asked why. "My mother. She had influenza. If I didn't come down with it after her, I can't catch it. Even the doctor told me that."

Phin shook harder, asking in stuttered speech, "How . . . how did she do? Your mother."

"Not as well as Charlie Carlisle." It was a quick reply, Esmerelda avoiding vivid images of her mother's death. She didn't think she could do it again, watch someone she cared for die. She touched him. Esmerelda had thought of doing this, but hadn't thought her first impression would be fire. His head felt hotter than her mother's ever had. She put on her best stage face. "Look at me." Tiny creases of eyes fluttered, a glimpse of blue-gray clouds. She'd be damned if they led to heaven. "Hassan!" Esmerelda spun toward him. "Find me some clean water and rags. When was the last time he ate or drank something? How long has he been like this?" Phin had no time for a language barrier. "And answer in words I can understand." For the most part, he did.

There was a small stool, and she pulled it to the side of the cot. She gagged on the butcher's shop air, which was saturated with the stench of carcasses and blood. Esmerelda tried not to see this as a foretelling. She pressed her fingertips to her head, recalling homemade treatments. "Cinnamon," she said to Hassan. "Do you think you can get me some cinnamon and milk? It will help the fever." She went on to tell the Indian to steal what he couldn't find and to be quick about it. He left, and Esmerelda went to work tending to Phin, who drifted in and out of consciousness. She paid attention to his wheezing breaths—that they were there—and wiped the bloody foam that dribbled over his lips.

Time drifted into something other than the space between sunrise and its setting. It moved past the moment a pocket watch might keep. Time became the moments that lived on Phin's shallow breaths. After each one, Esmerelda prayed hard for another. She assigned Hassan the task of keeping Phin's condition from the butcher. People would panic, and rightfully so. If the butcher knew influenza lurked in his back room, he'd toss Phin into the street. The day noises never stopped, and this was a good thing, whether it was the mayhem outside the shanty door or the butcher and his loud lot of customers.

Again and again, Phin's meager words were scratchy pleas for Esmerelda to leave. Eventually, her determination defeated his exhaustion. She placed cool cloths on his head and dribbled broth, stolen from butcher bones, down his throat. Hassan did manage to procure the cinnamon and milk. Esmerelda couldn't be certain it helped, but his head didn't get any hotter. Naturally, she considered medical aid, but a doctor would only sound another alarm. None would make a house call to this place. The only accessible doctors would be at Bellevue, the murky public hospital for the poor and insane. They'd only be happy to help him die.

After two days, Phin's body rattled with a sharp cough. She'd fallen asleep in the dim wedge of lantern light, curled on the floor beside him. Her head lay crooked in the belly of the cot, between Phin and its hard edge. She felt fingers move through her matted hair. Esmerelda lifted her head and blinked into daylight. He coughed again. It was a positive sign: the cough came with a strong breath, and even sputtering droplets of blood were a welcome thing. This was the most life she'd seen in days. Phin looked clearly into her eyes, the glassiness of his gone. For a moment, Esmerelda panicked, thinking he'd floated from this life and was simply smiling at her from the next. She had to touch his face, assure herself it was all real.

His creaky words moored them to Hell's Kitchen. "You're still here."

"Well, it wasn't as if I could leave you to the likes of Hassan." She glanced over her shoulder. He was gone now, his presence sporadic, or Esmerelda hadn't kept track. She shook her foggy head. After days and nights pinned to Phin's side, she was her own wobbly mess of exhaustion. But looking at him, all she felt was grateful. For the first time, sweat didn't cover Phin's brow. His face didn't feel like a lit stove. "You're awake—looking like you might stay that way."

He managed the smallest smile. "You mean alive."

He tried to raise himself up. It took no more than the faint pressure from Esmerelda's arms to get him to lie back.

"I wanted you to go."

"And I wanted to stay. Since it seems you'll be doing the same thing . . ." She blinked at wet lashes. "Staying around, that is . . . how about we get more than a few spoonfuls of broth into you? I'd wager you've lost ten pounds."

He nodded softly, his head sinking back onto the dirty cot. But the light was good, and so was the rise and fall of his chest. Phin Seaborn was alive, and this made her happy.

# CHAPTER
# TWELVE

*Long Island*
*Present Day*

A crease of light cut like jagged glass. Pete's head pounded and a gut-tural noise rose from his throat. He wiped his hand over bleary eyes and tried to focus. He'd once woken up in a spider hole in Kabul, cramped and camped with six marines. The ground above had swarmed with a Taliban insurgence. He hadn't felt this alarmed or disoriented. The horizon was lower than his body, and he saw sky and water meet. He groaned, thinking he might vomit. But where and onto what? He held up a hand, shielding sharp rays. Blinking, he glanced around. A truck. He was sitting in a truck. Weathered leather seats, the antiquated dash, numerous gearshifts.

Okay, he remembered getting into the truck in East Marion. He recalled the uncanny urge to drive forward, amazed the truck's engine turned over. That he knew how to drive it. While all this was curious recall, Pete couldn't explain how he'd arrived at the sight in front of him: a sandy beach. "How the fuck did I get . . ." Pete slid open the truck's door and essentially fell from the seat. "Here?"

His legs gave way and he crumpled to the ground. Gripping on to the truck door to pull himself up, Pete had the sensation of having traveled to some far-off place. Maybe the moon. He steadied himself and peered inside the truck, almost hoping to find an empty gin bottle. Drunken stupor would be a welcome explanation. There was nothing, and Pete didn't drink like that. The beach looked deserted, along with the dirt area where the truck was parked. He hung on to the door, turning in one direction, then the other. Gulls squawked and tiny waves lapped twenty yards away. Brown seaweed made for a messy shoreline, and across the water was a small strip of land. He wasn't looking at the sound; you couldn't see land across that body of water. *Where the fuck am I and how did I get here?* To the right was a row of shed-like structures, similar to those he'd discovered in Walberswick, England.

Oddly, Pete smiled. That memory, as opposed to this moment, was a good thing. Walberswick was from another era. Pete had flirted with peace on that timeless riverside respite. His dopey smile collapsed as his heart thundered. *Time.* The neatly painted beach shacks in front of him bore no sense of time. No girl in a bikini or blaring music. Waterfront, of course, was ageless—a wooden rowboat turned upside over told him nothing. Rising streaks of pink and orange gave way to a dome of blue. East. To his left was east. He considered approaching one of the small shacks, knocking on a door. He started in that direction and stopped. What if a door opened to someone from another century?

The question filtered through his woozy mind. He curled his toes into the soles of his sneakers. It seemed like ninety-dollar Nikes should indicate a firm grip on the twenty-first century. Yet the beach was uncannily familiar. Walking, he steered away from the huts and moved parallel with the shoreline. Irrational fear tugged at him like the tide. The idea of wandering in, vanishing, was also on Pete's mind. It would be one way to answer every confounding question that plagued his life.

*"Keep moving, Soldier . . . that's not your destiny . . ."* The trudge of Nikes stopped. The voice was the same one he'd imagined on Rocky

Neck beach. Or always thought he imagined. It belonged to his life-guard uncle.

He murmured to the horizon: "Lifeguard . . . lifeline. Something life affirming would be great right about now."

He turned in a three-sixty motion, staving off panic and the impossible. Several yards away, a wooden sign was staked in the earth. "Earth, sure. Circa . . . ?" He stumbled in a circle, reassessing the views. "Not a fucking clue."

Approaching the sign, improbability did not abate. Not until the wooden sign grew legible. It read: "Site of the Gillette Dock, taken to sea in the Great Hurricane of 1938. Bayport, New York." A few feet away was a discarded Starbucks cup. He sighed and squinted at the water. A bay. This was the—present-day—Great South Bay. Pete realized precisely where he was, positive of three things: One, he hadn't a clue how he ended up there. Two, this was the location depicted in his mother's ghost gift, the vintage postcard. Three, Esme had visited this place, taken in the same bay view a hundred years earlier. The view that had inspired her to write on the card: *When I spent two weeks on this beach, I didn't dream of you then. E.M.*

Pete spun toward the truck, frustration coming at him like a cavalry charge. He marched back with his fists clenched and his eyes on his sneakers. He couldn't process last night or this morning. Visits to another life via the portal of an unknown REM state and the gateway drug propofol, something pumped into him years before, he got that. His cumulative experiences were driven by a profound psychic gift—sure, fair enough. He could file all of it under old news. But now it seemed he could add blackouts to his otherworldly woes. A blackout that had dumped him on a beach illustrated on a ghost gift that belonged to his mother. Pete moved faster to the truck. From the relative safety of the cab, he stared at the wide span of water, tiny shacks, and the past, which—by his best guess—seemed to be overlapping with the present.

♦ ♦ ♦

With no GPS and a vehicle that didn't move over forty miles per hour, it took Pete a while to make it back to East Marion. Still, it was early morning as he bumped up the driveway. The old compact car caught his eye, but he motored along until he was back inside the barn. The lantern had been extinguished. He exited the truck and the dilapidated building. Then Pete shoved the wooden plank over the door—like maybe this would keep the truck from escaping or the past from entering. He leaned against the rough wood. Clear as the sky, behind his closed eyes, Pete saw a much smaller door, a plank sliding across it. A young man with two braids stood guard; he smiled at Pete.

*Am I in the room?*

His mental point of view was staring up at a crude ceiling, as if lying in a bed. The room was small, a hovel. Smells made him gag, rank odors of filth and illness. Pete lurched from the barn door, both his hands clamping onto his head. "Goddamn it!" he yelled. "Get the fuck out of my mind!" He was silenced by an internal flash of Esme; she too was in the shabby room.

He tried for logic again. It could be this new vision was aided by the photographs he'd discovered in the bungalow—Esme, beautiful and beaten. But Pete had never lost hours. Never woken up clueless about his location or how he'd arrived there. And not just anyplace, but a spot on the map where Esme had been a hundred years before. To a point, Pete was able to handle the haunting repetitive visits to his past. Hell, he'd been practicing most of his life. Upsetting as those occurrences were, they didn't bleed into this life. In fact, until this trip home, specters and his other life had been mutually exclusive. "Why?" he shouted to no one, lost to frustration. "Why are you doing this?"

Pete focused on the compact car. It was the only object that didn't make him feel like he wavered on complete madness. The car door creaked open, the front seat flipping forward, smacking against the steering wheel. The horn sounded, which only drilled into his aching head. The girl from yesterday stumbled out from the back seat like a lost clown, her deep red hair askew, her expression as bewildered as his.

"What the hell are you shouting about?" she said, her voice sleepy.

Pete fought the urge to ask why she'd slept in the car, woken up someplace other than her own bed. Or maybe she didn't know either, and they could explore this grand new fucked-up state of confusion together. Pete stood about twenty feet from her. He forced his staccato breaths and thoughts into a more stable rhythm. Scaring the shit out of her wouldn't be a great idea. "Sorry." He held up a hand. "I . . . a bat swooped at me."

She moved in a sleepy stagger, glancing up at overgrown trees. "Don't bats come out at dusk?"

"This one must have had a screw loose. Maybe I startled a nest." He thumbed over his shoulder. "The barn." She glanced that way but didn't come closer, and Pete figured he'd better find "normal" fast. "I looked for you last night. I came out here . . . late. I saw your car. You weren't in the house."

"Why were you looking for me?"

"I wasn't."

"But you just said—"

"I didn't come here looking for you. I saw the car and couldn't find you." Pete struggled for the thing that usually tripped him up—awareness of difficulties more precarious than his own. "I got worried after I looked everywhere."

She pointed toward the vehicle. "Obviously not everywhere. You didn't think to look in the car?"

The *"duh"* question triggered the concrete events connected to last night. He was about to look in her car, his phone had gone dead, then the light from the barn had caught his eye. Pete raised an arm, and it thudded against his khaki-covered thigh. "Just glad you're okay."

"Yes. Fine. A little stranded, maybe." She motioned to the car again. "It wouldn't start. I ended up calling Caroline." She tugged on a messy braid, which struck him as a sign of uncertainty. "She's my roommate. I was kind of desperate."

"Was she supposed to come get you?"

"Hardly. She wanted to send a car."

"Like a taxi?"

"Like a car and driver."

"You're kidding?"

"It's why I tried everything else first. Caroline comes from megam-oney. She likes to be in charge." He waited. "She enjoys being right—queen of passive-aggressive behavior. The luxury ride back to Manhattan would have turned into a fantastic 'I told you so.' She warned me not to borrow Lucy's car. She's a different friend."

"I see. Less bossy . . ."

"And less reliable transportation." She glanced at the car. "Caroline wouldn't have come herself, either way. Being in *Wicked* takes up her evenings."

"Geez, if wicked describes her, maybe you ought to rethink your room—"

"I didn't call her wicked. I said *she's in* Wicked. Caroline made ensemble last spring." The girl pulled a cell phone from her back pocket and poked at it. "Anyway, it got late, and I decided to wait until morn-ing to figure out a plan B. I thought about sleeping inside, but that place . . ." She cocked her chin at the house. "It's creepy."

"You're telling me."

"So why did you come back so late? Did you sleep here?"

Easy explanations continued to elude Pete. Instead, he gave in to exhaustion and asked, "Do, um . . . do you want to get some breakfast?"

# CHAPTER
# THIRTEEN

On his way back to the bungalow, Pete had passed a restaurant. He called Grace as they drove toward the North Fork Diner now, his phone charging in the Audi's console. Pete could imagine Grace's reaction, waking up and finding him gone. She'd probably alert the local police, maybe his mother. On the other hand, Grace didn't do anything before a three-mile run. His call went to voice mail. "Hey, I'm fine," he reported. "Sorry I was gone this morning. I went out to the house . . . early. I ran into, uh . . ." He glanced at the girl seated beside him. "Alice."

"Ailish." She said it curtly, insulted or amazed at his inability to recall.

"Right. Ailish." He glanced in her direction again; the name wouldn't stick. He spoke into the phone. "Montague." Her last name dropped in on his busy brain. "She had car trouble. We're getting break-fast. I'll be back . . . soon."

They turned into a dusty parking lot, and she hopped out when they rolled to a stop. Ailish swung her backpack over her shoulder, her messy braid flying in the opposite direction. Peering through the open car window, she hooked her finger around the bridge of wire-rimmed sunglasses, cobalt-blue lenses, and slid them down her nose. "Girlfriend keeps close tabs on you, huh?"

"She's not my girlfriend."

"Really?" She paused. "Wow. The hovering must have been claustrophobic when she *was* your girlfriend."

He got out, slamming the Audi's door with an annoyed thud. "What makes you say she used to be my girlfriend?"

"Evidentiary clues. For one, clearly you're sharing a room. *'Sorry I was gone this morning . . .'*"

He didn't say yes or no, yanking on the diner door, his hand sweeping by in an exaggerated gesture. "And the second reason, Miss Mind Reader?"

"I might have been in a whirlwind state yesterday, but I'm a good people observer."

"FBI profiler?"

"No. But it is part of my job." She glided past him, chin tilted upward. "Remember. I told you, I'm an actress."

No. He hadn't remembered, and he froze at the blip of information. Cold air rushed at him from the diner interior.

"Are you coming?"

Pete squeezed his eyes shut and breathed deep before following.

"As for . . . ?"

"Grace," he said, glad someone else could forget a name.

"Grace. I'm sure Grace is a lovely person, but after meeting you . . ." She slid the glasses down again. "She hasn't a thing to worry about from me."

Pete kept walking.

"Besides, as noted, I'm good at reading people."

Pete was about to object to her tarot-card opinion of Grace. Then he recalled the sexy blonde on the beach. In the moment, Pete had been fine with Grace's interruption, glad to be rid of the girl and her father's ghost. Of course, Grace's ploy had also removed any obstacle to her beach-blanket picnic for two. That motivation hadn't struck him, not until this girl unwittingly noted it. He moved deeper into the diner, Ailish leading the way. She was quirky but quick. He pointed toward a sign for the restroom. "Did you want to use the restroom? I'm guessing it was a long night in the car."

She looked that way but didn't budge. "No. When nature called at five a.m., I just went there . . . into the woods." She sang softly under her breath, some rhyming trill that repeated the phrase.

The soft sound of her voice penetrated, and for a second Pete felt like the whole diner went wonky. He shook it off and turned left. She went right.

"Oh, let's sit over here! In the sun. I love early morning sun. You don't get much of it in the city, with all the tall buildings. Our condo is like a tomb. Sun kind of makes you feel . . . *reborn*." She kept moving, forcing him in the opposite direction.

*Quick, quirky, and annoying,* he thought.

She slid into a booth, and Pete dropped onto the other seat, squinting at the harsh light. A waitress pounced, supplying thick laminated menus and pouring coffee. "Just leave the pot," Ailish instructed. Bossy too, but different from Grace—like maybe she wouldn't order for Pete. She perused food choices, flipping back and forth between the glossy pages. Pete opened his mouth; she held up her index finger, eyes never veering from the colorfully photographed food.

*Like a person can't picture pancakes . . .*

Whatever. He had nothing relevant to say to her. The only topic they might have in common was her dead uncle, and talking about Zeke Dublin didn't interest him either. Although on that front, Pete also realized zero spirits beckoned at him. He closed his eyes for a moment, only seeing oranges and reds blurred on the canvas of his brain. Endless days on assignment had the same effect, and mental fatigue had its perks. Pete tried to relax and chose to be grateful for the mental reprieve the universe currently allowed. He sipped black coffee, assuming his breakfast club guest was half-starved after being stuck at the bungalow since yesterday.

The waitress returned. "You folks ready to order?"

His dining partner flipped feverishly between two pages. Pete rolled his eyes. *Great . . . impulsive and indecisive.*

She closed the menu and folded her hands. "I'll have two eggs, sunny side up, with the Southern biscuits, gravy on the side, double bacon, and the sausage—I couldn't decide, they both looked so good. Make it rye toast, dark, with the Irish butter if you have it." She ran a bitten-nail finger over the silver caddy holding tiny plastic containers of jelly. "You're out of peach. Can you see if there's any peach jelly in the back?"

Pete's mouth gaped before he placed his order. "And I'll have . . ."

She shot him a look, holding him silent. "Could I also have a side of pancakes with fried bananas on top—do you have the silver dollar ones?" She jabbed a finger at the menu. "And the seasonal fruit to round it out."

Pete blinked, looking between her and the waitress, who wrote furiously. The server's pencil finally stopped moving, and she glared at Pete as if he needed to catch up.

"I'll have toast," he said.

"White, rye, wheat, pumpernickel, millet, gluten-free—"

"White. Just bring me white toast—dry." He said this before Ailish assaulted him with an assortment of jams and spreads from which to choose. The waitress hurried away, and Ailish chimed right in.

"Wow. Are you always like that?"

"Like what?"

"Like you're going to bite the head off the world, or at least the nearest snake."

"Sorry." Mostly sorry he'd suggested breakfast. "My work doesn't allow for much food indulgence."

She wriggled her nose. "Corporate type, chained to a desk, locked in a boardroom, intent on paying off your swanky Midtown condo before you're thirty? Maybe you're shooting for partner this year."

"No . . . ," he said slowly. "And so much for your people-reading skills. I'm a photojournalist. I travel most of the time. I'm either in an airport, where I wouldn't touch the food, or—"

"Oh." She nodded, sipping her coffee. "Fussy too. Interesting."

"Or hauling ass through a country where staying alive doesn't include an opportunity to sample the local cuisine." He realized his reply was largely acerbic. He didn't care. "At the moment, I have a bitch of a headache, which isn't lending itself to the coronary disease du jour offered in this fine establishment."

"Bender last night?"

"You've no idea."

That much didn't elicit a verbal volley. Instead, she rummaged through her backpack and plopped three bottles of pain reliever onto the table.

"Extra-strength ibuprofen, migraine-strength Excedrin, or plain old aspirin, which I don't recommend on a slush stomach. Of course, if you're into it, I have about a half ounce of weed in here too, but we'd do better out in your car with it."

"Yeah. My father would love that air freshener. You're kidding, right?"

"No. Why? Does weed insult your moral fiber?"

"Just my better sense." He'd experimented enough at Brown, but booze and pot in excess had never been the cure or even soothed Pete. "I outgrew it."

"Whatever." She shrugged. "I was just holding it for Caroline."

He snickered.

"What? The other day, Caroline took her dad to the airport, and she just figured . . . well, it could be a problem in some places."

"Try that excuse with the TSA at the gate in Logan, London, or Libya, see where you end up."

She made a face at him, reaching for her over-the-counter drugs.

"Wait." He grabbed the Excedrin, opened it, and popped three, washing them down with a gulp of coffee. "Nothing medicinal will fix what ails me, but it won't make it any worse."

Her expression changed. "You're not sick, are you?"

"Sick? No, not physically." He thought of the scars he couldn't explain. *Everything* he couldn't explain. "Not even in a way a good lobotomy might cure. More like permanently pissed off at life."

"Wow again."

He sighed, feeling like the germ under Ailish Montague's microscope.

"Are you always so cynical? You're young to have such a chip on your shoulder."

"Interesting choice of words. *Young* would be a relative description."

Her hazel gaze speared him.

"Some . . . *people* would define me as more of an 'old soul.'"

"And a really crabby one." Ailish tipped her head at the open palm of his hand. "What did you do to yourself?" She pointed to his blistered fingers. "Spend the night chopping wood?"

Pete stared at the raw spots. "I, uh . . . I accidentally touched something hot."

"Like what?"

"What?" He picked up his cup so the blisters wouldn't show.

"Most people wouldn't say they 'touched something hot.' Not unless they were avoiding the root cause. You know, like a battered child sidestepping the reason for a bruise. Marks like that"—she motioned to his hand with her cup—"a person would say they'd touched a hot pot . . . or an iron. Not . . . *something*."

"Just *something* I prefer not to talk about, okay?"

She raised her mug at him. "Freebasing cocaine it is!"

The pissed-off look on his face must have been clear.

"Sorry. My mention of an eyedropper's worth of weed seemed to get a rise out of you."

"So you're just pressing my buttons." Pete lowered his blistered hand beneath the table.

She cleared her throat and the silence grew awkward. Ailish fussed with a napkin, placing it on her lap, directing her words that way. "I . . . you're just very dark . . . brooding. I guess I was just trying to counteract it."

*Promise. Quit while you're ahead* . . . Instead of saying as much, Pete turned the question on her. "Why would you do that?"

"Because . . ." It shut her up and he was pleased. But something in Ailish's expression changed, a seriousness that she hadn't brought to the table. "Sorry about whatever it is in life that you find so disagreeable."

The waitress arrived with a jam-packed tray. Pete thought it was enough food to feed one of the third-world countries he often visited. Ailish only admired the dishes placed before her and hungrily dug in. She also ate like she'd been held captive for the past month, kept alive on a rice-and-dirt diet. The sight rocked his queasiness, and Pete turned his head toward the window.

"Sure you don't want a slice of bacon, maybe a biscuit?" From the corner of his eye, he saw a plate being inched across the table. "I've always had a big appetite. Lucky I got my dad's fast metabolism. My mum's too, I guess. Curious about parents, the things we inherit."

He absorbed that hit to the head of the nail and looked back at the buffet spread. "Nice their traits are compatible. Can't say the same about mine."

"Oh, they don't get along, your mum and dad?"

"No . . . I mean, yes. They get along fine. More like the poster couple for opposites attracting. However, put them in a blender and you . . ."

"End up with you?"

He didn't answer; she shrugged, never breaking rhythm with the food being ferried from her plate to her mouth.

"Let me guess," he said. "Your parents aren't much for standard social cues, maybe a bit Bohemian."

"Mmm . . . Mum for sure. She's never fit into anybody's pigeon-hole. My dad . . . well, if Ian Montague was a college professor, 'absent-minded' would be the sign on his door. Why do you ask?"

"No reason." Pete pointed to her morning smorgasbord. "I see you're not a slave to common social behaviors either. Refreshing, in a gluttonous sort of way."

"Meaning what?" She slathered a piece of toast with the requested peach jelly, then used it as a shovel, capturing the goopy egg. Shoving a wedge into her mouth, she caught a dribble of yolk with her finger, sucking it off.

"Nothing." Pete took another mouthful of coffee and poked at his plate of naked toast. "For sure this is my father's antiquated behavior talking, but isn't it some kind of girl etiquette, eating like a bird in . . ." He shuffled his hand between them. "Boy-girl situations?" He couldn't recall Grace ordering from anywhere but the salad selections, possibly even at breakfast.

"Situations like what?" She glanced around the diner. "This isn't a date. And—"

"Finally, something we agree on."

"I'd say so." She looked him up and down. "Difficult and disagree-able isn't my type."

Pete swallowed down his immediate reply with a gulp of coffee. "How about just finishing your one-of-everything-on-the-menu meal and we can conclude our very nondate."

She sobered and turned her attention to the silver dollar pancakes, dumping a river of syrup on top. Pete reverted to contemplating the blistering sunscape and shifted in his seat. After last night, he didn't think it possible to run into anything more uncomfortable than his own skin. Minutes passed. There was nothing but the clinking of cutlery, silence that hung like bad weather. And while it'd been some time since Pete was motivated by parental pressure, his mother's text did surface in his brain. *"Be nice . . ."* He faced her. "I found your photo album."

"Did you?" Her eyes went wide, though it didn't slow her inhale of food. She impaled a piece of melon, adding a chunk of gravy-covered biscuit. "My mother will be glad for that." At least she managed to hold a napkin to her full mouth.

"Uh, yeah." Pete closed his eyes lightly and shook his head. "Last night, before I . . ." He pursed his lips. "It's back at the bungalow, in one of the bedrooms."

"What else did you find?"

"What else?" The question didn't fit—anywhere. "Nothing," he said quickly. "Just some other photos. Nothing related to you."

"Are you certain of that?"

"Yes." He looked curiously at her. "Just photos. And they were much older—way before your uncle hooked up with . . ."

"Your mother?"

Her trickle of laughter ran like a faucet. It no longer felt reminiscent but had needled its way under his skin. "I was going to say the Heinz-Bodette troupe."

"My mistake."

She crunched down on what had to be her fourth slice of bacon. He couldn't stand to watch her consume a fifth, and plucked a crispy slice off the place.

"Good," she said. "Maybe low blood sugar isn't helping your disposition."

"I doubt it."

"Me too." She paused, sighing deeply at her plate. "Disappointing. So not what I imagined . . ."

It was barely audible. "What?"

"Nothing."

Uneasy silence sat again. It seemed like she wanted to say something but returned to her meal, consuming the rest, and Pete thought about offering up his toast. At the very least, her eating habits rivaled a carnie sideshow. He was about to ask if she'd ever considered the hot-dog-eating contest at Coney Island, but the thought of Coney Island stopped him cold.

*"If Paris is France, then Coney Island, between June and September, is the World."*

"Shut up," he murmured, though no voice had spoken the thought. It just wouldn't vacate his head.

"Excuse me?"

"Sorry. I had something else on my mind." He tapped the half-eaten strip of bacon on a plate. Ailish took out her phone and poked at it with one finger, tugging on the messy braid with the other hand. She was pretty—at least when she wasn't devouring food like a lioness. He shrugged. Maybe even then. Pretty in a redhead way that was hard to define. Too bad it all came to a crashing end when she opened her mouth.

People . . . *women* of color, dark hair and skin, dominated Pete's recent memories. Admittedly, there weren't many to recall. And she wasn't without a point. Pete's disposition, on this side of the world or the other, worked like a charm—an amulet for keeping most women away.

"So . . . I'll get you the album when we get back to the bungalow. I can take a look at your car, if you want. Give you a ride to the train station, whatever you need."

With her hand still wrapped around the thick plait of hair, her gaze moved to his. It was penetrating, different from the curious glances she'd peppered him with so far. "Okay. Thanks. That'd be . . . helpful."

Noises seeped into Pete's head, water spilling over an edge. The infinity pool of his mind. But the sounds were distant, he couldn't tell if they were music or words—maybe both. A subtle tremor rose upward, as if the diner sat on a fault line. But a glance at Ailish told Pete he was the only person aware of the vibrating sensation. He placed his palms flat on the table, a steadying gesture. When Pete closed his eyes, her voice severed the undulating lure.

"Can I ask you something?" He didn't say anything, and she went on. "Is it true?"

He opened his eyes. "Is what true?"

"That your mother speaks to the dead. That you can do the same."

It startled him. They'd gone hours between yesterday afternoon and today. They'd managed a damn good sparring match in a public place. Yet she hadn't hinted at his gift. But of course, she would know.

"You sort of looked like you were slipping into some sort of trance."

His low gaze was now one with the empty coffee cup, his grip around it choking. "Add blunt to your list of alluring qualities."

"It's just a question. Your gift. I didn't know it was a secret."

"It's not a secret." *I just prefer not being stared at like a Vegas lounge act.* "I, um. It's not something people know about me unless I do the telling. Which I don't very often. I guess your mother mentioned it."

"Mmm, Mum talks a blue streak on a quiet day."

"Big surprise." He rolled his eyes. "My gift, it's not a topic I enjoy talking about."

She sighed. "That's a hell of a list of grievances you've got going. I see why you spend most of your time in countries where you don't speak the language."

"So when did *Mum* tell you, before you headed out to the bungalow?"

"I'm not sure she ever did. It's more like your birthday—something I've just always known." She ignored any objection from him and moved right along. "So why don't you like to talk about it, your psychic gift?"

"Why? Because . . ." He blinked at her. "You know, I've never met anyone more obtuse than me."

"It seems to me if a person had such an amazing gift, they'd—"

"Want a reality TV show?"

She waited for more.

"Hardly worth it, in my experience. Look, let me give you the Psychic 101 crib notes: One of two things occurs when a gift like mine, or my mother's, becomes the focal point. People label you a freak, which is super fun finger-pointing when you're twelve or thirteen—even twenty. Trust me. Or you become this godlike being to people's worst suffering. And in my experience, no matter how much healing you're able to offer by way of communication, it's never enough. I can't bring back the dead."

"Can't you?"

The bizarre question caught him off guard, and Pete looked away. When he looked back, to his dismay, Ailish was still there. He didn't know if she was trying to be funny or looking for facts. Laughter rose, and he wasn't entirely sure it came from her.

"Of course you can't do that," she said. "Anyway . . . surely there must be something in the middle? Something positive."

He was amazed she didn't demand a demonstration. She seemed like a party trick kind of girl. But because she didn't do this, he answered. "On occasion, there have been moments when the benefit of my gift has outweighed the burden." Pete thought of the young girl in the Afghan village, others he plucked from precarious circumstances thanks to whispers from the dead. "Extremes are what keep my gift from being a great talking point. So if you don't mind . . ."

She held up her hands. "Forget I mentioned it. I didn't realize it was such a sore spot."

"It is." He looked around the diner. "Could we just get the check, get going? I'll buy."

"If you insist."

She didn't even make a faux reach for the backpack. Of course, she had a cell phone. If she had a dime, or a credit card, she could have called a tow service last night, an Uber ride at the very least. Pete reached for his wallet, never taking his eyes off her. Bothersome as she was, common as Uber drivers were, he didn't like the idea of a stranger having come to her aid. Not in such a remote location. Pete busied himself with his wallet, unsure why chivalrous behavior had cropped up. Whatever. He'd make sure she got somewhere safe, report that much to his mother. He looked hard over his shoulder; the waitress appeared to be nowhere. Then he looked at Ailish. She wasn't the easiest person to read either. But he did see that curiosity hadn't fallen from her face. "What?"

"Yesterday, I got the impression you didn't really want to be at the bungalow. This morning, you never really answered me."

"About what?"

"Why you came back—and in the middle of the night. Seems like a strange thing to do. So tell me, Peter St John . . ." Her smile was like a finger poke to his back. "What happened last night that makes you even testier today? Did you fall down a Rabbit Lane hole?"

# CHAPTER
# FOURTEEN

Cryptic or superfluously babbling—Pete couldn't pinpoint which behavior best described Ailish's inquiry about his psychic gift. Either way, her presence felt intrusive, and they drove back to the bungalow in silence.

Turning onto Rabbit Lane, she finally spoke. "Sorry if what I said . . . asked, pissed you off."

"Not at all." Quiet resumed, and Pete realized that he sounded like his father when clearly irritated by his mother.

"Because sometimes I do that, talk too much."

"I never would have guessed."

"Especially when I'm nervous."

"Why would I make you nervous?"

"You don't." Her attention stayed with the road in front of them. "I didn't mean nervous. I just meant uneasy, the house and all. Stuck there all night."

"And me." Pete couldn't get the photos of a beaten Esme out of his head. While Ailish wouldn't admit to Pete making her uneasy, he felt anxious enough for both of them. He gripped tighter to the steering wheel, and they turned down the bungalow's driveway.

"I should tell you," she said, cutting into the quiet, "yesterday, when I pulled up, I had the oddest sense of déjà vu. Has that ever happened to you—feeling like you've lived something already? Because this was incredibly intense."

"Déjà vu, huh?" The car rolled to a stop.

"Yes. Do you ever experience anything like that?"

With everything weighing on Pete's mind, talk of déjà vu struck him as wildly trite. He turned toward her. "You mean a phenomenon most easily explained by a flash of cross-wiring in the brain, mismatched memories? It's actually most common in individuals between the ages of sixteen and twenty-five—so I'm guessing you fall right into the mainstream. Small bits of real memories, smells, sights, sounds, are enough to elicit a detailed recollection, that while seemingly true—hence the déjà vu—have no actual substantive basis in fact."

She blinked at him. "My God, are you always like that?"

"What? Sort of a walking encyclopedia of information?"

"No. Such an ass."

His mouth gaped, and she got out of the car. Ailish strode to her vehicle and opened the door, rummaging through the car. He considered abandoning her, backing down the drive, leaving her there. Instead, Pete continued to idle, along with the motor. He rarely pursued arguments. There was enough war in his head. He wasn't about to get into it with someone he considered a passing acquaintance. Yet he moved on autopilot and exited the Audi. "What I just said is a fact," he insisted, coming across the driveway. "Look it up. Sorry if your déjà vu was no more than a textbook event of readily explained circumstance."

She whipped around from the car, holding a hairbrush. For a moment, Pete thought she might beat him with it. "I've got it. No one but you is allowed to experience anything mind-provoking—déjà vu or maybe even dreams. Clearly, compared to your *great psychic gift*, my experiences are laughable. Again, sorry I annoyed you back at the restaurant. That you feel so compelled to dismiss me."

"I'm not doing that."

"Aren't you?" She stabbed the hairbrush at him.

"Well, in most cases . . ." He flailed a hand toward the garage. "No. Make that all cases of déjà—"

"Seriously?" she snapped. "You're going to defend that snotty, hubristic statement? You may see ghosts clearly, Pete St John. But know you are straight-up dense when it comes to social skills."

He glared in the direction of the barn, his face warming at his most blatant shortcoming. Back to the point. "I'm sorry if I'm unimpressed with a singularity covered in a Psych 101 class."

"Oh, so it's just Basic Manners 101 you made an F in." Ailish shook the hairbrush: rapid, angry, thinking beats. "While it's against my better judgment, let me jump in here, educate you."

"Educate—" He thumbed at his chest.

"A common societal response, whether you disagree or not, is to exhibit a modicum of magnanimous behavior. This might include anything from a hum of acknowledgment to verbalizing a thought, like, 'Wow! That's interesting!' even if you're positive it's total bullshit."

"Really?" He crossed his arms. "And where did you get your degree in psychology?"

She'd turned for the car but spun back around, speaking in loud, staccato beats. "N. Y. U."

He blinked at her and shut up.

"You said you were an actress."

"One-note assumptions again. How thickheaded. Must be what you got your degree in."

Pete opened his mouth and closed it, stopped by his one-credit-shy exit from Brown. He'd never seen his father so livid.

"My degree"—she took a step toward Pete, who took one back—"didn't come with a disclaimer saying the two things were mutually exclusive. One can earn a degree in anything, then decide to pursue something else. Hardly a phenomenon. Just a stereotype."

"Yeah, but . . . well, I don't know that much about actresses, but I didn't think—"

"What? That we're educable?"

While he'd never thought about it, Pete felt committed to the ludicrous argument and splayed his hands wide in front of him.

"You're kidding, right? No one is that ignorant."

"Excuse me?" And now he was ready to fight, certain he could handle an intellectual argument—even one credit short.

She beat him out of the gate.

"Education was the agreement I made with my parents. Flighty as my mother can be, my father not such a great businessman, they insisted I earn a degree if I was going to pursue acting. It seemed reasonable to me and my 3.86 GPA. Average is 3.7." She smiled at his awed expression. "Oh, did I suddenly jump a notch on the brainiac meter? I might be something more than the niece of your mother's dead grifter lover." And for all her capricious humor, she appeared quite serious.

"Sorry. I didn't think—"

"No. You didn't."

And Pete felt himself lower a peg, maybe two. "Look, I'm sorry if my knee-jerk reaction to déjà vu came off as snobbish. It was a really long . . . strange night. But I think we've already covered my off-putting disposition." His stare shuffled between her and the barn.

She threw the hairbrush in through the open car window. "Why do you keep doing that?"

"What?"

"Looking toward the barn. While we've been duking it out here, you keep looking in that direction, like the barn is a third party in this argument. What's in there that's got you so spooked?"

He hesitated. A voice cut into their conversation, one to which Ailish wasn't privy. *"Do it . . . take her . . . show her . . . it has to start somewhere . . ."*

Great. Just what he needed—a rogue specter flickering. Pete shuffled his hand through his hair. But in an instant, he also understood that the spirit present was connected to Ailish—not him or the bungalow. This knowledge put him abnormally at ease. "I . . ." He pointed to the barn. As she'd noted, Pete didn't share well. Not with people he knew, never mind with an almost stranger, one who clearly didn't care for him.

*"Well, whose fault is that?"*

"Okay, that's just . . ." He looked around the thickly wooded yard. Specters rarely made it past surface thoughts, never mind offering an opinion. "Son of a . . . who are . . . ?" He concentrated, forcing the hovering ghost out of his mental line of vision. He turned his attention to a waiting Ailish. "I came back here last night because this place was gnawing at me. It wouldn't let go."

"What does this bungalow have to do with you? I thought your mother inherited it, and you were just here to do the math, see if there was anything she might want to keep."

"It's what got me here. But if I can step beyond déjà vu without insulting you . . . ?"

"Since you ask so nicely."

"The spirit world influences everyone—whether you have a gift like mine or not. And—"

"Do you really believe that?"

Again, what was with her probing, off-track questions? For the sake of getting on with it, Pete answered. "Yes. I do." He paused, seeing if she'd counter. "May I continue?"

"Please."

"In my experience, most people are unaware of otherworldly occurrences. Mostly because they're not open to it, because it's too outside the box for them. People are fearful of things not readily explained. What it might mean."

"Sometimes they are." She crossed her arms. "Déjà vu, maybe even dreams."

"Maybe even that. My point is, I believe a confluence of events, both earthly and otherwise, landed me here. You said you didn't sleep in the bungalow because it creeped you out."

She nodded.

"Multiply that by about a thousand for me. Of course, that's not the most intriguing or interesting part. That occurred this morning—or last night."

"What happened this morning . . . or last night?"

He gestured toward the barn. "Come with me." Hesitantly, she followed, and the two walked that way. Pete slid the wooden plank to the right. As he did, the past flashed before him, a foul-smelling room and near squalor. He had to stop, closing his eyes.

"Are you all right?"

He blinked. "No. It has to do with my permanent crab-ass disposition. Think of it as a lifelong hangover." Pete pulled on the barn door. "Grace and I found this yesterday. After I looked around the house, I came out here last night." He pointed. "That lantern was lit. I'm guessing you didn't light it."

"I never came out here." She didn't look at him, her attention tight on the truck. "I curled up in the back seat once I realized I was stuck for the night." Ailish closed in on the vehicle, running her hand over its battered paint: "Oscar Bodette's Traveling Extravaganza. Well . . ." She brushed her dusty hands together. "There's something you don't see every day. What is it about the truck that bothers you so much?"

"This morning, I woke up in it."

"Like me in Lucy's car?"

"Not exactly. I woke up in it parked near a deserted piece of bay. A sweet little beach, some town called Bayport."

"Bay . . . ?" Her face grew perplexed.

"Bayport. It's about an hour from here. Beyond getting in the truck, pulling out of the garage, I have no recollection of driving there."

"Like a blackout?" She looked between him and the truck.

"Would be my best interpretation. But it gets better. I knew the place, the beach."

"This, um . . . *Bayport*."

"Yes. Bayport." Pete opened his mouth, on the precipice of a blow-by-blow explanation. It was too much; he went with a simpler version. "The beach scene, it's among my mother's collection of . . . *ghost gifts*."

"Ghost gifts?" She smiled at him the way people did in instances like this, like he'd drifted into a fairy tale.

"Yes. Ghost gifts are objects my mother's collected since she was a girl—or more to the point, the objects . . . *gifts* find her. Trinkets, baubles . . . stuff. They connect to the spirit population she encounters. They're delivered to her by specters. Whatever the gift, it somehow ties to the ghosts and the living person she's likely to encounter."

"That's pretty fascinating."

"You mean unbelievable."

"No, fascinating. The story's not completely new to me."

"Your *mum*."

"Yes. Mum."

"My mother's ghost gifts, she's never been able to place some of them—their meaning or what they connect to. Among the rogue ghost gifts is an old postcard, a beach scene. It's dated from the early part of the last century."

"That's the beach where you woke up this morning?"

"Yes." He sighed, the exhaustion of attempting to get his point across.

"Huh. An oddity within an oddity." Ailish put her hand on the truck, and Pete waited for her NYU clinical diagnosis. "Did it ever occur to you that the card wasn't meant for your mother, but for you?"

"Actually, my mother and I talked about that right before I made this trip. With very old postcards, you didn't write on the back like you would nowadays. There's a tiny space on the bottom, on the front, for a message. My mother insisted that aside from the New York postmark, the card has always been blank. Two days ago, there was a short note on it—nothing mind-boggling, more the fact that it'd suddenly appeared there."

"That would be fairly amazing. Your mother's gift and yours, is it the same?"

"To a point. Generally, I don't encounter ghost gifts like she does. Of course, my grandfather was subjected to even stranger messages than . . ." Pete backtracked. Hearing his family history was a lot, even if you had insider information. "Our gifts. Mine, my mother's, her father, even my great-grandmother, they all translate differently. In fact, mine has facets we've yet to figure out. Peculiarities . . . tics."

"More peculiar than speaking to the dead in general?"

He didn't answer right away. Esme and his past life were too personal. The risk of disbelief was high, and guarding his secrets was paramount. "Let's just say, in my family, we've all had to travel a path to deciphering our gifts. Communicating with the dead is the baseline ability. The count-on-it rule seems to be that no matter the gift, it doesn't come without complications." They traded quizzical looks. "I'm a work in progress."

She brushed one hand over her other, as if mulling over dusty details. "It . . . it's all very curious. I don't know what to say." Ailish turned, walking at a sober pace toward the house. Pete nodded at her exit. At least she hadn't laughed in his face. Keeping to a simple story was the right decision. He wasn't just protecting himself; he was protecting Esme. He couldn't stand the idea of a near stranger speculating, drawing random conclusions. Even well-educated, open-minded people had their limits. Pete closed the barn door and followed.

Near the bungalow, Ailish stopped. She gripped her hand around the rotten wood post that supported a sagging overhang. With her other hand, she pulled her phone from her back pocket. Great. He'd managed to freak her out enough to call for assistance, maybe the police. *Help! I'm stranded with a nut who thinks he talks to the dead and suffers debilitating blackouts . . . "* She stood with her back to him, fiddling with her phone.

She pivoted, holding out the device. "Is this the beach where you woke up this morning? Is this the scene on the postcard, your mother's ghost gift?"

"What?" The photo in his face was identical to the place he'd woken up that morning—a glassy sea and a row of neat huts off to the right, the weathered sign noting the site of the destroyed dock.

He gripped his fingers around one end of the phone, both of them staring at the image. "How . . . where did you get this?"

"Seems it's a little more than déjà vu. You might find it interesting to know, I spent two weeks on this beach last summer."

# CHAPTER
# FIFTEEN

Ailish had gone inside the bungalow and it took Pete a few moments to follow. He shook off her beach photo. There was serious margin for error between the ethereal and coincidence. Surely that's all this was. The Bayport beach, it wasn't that far. It was plausible happenstance. She lived in the city. If you couldn't afford the Hamptons, the South Shore hamlet was a decent compromise.

For now, he let it go. Something more disturbing had been on Pete's mind since waking up that morning and finding the bungalow photos. He needed to follow through on a hunch. With his phone charged, Pete pursued a reluctant Google search. The photos of a beaten Esme had him recalling a class from Brown—Visual Art and Literature, a Litmus Test of Changing Sensibilities in Twentieth-Century American Culture.

Pete held his breath, clicking from one web page to another, eventually confirming a fear that caused his stomach to plummet. In the early part of the twentieth century, there was a strong market for perverted media of this kind. Newspapers had little hesitation publishing photographs of beaten women. In fact, they paid good money for them. And if newspapers didn't want them, underground nickelodeons were an equally strong venue. He found photos similar to the ones of

Esme—other women abused and exploited. He didn't know whether to be relieved or more anxious that none offered a photo credit.

Pete forced forward motion and went inside the bungalow. The room all but slugged him in the face, and the heinous photos ebbed. If the bungalow and its contents spoke to him yesterday, they were screaming at him now. A mixture of scents trounced Pete, sights rushing by like a high-speed carousel, sounds ringing in his ears—church bells.

"Are you all right?" Ailish stood near the saddle.

Her words were foggy, like she was the intangible thing. Balance wavered, Pete's grasp on this world turned slippery, and another grew more prevalent. He stood closest to the carousel pony and shakily shuffled forward. Touching the horse was out of the question, so he gripped a bookcase edge. He squeezed his eyes shut; sweat prickled from every pore. When Pete opened his eyes, the girl was in front of him. He took a step back, bumping into the carousel horse. He nearly panicked, feeling trapped between two places. He chose the girl. Concentrating on a single object was a go-to remedy, a trick his mother had taught him.

After a moment, things started to settle—a ship dodging weather. The surge quieted and the room steadied. Ailish's presence also clarified, and the assault on Pete's senses ceased. "Like I told you, this place creeps me out."

"No. I said this place creeps *me* out. You said it was a thousand times worse than that. Can I ask, is it like a spiritual presence or something more?"

There she was again, prodding at his most private thoughts. He wasn't about to share deeper confessions. What would that even sound like? *"Funny thing, it's not just plain old ghosts, Ailish. Everyday specters, they're a no-brainer. It's more about the woman I murdered in a past life. The fact that I found her photographs in this damn house. Maybe discovering that in addition to killing her, I beat the shit out of her. Then there's my handwriting, basically a signed confession. Aside from that, I'm cool."*

But the way she stared at him, Pete was compelled to offer an explanation for his acute moodiness. He relaxed his mind, and help arrived. The specter from earlier nudged at his subconscious, an otherworldly tap at his brain. He granted a sliver of an opening and the ghost grabbed at it. "Your uncle."

"What about him?"

"He's here."

"My uncle Zeke?" Her fair eyes drew full-moon wide.

"Unless you have another uncle who's passed."

She shook her head. "No. Although . . . actually, it was another—"

"Uncle that killed Zeke." Pete cocked his head, listening harder. The communique was marginally more interesting.

"Did your mother tell you that?"

"No. Zeke just did." Pete massaged two fingers into his brow. "Jesus, I know it was murder, but what did he do, shoot him in the head?" Pete's head throbbed more than usual. A bizarre fusion of smells filled his nose: popcorn and gunpowder. He tasted blood. Then he tasted cigarettes, coffee.

"Actually . . . yes." Now Ailish and the ghost had his attention. "Not really the kind of family history one likes to dwell on. It's ugly. My father's half-brother, Jude, was responsible. I don't know much more about the details. We don't discuss it. My uncle Jude is in prison. My mother does talk about Zeke, how much she misses him."

He guessed Ailish was unaware that her incarcerated uncle was also responsible for kidnapping a twelve-year-old Pete. He stayed away from it and concentrated on the ethereal. "Your grandparents." He stared at the beaten wood floor beneath his Nikes. Then he looked at Ailish. "Zeke wants you to tell your mother they're all together."

"My grandparents." She drew closer to Pete, who nodded in reply. "What else does he say?"

Her acknowledgment was all Pete needed, and communication with Zeke became a fluid thing. "He says to tell Nora none of the awfulness from this life moved with him to that one. Everything is peaceful and she shouldn't wonder or worry. He misses her too."

Ailish's cheekbones rose, a coy smile on her lips. "Oh. Okay."

"What?"

"Sorry. I don't mean to be skeptical, but that's just kind of . . . well, what you might expect a ghost to say. Kind of like saying if Mum sees a butterfly, he's thinking of her."

"Oh, I see. A doubter in our midst." Pete raked a hand over his stubble-covered jaw.

"Look, I don't mean to insult you. I'm sure you believe in what you think you're communicating."

He held up a hand. "I honestly don't think about it at all. It just exists." He smiled tightly. "You know what? I don't usually do dog and pony shows, but in your case, I'm going to make an exception."

"Really, you don't have to—"

Pete concentrated with superior effort, wanting this exchange to be flawless. "Uh . . . Zeke says something about rings. He's glad Nora gave you one, and not to forget what she told you about it."

"A ring."

He pointed to her left hand. "That ring."

On the fingers of her right hand were several rings. On the left there was one ring, a plain gold band around her thumb. "My mother gave it to me a few years ago. It was—"

"Your grandfather's. She wanted you to have something of his. Zeke gave her the rings years ago."

"How did you know . . . ?"

He tipped his head at her. "The inside of the band, it's engraved with a triple knot. The Holy Trinity."

"My mother's father, she told me he used to say . . ."

Pete and Ailish spoke simultaneously. "'May the hand of family always be near you.'"

Then he shrugged. "Guess Zeke is keeping up tradition."

"I'm sorry. It's just hard to get your head around unless you—"

"Experience it?" He snickered. "So before now, your brain said that what you heard about my mother, about me, was a wild story, something that grew like a fable."

"Not necessarily. But it is different to . . . well, like you said, 'experience it.'"

"So there you go. A post-this-world souvenir and message. Dog and pony show complete. Anyway . . ." Pete listened for another moment. "I think the rest of his message is for my mother."

"Really? Can I ask what it is?"

"Zeke says he'd visit more, but she knows how grifters and their souls are—wandering. He said that and . . ." Pete felt heat, redness rise in his face.

"What?"

"That, uh . . . that he still loves her. He also talks about the nature preserve behind our house. Weird. I don't know what that means."

"Sorry if this is a dumb question, but what's it sound like in your head? Do you really hear his voice, my uncle speaking to you?"

"In part. Like the Irish saying about family that he communicated. Zeke was very clear about that, verbal, if you like. The best way I can describe those messages is a movie clip. It just starts running in my head. Imagine yourself in a dark theater. All of a sudden, this piece of movie lights up from the middle. It's filled with someone else's life, the script that goes with it. It takes practice to capture the meaning, what it is they want. Sort of like learning another language. Other times, it's more the single frames of a film, like the ring he showed me, the symbol. It varies." Pete rolled his eyes. "Give me a minute, would you? I'm getting to it."

"Getting to what?"

"Zeke's shoving your family photo album at me. He says, 'Here's a visual for you.'"

"Does . . . could I ask, is it just my family photo album? Does he mention anything else?" She shrugged, but there was nothing casual about it. "Anything at all to do with me?"

"Nothing specific. He's very keyed in on your mother. Why, what is it you're anticipating?"

Her strawberry mouth gaped. Then she shut it, biting down on her lip. "Nothing." Ailish looked as if she was at a loss for words, which Pete assumed was an anomaly. "Makes sense, about my mother. I know he worried a lot about her."

"Sounds like he was a good brother."

Her confounded expression hung in there.

"Are you sure there wasn't something else? The spirit world doesn't entertain Q and As. But if there's something you wanted to know, stating it aloud will sometimes motivate—"

"No." She shook her head. "It wasn't anything. Not anything he could help me with."

"Okay. Sorry his communication wasn't more personal."

"It's fine." She smiled. "That was fascinating. Mum will be thrilled, and I have such vague memories of Zeke. I was only seven when he died. It would have been stranger if he had said something more personal."

Pete nodded, grateful that Ailish and her dead uncle had managed to quell the bungalow and its contents. "Let's get the photo album and we can get out of . . ." His words trailed off as Zeke Dublin's voice rose once more. But this message wasn't for Ailish, her mother, or his. It was directed at Pete.

*"Listen, kid."* Pete glanced about as if a fly were buzzing through. No one had referred to him as "kid" in ages. *"You're as smart and stubborn as your old man, gifted as your mother . . . even your grandfather. Don't let your mind fuck you up. It's no carnie sleight of hand. You have to pay attention. If you want your life back. If you want a murder solved."*

"Pete?" Ailish said, moving toward the bedroom.

"What the . . ."

"*Stop running. Start putting the pieces together. My niece can help, if you let her.*"

"She'll help?"

"I'll what?" Ailish said, having turned for the hallway.

But Pete wasn't tuned in to Ailish, and her uncle went on: "*One more thing. So we're clear, if you hurt her, I will haunt the living shit out of you.*"

Then the grifter was gone.

"Did Zeke say something else?"

Pete frowned, unsure how he could hurt Ailish Montague. His immediate thought was emotional pain, then he recalled the photos of a beaten Esme. Pete swallowed and took a step back. "Just know Zeke's watching over you. Like you said, common ghost notes."

She glanced around the room like people did, anticipating a figure under a sheet. "Oh. Still good to know."

"Depends on your perspective." He pointed toward the bedroom.

As they made their way past the boxes and racks of costumes, Pete considered Zeke's message. *What the hell does Zeke Dublin know about any other life of mine?* He looked at Ailish, in front of him. *And after I turn over this photo album, get her to a gas station, she and I, we're done.*

When it came to Zeke's niece, Pete was sure of three things: One, he harbored no desire to prolong their association. Second, that made the chances of harming her in any way nearly impossible. Third, Ailish Montague knew too much without really knowing a damn thing about him. He didn't need her BS in psychology to sort out his life.

Pete took a quick peek at his phone. Excellent. A message from Flagler. No doubt an assignment on the other side of the world awaited him. Only a little further back in his brain did Zeke Dublin's warning echo: "*Stop running. Start putting the pieces together.*" It sounded more like something his father would say. Maybe the exact advice his mother had shoved in his face before this wild ride. Pete pushed a heavier box out to the side and tried to clear his head. The girl stood near the rolltop desk and was saying something.

"You didn't mention this many photo albums. Is it—"

He lunged, grabbing the vintage, leather-bound photo album. "Don't touch that one!"

Any peace treaty they'd reached evaporated. She lurched back, knocking the photo album from the desk, Pete catching it like a glass vial. One that might contain an arsenic-laced potion.

She collided with the wall. "Jesus—what the hell is wrong with you!"

And they were back to that. "Nothing." He shook, internally and externally. Or at least Pete thought he did, from her wild-eyed look.

Moments like this, they were why Pete ran. Why he wasn't spurred on to an exploration for firm answers. He really didn't want to know the reason he'd woken up on a beach that clearly connected to his past life. And he certainly didn't desire further clarification about photos of a beaten Esme—how or why she'd ended up in such a state. Past life regression, even pedestrian tinkering with his other life, would be nothing but a great way to detonate a bomb.

It also seemed like a solid reason for Ailish Montague to steer clear of him. He sure as hell didn't want another puzzle piece, or to factor in a redheaded actress he didn't know before yesterday. Then her earlier words about the postcard rang louder than church bells: *I spent two weeks on this beach last summer.*

Pete realized why her comment resonated. They were nearly the same words that had mysteriously appeared on the postcard, his mother's ghost gift. He ignored it. "I'm sorry," he said, gathering his composure. "I didn't mean to snap." With the leather-bound album gripped tight in one hand, Pete pointed to the floral-patterned album on the desk. "That one. That's the photo album you were looking for."

Ailish never took her eyes off him. A wise girl wouldn't. But instead of grabbing up the photo album and fleeing, she touched his arm. Her fingers felt like silk over spikes, the hairs on his arm standing just that way. Pete's eyes drew wide, the way other people's did when he spoke of their dead loved ones. Her touch was intrinsic, surreal.

She'd touched him before.

"Whatever it is . . ."

Pete stepped away. For more reasons than he could process, he didn't want her to come closer. He didn't want to know anything else about her.

"Whatever it is," she repeated, "you should let someone help."

"You have no idea what you're talking about."

"You're right. I don't claim to understand the first thing about what's in your head, but nobody should live like this."

"Live like what?"

"So completely terrified of the unknown."

♦ ♦ ♦

"Pete?" Grace's voice called out as Ailish's phone rang.

"It's Caroline." She answered the call.

With the leather photo album in hand, Pete left the bedroom. Grace stood in the middle of the living room, arms folded, two fingers tapping rhythmically against her upper arm. It was old sign language for *"I'm really pissed off."*

"I left you a message." He peered around her, looking out the front window. "How did you get here?"

"Uber is handy. Why did you come out here last night?"

"Couldn't sleep. I was afraid if I stayed there . . ." Pete squeezed his hand into a shaky fist and stared at Grace's pretty, unmarred features. Postwar PTSD had always concerned him, and now he had hard-core evidence of how deep his defects went. "I went for a drive, ended up here." He didn't mention the truck or where he'd woken up that morning. "I told you about Ailish getting stuck here." As he spoke, Ailish came out of the bedroom, talking on her phone. Her hand tugged heavily on the plait of red hair and her smile looked forced.

"Okay. Yes. I know you warned me not to borrow Lucy's car, but I was in a hurry. No. Don't do that." She looked between Pete and Grace. "Please don't send a car, Caroline. That's ridiculous. I'll deal. If I can't get it fixed, I'll take the train back into the city." She hesitated for a moment. "Uh, well, goodbye then."

Pete thought the red of her hair seeped into her complexion.

"Passive-aggressive at its finest." Ailish smiled small. "I'll, um . . . I'll take a ride to a gas station, if you don't mind."

Before Pete could reply, Grace did. "Of course, we'd be glad to get you wherever you need to go."

They stood in a triangle, Pete sensing a different uneasiness. Something about territory.

"I see you found your photo album," Grace said to Ailish.

"Pete found it, actually . . . last night."

"So you were both here all night." Grace never stopped smiling, leaning left just enough to glance in the direction of the bedrooms. "How cozy. Or was it spooky out here in the dark, by yourselves?"

Ailish pointed at the front window. "Actually, I slept in my car. Pete didn't even know I was here until he . . ." He shot her a look that somehow was enough. She reversed her finger from pointing to the door to thumbing over her shoulder. "He slept in the bedroom. Or that's where he wandered out from when I came back inside earlier. Right?"

"I dozed off. Didn't even realize Ailish was here until morning."

"And you were okay with that?" Grace asked. "Sleeping here? That's seriously hard to believe, Pete." She looked between him, the room full of stuff, and Ailish. "Considering."

Pete sucked in a breath, guiltily aware that Ailish knew something Grace did not. He discounted the feeling, reminded now of the hovering Grace he'd left years ago. "I . . . it was fine."

"So," Ailish said, cutting in. "Are the two of you heading back home? Massachusetts, right?"

"Well, I'm not sure if . . ." Pete took a turn around the room, which suddenly lacked any sense of a past life. In fact, since Grace arrived, the crazed vibe of the room had fallen flat as a sidewalk.

"We do have a ferry reservation." Grace stood taller, brushing her hand over a crisp-looking outfit. "I've already checked out of the motel. Pete just needs to let that pushy New York lawyer know what he wants to do with this stuff. Are you both ready to go?" Grace talked as she moved toward the exit. "I've looked up the nearest gas station that does mechanic work. Five-star rating. I'm sure they'll be able to help you out."

"Oh, okay," she said. "That was nice of you . . . I guess."

Pete also moved to the exit, but his gaze stayed with the room, bumping over abandoned belongings—the saddle and carousel horse—bumping over Ailish Montague. He was strangely annoyed by the desertion of past life connections. In spite of his resistance, Pete was searching for them. At the door, gut instinct won out over deep-seated fears, and he announced, "We can go. But I'm telling the lawyer to back off. We're keeping the house." He looked at Ailish, who, like it or not, he associated with puzzle pieces and an uncle's cryptic warning. "For now, anyway."

# CHAPTER
# SIXTEEN

Compared to the past day and a half, the trip back to Surrey was uneventful. Pete kept conversation with Grace to small talk, first on the ferry, then in the car. He was subdued for many reasons, not the least of which was a new and heightened sense of anxiety that included Grace's safety. He counted on the public setting of the ferry, glad for the traffic on 95, which kept him focused on the highway. While Grace darted from subject to subject, Pete continued to roll events around his head. The bungalow and its contents, the old photos—the troubling ones and the tranquil image of Esme. Then there was the truck and the Bayport postcard, which it seemed—like it or not—connected to Ailish Montague.

*Ailish Montague* . . .

Pete turned onto Homestead Road and gripped tight to the Audi's steering wheel until the blisters forced him to ease up. Curbside, about a block back, was a good spot to mentally leave the NYU-educated, redheaded actress. Of course, he'd thought the same thing when boarding the ferry at Orient Point. Ailish had nothing to do with his past life. The Montague girl had claimed her prized family photo album. A quest and an object that had put her in Pete's path. She'd gone back to the city by car or train. She was irrelevant. He'd never see her again. He'd make sure of it.

He and Grace neared the house and Pete glanced over his shoulder. Like Ailish, he hadn't left the bungalow empty-handed. In the back seat, amid Grace's belongings, was the leather-bound photo album. He hadn't mentioned the album to Grace beyond, "I think my mother would like to flip through it."

Turning into the driveway, Pete prepared for an awkward exit. Grace, being Grace, saved him from it. "So give me a call if you want to talk any more about the bungalow . . . or this house." She pointed to the one that Pete still associated with home. "I wouldn't mind looking into its past."

"Grace, let it go." He glanced in the back seat. "I have enough house history to deal with. Besides . . ." He looked at the porch, where his parents sat. "All the weirdness here, I know where, or more to the point who," he said, returning his mother's wave, "it connects to."

She exited the vehicle and gathered her things, opening the door to her car, which was parked on an extended patch of driveway. Grace had insisted on dropping her car off before they left. Something about running errands that were closer to the St John house than hers. He watched her sharp movements, an efficient transfer of belongings that said she'd been gone a week, instead of overnight. "It was interesting, Pete." She slammed the car door, and any ruse of keeping things casual crumpled. "But I've got to get back to my reality. Tell your parents hi and bye for me."

He pointed to the porch. "Are you sure you don't want to say . . . ?"

But she was already in her car, adjusting her side-view mirror and sunglasses.

"Thanks for going with me, Grace. Look, I'm sorry if I did anything to . . ." He shoved his hands in his pockets. "We'll talk again before I leave for . . . wherever."

"Sure." She proceeded to back down the driveway.

Pete watched until Grace was out of sight. He leaned on the Audi and tapped his knuckles against it—code for flagrant self-doubt. Proof that his ability to handle relationships, in this life or the last, sucked beyond belief.

Pete gathered his duffel bag and the photo album and headed for the front porch and his parents. "Grace said to say hello . . . and goodbye."

Levi hummed under his breath. "I take it that part of the trip didn't go well."

"You could say that." Pete looked over his shoulder. "Honestly, it's just as well." He smiled stiffly. "Women. Not what I do best, for a million reasons."

"Like father, like . . ." Aubrey traded a smile with Levi. "You have to admit, the Levi St John learning curve was seriously steep."

"Maybe it just took the right woman." Levi cleared his throat and put aside his book. "So what did you learn about this Long Island house, which I believe was the point of the trip?"

"Maybe not the entire point," Aubrey said. "Was there more, Pete? Was there anything associated with an abandoned bungalow, other than carnie keepsakes?"

He hesitated. "More than I cared to know."

♦ ♦ ♦

Pete spent the next hour detailing his discoveries, the curious ones, like the vast array of paraphernalia left behind and how a crazy-eyed carousel horse and vintage saddle struck him as more than memorabilia. He talked about the old truck he and Grace discovered, his mother fascinated by its connection to Oscar Bodette. "Oscar?" she said. "As in Charley's second and fourth husband? That Oscar?" Pete assured her it was one and the same.

Levi adjusted his glasses and listened harder as Pete reached the more baffling part of his trip. He told them how he'd gotten into the truck but had no cognitive knowledge of how he'd ended up at a beach, miles away. Their expressions shifted from concerned to astonished when he explained that the beach was the same one pictured in Aubrey's postcard. The one that, according to her, bore no message before two days ago. He did not speak of the redheaded Ailish Montague.

Then, in his ambivalence, Pete made an attempt to brush it all off. "But you know, now that I've had a chance to think about it, put some distance between me and Long Island . . ." He drew a steady breath. "Compared to most life experiences, this was fairly tame. I don't know that it delivered the 'aha' moment you were hoping for, Mom."

She was silent, thrumming her fingers on the glossy magazine cover. "So you think it's coincidence." She shrugged her slim shoulders. "A fluke that somehow there's a connection between your past and Oscar Bodette."

"That's more or less what I'm saying." If Pete kept up the pretense and his mother agreed, they could move on.

He should have known better.

Aubrey fluttered her eyelids. "I don't know what's more appalling. Your desire that we go along with your faux naïveté, or the fact we should have realized a connection long before this."

"I'm willing to go with naïveté if you are," Pete said.

It was his father who moved on, pointing to the photo album he clutched. "What's that?"

He'd been standing, talking for so long, the object felt as if it'd blended into the rest of him—like maybe Pete camouflaged it. "This thing?" he said, holding it up.

"Yeah. That thing." Levi pointed again. "And why don't you sit?"

Levi had always possessed the ability to read Pete better than anyone. He moved slowly to the porch swing. "Well . . . this part. The photo album, it's curious. Maybe stranger than anything else that happened. You look."

Reluctantly, he passed the photo album to his mother, his father leaning over. She flipped through the first few pages, absorbing a younger Oscar Bodette. She pointed to one photo, reading the descriptive note. "'Oscar, Luna Park, 1922.'" She smiled at Pete. "That's a fine raccoon coat he's wearing. I wonder whatever happened to it?" She turned to the next page and more photos of Oscar, other people she couldn't identify. "Kind of crazy. Oscar wouldn't even meet Charley for another thirty years."

"Interesting," Levi said. "It's as if he lived an entire life before your grandmother."

"Before marrying Charley bound him to the Ellis clan." Pete murmured this, still connecting the dots.

"I wouldn't have recognized Oscar if these photos weren't marked. In every picture Charley had, he was an old man." Aubrey turned one more page and picked up the loose larger photo of the beautiful woman, posed on a chaise, holding roses, and wearing a tightly fitted gown with a train. "Oh my . . ."

"She's very pretty," Levi offered.

Aubrey's attention moved sharply to Pete. "She's also very warm . . . hot, even."

Pete unfurled his hand, palm open. While his right hand bore the effect of punching a mirror, it was his left that drew a gasp from Aubrey—the kind mothers made. "I'd call it blistering hot. My memento from having touched the photo at the bungalow." He cocked his chin at the picture, which he had serious reservations about touching again. "Turn it over."

Aubrey did this, but it was Levi who reacted, sucking in air as if he'd burned his own hand. No psychic perception was required. From the time Pete had learned to write in cursive, since the age of eight or nine, they'd all noted how the son's penmanship mirrored his father's—artistic and unique for a lefty. The three of them would know it anywhere, including writing on a photograph from 1917. "'Esmerelda Moon,'" Levi read, "'One year, five months before her death. August 1917.' That's quite a notation."

And Pete wasn't sure if he was commenting on a chilling caption, or a chilling caption that it appeared his son had written. He doubted Levi knew either.

"Pete. I thought maybe you'd find a connection," Aubrey said. "I never imagined you'd find a photograph—or a whole name."

"So then you know who she is? Do you recognize her?"

"No. Not physically. Just a guess," she said. "Esmerelda . . . Esme. They're one and the same."

"That's right. They are."

"What am I missing?" his father asked.

"Esme, Pa." Pete blinked back a drop of frustration that seeped through the cracks—in his mind, in the universe. "That's a photograph of Esme, and I took it."

He felt as if someone should jump in with *The year before you killed her . . .* But it wasn't the kind of thing parents would say, even if they'd been presented with smoking gun evidence. "It gets better. Turn the page."

His mother obliged.

"Oh my God." Aubrey picked up the smaller but telling strip of photos, her fingertips hovering over the battered images—all posed slightly different, a clear record. "Pete, you don't think . . ."

"That I did that to her and then I documented it by taking photos of my handiwork?" His shoulders curled forward, his chest sinking. "Well, Mom, I suppose that depends on just how much of a twisted bastard I was. Look at the back." She did, revealing more of the same handwriting—Esme's name, the words "Just to show," and a date: January 1919.

"Pete. Come on," Levi said. "You don't seriously believe that you did this, or took these photos?"

"Wet plate photography."

"What?" he said.

"Wet plate photography. It's how you produced a strip of photos like that in 1919. I can tell you anything you want to know about modern photography, image processing, and digital asset management. The software I work with that allows me to connect what my eye sees and what the camera records. But how I know the process for wet plate photography, the tedious procedure for producing photos like that . . ." There was a disbelieving shake of his head. "It's as present and mysterious as my knowledge of World War I."

"The photography," Levi said. "You could have read it online or in a book, and you're just not recalling—"

"Wet plate is a painstaking, complex chemical process that's obsolete to modern photography. Yet I could take you into a darkroom—assuming we could find one—and repeat the process on demand." Pete paused, letting the photos and information sink in. "And there's something else to consider. During this time period, there was a market for sick photos like this, beaten women, bloodied dead bodies."

Levi was quiet for a moment. "Unfortunately, I'm aware of that dark fact."

"So add that bit of history to my motives."

"Pete, stop," Aubrey said. "Let's not make assumptions—"

"Assumptions?" he said. "Looks to me like we have more facts than ever. The only conclusion I can draw: maybe Esme has moved on to gaslighting me. Haven't you said it yourself, Mom?" Pete's gaze dropped to her pockmarked arm, and she clamped her other hand around it. "Not all spirits come for the benefit of closure. You're proof of that."

Aubrey reached to the scar on her chin. Along with the ones on her arm, it was a permanent souvenir of her encounter with evil.

"The specter responsible for those." Pete pointed to marks she could not deny. "According to you, it was a complete stranger. Imagine the justification if you'd killed someone, the vengeance their spirit might bring."

Levi inhaled hard, running a hand through his hair—a thinking gesture. The processing of tough information. Pete was curious. Could they manage the positive spin only parents could put on things? Levi removed his glasses, rubbing two fingers across his eyes until they pinched the bridge of his nose. When his father didn't speak, Pete's pulse pounded harder. "Say it," Pete demanded. "It's even too fucked up for you, isn't it? There's nothing good here. Maybe reliving my past like I do is the lesser evil."

Levi blinked at his son. "I wasn't going to say anything like that, Pete. I'm just trying to absorb—"

"The impossible. Which is suddenly looking damned probable." Pete surprised himself, leaning back, feeling smug, as if he'd discovered all the answers—even if it was just the vile truth. Then he glanced at the photo album and a battered Esme. Smugness evaporated, and he was solemn, thinking about the pain she must have endured.

"Pete," Levi said. "You're taking fragments of a story and assuming the whole. You don't know what led to—"

"Murder?" He snickered. "Geez, Pa, if this were your story, these were your leads—would you expect to find facts that supported exoneration or guilt?"

Levi took a different tactic, one that seemed to imply that he was considering the idea. "Look, son, whatever occurred back then . . . you're not that person anymore."

"Maybe not yet. But every time I come back from that life, I can't help but think I drag another piece of *him* into this one. Who's to say we don't merge? We know I've been strangely attracted to war and conflict my whole life. That's something we can prove—a World War I medal with my initials, scars I can't identify. A basement full of models that are one battle scene after another." Pete flailed his hand at the house. "What if *all* the events of that life continue to surface in this one?"

Levi turned the photo over again to stare at handwriting he couldn't argue against.

"If PTSD was my trigger in that life, how long until I come off the hinges in this one? What *lucky* woman gets to play Esme's part?"

"Pete, could you give us a minute?" Levi held up a hand as if this might hold off his son's darkest conclusions. "I'm trying to think it through. There must be a logical way to—"

"What? Find a new way around what I've known since I was how old, ten or twelve?"

"Twelve," Aubrey said absently.

"Whatever age. It doesn't matter."

"I think it does. If you recall, Pete, there was a catalyst for the Esme part of your past. Your innate knowledge of war is something you seemed to know since the time you could talk. But you didn't speak Esme's name, you never experienced the visual of . . ." His mother's voice dropped to a whisper. "*Taking her life . . .* until after you were kidnapped, drugged."

"Your mother's right. We've always viewed that as the trigger." Levi pointed to the photo album. "What you perceive as the memories linked to this."

Pete hadn't thought about that, or how events and people connected to this life might have affected his reliving of that one. He leaned back on the swing as if widening his personal space, maybe his mind. "The kidnapping. Bottom line. It all goes back to Zeke Dublin, doesn't it?"

"Zeke didn't kidnap you, but yes . . ." His mother glanced at Levi, who wore a "he's just as guilty" expression. "The motive for your kidnapping was connected to the man Zeke worked for. It was all part of a blackmail scheme, tied to your grandfather's box of ghost gifts."

"And both those men, they're related to Nora Montague's daughter?"

His mother's weary frame tightened. "Yes. She's their niece. Pete, where are you going with this?"

"There's a piece to the story I haven't told you. Because I didn't think it mattered." His body tightened too. "That's a lie. I didn't tell you because I can't figure out why it . . . *she* matters."

"'She' being?"

"Zeke's niece. She showed up at the bungalow, looking for a different photo album."

"Oh, you hadn't mentioned her, and I assumed she never showed up. Nora wasn't sure how quickly her daughter would make the trip. She certainly acted fast."

"Yeah, well, it'd be the least annoying thing she did."

"What does that mean?" Levi said, still examining the photo.

"Nothing. She was just assertive . . . abrupt. Ravenous," he said, tapping his knuckles to a knee that now bounced. "Aggravating, if you want another word. That and she . . ." He stopped, mulling facts once more before saying it aloud. "The most disturbing thing about Zeke's niece was a photo she had on her phone. It was of the Great South Bay—the one in Bayport, from your postcard."

"You're kidding," Aubrey said.

"Not so much. Even better, she showed me the photo *after* I told her where I woke up this morning. Then she said, and I quote, 'I spent two weeks on this beach last summer.'"

Levi looked between mother and son. "And other than an offbeat, coincidental vacation spot, that's fascinating because . . . ?"

"Because it's more or less what's written on the bottom of the postcard. I told you this yesterday," Aubrey said.

"Right. Slipped my mind." Levi put down the photo and gave his complete attention to the conversation. "This girl, she repeated the words on the postcard with no prompting from you?"

"None. I suppose if you want to apply a rational explanation, we could assume it's a fluke on top of coincidence. That's where you'd go with it, right, Pa?" His father's jaw slacked, but he didn't jump to agree. And right now, Pete needed more than a drop of his father's logical nature. It was something Pete had counted on from Levi his entire life—especially when he began to recall another. "I mean, this ballsy, basically pain-in-the-ass girl shows up. It's clear she has some freakish six-degrees-of-separation connection to me. I'll admit that much. But then the photo she has on her phone . . . the words she said. I mean, it's not like I'd ever seen Zeke's niece before yesterday—anywhere."

Aubrey ran her finger over the earrings lining her lobe. "That's not quite true."

"How's it not true?" Pete's everyday frustration edged toward fitful.

"Shortly after the kidnapping, not long after you came home from the hospital, Nora and her daughter were here."

Pete pointed at the craftsman's front door. "Here. That girl was here, in our house?"

"Well, yes. But that's exactly what she would have been, a little girl. It's probably why you don't remember."

"Or," his father said, "maybe she didn't stick in Pete's memory because of the ordeal he'd been through, the drugs pumped into him. All of which also connects to Zeke Dublin."

"I don't remember any of it, not the Montagues being here."

"It was a brief visit," Aubrey said. "Aside from Nora being upset about Zeke's death, nothing of great interest transpired." She paused. "I do remember her daughter sitting in the living room, holding a baby doll." Aubrey leaned back in the chair. "Although, if I recall, she couldn't get your name right."

Pete stared at his blistered hand, unable to make a clear connection between events from when he was twelve, this morning, and a hundred years ago.

"Pete?" they said simultaneously.

He looked up. While the information his mother offered was disturbing, it was the concerned look on his parents' faces that hit him harder. He was approaching thirty years old, and he was still dumping the debris from his life in their path. After the trip to Long Island, it'd only grown messier. They didn't deserve it. "Nothing," he said quickly. "Just something Esme said."

"Your mother said you heard her speak. If she did, seems like that's a milestone worth discussing. Maybe if we put our heads together, deconstruct your trip to Long Island . . ."

Pete stood. Then he lied. "No. I'm fine. You guys have done enough. More than any parents should need to." He stared at the photo album, seriously considering burning the damn thing. He knew better. You couldn't set fire to ghosts. He needed to handle this himself. "Right now, I just want to get a shower," he said dismissively. "Check my messages. Flagler called." He moved toward the front door. "Really, I've got this. You don't need to worry."

"Pete." The tone in his mother's voice, it resulted in the same halt of forward motion as it had when he was a kid. "You're not burdening us with this, if that's what you're thinking. We want to help."

He looked at them. Tired. When did they ever look so tired? "I know. I appreciate it—more than you can imagine." He turned for the door but twisted back. "Oh, about Zeke's niece. The only relevant thing you need to know is that when I saw her at the bungalow, Zeke showed up too."

"Did he?"

"Did he?" Levi repeated in a decidedly different pitch. "I don't suppose he offered you the apology he owes for the hell two uncles put you through."

"No. In fact, he was fairly in my face, ballsy as the niece."

"Sounds like Zeke," Aubrey said, avoiding Levi's glance. "What did he say?"

"Mostly his message was for Nora Montague. The usual comfort memo," Pete said. "But he did ask that I tell you something."

"What was that?" she said, smiling.

"He said he'd visit more often, but you know how grifters' souls are, more wandering than lingering."

"Anything else?"

With his parents seated side by side, Pete rethought the rest of Zeke's message—how he still loved his mother. He considered relationships in the here and now. He reached for yet one more white lie. "No. Nothing else." Pete left them there. He went inside to do what he said, take a shower and listen to his messages—those from the living and the dead.

## ACT IV, SCENE I
## NEW YORK
## 1917

The sun sat lopsided over the earth. This was Esmerelda's impression as she peered upward, through the hotel room window. To see any sky at all, one had to bend over and look up, the building across the alleyway so tight to hers. Since midsummer, this had been her view.

On the verge of fall, Luna Park had cut back on its acts. The Coney Island landmark would officially close for the season in days. Only Barney and Bill's soft shoe and Jimmie's dramatic reading remained on the bill. This meant Oscar's Traveling Extravaganza could only be in one place and Cora had to find other means of employment. She'd taken a job cleaning the bathhouses, remarking to Esmerelda, "It's no matter. Oscar will be movin' us all on to other shows. He'll have to. Only that Elephant Hotel stays open year-round." Esmerelda's situation gave Cora a place to sleep, but it was wages Oscar needed to see—whether you earned your nickels juggling cups and saucers and a cat or by scrubbing sand and piss.

Cora said she didn't mind about the bathhouses. But Esmerelda could see she'd been crying after returning late at night. She also had to insist that Cora bathe before getting into bed. She reeked of urine, sweat, and lye soap.

"Bathe more than once a week? Who ever heard of such a thing?" she said. Esmerelda had draped Cora's undergarments over a chair, shoving them under her clearer nose the next morning. After this, Cora would wash herself and Esmerelda would scrub her clothes in the sink, hanging them on the indoor clothesline.

Dwindling Luna Park crowds also meant Henry Erlanger no longer needed a solo songstress. Esmerelda was fortunate to remain in Benjamin Hupp's employ. So she told herself it was good news when he decided to experiment with the shift in patronage that came with cooler weather. Benjamin added a pricey luncheon menu to the supper club, envisioning businessmen and Upper East Side ladies' groups taking advantage. Esmerelda provided background music—a softer version of her evening fare. Not long into the new schedule, the idea seemed to be taking hold.

It left Esmerelda exhausted, performing from noon until three, then again in the evenings. But the change she found most disturbing was the amount of time she spent inside the hotel. She looked up at the crack of sky and then across the alleyway.

The Hupps had opened their fancier hotel next door. Benjamin had prattled on about the finished project, also boasting to Esmerelda that he'd taken up residence there—a suite, located directly across from her room. This was during a hotel tour he'd insisted on, showing off the lobby floor, where a sweetshop, haberdashery, and photography studio had rented space. Gazing in the window of the photo studio, she'd smiled at Benjamin, thinking how much she'd like to tell Phin about it.

This morning, Licorice sat on the windowsill. She scratched his head and he jumped down, darting under the bed—his favorite spot. Despite the fanfare of a new hotel, the alley had become dull, dominant scenery. She yawned. Usually, Esmerelda didn't get to bed until after one in the morning, making it difficult to rise and shine, to do something other than sit and wait for the next performance. Almost always, Benjamin was a front-row patron, smiling and applauding.

Today, however, offered a respite from the monotony. A new stove was being installed in the hotel kitchen. Hupp's restaurant would be closed and, in turn, entertainment unnecessary. Circumstance provided a full day and a half of freedom. Turning away from the window, Esmerelda scooped Marigold up from her rocking-chair perch, straightening the doll's bowed bonnet. "I suppose it's too much to imagine Phin turning up in the alley." She hugged the doll. "If he did, the scenery would change considerably." Esmerelda returned to the window. She smiled at Marigold as if she might agree. "Maybe he's not well enough yet. Maybe I should never mind what he last said and go see him."

It'd been an equal amount of time since Phin's near-miraculous recovery from influenza and her busier schedule. Esmerelda wasn't foolish enough to go to Hell's Kitchen without Hassan. As Phin improved, he'd insisted she not come at all, even with Hassan as a chaperone. "Thieving won't get you more than a fistful of lint down here," he'd said, propped on a pillow she'd smuggled from the hotel. Phin coughed and he drew air into his still-weak lungs before finishing his opinion. "Raping. That's easier to come by. Some men won't think twice about it."

She offered no outward reaction to the observation, refilling his mug of weak tea.

Phin had gone on, chiding Hassan. "You're not to bring her again. Your kind might swing tomahawks, but you're no fighter, Hassan. It's not what the army wants from you." Hassan had said something in his native Choctaw, a word which by then she knew was agreement. Instead, Phin had made Esmerelda a promise: the moment he was well enough, he would come to her. He'd squeezed her hand before she left, and Esmerelda took it as a blood-sworn oath. She'd returned to the hotel, having to answer to Oscar for her absence. In the meantime, he'd been quick enough to lie to Benjamin—insisting that Esmerelda had been battling a fever of her own.

Since leaving Phin's side, Esmerelda had seen Hassan twice at her Luna Park show. She imagined the braided-haired Indian felt comfortable in a park filled with human acts that would draw glances on ordinary streets. "Might as well get paid for life's little curse," Diego would say, laughing. He was a Negro midget from the French Quarter who amazed audiences by adding any set of numbers in his head. The first time Esmerelda saw Hassan, he assured her that Phin was gaining strength. The second time, he told her Phin had returned to work.

Hassan also confided, in broken English, a story that had Esmerelda spellbound: At the age of six, Phin was left at New York's Children's Aid Society. At nine he ran away from the home. This came after a group of older boys stole Phin from his straw mattress and locked him in an outhouse, but not before dumping in a sack of rats. Since then, he'd lived off the streets, determined to overcome abandonment and a rat-infested past.

This told Esmerelda a great deal about Phin's pride. The reason working delivery for the *Tribune* would never satisfy him. In her mind, it also separated Phin from any man she'd known—he viewed the value of money and emotion as two different things: the necessity for one and the aesthetic worth of the other. Hassan had broken a confidence by telling Esmerelda about Phin's past, but his intentions were honest. He wanted to give Esmerelda cause to be patient.

Sitting at the hotel window, she sighed at the circumstances surrounding her. What did any of it matter, and why did she keep dwelling on it? What would any man want with her? Technically—since the night of the pie—she was as used as the girls who worked at the Elephant Hotel. Her face warmed; she was lucky to have a life as good as she did.

A knock at the door disrupted further brooding. She didn't respond at first, not terribly anxious to see Benjamin, who was surely on the other side. Cora had gone to run an errand for Oscar, who planned to meet her at the trolley stop near Luna Park. It was one of a few times Esmerelda was alone, and she wondered if Benjamin knew as much.

To her surprise, her employer and admirer hadn't grown exasperated with Esmerelda's polite but never inviting behavior, even after

Oscar's warning. She'd even grown brave enough to ask Benjamin about Ingrid, the German immigrant girl he'd favored and Oscar had mentioned. Benjamin was quick to disclose to Esmerelda that he'd been smitten. "Of course, I realized we were to be no more than friends, especially after learning Ingrid steadily corresponded with a soldier from Cologne." He admitted a slight heartbreak over the girl, but was moved by her story. Enough to see to it that Ingrid returned home to her beau.

Esmerelda had smiled at Benjamin's generosity, though she remained hesitant about accepting his Palace proposal, which he offered just as Oscar said he would. So far Esmerelda hadn't said yes or no, only that she was flattered. If she accepted the job, she'd be out of Benjamin's employ, yet still indebted. It seemed a quandary either way.

As for today's free time, she guessed Benjamin had an idea or two about how she might spend it. She paced slowly to the door, arranging excuses. *"Thank you, Benjamin, I'd love to join you for a picnic in the park, but Oscar needs me to attend rehearsal—a winter act we're preparing . . ."* *"Oh, Benjamin, you're forever thoughtful . . . the flowers . . . champagne, roof over my head . . . but you see . . ."* And that's where Esmerelda got stuck. She suspected words about her affection for Phin would not be well received.

The knocking persisted, and she moved across the room. Esmerelda smoothed her skirt. She swung the door wide and began with a lie. "How lovely to see you this time of day . . ." Her words fell away, landing softly in the truth. She smiled. "You're back on your feet."

"I'd have come sooner, but I wanted to make certain I had the strength to carry this thing across the city."

Phin stood before her, thinner, cheekbones jutting in a way that made him look both hungry and elegant. Someone had cut his wavy, dark hair. In his arms was a burlap-covered object, though she guessed what it was. While propriety dominated Benjamin's visits, she clasped

Phin's arm, quickly guiding him past proper decorum and into the room. It wouldn't do for anyone to catch him in the hall.

She leaned against the closed door, her heart moving as if she'd been the one to rush up three flights of stairs, a bulky sack in hand. "I saw Hassan. He said you were better. He said you went back to work."

"I was lucky to get my spot back. They're hiring ten- and twelve-year-olds at half the pay. Likely the only thing that saved me is knowing how to drive their trucks." His forehead scrunched. "Maybe the fact that I can reach the pedals."

"Or you're such a good photographer the *Tribune* wanted to keep you in their employ. I want to tell you about—"

"Don't boast, Esme. Or make me out to be something I'm not. Mostly I work distribution. It'd take a lot for *Tribune* brass to make riffraff like me a real photographer." He took a slow turn around the room. "I imagined it'd be a nice place." He stopped moving and his gaze landed on her. "Nice as you should have."

His reaction wasn't without reason, and Esmerelda defaulted to caution. The home she'd left wasn't rich, but they had nice things, like the glass globe lamp her father gave her mother one Christmas—a time before he drank so much and her mother wasn't dead. Before the pie and the night her sister had gone to stay with a sick friend. There were dyed rugs, store-bought linens, and china dishes. Her life with Oscar had exposed Esmerelda to the gap, the seediness of city streets, an underbelly that many, including Phin, called shelter. She lied. "I was surprised as you first time I saw the room."

"Were you?" Phin leaned and pointed. "A water closet and all—just for yourself?"

"Cora too." But it wasn't what he meant. Esmerelda grasped the bedpost as if she and it might hide the fat feather mattress. "None of it's mine. The hotel room is part of my agreement with . . ."

He shimmied the burlap-covered object from one arm to the other.

"It's Oscar's agreement with Hupp."

He stared at her and, subsequently, the bed. "But it's not Oscar who sleeps here every night."

"No. I suppose it isn't. But Cora's here every night." She dove at a change of subject. "What did you bring?"

"Seems silly now, here with all this." He looked to the fireplace. Over it hung a painting of English lords in top hats, dogs at their feet, one little fox trying to make its escape.

She gestured to the window. "This place isn't so grand, Phin." Benjamin had said exactly this, referring to more luxurious rooms across the alleyway. "Hotels are Hupp's business. I can't help that."

"I'm not sure objecting to any of it is my business. Better still, why a palooka like me would deny you all . . . *this*. Why I'd rather see you camped on the Flats with Oscar." Phin perused the room, but again and again, his gaze returned to Esmerelda, posed by the bed.

She was an idiot. Why hadn't she sat in the chair, stood near the window? Anywhere but near the bed. She rushed toward him. "Are you going to show me what you've brought?"

Begrudgingly Phin handed over his gift. Esmerelda let the rough sack drop, revealing the sparkling mermaid painting.

"It's even more beautiful than it was on the beach."

"It wasn't finished on the beach."

"Thank you." She placed Phin's painting atop the mantel, occluding the hunting scene. Esmerelda stepped back and admired his work. No, of course, a mermaid didn't belong in a hotel room. It should be free, like the carousel horse. Esmerelda turned to tell him as much, or at least how much she loved the painting.

When she did, words melded into a kiss. The unexpected moment dominated everything, including societal propriety or what Phin thought Esmerelda should have. She'd never kissed a boy of her own choosing, and Esmerelda thought it more luxurious than the hotel room. Inviting in a different way. The closeness spun the ground on which she stood. It was only a single kiss, though Esmerelda saw it as the most heavenly moment of her life. She wanted the kiss to go on or repeat, the sensations as mesmerizing as a dream. Phin didn't kiss her again but lingered, his forehead pressed to hers. Then he looked past Esmerelda, blinking hard at the bed, quickly—though stumbling over his words—insisting they should be on their way. "We . . . we'd best go before I forget the little I know about being a proper gentleman." She followed, nearly floating, the breadth of the kiss surpassing the few amazing things she knew of: paintings and Paris, France, Coney Island, and the rest of the World.

◆ ◆ ◆

Phin suggested a walk through Manhattan. After several blocks, in the open air and crowded streets, the feeling attached to the kiss began to ebb. Sadly, she supposed it had to—it was that or be trampled. Avenues were thick with an eclectic mix of pedestrians: ladies dressed in their finest, arms looped through their husbands', and then a girl who sang for her supper, side by side with a boy who scavenged for survival. She and Phin walked until they reached the far side of the Brooklyn Bridge.

Conversation picked up as they made their way across metal that bound the two boroughs. Modes of transportation competed tightly here: foot, horse, motorcar, trolley. While there was new familiarity between Phin and Esmerelda, talk remained generic: the weather and the Brooklyn Robins, then Phin saying how the army had come through Hell's Kitchen recruiting soldiers. For the promise of a meal, many went.

The trolley clanged as Esmerelda explained how she and Cora would often take the streetcar to meet up with Oscar, the boys, and the wagon on Brooklyn's Stillwell Avenue. She said something about the fall weather coming and that soon Coney Island beaches would be uninviting. Phin insisted the day's bright weather and their mutual free time was an invitation to the shore. Maybe they could even rent bathing costumes. Moments later, the two were aboard the trolley, moving toward its Coney Island stop.

When Phin and Esmerelda exited from the front of the car in Brooklyn, Cora came clamoring off the rear. They hadn't spotted each other aboard the crowded trolley. Oscar was waiting with the horses and wagon. "Lordy," Cora said, catching up to the group. "I had to run six blocks from Oscar's errand to make the trolley!" She pushed in between Phin and Esmerelda, huffing for air.

In the meantime, Oscar had narrowed his eyes at Esmerelda and her companion, the look shifting onto Cora. "Did you get what I sent you for?"

She nodded, holding a yellow envelope up to Oscar.

"Good girl. I'd almost let you skip your job this evening."

"Would you?" she asked as if Oscar was the least bit serious. "Because if you don't—"

"And what would you show me for earnings, Cora? It's why we work, girl." But his look did soften as she handed over the envelope. "The fall circuit will pick up soon. We'll find you something more . . . suited to your talents."

Bill and Jimmie poked their heads through the wagon cover, saying hello to Esmerelda. She missed them, being so bound to Hupp's hotel. Esmerelda pointed to the envelope. "What's that?"

Oscar tore at the flap. "It's the future."

She cocked her head at the paper he withdrew, imagining it foretold such a thing.

"Is it something for a new act?" Bill asked, peering over Oscar's shoulder.

"Cohans added a bit that cuts a lady right in two," Jimmie said. "I seen it. Does that paper tell you how to go about doing such a thing?"

Barney's head popped through the canvas hole, completing the curious sets of eyes, all of them peering over Oscar's wide shoulders. "And what kind of date are you?" Barney asked. "You talk like we'd really be cuttin' Esmerelda or Cora in two!" He knocked his elbow into Jimmie and ducked back into the wagon. Between Barney and Bill, he was the crankier of the two.

"You're all a bunch of blockheads," Oscar groused. "Like a single act would help us out. But this will. It's the ownership papers to a truck." Hums radiated like the warm-up for a three-part harmony as Barney's head popped back through the canvas hood.

"A motor truck?" he asked.

"Now who's dull in the mind?" Jimmie elbowed him back.

"If you'll all quit your blathering . . ."

On Stillwell Avenue, with his troupe surrounding him, Oscar went into great detail about his new truck—how he'd scrimped and saved and struck a deal, trading Go and Fish as the final payment. Esmerelda patted Fish's nose, sorry to hear that the future meant saying goodbye to the beloved team. Oscar captivated the group with his long-kept secret—a near-new Ford double TT truck—then he arrived at his one problem. "I don't know how to drive."

"What?" Esmerelda said. "You bought a truck with your last dime, traded the team, and don't know how to operate what you've bought! Oscar—"

"I don't need backtalk from you, Esmerelda. Seems I'm not the only one choosin' things that I've not thought through." He cocked his chin at Phin. "I figured somehow I'd learn between wanting a truck and owning one. But the fact of it is Go and Fish need to be to the Queens line by two."

"And then what?" she asked.

"And then we make the trade. The papers are from a solicitor who handled the owner's estate. The fellow that owned the truck was killed aboard one of America's new warships. His wife sold it to me." Oscar glanced over his shoulder. "I don't suppose you boys, Barney and Bill, have any more useful secrets?"

Esmerelda cleared her throat and glanced away from Phin.

"None of you knows how to drive, do you?"

It was strange to hear Oscar ask for help. It was stranger still when Phin spoke up. "I know how to drive." Stares shifted from the paper Oscar held to Phin. "I was telling Esme earlier. The *Tribune* will employ boys to do the newspaper selling. But they need a man to drive their delivery trucks."

"I'll be damned." It was Oscar's initial response, before saying he had no intention of allowing Phin to retrieve his new purchase. But after some back-and-forth (Esmerelda agreeing to accompany Phin), and the clock ticking on Luna Park showtimes, Oscar had little choice. As Esmerelda climbed into the buckboard, she squeezed Cora's hand. "See. It's all getting better. You won't be scrubbing floors forever."

"For me, it's going to get better today. I've seen to it."

"What are you talking about?" Cora left to her own devices, Esmerelda didn't like the sound of that.

"Compared to what I've been doin' . . . I've found different work, if it must be at Coney Island."

"What is it? Did Oscar find you something?"

"No. But Oscar . . . other patrons, they gave me the idea. I've decided this on my own." In the bright sun, Cora's eyes pinched narrow as her face and her ears seemed to offer a victorious wave.

"Cora, what are you going to do?" Before she could reply, Oscar was giving Phin a slip of paper with the address and urging them on.

"You can drive a wagon, can't you?" The question from Oscar seemed reasonable as Phin looked leery sitting over Go and Fish and their formidable size.

"I can manage. I only have to get them to Queens, right?"

Oscar nodded at Phin's question, but he was quiet, bowing his head into the noses of his dedicated team.

"Your truck will be in capable hands."

They pulled away from Stillwell Avenue, and Esmerelda found herself turning hard to the right, where Oscar and the troupe stood. She nearly fell out, seeing Oscar dab at an eye. Phin grabbed her arm. But Esmerelda stayed in her twisted pose, rapt by the scene. Finally, the hodgepodge cluster faded from view as Go and Fish, she and Phin, clopped along, deeper into Brooklyn.

# ACT IV, SCENE II

The transaction of exchanging the horses and wagon for Oscar's new truck went smoothly. It seemed the war widow had gotten herself a new husband. He\farmed potatoes farther out on Long Island and appeared glad to have such a fine team. It was only Esmerelda who cried, saying goodbye to Go and Fish, as Phin inspected the new truck, which was far larger than Esmerelda had imagined.

"Don't worry," Phin said as they climbed inside the truck. "The farmer will see to the horses' care. He needs them healthy and well fed."

"But who will love them?"

Phin's mouth gaped. "You're a curious thinker, Esme. A thought I wouldn't have considered before knowing you." He fiddled with the foot pedals, and Esmerelda was amazed how a person could know which one to step on. Phin paused at the horses being led away. "Oscar was wise to make the deal. Practical. A truck, not steeds, will be a boon to his trade."

She was surprised to see him step on a small button, making the engine rumble. "Is that how it works?" She tipped her head at the floor-boards. "Then what are all those pedals for?"

"The two on the left are the gears. The one on the right's the brake. And this here," he said, squeezing a lever near the steering wheel, "is the accelerator." With his foot on the right pedal, the engine roared in place. "Have you never been in a motorcar . . . truck?"

"Yes. Last summer. Oscar has a friend out on Long Island. He runs a restaurant and wanted to add entertainment. It only lasted a few weeks. Country folks won't pay for shows like Manhattan or Brooklyn crowds. But he did have a fancy car and he took us for rides in it."

"And what did you think?"

"I thought it was remarkable, how fast a person could get somewhere. Oscar's friend took us to a lovely beach." Thoughts of the horses faded and Esmerelda smiled at the memory. "It wasn't anything like Coney Island's beach, so crowded." She looked in the direction they'd come. "I'm sorry. We got so wrapped up in Oscar's truck dilemma, I forgot about our plans."

"Maybe we can still make a shoreline trip out of the day. Tell me about this lovely beach and how to get there."

◆　◆　◆

They motored east for a time, until Esmerelda recalled the small town; she even remembered the name of the restaurant—L'Azur. The French name had left Cora and the boys scratching their heads, unaccustomed to heavy sauces covering what Barney had called "an otherwise decent pork chop."

It was late afternoon when she and Phin arrived, and she thought he might ask if she wanted to have a meal there. This made her nervous, as she also recalled Oscar saying his friend overcharged for a lunch plate. She wasn't sure what to think when Phin told her to wait while he went inside. Perhaps he wanted to see if he could afford two meals before inviting her to one. He returned carrying a sack. Climbing back into the truck, he said, "Now, do you remember the way to this beach?"

Esmerelda pointed south, her heart fluttering like the wind. "That way. It's just a block or two that way."

The beach was exactly as she recalled, gentle waves and soft sand, the tranquil bay. Seaweed. There was a good bit of brown seaweed, but she thought it only added texture to the scene and that Phin might like to paint it. Rickety huts lined the upper shore. Even though it was a warm September day, they appeared empty. Overturned canoes and old campfires dotted the beach. An impossibly long dock stretched out into the water, a gazebo denoting its point.

The gazebo turned into their picnic area, Phin having found a cloth tarp the widow wife had forgotten. Esmerelda tried not to look amazed when Phin reached into the restaurant sack, producing roast duck, fancy potatoes, plates, and a bottle of wine. "I couldn't get any cups. I hope you don't mind sharing from the bottle." He plucked the cork with his teeth and offered her the first taste.

Esmerelda laughed before she had a chance to get drunk on the moment or wine. She took her swig and handed it back. "I think I'd share most anything with you, Phin."

After the duck and potatoes and most of the wine were gone, a couple of local fishermen arrived, saying the catches were best at sunset. Phin's hand caught around Esmerelda's as they left the pier and unwanted company. Halfway across the beach, with the truck in sight, she spoke. "It will be close to midnight before Oscar has a chance to look for us and his new truck. If it were Go and Fish, we would have needed to be on our way hours ago, if not yesterday."

"But with the truck," he said, "we have hours to spare."

She took the canvas tarp from him and laid it out on the beach. Phin busied himself rekindling one of the fires. They talked until the sun dipped and the fishermen left. Phin had stretched out on the canvas, fingers laced behind his head, commenting on stars as they lit the private setting one by one. "It's an interesting thing. This sky or a sky thousands of miles away. The sight is the same—a mirror moon to wherever you might be. Remember what I'm telling you, Esme."

The thought puzzled her, but she stayed quiet, admiring him. Lying stretched out that way, it was a simple thing for a man to do. For a girl, it would be a bold invitation—the way a proper girl shouldn't behave. "A mirror moon. What does that mean?"

"That one." He pointed to it. "This one." His hand lightly touched hers. "You're my compass—you'll both lead me home."

*Home* . . . She pictured it so clearly—anywhere Phin was, that's what such a place would be. The enticement was too much, and Esmerelda lay alongside him. Phin didn't appear shocked. But he did roll onto his side, moving his fingers through her wind-whipped tangles of hair. "I like the sound of that."

"Do you?" He shimmied closer, their noses almost touching. "We might steal Oscar's truck, plant whatever they grow here, and call this place home. What do you think, Esme?"

"I couldn't steal Oscar's truck."

"No." He smiled, kissing her. "I don't suppose you would. It means we'll have to go back."

"I don't want to go back."

"You don't want to be a great singer with the world as her stage? That could happen."

"That's what Oscar says . . . if I wanted it."

"And you don't want that?"

Esmerelda shook her head.

"Good to know. Helps a fellow think things through." Phin lightly gripped her chin, touching her cheek. He kissed her again.

And like a potion, with the kiss came all the knowledge Esmerelda needed. She knew exactly what she wanted. They were all the things she suspected she couldn't have.

"I need to tell you something." She put her hand to his chest. Phin didn't move a muscle, and Esmerelda felt dizzy and breathless, though what she had to say was anvil heavy. "It, um . . . it has to do with this." She moved her hand in the mere inches between them. "Why I can't . . . why you won't want to . . ." Esmerelda squeezed her eyes closed. Speaking it aloud was more vile than she'd imagined. Of course, she'd never imagined confessing her past under these exact conditions.

"Let me say it for you."

She opened her eyes, blinking into what looked like Phin's angry expression.

"You shouldn't be here, can't talk about a future, because you've promised—maybe even *committed*," he said, using the word in a way that translated as only one thing, "yourself to Benjamin Hupp."

Benjamin couldn't have been further from Esmerelda's mind. She shook her head fervently. "No. This has nothing to do with Benjamin. I don't care for him. I've told you that."

"Then what?"

Tears began to drip. The ones she'd wondered about since the night she'd left her home. How such a horrid thing could have happened and Esmerelda had never cried a tear, not while her sister's husband had ripped at her nightclothes. Not when Lowell had informed her how much and for how long he'd imagined the chance. Not afterward, when she'd thrown a doll and a dress into a bag and left.

Phin's fingers were fast around her chin again. "You'll tell me this moment, whatever it is. Because whatever it is can't be worse than what's going through my mind."

"Yes it can," she whispered. And the story spilled out as if Esmerelda had been waiting to share it with him. It was a night that she still perceived as inconceivable. Phin listened as she retraced the wretched details. How, on a spring evening, Esmerelda had baked a cherry pie, and her sister, Hazel, had gone to stay with a sick friend. Her father was passed out, stone-cold drunk. Lowell had entered her bedroom and her body. Through weeping gasps, Esmerelda told Phin how he'd lorded over the act, describing his new home as communal, biting down on Esmerelda's ear and telling her that *everything* in the house now belonged to him. How he looked forward to such fine property and sisterly options. That Esmerelda wouldn't say a word because Hazel was an obedient wife who would never disbelieve her husband.

"Hazel, she's never had much of a backbone. She's more like our father than our mother. Her husband was right. Hazel would never challenge his word. After Lowell left my room, I knew two things. It would happen again. And the only way to stop it was to not be there next time. So I left."

Phin's eyes rivaled his great white moon. Everything was so still, as if only her heart moved, waiting for his reaction. She couldn't stand it. "So you see," she said, forcing her pragmatic side center. "If things were to progress, from now to a proper time . . . well, I thought I should save you the shock of not finding me in the expected state. To know you wouldn't be the first to . . ."

Phin sat up, his fingertips pressed to his forehead. Esmerelda sat too, prepared for what she'd been warned of if something like that happened to a girl, a man forcing himself on her. It was true. The girl must have done something to encourage the act. Although, in the two years since that night, Esmerelda could not think of a single thing she had done to embolden Lowell. She defaulted to the pie. It must have been the pie.

"Expected state?" he said. She waited for more. The more turned out to be Phin lurching to his feet, trundling through sand toward the truck. Her heart shattered into something smaller than the grains of sand beneath her. Maybe the pieces would wash out to sea, sink to the bay's bottom. He spun back around. In the moonlight, she could see every raw feature. "I don't know the address. Tell me how to find him."

"Who?"

"Your brother-in-law."

"Why?"

"Because I'm going to skin the son of a bitch alive, then I'm going to kill him."

And while she was certain Phin meant it, she only needed to hear him say it. It no longer mattered what the world might think. Phin Seaborn believed, as Esmerelda had deep down, that what happened with Lowell was not her fault. She tore across the beach. Phin's arms folded around her, and he held on so tight this act alone made them one inseparable person. "No. You won't," she said. "I'll not further that memory by dragging you into it."

They stood that way for some time, until night air and confessions had them both shivering. But it was all fine as long as Phin was there. For so long, in spite of Oscar's steadying presence, Esmerelda had stood on her own, kept the burden of that night from crushing her. The embrace hadn't lessened, and Phin wove his hand through her hair.

"So the rest is simple enough," he said. "We'll save it for a wedding night. We'll make certain it's the way I suspect you saw such a night in your mind."

And the embrace broke, Esmerelda stepping back. "Whose wedding night?"

"Esme, for a smart girl, you can be as silly as Cora. Did you think for a moment, had we even considered . . . well, what it is married people do, on this beach, I wouldn't be making a bride out of you? What sort of common lowlife do you take me for?"

Certainly not the kind Phin's troubled life, his harsh existence, should have produced. She didn't reply with a yes or no, because somehow the question of marriage seemed asked and answered. Esmerelda just held on to him.

On the way back into the city, they didn't speak any more about Lowell or that night. Phin only insisted that, should she need it, he'd always be her ear. Esmerelda was quiet, never picturing the day unfolding as it had—an act and a confession she wore like an inner wound being healed from the outside in. The boy she loved proposing, indifferent to things she was sure any decent man would perceive as a ruined girl.

As the blur of city lights drew closer—an astounding sight when moving at such speed—Phin spoke. "And now," he said, his voice just as serious as it'd been on the beach, "I have something I need to tell you."

# CHAPTER SEVENTEEN

*Surrey, Massachusetts*
*Present Day*

Flagler had only called to tell Pete the airspace over Reykjanes remained a volcanic no-fly zone. That and he had no other immediate assignments abroad. "It's economics, St John. I should fly you in from the States when I have a pool right here? I have bosses too."

Pete paced his bedroom and thought about telling Flagler he'd fly back on his own dime. He realized how desperate it sounded, slightly unstable if his editor knew Pete's underlying motivation. *"You see, Austin, I'm more or less afraid to spend the night in my own bed."* The last thing anyone needed in a volatile region was a guy with a foot on the ledge.

Pete rolled his eyes and plopped into a chair. He ended the call and hung his head. Flagler's last words were about the upcoming One Direction assignment in New York. "Over my dead body . . ." He stood, muttering at his own threat, "Are we seeing a theme here?" *Not existing.* It was sarcasm, but it wasn't the first time a thought like this had crossed Pete's mind.

He threw the phone onto the mattress. Lacing his fingers behind his head, Pete stared at a queen-size bed. All he could think about was getting the hell out of there. He'd barely touched months of accumulated vacation. He could drive north to Montreal or Toronto. He was a fan of both cities. But sightseeing had zero appeal, and he doubted his street photography or even painting would distract him. Too much—in both his lives—had shifted on this trip home. Leaving like that would only prove his parents and Zeke Dublin's ghost right. He was running from his otherworldly problems, not solving them.

A few hours later, dinner ended, and Levi did a poor job of hiding his surprise when Pete announced: "I'll stay. I can't remember having two bad nights in a row here."

Levi returned his car keys to the blond sideboard. In the kitchen, they could hear the clanking of pots, the running faucet. "I thought for sure I'd be making a trip to Logan this evening."

"Yeah. Me too. Well, Mom will be glad to hear it." He leaned away from the dining room table, looking into the kitchen. "How about we make her totally giddy? You and I can do the dishes."

Levi laughed. "Okay. Sounds like a deal."

It was Christmas in July; at least, that's how Pete viewed his mother's reaction to the news that he'd be staying another night. Aubrey said she'd pick out a movie they could all watch, as husband and son took over kitchen duty. A short while later, they settled into the living room. Pete had seen the comedy she'd chosen, on three different flights, but he kept silent and watched with feigned interest, doing some miscellaneous texting in between. It worked for a few hours: life as a normal family, sharing a bowl of popcorn, Pete laughing on cue, though his mind never really left his troubles.

The house was quiet and home sort of felt like home. It helped Pete's reservations about staying when his mother went to bed looking happy. He was surprised by his own sleepy state. As his head hit the pillow, Pete did not think about his mother's close proximity or how her energy aggravated his burdens. He just thought of her as "down the hall." After turning out the light, he stayed away from thoughts of Esme. Sleep came silently, like vapor under his door. The bells from Our Lady of the Redeemer chimed, a reminiscent drill.

Conscious thoughts gave way, and Pete drifted, sensing a shift. On nights like this, his last purposeful thought always mirrored: When you died, did the world fall away? Did your mind, body, and soul surrender to something from which you couldn't turn back? This was what Pete felt when his everyday life transformed. It was the divide he crossed, finding himself hapless and helpless, slipping into an ever-after murderous rampage.

He gasped as if water filled his lungs, air not a sure thing—his whole body panicked, having no chance of escape. In the bedroom was a clothesline and a china-faced doll with heavy closed eyelids. He spied a cat; its tail flicked from beneath the bed. His gaze moved to a fireplace where embers smoldered, sparks crackled. Above the fireplace hung the hunting scene. As always, his point of view was limited. But the fire. Something was different. He knew the pattern of lapping flames, could anticipate the crackle of wood. It all came right before gunfire, which he had no prayer of stopping. The fire raged larger, angrier, as if fuel had been added. Flames sparked, and he swore he saw the image of a mermaid burning. Mostly, he saw Esme.

Stepping deeper into the moment, he raised the gun and squeezed the trigger. The dispassion with which he fired the weapon conflicted with what he felt for the girl. It differed greatly from the impulse present when aiming a gun on a battlefield. Why? Why was he doing this? Yet the bullet met its target. Smoke rose. It wasn't thick enough to hide the horrified look on Esme's face. She made no attempt to save herself, dodge the fatal shot. Emotions trounced him—absolute terror as blood spilled from her middle, her small hands clutching the white beaded gown. Esme fell. He dropped the gun and caught her, all before a church bell chimed. His grip was nervous, and she fell to the floor. He scooped her up. Even after killing her, he was consumed by the feeling of how much he loved her.

Pete turned to the room's single window, perhaps looking for a coward's way out. Then his view shifted, moving from the darkened window to the dresser mirror. The eyes of a killer looked back. He exited the scene carrying a lifeless Esme. The body. *What would he do with the body?*

Before he found out, the reverse slide began, Pete's arms and legs flailing as he fell back toward the present. Nothing to grasp. In the distance, a brighter light flickered. A tunnel; a way out. He'd never seen this before. Struggling past fiery desperation, he aimed for it. But the dishonor of the act clung like a cloak made of metal, something that wouldn't burn. Something holding him to what he'd done. The feeling didn't ease as he moved through time, traveling from one unwanted wanderlust to the next. From killer to the ritual punishment of guilt. A physical thud hit, like he'd fallen from a tree. Vaguely aware of his surroundings, Pete wiped his hands on fabric, screaming, "Get it off—get it off me!"

It took light to comprehend the transfer, whether it was sunrise in a bunker in Mosel, a hotel room in Paris, or a boyhood bedroom. He needed light to see that the wetness on his hands was not blood, but sweat like a raging fever.

Someone disrupted the chaos. Things escalated fast; he was awake but not cognizant. A physical assault ensued, and seconds later it was a full-on brawl. Pete swung and felt his fist connect. Another blow was blocked, an arm nearly as strong as his. When a lamp smashed onto the floor, he heard his mother scream. Pete blinked into his father's face.

The mayhem rivaled that of an intruder, but it was only their son. Blood trailed over Levi's lip, yet Pete's mind was moving beyond his control, his heart whacking against his chest. He couldn't process the horrible thing he was doing now, so consumed by the act he'd committed moments ago. Levi came forward, and Pete used his rigid stance, pushing against his father and jackknifing himself into the wall. His shoulder busted through thick plaster, completing the wakeup call.

Pete blinked into the bright bedroom, fully aware. Plaster flaked and he reached for his throbbing shoulder. "Son of a bitch." He bent at the waist, absorbing the wicked ache. "Pa . . . you okay?" The blood dripping from Levi's lip was answer enough, having splattered his white T-shirt. His mother stood in the doorway, one hand clamped to her mouth, the other flat against her heart. Her eyes—Pete's eyes—awash with terror.

Welcome home—again.

A short time later, they all sat in the living room. Aubrey had applied one ice pack to Levi's bruised mouth and chin, another to Pete's swollen shoulder. Over the years, they'd amassed a fine collection of first-aid treatments. She hadn't said a word and neither had Pete.

Levi sat in the leather recliner that Pete viewed as a part of him. Yet he looked so uncomfortable, in pain. A piece of this was surely his puffy mouth, a red and misshapen jaw. The rest of Levi's upset was surely knowing how little he could help his son. His mother's silent state rang loudest. Normally her soothing words would meld into Pete's ears, combatting the experience he carried from that life into this one. Aubrey would insist that everything could be fine and that there were no rules. Things might change tomorrow.

But there was nothing.

Pete winced at his achy shoulder and shifted the ice. He was reminded, once again, of his greatest reasons for leaving home: What if he injured his father to the point of unconsciousness? It was within the realm of possibility. He'd inherited Levi's stature. He'd surpassed him in strength. Worse, what if Pete did this and then moved on to his mother? She was already so thin and frail. What if Pete attacked the one other person who, somehow, loved him regardless of the misery he brought to their lives? In the dimly lit living room, Pete stared at nothing. Aubrey sat across from him, though her head was turned, her gaze fixed on the cold fireplace. He adjusted the ice pack again, searching for words to comfort her. "Mom, listen—"

Aubrey held up a hand. She didn't face him. "I think you should leave."

Pete's gaze dropped to the floor. "Because you think I'm going to hurt Pa . . ."

"Aubrey . . ." Pete glanced at his father, who'd removed his ice pack from his face but was resigned to putting it back. "Let's not—"

Pete cut him off, talking to his mother. "You're thinking it too, that I might hurt you."

She turned slowly, like she hadn't the strength to run if the house were on fire. "Do you think I give a damn what happens to me?" Her voice was raspy, as if she'd been screaming in her own nightmare. "I won't do this to you anymore. I don't want to be the cause of this . . ." In a limp motion, she gestured to father and son. "I can't fix it. I can't do it anymore. I can't make us—*our family*—live like this."

Pete's first thought was of the normal life she'd fought so hard for, the one that seemed forever beyond her reach. His second thought was that of an addict son. Parents who would go to the end of the earth for a cure. The ones who realized they'd failed. Their son beyond conceivable help. All they could do—for their own sanity—was let go. Pete looked at his father. He believed what his mother said; she didn't give a damn about herself. But she did care a great deal about Levi. Maybe she thought the poor son of a bitch had suffered enough, bound to psychic mysteries that challenged the toughest, most resilient man Pete had ever known.

"Just leave, Pete," she repeated.

"Go. You want me to . . ." Pete's shoulder hurt less. A sudden ache took up all the space in his throat. "Now?" In the irrationality of his life, this was a scenario he'd never envisioned—being tossed from the one place where they wanted you unconditionally.

"As soon as possible, I think."

"Aubrey," Levi said, "come on. You don't mean that. Pete, you're not going—"

She stood. "Yes. He is. And let me be clear . . ." She wore a short cotton nightgown. Her long limbs trembled, one hand gripped over her scarred arm. In the tendons of her neck, the pound of her pulse was visible. "You're not to come back—ever." She moved her attention to Levi. "If Pete is no longer bound to me, obligated, whatever channel my presence provides is severed. It's as logical as anything else. If my connection to Pete no longer exists, specters, Esme, visitant nights have no path. Whatever conduit I provide to his other life is thwarted."

"Mom, you don't . . ." Pete was about to object, but her theory made basic sense. "Do you really believe something like that could work?"

Through the silence came a speech Aubrey clearly did not want to make. "I've been doing this awhile now, Pete. I know what ghosts want. I have respect for their tenacity." Her words gained momentum. "I understand every nook and cranny they'll squeeze through—like mice under a wall. I know the evil spirits' harbor. How they can draw you in, make you their mark.

"And even the good ones, they're so clever. Zeke Dublin's ghost was present for weeks before I realized there was a specter under my nose. It's my fault." His mother's gaze connected to a photo of her long-dead father. "I've denied it, wouldn't say it out loud, but I've been *aware* of the idea for years."

"Really?" Pete said this softly. "Tell me more. What else do you know about ghosts that would never fit into a normal family conversation?"

"Aubrey, Pete," Levi said.

His mother held up her trembling hand. She edged closer to the mantel. When she spoke, her words were like an incantation. "When it comes to evil, I know three kinds of specters. There's the ghost that will haunt you. Annoying, but not deadly. Common as poison ivy. It makes me think of Eli Serino.

"The second apparition, this one feeds off physical harm—whether it's you or your father who ends up injured." She held out her pock-marked arm. "Or even me. Their actions are fueled by anger, disappointments from their earthly existence. They don't seek closure. They only want to howl." Her brow knotted, her attention still on the mantel. "And they're not really after you, your life. You become their target by default, because they can get to you.

"After this, there's one more phantasm. I've never encountered it, but your grandfather surely did. This is the ghost that should instill the greatest fear. This apparition has the desire and the means to drive you completely mad. Enough to make you welcome insanity or maybe seek solace by plunging a car off a cliff."

"That's what your father did, how he died." Pete looked into his mother's eyes, his own eyes. "And now you're thinking whatever haunted him, it's not half as bad as the ghost that's chasing me."

"After tonight, I believe whatever is haunting you possesses the power of all three. What you've said about my presence exacerbating that influence . . . you couldn't be more right."

Pete swiped at a sweaty brow. He'd never heard his mother talk like this, and clearly his father was thinking the same thing.

"Aubrey," Levi said, "let's back this up a minute. You don't—"

"No, Pa. Listen to her. It's what harsh truth sounds like." He looked at his father. "Nothing a person ever wants to hear."

"Yes, but . . ." Levi, who'd been sitting cautiously on the edge of his chair, stood. He pointed at Pete. "News flash for both of you: the son's father gets a say in excommunicating him from our lives. If the two of you think I'm going to allow psychic speculation to run my son out of my—"

"Levi." Aubrey's tone silenced him. "This is fairly straightforward." She stepped in his direction. "You're far too connected to me, and ghosts aren't easily fooled. Surely, that's the least of what you've learned when it comes to psychic phenomena. If Pete is going to have a chance at normal, the break has to be from both of us." She paused. "It's the only thing we haven't tried."

"Not true. Pete's spent the last six years halfway around the world, away from both of us. As a family, we've been separated."

"That's subject to interpretation." Pete delved deeper into his mother's suggestion. "What I did was find a way to live a life and stay connected to both of you."

"He's right, Levi. It's all about communication—whether it's modern technology or even a passé postcard. Anything that's a conduit. Specters that have nothing to do but search for energy, a way in."

"The two of you can't be serious."

"I've never been more serious about anything." Aubrey turned back to Pete. "And imagine the energy between mother and son, particularly considering the traits Pete and I do share."

"It makes sense." Pete drew a shaky breath. "The only way to break the cycle is to break the bond—our bond." Pete's mind and heart raced. He didn't want to say or do any of it. They were his parents. She was his champion. But like a complex math equation, the theory had merit.

Levi clung to less drastic options. "So we, what? Toss Pete from our lives without even . . ." He flailed a hand at Aubrey. "I don't know, at least insisting he attempt past life regression therapy? Shouldn't we at least consider avenues like Dr. Kapoor before we go to such an extreme?"

"It's not the answer, Pa. Nobody's wanted to admit it or go there . . . but Mom's right."

"It's not all bad," Aubrey said. "Don't you see? By doing this, Pete will have a chance at a normal life. Isn't that the bottom line, what we want for him?"

"That's not fair, Aubrey. We shouldn't have to choose." Levi slammed the ice pack onto a side table. "This is just great—fucking great." He turned and headed for the front porch, nearly removing the screen door from its hinges as he went.

"Let me talk to him." Aubrey exited and their angry whispers rose into the night air.

As agonizing as his mother's conclusion was, Pete comprehended the rationale. The blood-smeared ice pack caught his eye, and a ghostly thought interceded; it was Zeke Dublin's advice: *"Stop running, kid. Start putting the pieces together if you want your life back."*

Maybe the grifter had been a step ahead, projecting the life Pete would want back.

He pressed his fingertips to his head, and the movement sent a zing of pain through Pete's shoulder. The hell with this. He wasn't twelve. He wasn't standing in his own fucking living room while his parents fought over his future. His mother might have initiated the idea, but this was his decision.

Pete moved toward the door, hearing the last of his mother's tense words: "I know what I felt, Levi. After all these years, do you really want to argue a presence? I know it was Esme."

"Tell Pete that now and you only—"

"Cement my argument?"

"What was Esme?" Pete pushed open the screen and stepped onto the porch.

Levi flailed an arm at Pete. "Go for it, Aubrey. You're so determined to drive him away . . ." His parents traded a fierce look, Levi narrowing his eyes at Aubrey. "Damn you."

And Levi's anger was almost enough to make Pete reconsider. He looked warily between his parents. "Mom, what about Esme?"

She turned, her dark hair whipping over her shoulder. "I woke up not long before you did tonight. And not for any of the usual reasons— I wasn't thirsty, I didn't need to use the bathroom. There was no dream, good or bad. I woke because there was a presence. She guided me into the hall, toward the hall bath."

"She?"

"She." Aubrey folded her arms. "When I got to the bathroom, her presence intensified—kind of like a Wi-Fi hot spot."

"I know the feeling."

"I'm sure you do. That said, she was still distant, not terribly forthcoming. But I believe it was Esme."

"How do you know that?"

She hesitated as if they'd reached the part Aubrey didn't wish to share. "The photo album you brought, the pictures of Esme."

"A ghost gift, hand delivered by her killer," Pete said dully. "A larger, wider channel of communication. That's what pushed you over the edge tonight. Esme."

"Yes." She looked nervous, clearly aware of the marital discourse she was inciting. Regardless, his mother went on. "I believe the photos you brought here enhance her ability to communicate. Assume the postcard was always a ghost gift that connected to Esme. Before today, the card alone didn't harbor enough energy to facilitate communication."

"But now she's managed to add a note to a once-blank card."

"We'd be foolish to ignore it. The photographs represent even a more personal point of access."

"What did she want?" Pete said, unsure what to do with the idea of someone else channeling his ghost. "Did Esme make a threat?"

"Does she really need to? You've known about Esme since you were twelve. But there's always been a distinction between your other life and the ghosts in this one. She didn't communicate anything to me, but her presence was enough."

"Something else that's changed with this trip home, along with my encounter with her spirit and hearing her voice."

"Then we agree." She glanced at Levi, who'd retreated to the porch rail, leaning against it, his arms crossed tight. "Two worlds . . ."

"Are bleeding into one. I thought the same thing back on Long Island, almost from the moment I walked into that bungalow."

"As it is, Esme is on to me—the person who intensifies visits to your other life." She moved away from Pete, the three of them caught in a tight triangle. "I know the terror that lives in your nights. I don't want to know what happens if it converges with your waking hours. Think carefully about those three kinds of specters, Pete. I've no idea what Esme wants. But I do think we're at a point where we need to be on the offense." She held out her pockmarked, teeth-bitten arm, doused in the gold glow of porch lights. Levi looked too, and his expression turned grim. Her scars were a sobering reminder of the potential of evil. "Bottom line, I will not give any ghost the chance to do *this*, or worse, to my son. Not while I'm on this side of the fight."

# CHAPTER EIGHTEEN

Back inside the house, the battle continued, but it was only Aubrey and Levi caught up in an all-out shouting match. Pete had moved on, methodically and mechanically heading into his room, stuffing his belongings into the canvas duffel bag. While there was panic and anger all around, Pete was determined to follow through. As long as his mother remained a conduit, Esme or any other spirit would have an open channel. And now, so it seemed, a greater one.

Pete intervened only long enough to tell them both to stop. "Pa," he said, going into the hall where both his parents stood. "Listen to me. It's not so different from when I left at twenty-two. This is what I want." While the statement wasn't quite true or the circumstances the same, the mandate subdued Levi.

Pete also considered something Aubrey hadn't brought up. If his mother appeared ill when Pete arrived, she looked even more fragile now. Her health, mentally and physically, superseded everything—even Esme. In time, Levi would see this; he'd agree. Pete grabbed his camera gear and laptop and quickly packed them, fueled by the notion of having killed one woman he loved. He'd proven his penchant for violence in this life and his last. Pete wouldn't test the possibilities.

That kind of tragedy wouldn't occur a second time, not if he could help it. Pete wouldn't Skype, e-mail, or Snapchat. Hell, he'd cancel their *New York Times* subscription to keep his photos from coming into the house.

Pete kept moving, taking out his phone and connecting to Uber. A blip of positive news—a driver was two minutes away. With the duffel bag over his good shoulder, the camera bag strap dug hard into his injured one. Good. It mirrored the pressure to get the hell out of their lives. He pounded down the stairs. The argument upstairs reignited, long enough for Pete to spy the photo album on the coffee table and his mother's box of ghost gifts. It seemed in everyone's best interest that, along with himself, Pete remove the eerie chattels. He tucked the single ghost gift and photos into his duffel bag.

Hearing Levi follow, Pete darted out the front door. "Pete, don't listen to this." Levi was steps behind. "She's not thinking straight—neither of you are. This is not the answer!"

From the porch, Pete whipped around to face his father. "Do you have a better one?" Murky mist covered the predawn, making for dull, poignant light. He'd never seen fear in his father's face, and his swollen jaw trembled. He'd never seen him cry—that wasn't his father, but it's what their family had come to. His eyes were wet, dark lashes batting at Pete.

"Don't do this." His mouth gaped—an *O* of vagueness posing for a lack of argument. Then he came up with a truth that cut Levi so deep, his always self-possessed father could barely find words. "I lost my brother. When Brody . . . *died* . . ." Levi never could say it, that Brody had taken his own life—his father's hero, his lifeguard and mentor. He started again. "Since you left home, I've lived with the fear of losing you to a battlefield. There," he said, pointing to the physical world, "or to the places in your mind. I can't lose you this way, Pete. Not because the ghosts chased you away. Please."

Pete wavered, but he couldn't see any alternative. "I . . . I'm sorry this happened to you, Pa. I'm sorry this is what you ended up with. You didn't deserve to lose a brother the way you did. You don't deserve to have ended up with me for a son."

"You know that's not how I feel."

"No. It's how I feel."

In the tightest embrace, Levi gripped his son. Pete buried his nose in Levi's undershirt. It smelled of love and family history—the frightened little boy who'd traveled endless violent journeys. The father who held him, just like this, willing him home. It wasn't to be. It occurred to Pete that he hadn't said goodbye to his mother. He couldn't do it. Mercifully, a horn honked. "I have to go." He glanced at the house. "For all our sakes." Pete stepped back, both their faces veiled in tears. Pete swiped at his. "Know you're the best father a son could ask for."

"Pete . . ."

He shifted his aching shoulder. "After that, there'd be too much to say, so I'll only say goodbye."

♦ ♦ ♦

The Uber driver double-checked the destination. Pete winced at his throbbing shoulder and wanted to say, *"Well, I'm already on the road to hell. What happens if we make a right at the end of the street?"* Without thinking, he confirmed Grace's address.

It wasn't quite seven a.m. when he knocked on Grace's front door. For a second, Pete really lost touch, picturing a half-asleep Grace cracking open the door, one eye squinting at him, bloodshot and mascara smudged. No such thing. She swung the door wide, wearing a chipper blue dress and disposition, a steaming cup of coffee in her hand, every hair in place. "Pete! What in the world are you doing here?"

And Pete didn't have a clue, other than his sudden state of homelessness. "I, uh . . . I just came to say goodbye. I'm heading out."

"To where?" She put the cup on a table and opened the door wider. He didn't go in. "When we texted last night, you said your managing editor didn't have an assignment for you yet."

Damn. He'd forgotten the autopilot texts he'd traded with Grace while the trivial rom-com had played. "Last-minute change in plans. Listen, I wanted to ask you something, a favor."

Her blue eyes beamed—emotion filled. "Anything, Pete. I mean, okay, so it wasn't the most pleasant parting yesterday. I overreacted. But I'm here for you—always. You know that, right?"

And if he felt shitty twenty minutes ago, he felt worse now. Technically. No. Quite literally, he was using Grace. He reasoned it out: maybe the thing he wanted justified the means. "It's important." She nodded dutifully, and Pete was surprised Grace didn't grab a pen and paper to take notes. "My *departure* from home wasn't good. I'll let my mother fill in the details if she wants . . . if she needs to. I'm not sure how much communication there's going to be between Levi and her in the near future. I don't want her to be alone . . . emotionally." Pete tightened his fingers around the strap of the duffel bag, a strangling hold. As he'd grown into adulthood, it occurred to Pete that if anything were to come between his parents, it would probably be him. *Prophecy fulfilled.* "Would you mind checking in on my mother? Could you stop by in a week or so, maybe see if she's done reading that paperback? You know, keep it casual."

"Of course. But whatever's happened, surely it'll blow over. You'll be talking to one of them in—"

"No. I won't. Could you do that for me?" She nodded solemnly. He looked at his leather-banded watch like he had somewhere to be. "Thanks, Grace. I appreciate it." Pete turned to leave but pivoted back around. "And this might sound really strange, but I don't want to know anything, what you talk about or how they are."

"Pete, that's crazy."

"You're catching on." He sucked in stagnant morning air. "Can you please do that? Nothing. I don't want to know anything, unless . . ."

"Unless what?"

"Unless you get to a point where you think you might not see one of them again. It's my mother I'm particularly concerned about." She blinked at him. Her curiosity was evident, but so was the fact that she'd hit a wall when it came to Pete being forthcoming. It didn't matter. Knowing Grace, surely she was ten steps ahead, already determining how and when she'd approach Aubrey. "Thanks again. You're a good person, Grace. Don't ever think otherwise, not for a second."

"Uh, who are you and what have you done with Peter St John? Come on, Pete. I can live with the cryptic request, but why a compliment like I'm never going to see you . . ." He turned and walked down the front steps. "Pete!"

He kept moving; he'd call for another Uber ride from around the corner. But in true Grace fashion, she couldn't let him go. Not without a last word. Her light steps came up fast behind him. "Here." He stopped and pivoted. "Since clearly I'm being cut off, at least take this. I did the homework. It might be of interest."

She shoved a white envelope at him, the preprinted return address noting "Town of Surrey."

"What's this?"

"Some research I did on your house. Nothing stuck out to me, but I thought maybe you'd want it."

Because he didn't want to prolong the moment or chide Grace for doing the opposite of what he'd asked, Pete accepted the envelope. "Thanks. I guess."

She stood on the sidewalk, hands tucked behind her back, looking disappointed when he only shoved it into his camera bag.

"I've got to get going. I've got a . . ." He couldn't think.

"Plane to catch?"

"Sure." He turned and headed for the corner.

# CHAPTER
# NINETEEN

*Plane, train, automobile, slow boat to China . . .* Throw a dart at a map. Pete chose automobile, asking the Uber driver to take him to the nearest car rental agency. Once there, he filled out paperwork and selected a modest sedan. Pete threw his duffel and camera bags into the back seat and slid into the already sweltering front. In seconds his hands were reduced to a slippery grip around the steering wheel. In moments, the car was suffocating. Yet Pete sat, the black interior closing in around him. He didn't possess the wherewithal to move.

He'd flirted with heatstroke in any number of Middle East countries, a common hazard. A person's mind would cloud as neurological dysfunction set in, nausea, disorientation, followed by delirium and seizures—Jesus, it sounded remarkably similar to his everyday life. None of this motivated Pete to move, not to turn on the air-conditioning or even roll down a window. If he stayed this way, dehydration and electrolyte abnormalities would follow, the latter sparking a cardiac arrhythmia. He sucked in air so hot it was like kissing a lit oven. Pete remained frozen in the melting car rental lot, parked on the edge of desperation.

A knock on the car window startled him, a clerk making a fast "roll down the window" motion with his hand. Pete complied.

"Hey, man, you okay?"

The rush of humid July air felt like a sea breeze. A beach and a jetty flashed through Pete's head—crystal clear. He associated it with the young man in front of him, who gripped a clipboard, wearing a white T-shirt and red shorts. Pete blinked at him—his blond buzz cut and mirrored sunglasses, in which Pete saw his own image. Chances were Pete was as crazy as his reflection looked: unshaven, sweat-soaked—lost. He could even make out his blotchy red face. "Uh, yeah. I'm fine."

"You don't look fine." The young man cocked a chin at the car's console. "Complimentary bottle of water there. I'm sure the AC works. Why don't you give it a try—along with the engine?"

"Right." Pete started the car. "Sorry. I, uh . . . I couldn't figure out my direction."

"I know. It's why I'm here." He made a humming noise, like he encountered desperate travelers and lost souls on a daily basis. Regardless of the heat, his white T-shirt was smooth and pristine. He looked like a fitness freak, taut muscles, not an ounce of fat. His haircut read as more military than trendy. And the red shorts, not exactly standard car rental clerk attire. He pulled the sunglasses off his face and Pete blinked into eyes the color of fallen sky. The man smiled—a deep dimple on one side. It was a trait that, to Pete, read as both uncanny and familiar. The young man pointed with his sunglasses. "That way's 95 north, if that's the direction you want to go." He paused. "Is it?"

Pete didn't respond. The man pivoted on what seemed like an airy glide. Pete brushed an arm across his brow, an attempt to wipe away the heat, which was clearly getting to him.

"'Course, that way is south, straight shot into Connecticut. You'll hit the beach if you follow it to the coast. After that, keep going. You'll end up in New York City. Big city. A person never knows what a place like that might unearth."

The way he spoke, it sounded more like instructions than direc-tions. Either way, Pete nodded as if he'd never been outside Surrey. "Sure. The beach. Maybe the city."

"The beach is a start. Can help clear your head, put things in per-spective. More so than a suffocating car. I always loved the beach." As he talked, a gold chain glinted from around his neck. A cross dangled from it—fatter, not necessarily a religious symbol.

Pete recognized it. "You're a lifeguard."

"Used to be. Still am, some days." He slapped his hand on the edge of the open car window. "You take care now, Pete." The lifeguard stepped back. "Tell your old man I said hello. Tell him I watch him all the time."

Pete took his last words to mean *Ink on Air*, seeing Levi on his television newsmagazine program. He blinked at the lifeguard-turned-car-attendant. Pete proceeded to move without further instruction. He turned on the air and put the car in drive, stepping on the gas. The vehicle moved forward, but Pete's gaze darted to the side mirror as the young man in red shorts grew ever distant. At the gate, he glanced in his rearview mirror. The lifeguard was gone. He hit the brakes hard and sucked in a breath of cooler manufactured air. "No way." He twisted around, looking through the car's back window. "That couldn't have been . . ."

Another man's muffled voice cut in. At the exit was a car rental agent, this one dressed in khaki pants, a green polo, black nametag, and visor—clearly the Enterprise uniform. He urged him on. "Keep it moving, please."

The attendant pointed to the exit; the car behind him honked. "I'll be a son of a . . ."

Pete drove for miles without a clear destination, taking 95 south, more or less following the lifeguard's direction. He prodded himself to pay attention to the traffic, his concentration eclipsed by his wonky mood. He wasn't sure if he'd just encountered his dead uncle, or if he'd sat so long in a sweltering car that his mind had dipped into more mainstream mirages. Taking the exit for Rocky Neck, Pete concluded either option was enough to spirit him out of the car.

The Connecticut beach was the only setting where Levi spoke openly or easily about his brother. It was all in the context of good memories. Not the uncle who'd taken his own life.

A jetty of rocks stretched out to the ocean. Pete headed for it, passing by a sign that warned visitors to stay back. The tide was high and the rocks slippery, as cautioned. It was a cagey balancing act. Pete teetered on the jetty point, a rough ocean before him with a view both boundless and finite.

Beneath his Nikes, the earth was slick, and the shadowy thoughts in Pete's head slithered toward even darker ones. He had nowhere to go, no place to be. Salt water washed over his sneakers, the pain he'd caused washing over his mind. The plain truth was that if Pete had never existed, a childless Aubrey and Levi would have lived far easier lives. They surely wouldn't be at each other's throats, which was where he'd left them. Well, clearly there was no turning back that clock.

The sea rose up, distracting him, presenting an alternative option. If Pete walked past one more rock, he'd be out of land. Dropped into the sound. He wouldn't swim long before exhaustion won out. Hell. His shoulder hurt so much he wasn't sure he could produce a stroke to save himself. There was nothing in front of him, and now not even his parents. Pete closed his eyes, imagining which would be less painful: to exile the son they loved or simply have no son at all.

He sighed into the sea air. His mother's plan wasn't a sufficient means to an end. There was no guarantee it would even work, just more speculation. And if he was being truthful, it was more than that. Pete was tired—so tired of fighting a gift he didn't want. He didn't possess the wherewithal to face a future, minus his parents, filled with more uncertainties. What if his violent behavior, along with Esme and other pieces of his past, overtook his present-day life? It appeared to be the exact path he was on. But if Pete were gone, beyond state lines and landlines, the chance of hurting anyone else—emotionally or physically—would be erased. He'd be at peace. He wouldn't have to get up tomorrow in a place where his sole objective was to remain a decent human being. He wouldn't have to wage a never-ending battle for normal.

Pete's ability to cope had hit bottom. His life and his mind were like a Russian nesting doll, one devastating discovery opening to the next. He inched forward, unsteady but more sure. This was the right option. Another violent spray of salt water shot up, slapping him in the face.

*A slippery slope . . .*

One more step.

*A means to an end . . .*

Out of nowhere, a force batted at him. It was far more than a breeze, beyond a shove. Pete fell inland, onto the rock-filled jetty. "What the hell . . ." He landed on his backside, his bruised shoulder hitting hard. Pete sat up to dizzying stars, seeing nothing but the swelling whitecaps of water. The sky dominated his sight lines, a vivid blue hue. The same color as the eyes of the lifeguard.

Pete crab-crawled backward. The violent churn of sea slapped his face. He considered the energy it took for a specter to offer a visual presence, never mind take action—a ghost who'd clearly come to intervene. Pete stood, gazing at the choppy sound, his heart picking up on the panic of having almost thrown himself into it. What the fuck was he doing? He feared his past life. He couldn't fathom his purpose in this one. But if Pete didn't get the message in the car rental lot, he got it now. His soul would be an unwelcome addition to the place ghosts lived, those born out of a reckless death.

Pete hurried from the jetty, jumping slippery rocks with a steadier, life-jarring gait. *Keep moving, Soldier . . .* The phrase reverberated; it was familiar. Something Levi had said on occasion, an otherworldly echo of the St John family mantra.

By the time he reached the car, Pete's acute awareness of the value of life kicked into gear. In the mess of his, he'd nearly dismissed the worth—even if it was totally fucked up. He leaned against the hood, his hands pressed into denim-covered thighs. Esme produced a hollow sense of longing, but she'd also ignited more fear than motivation. It was time for that to stop, and it was up to Pete to figure out how.

His mother's conclusion fell beyond tough love, but it also provided Pete with new incentive. If he could figure things out, somehow make peace with his other life, maybe he'd get this one back. It wasn't a life he loved, but clearly giving up on it was not the answer. Pete heaved a breath at the sound-soaked jetty, slightly surprised his lungs were filled with air, not water. He'd come that close. He was ashamed at having flirted with the idea of putting his parents through that. He needed to find a way to resolve his past and redirect his future—for his own sake. Pete closed his eyes, maybe asking God or time if it would backpedal just a little, erase the past hour. When he opened them, his gaze was stuck on the rocky ledge. No. Pete needed this, to smack hard into the bottom. It was the only way back up.

The most immediate question: How and where to start? It didn't seem as if the answer was in a bungalow on Long Island. The bungalow was important, but more like a giant puzzle piece, a place that held nuggets from the past and confirmations. Ultimately, the things found there only widened the breadth of his plight. Of course, he had taken the most telling pieces of information with him. Pete fished the keys from his pocket and unlocked the car. He reached into the camera bag. As much as he didn't want to look, he needed to see the photos of Esme—the beautiful image of her stretched out like a silent film star on a chaise. The far more disturbing visuals of her bruised face. Turning the photos over, Pete realized the clue—perhaps one he'd left for himself. He read aloud: "'Esmerelda Moon. One year, five months before her death. August 1917.'" And the others: "'Esme. Just to show. January 1919.'"

He rolled his eyes at his own thickheadedness. Two days ago, she was no one but Esme. Now he had a whole name. If Esmerelda Moon existed, maybe her history did too. All these years, it was the first promise of real hope—finding Esme's past. Pete put the photo back. Something else occurred to him. It seemed he had not one, but two ghosts conspiring on his behalf—Brody St John and Zeke Dublin. He mentally rewound the message Zeke had offered at the bungalow: *"It's no carnie sleight of hand. You have to pay attention. If you want your life back. If you want a murder solved."*

What the hell did a dead grifter, far more associated with his mother than Pete, have to do with any of this? He closed the car door. "Holy. Shit." His gaze scanned the sea. "Connected to my mother, but maybe even more connected to his niece. Ailish Montague." He hurried around to the driver's side and got in. "She's more than a bit player in this ghost hunt."

Before backing out of the spot, turning away from the sound, Pete looked once more at the sun-soaked view. The beach his uncle had patrolled, the *"Move it, Soldier"* advice Brody had given. Pete needed to heed it, not just for the sake of the past, but to recover his family in the present. "Thanks," he said. "You may very well have saved two St Johns." Like the lifeguard advised, if you kept driving, you'd run right into New York City.

## Act V, Scene I
## New York City
## September 1917

They drove in the truck from Long Island to the city line. Along the way, Phin shared his news with Esmerelda. By the time they reached the Brooklyn Bridge, the two were silent, Esmerelda mentally floundering with what he'd told her: Phin's number had been called up, along with Hassan's. Tomorrow they'd leave for Camp Upton.

"Camp Upton?" Her emotions had spiraled from the happiest of news to facts she did not want to be true.

"Camp Upton. It's not far from where we were today, out on Long Island—some town called Yaphank. It's the training camp for enlisted men. It's where they teach soldiering, how to fight, win battles."

"How to kill," she said.

"I suppose there'll be that."

After his training, Phin, Hassan, and thousands of other men would board ships like the ones she and Cora had seen, delivering them all to Europe and the conflict that raged. Rally cries had become war cries. Phin and Hassan would answer. So it was silence that dominated as they drove west in the truck of a man whose life had been taken by the war.

The vehicle rumbled to the foot of the bridge, where Oscar and company had agreed to meet them. Phin said one more thing before exiting the truck. "It's you, Esme, I'll be thinking of when I look upward at night. Heaven has its moon, and I'll have mine. No world can exist without either."

Oscar was waiting. His hulking frame appeared slightly less large without his team and wagon. It took Esmerelda's best dramatic performance to hide her joy and upset. But Oscar was too taken by his new vehicle and paid her no mind. As Phin gave him a quick lesson, pointing out the gear pedals and starter button, all-important brakes, and accelerator lever, it was Esmerelda who noticed Cora. She looked a mess, the way she did after her bathhouse duties. But there was something different, and a good whiff piqued Esmerelda's curiosity. The girl didn't smell of piss and lye soap. She smelled of tobacco and whiskey.

"Cora, what did you do?"

Cora only wrapped her arms tighter around herself, tugging on a threadbare shawl. She stared straight ahead. But from her skirt pocket, Cora withdrew the edge of paper money—more than Esmerelda herself had ever carried.

"I earned a decent wage," she said.

Esmerelda's heart pounded harder than it had on the beach. *The Elephant Hotel . . .* She knew instantly the kind of work to which Cora had succumbed. The girl moved away from the group, pulling harder on the shawl, and waited on the bridge's narrow catwalk. Motor vehicles buzzed by, even at the late hour. The boys—Barney, Bill, and Jimmie—offered strange looks but kept mum as they turned for the back of the truck. Oscar was lost in the excitement and a fear of smashing up his new vehicle. He noticed nothing—certainly not the feelings of a girl he saw, at best, as a burden.

Oscar took in the last of his instructions and Cora made an abrupt move. Esmerelda leaped forward, sure she was about to throw herself into the heavy traffic. It turned into a chain reaction as Phin hurled himself in her direction, shouting, "Esme!" He grabbed her, and Esmerelda saw *his* life flash before her eyes. A truck as large as Oscar's nearly clipped him. In turn, Cora looked at them as if they'd lost their minds. She did not thrust herself into the traffic but turned and walked idly toward the truck.

# ACT V, SCENE II

The next day, Esmerelda waited at the alley entrance between Hupp's Supper Club and its new next-door hotel. She'd all but begged Phin to stay the night before; she'd asked to go with him to Hell's Kitchen. He wouldn't consider either.

"It's not proper, Esme," he'd said. "If I'd known what today would bring—me asking for your hand, you saying yes . . ." His forehead pressed to hers. "I would have come a week ago. We could have seen a city preacher today and made tonight a honeymoon." He laughed. "Though I doubt Mr. Hupp would be keen on us making a lovebird's nest out of his hotel room." The deep kiss he'd left her with was meant to suffice. It didn't, not hardly. But if Phin's artistic sensibilities were his flesh, integrity was his bone. She also knew stubbornness claimed a good bit of his mind.

The September air could have been mistaken for mid-August that morning, and the sun seemed to glint off him as he walked toward her now. Over his shoulder was a small sack—all his worldly belongings, she thought. *Except one.* There weren't many words—what could one say in a moment when it was a lifetime they needed? But Phin was quick to maneuver them into the alleyway, where crates were stacked. Tucked beside them, he kissed her like he might never on the open street.

Esmerelda absorbed the feel of his arms, solidly around her. And his eyes, filled with the color of a brewing storm. She looked away, thinking only of the storm for which he was headed. "How . . . do you have any idea how long you'll be gone? Do you stay until the war is over? If you do, I'll start going to church tomorrow, see if any of the saints my mother used to pray to might move things along."

"I don't know. I imagine once the army goes to all the trouble of getting you there, using a man where he's needed . . . as long as he stays a—" He pulled her closer. "I would think until I've been there longer than those ahead of me. It'd only be fair."

Esmerelda's chin quivered, the movement out of sync with the rest of her trembling body. Yesterday, miraculously, everything she wanted seemed to fall at her feet. Today it was a rug being yanked out from under her. She coaxed words from her tight throat, ones that might distract. "Did I tell you?" she said cheerily, pointing to the hotel across the alley. "The lobby has a photographer's studio. In fact, it has several shops. It's a new idea, offering guests merchandise so they don't go miles to spend their money. When I saw the studio, I thought one day you could inquire about a position."

"How, um . . . how did you come by that bit of knowledge, the idea about commerce?"

Esmerelda cast her gaze downward.

"All right. Let's get it out of the way. If we were married, I'm not sure leaving you to sing in Hupp's club or traveling with Oscar is a suitable way of life. But seeing as we aren't married, I can't really say that. 'Course, if you were my wife, the prospects of what I'd be leaving you with are even dimmer." Phin stared at the alley's dirt lane. "A hovel behind a butcher shop in Hell's Kitchen would make you no more than a pauper's better half. So let me be blunt, since we've no time for bush beating. I don't like leaving with circumstances as they are."

Wanting to reassure him, Esmerelda dove at a dubious solution. "I could go home." Her gaze shot from the buttons on his shirt to Phin's face. "I could wire my sister, Hazel. It would get me out of New York. As it is, you've no need to be concerned about Benjamin Hupp, but if it'd ease your mind . . ."

"Have you go back to a house where your brother-in-law considers everything in it his property? Don't be ridiculous."

"It's been nearly three years. Perhaps Lowell has changed, or my resolve has. Who knows, maybe he's gone off to war. I could tell Hazel what he did, why I left."

"You didn't tell her when it happened. You think she'd believe you now? She'd take your word over her husband's—a man bold and unprincipled enough to . . . no, Esme. You won't be going back to New England."

"Then the answer is simple. I'll tell Benjamin I've accepted your proposal. That we're to be married at the first chance. Wouldn't that settle things?"

"It might," he said. "It'll also likely get you booted from the supper club's billing." He held up a hand. "We don't have time to argue your talent versus Hupp's objective. Shun his affections like that and you'll likely be working alongside Cora by week's end."

Esmerelda's mouth clamped shut. He'd meant cleaning bathhouses. Phin would be shocked to learn the depths to which Cora had sunk. Bells from the Church of the Resurrection tolled. Noon. Phin looked over his shoulder. "Hassan will be here any moment. Look, we haven't any time—"

She kissed him—a wanton but tender meeting of lips. It left Esmerelda with no chance to launch into a persuasive argument about how Oscar would find her other work. Conversely, Oscar also wouldn't find much favor if she were to get herself fired from Hupp's or if she were to turn down Benjamin's lucrative offer of Palace billing. With no time to weigh the risks, Esmerelda settled on a lie, meant only to lessen Phin's burdens. "I've had another job offer," she said. "At the Palace."

"The Palace?"

"Yes." She forced a tight smile into her cheeks. "I didn't say anything at first . . . well, because if we were married, you didn't seem to be in agreement about my performing. I believe I'm clear on all the current obstacles. Regardless, one has to earn a living. I see no reason not to accept an offer of employment that would resolve everything for now . . . until you come back. Your focus, Phin. It's the most important thing. It could be the difference between life and death. That said, where's the harm in taking the Palace's offer?"

His expression turned contemplative. Phin let go of her, scrubbing a hand around the back of his neck. "I suspect this is why I've the good sense to marry you, Esmerelda Moon. You're able to sort out the answer to any question in my head." His whole being lightened. He kissed her one last time. She wanted to live in it forever. But as the kiss ended and the embrace held, Hassan was standing at the edge of the alleyway. Time was up and Phin needed to go. He moved to the edge of the alley, their twined gazes the last thing to let go as Phin vanished, for now, from Esmerelda's life.

◆ ◆ ◆

Several days passed. It took that long for Esmerelda to settle herself. It wasn't anything like the shame-filled, haunted feeling with which she'd left home. Then, she'd spent two nights in an old barn only a mile or two from her house. It had taken that much time to gather her wits, the instinct that said she would survive Lowell's attack. This pain was more of a tender ache, mostly tied to Phin leaving, perhaps the slight underbelly of the lie she'd told. The one he'd taken with him to war.

Not unlike when she first set out on her own, Esmerelda left home with fierce determination—even if that determination was all pretense. After the initial wave of melancholy, she decided her most immediate action should be coming clean with Oscar. He'd have good advice, while surely at the same time calculating his commission for accepting a Palace billing. At worst, he'd tell Esmerelda what she already knew: taking Benjamin Hupp up on his offer would tighten the marionette strings.

Surprisingly, Oscar's opinion fell to the middle. "So this is what you want. To marry a boy with nothing, less than the gypsies we look down on?"

"You don't know him, Oscar. I understand that it's money that drives you—"

"It's money that feeds me, girl—all of us." He sighed heavily, a sure indication he was irritated but also working the problem. "So why not fall back in with the troupe? Thanks to the truck, I've got a new plan for this winter. We'll get out of New York, head south."

"Oscar, why is it the draft doesn't find you or the boys?"

He smiled. "If it gets much worse, we'll likely sign ourselves up. As it is, I'm not sure Mr. Wilson's army is a good fit for Barney or Bill. That and it's difficult to draft men with no permanent address." He chuckled, folding his husky arms. "But I'm not the point. You are. I'm already negotiating dates south of here. New Orleans has a fine theater district, riverboats, and—"

"I can't go to New Orleans. I have to stay here. This is where Phin will expect to find me."

Oscar spit a wad of tobacco harder and farther than she'd ever seen. "This is why I've no use for permanent things. Women being one of them. I can't conceive of a one that'd make me put down stakes."

"One day you might."

Oscar didn't continue that argument but listened intently as Esmerelda went on to explain her motivation. "If I have a contract with the Palace, I'd no longer be in Benjamin's employ. Isn't that better than the situation I have now, beholden to the supper club?"

"And when Hupp learns you've accepted another man's offer of marriage, you don't think that will change his willingness to follow through?"

"I've considered that. I suspect Benjamin would rescind his offer quicker than you'd run from a good woman." He started to agree, but the rest of her strategy silenced him. "So what I'm wondering is how much worse do you think things would be if I don't tell Benjamin about Phin. Not until I secure an audience at the Palace, let my talents speak for me?"

Oscar snickered. "Fancy yourself pretty clever, don't you, Miss Moon?" He considered her plan before carving an answer out of experience. "There's only enough age between us, Esmerelda, that you couldn't be more than my younger sister." He leaned against the truck, tapping his knuckles against the shiny black paint, his newly adorned bright yellow advertisement: *Oscar Bodette's Traveling Extravaganza*. "If I'd had a younger sister, I couldn't care more for her well-being than I do yours. The last thing I'd want is for that sister to end up in a spot like Cora."

"Like Cora?" Apparently Oscar had also discovered Cora's new line of work. Esmerelda was regretful. In her own commotion, she'd so far neglected Cora's fateful choice.

"I'm not sure who was more shocked when we spied one another at the Elephant."

"What are you going to do about it?"

His wide shoulders shifted. "The girl's made her bed, so to speak. She won't be climbing back into my truck."

"Oh, that's fine, Oscar. You'll sleep with whores, but you—"

"Won't have one in my troupe," he said, speaking louder than she did. "That's the way of it, Esmerelda. I'm not interested in your thoughts. It's not my job to keep her . . . *decent*. You all make your own decisions—Barney, Bill . . . Jimmie. There are things I'll tolerate. Things I don't see as a choice." Esmerelda guessed this was in reference to Barney and Bill's unorthodox relationship. "Other ways of life are just that. It's no more than wantin' out from scrubbin' toilets. Cora's not my concern any longer." He removed his derby hat, tapping the brim against the thigh of his thick leg. "I'm only sharing this much because I want you to realize that I see precarious choices. You're about to make your own. Because it's you, I'll do what I can to keep your secrets from sinking you. But I'll also warn you. You're about to roll the dice in a chancy game. My advice is to keep your eyes on your lie while saying a prayer."

"What is it I should pray for?"

"Pray for a short war. Pray that Hupp remains the gentleman."

"Which thing do you think has a better chance of coming to pass?"

"I should say war, but for your sake, I'll say the gentleman."

Phin was gone no more than ten days and Esmerelda had already written him three times. Before writing a fourth letter, she approached Benjamin. That morning's frost appeared like a stage cue, alerting her to the movement of time. She hadn't seen Benjamin in recent days—not in attendance during any shows. But she did catch him one afternoon in the supper club lobby. In an attempt to get his attention, Esmerelda lightly touched his coat. It was hard not to notice the smooth fabric, well-crafted fit. She asked if he'd been ill, and her concern was true enough.

"Ill?" He shook his head, looking detached from his usual buoyant self. "No. I've not been ill. I've been inside my hotel suite, looking out the windows . . . thinking." His nostrils flared with the breath he drew. If his deep dimples hadn't emerged, she might have felt uneasy. "War and business. Both have kept me occupied. Did you miss me at your performances?"

Her hesitation equaled his. "I surely noticed you weren't on hand." The afternoon crowd continued to filter out, squeezing them into a tight corner. She nodded and waved to a few patrons, all of them complimenting her performance. Esmerelda was mindful of Oscar's warning and literally kept her eyes on Benjamin. "You mentioned the war. Has your number come up?"

"It's been delayed, but only for a short time. I suspect I'll be in the thick of it soon." His dimples vanished. "Would that bother you, Esmerelda, if I were sent to the front line?"

"Of course. I don't want to see any of our boys in a war, much less on the front line."

"I see."

"I'm praying for all of you."

"I've no doubt about that."

Silence, marked by the rest of the buzzing lobby, grew. "I was wondering." There was no way to proceed without at least returning his smile. "Weeks ago, you mentioned billing at the Palace. Would that still be a possibility?"

"The Palace?" His dark eyebrows encroached on one another as if he didn't recall the offer. Benjamin's gaze moved over her and the white, beaded gown she wore. He'd insisted on the gown, explaining that the demureness of white better suited the ladies' groups that attended afternoon shows. He'd been openly bedazzled the first time Esmerelda had performed wearing it.

Esmerelda didn't care to agree with Benjamin, but she could not argue. It was a beautiful gown. It had the most exquisite fitted bodice and long organza sleeves, the tight cuff connecting to a finger loop on each hand, pearly beads delicately threaded to connect gown to fingertips. Clearly, the gown was on his mind too.

"I simply knew that dress was made for you. Naturally, you look fetching in everything, but that gown in particular. I do so . . . *love you in it.*"

She nearly changed her mind. Benjamin's words wafted uncomfortably into her ears, made her breath rattle. Oscar and the boys were heading off in the truck for New Orleans that evening. She had time to catch them. He'd booked dates that would take them right through the coldest months. Surely he could squeeze a singer onto the bill. But

Esmerelda couldn't do it; she couldn't go that far away. Mail was so erratic. What if Phin returned and she was nowhere to be found?

"The Palace," Benjamin was saying.

His dimples materialized again. She reasoned it out: a man with such sweet dimples couldn't have an unkind heart.

"You hadn't mentioned it. It interests you?"

"It does. I'm sorry it's taken so long for me to reply. I'm very interested—in playing the Palace."

"In that case . . ." His smile broadened and she thought maybe his heart swelled. "I'd love to help you out, Esmerelda. I'm certain something can be arranged."

# CHAPTER TWENTY

*New York City*
*Present Day*

Sitting in the rental car, Pete squinted up into stingy pieces of sky, century-old Midtown buildings surrounding him. It was like being trapped inside a tin can, even with the AC running full blast. He was accustomed to hot places, he was well versed in busy cities, but he'd never been a fan of New York. Honestly? He'd be more comfortable crouched in a tank, trekking across the Thal Desert. He'd always suspected his New York uneasiness connected to Esme.

Traffic moved in spurts, and on his drive into Manhattan, he'd reasoned through his options. He could dive right into a search for the long-dead Esme or attempt to enlist the help of Ailish Montague. She might label his quest absurd, but Pete went with his gut—that Ailish would be willing to listen. Regardless, the problem with both women was the same. How the hell would he find either one?

A cab darted from a tight spot, and Pete slammed on his brakes, setting off a chain reaction of blaring horns. Mercifully, moving fast in tight spots was part of his job. He parallel parked, snug and smooth as a snail in its shell. He got out of the car and began with obvious Internet routes: Google and the white pages, other people-searching sites. There was the option of a deeper Internet quest for a fifty-dollar fee. It was too creepy. He passed. He kept at it. "She's an actress, shouldn't she have a website?" he said to himself. PressCorp had been urging him for years to get one. Nothing came up for Ailish Montague. Pete couldn't locate her through the NYU alumni site or even find a Facebook page. Almost every "Ailish" he came across lived in Cork or Kilkenny.

Pete glanced up; a wider patch of blue domed. "Hey, Uncle Zeke, I heard you ran the tables back in the day. I don't suppose dropping me the numbers for her phone occurred to you?" There was nothing. "Thanks. All you ghosts are the same. Show up when *you* want something."

At least he knew she lived in Manhattan—excluding four other boroughs was a plus. Her mother. He could call Nora Montague. But attempts to locate her proved equally futile, unlisted and unfindable. He guessed having one family member in jail for killing another might drive you under the radar. His own mother—she could get to Ailish's mother. His thumb hovered over "Favorites" on his phone and the very few contacts it held. The aching pit returned to his stomach. He wondered if the first thing his mother had done, after expelling him, was change their phone numbers or block his. No. Calling home wasn't an option. Not until he could assure his mother there was a reason to let him back in.

Pete turned in a tight circle; the island around him seemed overwhelming. He tapped his knuckles on the car hood. *Kimball . . .* Ailish said that Kimball Studios had arranged an audition for her, the one that she'd missed. Another Google search produced good information: Kimball Studios, a prominent acting school. A solid lead, but Pete would need a ruse. Kimball Studios wasn't going to hand over a name or address because he asked. Although surely anxious acting students could be enticed. He texted Flagler.

I'm in NY. I'll shoot the One Direction concert. I'll need
credentials.

While he waited for a reply text, Pete took a chance and googled
Esmerelda Moon, not terribly surprised when search engines turned up
nothing. His phone pinged with Flagler's reply. The editorial desk would
have credentials waiting. Pete drove to a parking garage near the Press-
Corp office. Once there, he picked up the official concert pass, adding
it to his general press authorization, and looped both around his neck.
Before heading to Kimball Studios, he hit the restroom. Pete splashed
cold water on his face and finger combed his hair. He supposed the scruff
was fashionable; the wrinkled polo would have to do. Before looking
away from the mirror, Pete took a genetic inventory—physically, he
saw Levi. Pete's eyes and the more curious parts were all his mother. He
missed them both already. There was an acute difference between travel
for work—hell, wasn't that in Pete's blood too?—and being banished
from his parents' lives.

Blocks later, he was inside the doors of Kimball Studios. "Hi!" It
came out of his mouth overly cheery, startling the girl at the front desk.
"I'm Pete St John."

"Good for you." She cracked a piece of gum and continued to scroll
through her phone. "We don't take walk-ins." She slapped a sheet of
paper on the counter. "Submit your application by snail mail or online,
include head shots and a bio, plus a personal mission statement about
why you want to be an actor." She finally offered him a fast glance.
"Hint. Don't start with 'I've dreamed about this my whole life.' You
and about two million other people in this city."

"You don't understand. I'm with PressCorp." He flashed the credentials in her face. "I'm covering a One Direction surprise reunion
concert."

"A surprise One Direction reunion concert?" He had her attention.
"You're kidding."

"Hence the 'surprise' part." Pete finger quoted the air as he spoke. "PressCorp is covering it for . . ." He had no idea why they would cover it. Pete clung to his smile and swept his hand past her. "Shampoo. One Direction is doing a series of shampoo print ads. And toothpaste," he hurriedly added. "Procter & Gamble spread. Huge."

She crinkled her brow.

"Anyway . . . my crew, they're outside." He pointed to the busy Manhattan street. "We need some crowd talent. One Direction management was supposed to have this all set, but somebody screwed up royally. My managing editor can e-mail you a complete list of what we're looking for." Pete picked up a business card. "Should I have him send the details here?"

"I guess, but usually—"

"Great." He pretended to punch Kimball's contact info into his phone. "Since I'm here, I happen to know they want a few redheads. Redheads, they, uh . . . they shoot well with the band." He was unsure if the statement made sense but continued to embellish. "From a photographic standpoint, the saturation level and contrast of redheads with the time of day, live and photo-shopped backgrounds are most amenable to print."

The receptionist looked at him queerly.

"Do you have anybody like that . . . handy? Redheads? Girls."

"Redheads?" She folded her arms. "Girls?"

"Yeah. The band's management wanted a safety net, in case there's not much of a crowd."

She laughed. "Fascinating. The last guy like you wanted Asian girls only. Listen, if One Direction were having a 'surprise concert'"—this time she finger quoted the air—"they wouldn't need *extras* to do the drooling and gaping. We get our share of scammers in here. Guys just looking for . . . you know." She grabbed at his ID. "I suggest you hit the road, Peter St John of PressCorp, ID number TAB-147—if any of that is even real—before I call security."

He left, assured his foreign investigative skills did not lend themselves to American pop culture. Pete leaned against the outside of the building, staying out of the receptionist's sight lines. He was formulating a plan B when the door to Kimball Studios swung open. A small group walked past, talking and laughing. From them, a single laugh stood out. "Ailish!"

They stopped—two other girls, one guy. "Pete. What are you doing here?"

"Trying to find you." He looked at her friends. The girls looked like pipe cleaners with arms, their features photo ready. In fact, he thought no two girls could have noses that perfect or cheekbones that high.

"Ailish, who's this?" The guy was commanding, like he'd just come from Leading Man class.

"This is Pete St John. I mentioned him from my trip out east."

"Right. The Lucy car debacle." He and the pipe-cleaner girls laughed. "Can't say Caroline didn't warn you." He extended a hand to Pete. "Topher Richards. This is Zamara Witherspoon."

"Distant cousin," she said.

"To what?" Pete asked. The threesome laughed again.

"And Evangeline Aires." He motioned to the third girl. "What brings you into Manhattan?"

"Her." He pointed at Ailish. "I need to talk to you."

"Why?" The question came from Ailish, and Pete started to answer. The curious stares and breadth of his mission stopped him, the possibility that her friends might intervene. Then Pete had a much simpler idea. He flashed the press credentials at them. "Would you all like to go to a concert?"

◆ ◆ ◆

It worked. The inside track and press credentials swayed Ailish's friends, who were standing up front near a Times Square stage, rapt when

One Direction stepped out. The receptionist was right; the crowd was instantly elbow to elbow, the noise earsplitting. One girl fainted on sight.

After a moment to gain his bearings, Pete went to work. He needed to turn something in to Flagler. Ailish's friends proved useful as props, and he fired off about ten shots per second in burst mode. The band was only into their second number when Pete felt confident he'd captured enough images to satisfy PressCorp's needs. He leaned over, asking Ailish if she wanted to get out of there. She pointed to her ear, indicating she couldn't hear him.

She'd been smiling, clapping along with the music. But as they looked at one another, her expression turned solemn. She grabbed Pete's hand and started guiding him away from the stage. He read her lips: "Let's go." When she took his hand, the powerful noise was reduced to garbled background music—the overpowering sound you'd hear if standing near an ocean, everything swallowed by its roar.

Pete took the lead and she followed, a serpentine escape through blocks of crazed fans, past police barricades and other media. Surreal as it was, above the mania, Pete heard only his footsteps and hers. He held tighter to her hand, and a bond that exceeded not getting lost in a crowd was evident. Pedestrian noise filtered back in when they reached the street corner, and he stopped.

"Can we go somewhere?" Looking around, he saw nothing, not a café or green space. Almost anywhere in Europe they would have tripped over both. "I need to tell you—"

"I live that way." She pointed northeast. "Do you want to come to my apartment?"

He nodded. "Yes."

They didn't speak, walking down one block and up the next. She was holding his hand now, showing him the way. They moved deeper into a catacomb of buildings. After the seventh or eighth block, Pete had to stop. He bent at the waist. "Wait." Nausea wove through him, the sun blistering. Ailish turned. Her face didn't look overheated. She just looked anxious. "Sorry," he said, feeling like a fine example of a weakling. "It was a long night before I even got to today—which hasn't been short . . . or easy."

He thought how fast she'd run if he confessed the day's agenda: tossed from his parents' lives, contemplating suicide, and a verbal exchange with his dead uncle. Pete stood straight and a curious addendum occurred to him. They both had dead uncles who wanted in on their fates.

Earthly smells distracted him. Pete and Ailish stood outside a Greek deli, the scents from which only stirred his nausea.

"Wait here a second," she said.

Ailish went in the deli as Pete recalled her ravenous appetite. If she came back with a gyro and today's baklava, he'd lose it all over the sidewalk. In anticipation, he eyed a sewer drain. Thankfully, she returned with only a bottle of water.

"Here. And give me the camera equipment to carry. We have a few more blocks to go."

"I'm fine." But he did take the water from her. "Thank you. I've got the equipment. You don't need to carry it."

She smiled at him. "Forever the hero."

Pete stopped drinking and swiped the back of a hand across his mouth. "Me? What does that—"

"Come on. I'm starting to wilt out here too."

Finally they reached a building fronted by brick steps and a wrought iron rail, a wide awning, and planted urns. It was more upscale than he'd expected. Definitely in a part of the city he didn't imagine she could afford. Ailish buzzed them in. The elevator delivered them to the third floor, and she retrieved a key from her cloth purse. Ailish and her accessories appeared more hippy than the designer ensembles her two friends wore. The back of her red head faced him, the thin cotton top she wore sticking to her. A glimpse of a small tattoo peeked out from between her strappy shirt and thick hair. He couldn't make out the symbol. "Just out of curiosity," he said, "is your roommate home?"

With the key in the lock, her hand froze. He realized how it sounded. "I mean, what I want to talk to you about is private. The lobby's fine if she's home. I saw a sofa down there. No people."

The space was tight, the hallway dim and hot. Ailish turned and leaned her head against the door. "Caroline isn't home. But here is fine. Just come in."

Pete assumed it was trust by association, their mothers having known each other for years. He followed, but he also fought the urge to warn her. She shouldn't be so inviting, even if the guy wasn't a complete stranger. The inside of the apartment caught him off guard—cool air and ultramodern decor, though it was New York tiny. It was a mix of glass and stainless steel, the small sofa in the living room covered in expensive-looking white leather.

"It's all Caroline's."

"You mentioned that her father footed the bill."

"For everything, including her taste. To be honest, I'm roommate number four or five."

"So, easy to get along with." He found himself smiling. "Got it."

"The rent is dirt cheap—Caroline's okay. Just used to having her own way. It feels more like I rent a bedroom, have kitchen privileges. Do you want to sit?"

He did, though a Siamese cat eyed him from the sofa, spitting before it darted away. "Hello to you too." Ailish busied herself in the kitchen and he tried to keep conversation going. "I'm guessing the cat belongs to your roomie."

"How did you know?" She was getting ice from the freezer, filling glasses at the sink.

Once she settled onto the sofa, silence took over. On their journey through the city, they hadn't talked beyond lefts and rights, and silence slipped to awkwardness. For a second, Pete considered leaving. *"Sorry—this was a mistake. I shouldn't drag you into my mess . . ."*

He imagined how everything would hit her ears. And it would have to be everything. Then Pete thought of his mother's declaration and his own need to break from the vicious cycle of his life. Pete squeezed his fist and stared at his hand. The photos of a battered Esme stood out in his mind; so did her newer ethereal presence. Motivation had definitely been piqued.

Ailish smiled uneasily and placed her glass on a coaster. Pete held on to his, the coolness soothing on his blistered fingers. "So," he said. "I guess you're wondering what this is all about."

"To a point. When I left you back in East Marion, I had a feeling I'd see you again."

"Did you?" He hesitated when she didn't expound. "Sorry. What I have to say, I don't know how it will go over. I'm also not exactly sure why I need to tell you."

"Then I guess it's best to get on with it. See where we end up."

She was being more cryptic than he was, and this made him curious. It also helped, and Pete started an arduous story that began with a war, his profound knowledge of things a boy of six, then ten, shouldn't know. The age of twelve took longer to convey. Pete talked about his kidnapping, moving quickly past her uncle's involvement. He detailed the injections of propofol and how Pete and his parents viewed this as a trigger, opening his mind to even deeper encounters. "My parents and I, we've agreed for years that this all comes down to some form of . . . *reincarnation.*" He anticipated a snigger, maybe an outright belly laugh. There was a reason he didn't bring it up at dinner parties—if he went to dinner parties.

Ailish drew a long, low breath. "These are dreams."

"No. Not hardly. Not at all. We suspect my psychic gift allows me to unveil or . . ." He slowed down. This is where he drew the crazy look. "Best we can determine is my gift allows me to enter a past life that would otherwise remain hidden to the average person."

She held up a hand. "Whoa. I was with you until time travel. So . . . black holes, wormholes . . . string theory, is that where we're headed?"

Pete stopped talking and stared at his sneakers, feeling like a guest star on the set of *Doctor Who*. But skepticism was understandable. Having studied numerous time-travel theories, Pete honestly didn't buy into any of them either—at least, he did not perceive them to be the explanation that applied to him.

But because he also couldn't shake the feeling that Ailish wasn't simply *any person*, Pete countered, "Einstein himself professed that time is an illusion. Relative, 'it can vary for different observers.' Let me, uh . . . let me show you something." Cautiously, Pete pulled up the edge of his shirt, poking at the knot of flesh in his abdomen, revealing multiple scars. "I can't explain any of them. Not in a way that can be defined by the things we know or accept. But it seems, I am that observer."

She considered the visible marks from another life but said nothing.

"Obviously, I can't prove the origin of what you see. And it's asking a lot for someone to believe these scars aren't the aftermath of my present-day war zone encounters."

Her questioning expression didn't shift.

"I do have documented blood work from years ago. There are antibodies in my blood that belong to an eradicated strain of influenza and even traces of a crude tetanus vaccine." He paused, giving her a moment to rebuff him. "So . . . what the world would label impossible, the St John household attributes to another life—one I lived about a hundred years ago." Conveying deeper facts to someone he barely knew, Pete felt stripped bare. He exhaled the breath he'd been holding. "Are you ready to toss me curbside?"

She tucked a piece of wavy red hair behind her ear. "Is there more?"

He was taken aback. It seemed like that should be enough. "Well, like I said, the drug from the kidnapping, it had an uncanny effect. Not only did it widen whatever portal I have access to, it triggered other . . . events."

"Events?"

"Another person."

"What sort of . . . *person*?"

"A woman. After the propofol episode, I began to experience profound visions . . ."

"Or visits."

Her acceptance surprised him. "Yes. Since that time, I've experienced a deep loop of recurrent visits. They all involve the same person, a single sequence of events . . . and outcome."

She shifted on the sofa, the leather crunching beneath her.

"Her name is Esme. And I . . ." Pete ran a hand through his hair. "She meant . . . *means* a great deal to me." He was back to staring, her hazel eyes doing the same. Hell, if it were all in reverse, if this were Ailish Montague's story, he might have quit at the kidnapping part of the tale. Of course, she wasn't entirely removed from the things he said. With the visit from Zeke, she'd had her own vague taste of the ethereal and enigmatic. Verbally, he trod forward.

"The thing is, I believe Esme is someone I loved very much in that other life."

"Esme." The way she repeated her name, it sounded like she was trying it on.

"She was beautiful and fiery. Hair," he said, his hand coming forward of its own volition, almost touching hers, "shades lighter than yours. Until recently, I didn't know much else about her. What I felt . . . feel for her drives a lot of emotion. That and . . . well, the one episode I continue to relive."

"You're saying she doesn't appear like an apparition."

He shook his head. "That's the thing, much of what's frustrated me for years. There's a distinct divide between Esme and the war versus present-day spiritual entities. There were no ghosts connected to her or that period. Not until recently."

Pete explained how this trip home had prompted something new. That Esme's spirit had spoken, been present, even if it was ever so brief. "And then there's the house."

"The one in East Marion."

"That's where memories and ghosts started to collide. I can connect certain objects inside that house to my other life: the saddle and the truck. The postcard and the beach you were on last summer. The one you photographed."

Having reached the part where Zeke's niece seemed to play a part, Pete opened the camera bag and inside zipper. He withdrew the post-card. "I visited a place called Walberswick a couple of years ago. It's in England. While there, I created some images similar to this one." He handed her the old postcard, his mother's ghost gift.

"*When I spent two weeks on this beach, I didn't dream of you then. E.M.*" She didn't move, other than the bob that swam through her throat. "Interesting coincidence."

"What you said to me outside the bungalow, the phrasing on the card?"

"I was thinking more about the initials."

"E.M. Esme. Actually, Esmerelda Moon. That's her name."

Ailish's hazel irises looked into his. "And the same initials as mine."

"Yours? How so?"

"When I introduced myself at the bungalow, I said my given name—you didn't catch it?" He shook his head. "Ailish is my stage name. My agent, Kimball Studios, thought it had better cachet."

He furrowed his brow.

"It's my middle name. Everybody—well, everybody who's not Topher or Evangeline or looking to hire me . . ." She fidgeted. "Everyone else, my parents, friends from home, they call me Em." She made eye contact with Pete. "My name, it's *Emerald* Ailish Montague."

# CHAPTER TWENTY-ONE

Pete had no chance to respond to her bombshell. The apartment door opened and he startled as if being woken from a dream. A woman dressed in high heels and attitude slinked forward, a shopping bag hung from each arm. She stopped, hooking a finger around the bridge of her trendy sunglasses and drawing them down her thin nose. "Oh. You didn't say anything about company."

"Caroline." Ailish . . . *Emerald* stood. "I ran into . . . an old friend of the family. This is Pete St John."

She removed the glasses, looking him over. "You're from Vegas too?"

Pete glanced back. She wasn't model ready, unlike Ailish's other friends. Tiny brown eyes and fine hair, features that rendered as unremarkable. She had wide ears and wore a form-fitting red dress.

"I'm stereotyping," Caroline went on, "but who's really *from Vegas*, right?" She laughed. "Other than Em, of course."

The use of Ailish's given name made Pete pay attention, and her roommate kept right on going.

"Personally, I'm not sure there's such a thing as 'Vegas roots.' It's not like my family. We can document our lineage all the way to my father's great-grandmother—New Yorkers through and through."

"Well, I'm not from Vegas."

It was like he hadn't said a word.

"That's where I get my performance gene. My great-great-grand-mother was in vaudeville. Did Em mention I'm in *Wicked*? That said, I'd love to chat, but I have—"

"Call is at six."

Ailish . . . Emerald, the way she spoke, Pete could see her teeth grit a bit.

"I'll need to meditate—in here."

Em pointed to a door so narrow, surely it violated the fire code. "We can go to my room."

Caroline grabbed a bottle of Hildon from the refrigerator and brushed by them, turning as she talked. "I simply can't break from my routine. Broadway expects your best every night!"

They exchanged places, Pete reaching for his camera bag, which she nearly sat on.

"If the two of you can keep it down. Noise is terribly disruptive to the creative process." And with that she turned on the television.

Pete glanced back at the roommate but followed Em. She shut the bedroom door and they were in total darkness. "What the . . . ?"

"Hang on." A twinkling rope of lights lit, outlining the minuscule space.

At least he could see her. "Are you sure you're not roommate four or five hundred?"

"You get what you pay for, and Caroline is what I can afford."

"I think I'd rather get a room at the Y."

"I checked. They won't rent you one long-term. Anyway, $400 a month is unheard of in this city. I get to live in Manhattan, in a place that my parents don't worry about."

"That much I can understand." The television volume rose and Pete thumbed over his shoulder. "I thought she was going to meditate?"

"Caroline thinks she meditates. Translation, three hours of binge-watching *Dexter*."

"So a total slave to her craft." He looked at the wall separating them. Then he looked back at her. Pete let the irritating roommate go and refocused. "Okay, so tell me which name you go by. Ailish or Emerald?"

"I'll answer to either—or at least I'm trying to. But people who really know me, they call me Em. Caroline does because . . . well, it keeps me tied to my Vegas roots, and you see how much she gets off on stirring the pot."

"Em," he said.

"Em," she repeated, as if it were permission.

Pete turned away from her and nearly collided with a wall. With no window, it felt like a walk-in closet and surely smaller than his parents'.

But the room was more than tight quarters. It was like a time capsule. The rest of the apartment was all Caroline. But this space was Em, and Pete felt as if he would have known it anywhere. It was Bohemian and bold, even in semidarkness, with swags of printed fabric hanging from the ceiling and an old leather-armed daybed as the only real piece of furniture. Stacked books served as a table. Above it was a low-hanging fluorescent light, and Em turned it on, providing a life source for a row of small potted plants. Where there wasn't draping fabric, sketches were tacked to the walls, nudes and costumed figures. They fascinated his photographer's eye. "You drew all these?"

"There's no cable in my room. Internet is spotty." She picked up a tiny mister, spraying the plants. "I spend a lot of time in here."

"I'll bet you do." He continued to take in the tight but busy space. Aside from eclectic, the room was a slight mess. Em shuffled by folded clothes stacked on the floor, and he looked away as she plucked three bras from a stretch of white string. It ran from the edge of one swag and was tacked to the outer wall in clothesline fashion.

"Sorry. Yesterday was laundry day."

Pete forced in a deep breath. "There's not a fireplace behind one of these walls, is there?"

"What?"

"Nothing."

The narrow bed was unmade, and she threw the covers up, attempting to straighten the tangle of sheets. He thought maybe it was the surprise of an unexpected guest, but it looked more like fidgety nerves, maybe the things he'd told her so far. The photo album Em had taken from the bungalow sat on a vintage steamer trunk, along with a mug, an empty yogurt container, and a script.

"I'd say it's usually not such a mess in here, but that'd be a lie." She turned toward him. "I haven't told you one yet."

"Neither have I." *Of course, I haven't gotten to the worst part either . . .*

She pointed to the daybed. Unless their location was an elevator, it seemed awkward to remain standing, and Pete wondered if he should have insisted on the lobby. Yet the room seeped into his senses, and Pete sat on one end of the daybed. Em sat at the other, pulling a throw pillow onto her lap. The postcard remained in her hand.

"So you see how it's almost the same," Pete noted, "what you said to me at the bungalow. *I spent two weeks on this beach . . .*"

"I agree. I also forgot I said that to you, my exact words. But now, seeing the postcard . . ." She looked from the card to him. "At the time, my remark was just flip. Now it doesn't seem so . . ."

"Random?"

"Something like that."

A closet was located opposite the bed. She kept glancing toward it, the same way Pete had looked again and again at the old barn. While Em's gaze was on alert, her body relaxed, sinking farther into the corner of the daybed. Pete sat in almost a military pose, acutely tuned in to the things he was beginning to fear about himself.

"I agree that what I said about the beach was more than coincidence. But I'm not sure what you want from me."

He reached for the camera bag and slipped his hand inside—carefully. The picture of Esme was room temperature. "To start with, I want to show you this." He withdrew the beautiful black-and-white photo. "It's Esme." They traded paper images.

"Esme," she said, the pitch in her voice rising. "She's pretty—delicate."

He glanced between Em and the photograph. The two women didn't favor each other physically—Esme so fair and fragile, but maybe that was her pose on the chaise, the deadly memory in his mind. Em's presence was more in line with her personality: bold, verbose, striking. She ran her fingers, blunt-tip nails, over the embossed corner of the picture.

"Royal Photography, NYC. They did good work." Her nervous smile flickered at Pete. "Can't imagine what a portfolio shot like this would cost nowadays." She turned over the photograph. "'Esmerelda Moon. One year, five months before her death. August 1917.' Wow. That's, uh . . . so she died, this Esmerelda Moon—and so young?"

"She did. When I was going through the rolltop desk, I found that photo in a different album."

"Is that why you freaked out when I touched it? You didn't want me to see it. Why?"

"Not because of that photo." Pete reached into the camera bag again. "These are the pictures I didn't want you to see." He held the strip out to her.

"Oh my God. How incredibly awful." After absorbing the front, she turned it over. "'Esme. Just to show. January 1919.' Who would do this to her, and why would they photograph—" Her gaze shot from the images to Pete's. "Wait. You don't think you . . . ?"

He tried to shuffle farther down the bed, but Pete was already pinned to the footboard. "I have no memory of it. I don't relive doing that to her." He said this as if in defense, pointing to the raw images. "But I am positive I took those photos—believe me, I recognize my work and handwriting." On the steamer trunk were a pen and pad of paper. He picked them up and wrote Esmerelda's name in cursive.

"Oh geez. It's . . ."

"Identical."

She nodded, and Pete sucked in a breath, his smaller confession coming on the exhale: "It only seems logical that I'm also the one who . . ." He hesitated. "Did that to her."

Em didn't say anything, but she sat up tall, her surprised look saying, *"Maybe we should have gone to the lobby."*

"Add it to other things I've learned in recent days. I know Esme's whole name and where that photo was taken. I know the month of her death, the year. And now I know her ghost—something that never occurred prior to this trip home. I need to figure it out, the specifics."

"Have you tried googling her?"

"Actually, yes. Unless you're interested in larger period events, like the sinking of the *Titanic* or the crash of twenty-nine, the Internet isn't very useful."

"I see your point. But why would you need me for any search pertaining to Esmerelda Moon?" It sounded more like a challenge than a question.

Pete didn't have an answer for her, just an instinct. He also knew he was holding out on the worst part of his story.

He was quiet and Em continued to stress her lack of relevancy. "I'm not like you, Pete. I don't see the past or the dead. I'm just a girl trying to make it as an actress in New York."

"Maybe," he said softly. "Or maybe you're a puzzle piece. A big one."

"Okay, forget me for a second. Explain your theory. You must have one. In your past life, why do you think you would have . . ." She held out the photo, avoiding the words. "Done this to Esmerelda Moon?"

"There are the go-to reasons, hot temper, jealousy, an out-of-control fight. But more recently . . . well, I'm starting to think a different theory plays into my actions."

"And that would be?"

"PTSD. Something I've seen in my travels as a photojournalist. Something a soldier from World War I might have suffered." He paused. She continued to stare, willing words from his mouth. "A condition and mind-set that isn't absent from my present-day life."

"How so?"

"When I return from visitant episodes, the reentry is always shrouded in violence . . . out of control."

She bit down on a thumbnail, her fair brow knotting. "And your new evidence, the postcard and me, that's the only thing linking your past life to me?"

"Well . . . yes." While Pete believed that Em was somehow connected, he couldn't quite put his finger on her persistence—like there was more. "Look, I'm a fairly solitary creature—someone who lives with so many ghosts, it doesn't make me a good candidate for most relationships. And that's okay. I have my work. Up until this morning, I had my parents."

Em clutched the toss pillow tighter. "What did you do to them?"

Pete ran two fingers across his forehead; her grim conclusion made him shudder. Was she really so far off? "Nothing. They're fine." He thought it prudent to skip over his father's bruised jaw. "It's more about . . . let me try this from a different angle. It's always been my belief that my mother's presence, her gift—combined with mine— aggravates my proclivity to venture into a past life."

"Spontaneous human combustion, less the fire."

"Of the most unusual sort. Earlier today, it was a pure shock to the system when my mother finally agreed." Pete paused. "My father wasn't exactly on board, but my mother and I concluded that removing myself from their lives is the only realistic solution, unless . . ."

"Unless what?"

"Unless I can fix it—my past. Until now, I've managed my past life by running, mostly into present-day war zones. It wasn't the greatest plan." A false smile rode his face. "Whatever gets you through the night, right? I never imagined the thing that would push me over the edge, make me seek the whole truth, would be losing my family." Pete's voice cracked in a way he hadn't heard since he was thirteen. "It can't be the answer. There has to be a greater purpose to everything I've endured—*if I want my life back. If I want a murder solved,*" he said, paraphrasing her uncle's words.

Apprehension turned to concern. Em shuffled from her end of the mattress to his. Her hand folded over Pete's, and he felt the connection again, something beyond conventional touch.

"I don't believe I can alter the past. But if I could find closure, maybe at least the past stops showing up." He looked at the floor. "I might get my family back. Maybe I figure out how to keep from turning into the man . . . *monster* who did that."

Em started and stopped several sentences. "You said you only relive one scene with Esme. What happens there?"

"It, uh . . . it takes place in a single room. It's both surreal and vivid." As he spoke, Em's hand had stayed tight around his. "Objects are a big part of what I see, but my point of view is limited."

"Okay, so tell me about the things in the room, if that's an easier place to start."

He nodded, guessing this was her psych-educated NYU persona talking. "There's an English painting over the mantel. Then a cat and a clothesline. The clothesline goes from the window to the bedpost." He pointed to the one Em had fashioned. "There's a mirror—I see my own eyes, look right into them after I . . ." He couldn't say it, taking a cowardly detour. "The doll. Of course. I almost forgot to tell you about the doll."

On the benign mention of a doll, Em let go of his hand. Anxiety shifted from him to her. She spoke slowly, a question she didn't want to ask. "What, um . . . what doll?"

Pete shrugged at the memory he considered least offensive. "In the room, there's a china doll on a chair. Another reminder of who Esme was, or just a thing she loved. I say that because I don't have the same feeling of attachment about the cat. But the doll." He sighed. "I know how much the doll meant to Esme."

Em catapulted from the bed, abrupt enough to make Pete stand too. In one step, she was at the closet. She opened the door to a narrow hole, as jam-packed as the room—clothes, a pile of shoes at the bottom. But it was an upper shelf she reached for. Turning, she held a china-faced doll that he recognized. His mouth gaped, though air stopped moving in or out of him.

"The doll doesn't belong to Esme, Pete. She belongs to me."

# CHAPTER
# TWENTY-TWO

Pete had seen the doll hundreds of times, maybe a thousand. He'd know the doll anywhere. But Pete had never touched the china-faced doll, and he was cautious. He wasn't sure if it was a ghost gift that had fallen into the wrong hands, or even more unlikely, if it rested in the hands of the rightful owner. Em cradled the doll; it wore the layered gown, though admittedly it was yellowed. Its pleated bonnet was as he'd seen it, bowed under the doll's chin. The lashes looked real, and the glass of her aqua eyes was like a crystal ball, so telling.

He imagined the sight couldn't resonate more if Em held a real infant that belonged to him. Pointing a shaking finger at it, Pete quickly retracted his hand. His throat went dry and his mind dizzied. "Where . . . where did you get that?"

"My uncle. Zeke gave her to me when I was five or six. Being she was an antique, he impressed upon me how valuable she was. Every time I saw him, he'd ask if I was taking care of her. Kind of an unusual thing for a grifter uncle to say, don't you think?"

"Yeah. Kind of. Where . . . do you know where he got it? Was it here, New York?"

"My mother always insisted he bought her in an antique store in Boston."

"Unusual place for a grifter uncle to shop."

"Yeah. Kind of."

"And you kept the doll all these years?"

"Amazing how the value of something increases when the giver is dead. For more than a few reasons, I've always felt attached to the doll. Mary—that's what I call her—we go way back. But . . . maybe not as far as the two of you. Could you tell me, Pete?" Her voice strained. "Is this the doll in Esme's world?"

"I . . . yes." He gulped. "It's the doll in the room."

"Great. One small mystery solved."

"Or we just made a huge one even larger."

"You have a point. Would you like to hold her? Mary?" She held out the doll.

"You mean touch her." Pete stared at Esme's doll. He viewed her as greater proof of his other life, even more so than the influenza antibodies found in his blood. The cloth-covered keepsake in front of him resonated differently compared to the blood in his veins or the war medal that bore his initials. Em had pulled the doll close again, crooked in her freckled arm.

Tentatively, he reached. The raw mark of his blistered fingertips stopped him. He balled his hand into a fist. "No. I don't think so. I don't want to touch her." He retreated to the bed and started to tuck the photos of Esme back into the camera bag. Em stood there, stiff as the damn doll. "I can't do this."

"Like hell. You're going to do this." Her abruptness was unnerving, like this was somehow her problem. "I haven't even gotten to the best part, Pete St John, and I've been waiting a while now. A good long while."

"Listen, I'm usually the one who does the creeping out, so—"

"So welcome to a turn from the other end." Em came closer, and the doll remained like a fragile infant in her arms, her protectiveness obvious.

Maybe this was why he gasped out loud when she pushed up its dress and snapped the doll's leg from its body.

"Don't worry. It goes right back on." Its insides were connected by cording, keeping the leg attached like a lifeline.

He half expected the doll to cry out, but it stayed like the physical dead, still and wide-eyed.

"I've taken her leg off many times," Em said. "The first time, though, that's the one I remember most clearly. It's the one I want to tell you about.

"I was seven. My mother and father, my brother, Kieran, we flew from Las Vegas to Boston. I got bored on the plane, started fiddling with the doll. You know, the way a little girl might. My mother was asleep next to me. I imagined I was in a good bit of trouble. At first I thought I'd broken Mary. Sitting there like that, I held Mary straight up over me, her leg dangling. When I did, this fell out." With two fingers, Em reached inside the small, hollow body. Retracting her hand, pinched between her index and middle fingers was a folded piece of paper. It was as yellowed as the doll's dress. "I can open it and read it, or I can just tell you what it says."

Hot. When did the room get so fucking hot? Sweat prickled on Pete's back and dripped from his brow. The bedroom flipped from eclectic to suffocating.

"I've read it so many times. Of course, it only took once to memorize it." She opened the note anyway, and he could make out words, printed in pencil. "*Emerald, today you meet Phin. Solve his troubles. Where Esme failed, you must succeed. Don't let his past prevent your future.*' An attention getter, don't you think? Even at seven."

She followed the creases on the paper and refolded the note, tucking it back inside the doll, adjusting the leg. Her whole face had gone solemn; even the freckles seemed to pale. "I've never told anyone about the note. Not until this moment. I'm not sure why—maybe it felt like a secret I was supposed to keep. Until now."

Pete's stomach took a hard roil.

She continued on, like she'd been rehearsing the scene for some time. "To be clear, I don't speak to the dead, and I can't tell the future. But I have been hauling this doll—and a few other things—around most of my life. I couldn't leave her behind when I came to New York. In fact, I'd go as far as to say she's the reason I was so adamant about coming here. God knows Vegas has its share of onstage opportunities. LA is a hell of a lot closer to home. You don't have to come to New York to get a degree in psychology. Yet here is where I ended up." He started to speak; she cut him off. "And I'll tell you one more thing. I've always strongly suspected that the doll connects to you."

"Phin. You've said that name to me before." He widened his eyes, a small memory pushing back into his brain. Something his own mother had recently recalled. "When you flew to Boston, you came to my house. I remember. It was right after Zeke died. You were out on the porch. You had the doll with you then. There was so much going on, so much in my head. But I remember that you freaked me out. You called me—"

"Phin," she said matter-of-factly. "And you might explain it as a slip of the tongue by a little girl who'd read that name a few hours earlier." She held the doll up as if in evidence. "It'd be the rational explanation, if it wasn't for—"

"Your name. It's written on that piece of paper."

"Exceeds a little weird," she said, the relief of her long-awaited announcement evident.

"You knew all this back at the bungalow, in the diner."

"News flash, Pete. You don't make a great first impression. And since I've been in possession of a note claiming that my future hinges to your past, or Phin's . . . well, you can see my—"

"Disbelief?"

"I was going to say 'hesitation,' but okay. While you've offered me a lot of information, apparently I've brought my own to the table."

"Which seems to keep turning." He paused. "All this time, while I sat here and told you this story, you knew about Esme."

"Apparently before you ever did. Phin too. Care to enlighten me? Because I've been really curious about him."

"Phin. I've never heard the name before. Esme, she doesn't speak when I'm . . . *there*. I mean, you said the name to me years ago, but it didn't mean anything then."

"Does it now? Now that you've had . . . what? Sixteen years or so to process your past? Because I've had plenty of time. Added to everything you've told me and the things I didn't know, it seems like Phin can only be one person."

"Me," he said softly. "Who I was. The name I went by. The same first initial on the war medal, a *P*."

"Well, doesn't this give new meaning to putting a face to a name? As for what I knew . . . yes. I wanted to hear your side before I shared mine."

"Feels good, doesn't it?"

"What's that?"

"To have crazy validated."

"I can't disagree. But I want to know something else. I want you to confirm bits and pieces of stories I've heard. It has to do with my cryptic note, how or why it might exist." She hugged the doll and its insider secrets. "The one that appears to be—"

"A foretelling."

"Interesting word choice. Any idea how something like that might work? How a seven-year-old girl ends up with a note hidden in a doll that would rival any message in a bottle."

"Yes."

"Yes?" She looked unprepared for the confirmation.

"My grandfather. The note does seem like something he would have recorded. It's, um . . . messages that predicted future events, provided by specters. He kept them all in a leather-bound letter box that . . ." He stopped; it was too cumbersome. "Prognostications. That's basically how Peter Ellis's gift worked. He recorded messages from the dead."

"You're named after him. Charming footnote."

Pete made a face. When his hand wasn't touching hers, or Em's touching his, "simpatico" definitely wasn't the go-to word between them. "But even if my grandfather did write the note, which does seem addressed to you . . ."

"Seem? Let me know when you meet your next Emerald."

"Okay, it is written to you. But how does a note end up inside a doll that in all likelihood Peter Ellis never came in contact with?"

"The doll did exist during his lifetime."

Pete shook his head. "No. He didn't put it there. All his ghost gifts, they live in the letter box. My grandfather, he was . . . well, society labeled him as disturbed. I can't imagine he had the forethought to put one of his messages inside a doll. One that ultimately ended up in your possession."

"This letter box. Is it still around?"

"Yes. My mother has it. Before that, her grandmother, Charley, was the box's caretaker. I don't know its origin. As for any message . . ." Pete paused, the ethereal world smacking him upside the head. "Your uncle."

"Zeke?"

"Yes. He stole ghost gifts from the letter box."

"Excuse me?"

"It's true. Stole . . . borrowed with intent, however you want to put it. It all ties to what got him killed. Zeke made a career out of taking and benefiting from my grandfather's predictions. It's not such a leap. What if he came across that note, with your name on it? Like you said, Emerald isn't so common. But it is *your* name."

"It would have caught his eye, been a red flag."

"And with his grifter life, he may have put a note—that he couldn't make sense of—in what he deemed a safe place."

"I see your point. It's not like the note says I should avoid deep-sea diving or taking a trip to Europe."

"But Zeke knew enough to realize the note meant something. Is there a reason he wouldn't have given it to your mother?"

"Uh, more than I care to count." She arched her fair eyebrows. "Take your pick: lifelong anxiety issues, depression, to wildly scattered on a good day."

"I see. So the doll, at the very least, is a gift that was also a hiding place. But then, when you end up a murder victim . . ."

"The best-laid plans . . ."

"Can go awry."

Em squeezed the doll tighter and looked at Pete. "Okay, so if we put it all together . . ."

And this time, Pete felt something in her gaze that was as profound as her touch. "Wait. You don't have all the pieces. You don't know what I did to Esme."

"It's not . . ." Em glanced at the strip of photos, Esme's battered face. "That?"

He shook his head in the smallest stroke. "There's a reason I recorded the date of her death, Em, took those pictures. They're mementos. The things a depraved mind will turn into keepsakes. Esmerelda Moon died young, so tragically . . ." The tight room seemed to be out of breathable air. "Because I killed her. That's what I relive over and over."

Her gasp was small, but she couldn't hide white-knuckled fingers in a death grip around the doll. "You killed her?"

"I shot her. I relive that scene clearly as I'm living this present-day moment with you." Pete went on, filling in the rest, how Esme would fall to the floor, the way he'd scoop up her bloodied body and carry her to the door. "Right there, every time, it all slips the other way, and my equally violent reentry to this life begins."

"I, um . . . I'm not sure what to say."

"The smart thing to say is that you want to think this through. Put all your pieces together. I've deciphered my share of messages from the dead, Em. I know their validity. I'm well aware what I'm capable of. Your note, that prognostication, what if it refers to a future I might steal, the same way I stole Esmerelda Moon's?"

She looked between Pete and her own exit. "What was your grandfather's track record with prognostications? Did many come to pass?"

"Accurate. They were pretty damn accurate."

Em considered the doll and the paper prognostication that bound the two of them. Then she looked at Pete. "I don't need to think about it. I've had plenty of time to live with that note, what it implies. *Don't let his past prevent your future.*' You've presented some unexpected possibilities, Pete. But if my future is at stake, the last thing I'm going to do is nothing."

# CHAPTER
# TWENTY-THREE

It didn't take long for Pete and Em to formulate a plan, which centered on locating death records from January 1919. For such a large place, New York was fairly organized, and the quest landed the two at New York City's municipal archives. But hours later, a microfilm search had yielded little more than sore necks and tired eyes. Pete leaned back, having scoured records from Brooklyn and Queens while Em fished through Manhattan, Staten Island, and the Bronx. "I thought for sure we'd find something. Not a name, nothing." He shoved closed the drawer of reels that exceeded their target year. "Not one moon among a million stars."

Em rested back in her chair and rubbed her hand around her shoulder. She smiled at him.

"What?"

"That was kind of poetic. Not one moon . . ." She cleared her throat. "Sorry. Off track."

"No. Maybe we are—way off track. Think about it. If I'm reading my past life actions accurately . . ." Pete struggled for the steps that might have followed murder. "It could be there's no record of Esme's death because . . . well, maybe I dumped her body in the East River, buried her in some patch of field just past Brooklyn."

"Transporting her how? It might have been 1919. It may even have been nighttime. But to carry a bleeding body through city streets unnoticed?" She shook her head at him. "Unless you had an accomplice."

Her words prompted an image in Pete's head: Oscar Bodette wearing his raccoon coat. He shook it off, the photos he found obviously creating a moment of déjà vu. "As far as I know, I acted alone." Then he said in a flip tone, "Wouldn't that be the MO for any good sociopath?"

She squinted back at her microfilm machine. "I can't speak for PTSD, but you don't fit the sociopath mold. Most are deceivingly charming."

"Thanks. I think."

She leaned back again. "You've explained the scenario, but I'm wondering if you're missing something. Have you ever considered—"

"If your next words are 'past life regression' . . ." He also leaned back into his machine.

"Nah. Not with you. I doubt anything so common to this life would be capable of tapping into something that complex in your past one."

"Is that your NYU psych degree talking?"

"Partially. Apply what you do know in a way you haven't before. I think that's logical."

"Logic. I'll introduce you to my father some . . ." The thought petered out as Pete was reminded of his choice to sever family ties.

"Well, there's a lot here that invites speculation, so let's put some basic challenge questions to what you do and don't know."

"For example?"

Em bit down on a thumbnail. The thinking gesture morphed into her finger wagging at him. "You insist it's a bedroom. You see it clearly. But you also say your point of view is limited. What's there besides the things you've mentioned? You must know it well enough to pick out specifics."

Pete wanted to insist that like his actions, his line of vision was predetermined. But instead of defending his finite perspective, he went along with Em's suggestion. He started to note less obvious details, but a different thought interrupted. Pete drew his hands into a prayerful fold. "This is going to sound strange."

She narrowed her eyes. "Compared to . . . ?"

"My father runs on pure logic. He's married to a woman whose gifts defy any semblance of logic. He, uh . . . he's the person who brought . . ." Pete thought for a moment. "A healing component of logic into her life." He unknotted his fingers. "I've given you plenty of reason to be cautious, but when I held your hand, walking through the concert crowd—before that, when you touched me at the bungalow. Then, in your bedroom, when you put your hand over mine, I sensed . . ."

"That sort of feeling, something healing?"

"Something different." It was as far as he was willing to go.

Em glanced around the safety of the public setting and slowly she offered him her hand. On contact, the sensations from before reprised. Pete closed his eyes lightly and attempted to step away from the viewfinder in his head. He began with the repetitive visuals: "The bed. A clothesline, single window—with curtains." He furrowed his brow. "They're kind of lacy, see-through. But it doesn't matter. They're pushed to the sides. I don't think I ever mentioned that."

"Go on," she said.

He kept his eyes closed and gripped tighter to her hand. "There's the cat, an English hunting scene over the mantel, a fire . . . and the doll." Pete said this with new confidence. It was validating to have someone who could relate to the doll's existence. His mind veered onto the fire. "Since this trip home, those visitant episodes . . . the fire is different. Like someone added fuel to it. It's burning brighter."

"So the basic scene, there's been a recent change to it?"

He opened his eyes for a moment. "Yes. But it doesn't alter what happens. It doesn't strike me as important—more of an inconsequential addendum."

"Okay, can you stop focusing on the events or your strongest repetitive impressions of what's there?"

Pete closed his eyes again.

"Go past the cat, the clothesline . . . the doll. Keep going. What else has been in the room all this time? Things you don't normally talk about."

"A bathroom," he said abruptly. "I know there's a door that opens to a bathroom. It's always been more about background than part of what's happening."

"Good. And the other door. The one you always exit through, where your experience ends. What does the door lead to, Pete? Another room, a hallway?"

"Darkness. Whatever it is, it's even more dim than the room. But you have a point, it's more of a hallway than an adjoining room or an exit."

"All right. So to my fresh set of ears, two things jump out at me, based on the time period and your recollections. Unless it's a grand home—"

"No. It's not. It can't be." Her touch and voice were so leading he spoke without thinking—a fact he knew, but he'd never paid attention to it. "The windows across the way, they're way too close."

"Across the way. An alley? So it's more of a city setting?"

A small smile crept onto his face. "Yes. An alley in a city. This city, I assume."

"Okay, come back to the bedroom with its own bath. I think that's a big clue. You say you don't exit into another room, but more interesting, you don't exit to the outside either."

He blinked at her. "It's a hotel room."

"It might be."

And for a moment, Pete felt as if he'd discovered the Holy Grail. He let go of Em's hand and rolled forward on the wheeled chair. He could have kissed her. Well, kissed her for clarifying—bringing a layer of logic—to what he'd perceived as a finite point of view. Then Pete looked at the microfilm machine, the drawers and drawers of recorded deaths, the hundred years between his memory and a city the size of Manhattan. He looked at Em's freckled hands. "It's good information, but how does it get us to a physical location? A hotel, somewhere in New York City, from a century ago." He raised his arms in defeat, dropping them onto his lap.

"Don't be so quick to give up on the research. We still have Royal Photography. Maybe we should have started there." Em looked at her watch. "Gosh, I didn't realize how long we've been here."

"Do you have to be somewhere? I should have asked earlier."

"Just a voice lesson. I can reschedule. It's fine."

"Voice lesson, huh?" Pete gnawed on his lip. "I'm guessing those don't come cheap."

"Believe me, one voice lesson won't make or break me."

"Tough business, show business." Pete kept the conversation moving away from their pursuit. It felt safer. "But it sounds like something you've always wanted to do."

"Definitely. But I'm not even sure why. There's no theater in my blood. My dad graduated from the London School of Economics, and Mum . . . well, she does best functioning inside our small family circle. I couldn't imagine her up on a stage."

"I can relate. Obviously, I get my desire to chase a story from my parents. But the photographic eye is all mine." He thought for a moment. "Painting would be my talent that seems to come from nowhere."

"So based on your larger psychic gift, do you see yourself as more like your mom than your dad?"

"Actually, it's more like possessing my mother's inexplicable gift trapped in my father's logical mind." Pete crinkled his brow at the observation. His circumstances had always been about his mother, never relating anything inherent from his father to his experiences.

"Interesting interpretation," she said.

Pete also had to admit that for someone who should be running from him, Em was decidedly drilled into Pete St John. He shifted in his seat. The intimacy felt off-putting. In a casual motion, Pete stretched his arms over his head. "Back to your voice lesson. If you can't reschedule, at least let me pay for it."

"No. That's ridiculous. You're not paying for my voice lesson."

"Then dinner. Let me buy you dinner." Pete splayed his hands out in front of him. "Public setting. Worst-case scenario, I take you to your favorite restaurant. You order one of everything on the menu. I watch in sideshow amazement."

Em folded her arms, her gaze examining. "My favorite restaurant makes at least fifteen desserts. I never can decide."

Pete stood, an arm gesturing smoothly toward the exit. "Then I suggest you save room."

# CHAPTER
# TWENTY-FOUR

Her favorite restaurant turned out to be, almost literally, a hole-in-the-wall fondue place just outside the theater district. Pete couldn't recall the last time he'd eaten fondue, or if he'd ever eaten it. The restaurant was a perfect Em fit—as was her name. If the finicky world of theater felt "Ailish" made her more attractive, fine. "Em" suited him.

He glanced between her and the menu, in which she was naturally engrossed. He saw the method to her madness: the menu was composed of forty-seven different fondues, applicable to nearly as many dipping items. After Em's à la carte selections were made, the waiter had to bring a tiny side table to accommodate her choices. Pete anticipated the assault on his senses, how unappealing he'd find the plethora of food. Surprisingly, that didn't happen. Having experienced her eating habits, he was more amused than shocked. Pete was even intrigued when Em pointed to the fried squid and said, "Everybody thinks the mint fondue is for the lamb. It's unbelievably good with the squid."

He shuddered internally but stabbed at the squid, swiping it through a green-gray fondue. It wasn't half bad. He washed it down with a mouthful of beer and retrieved an iPad from his camera bag.

"Ah, I almost forgot this was a *working dinner*." Em reached with her fondue fork, spearing a morsel of beef. She scooped it through a white fondue and popped it in her mouth, eyes watering. "Oh my God, that's so good!"

"Enough to make you cry?"

"No. It's the double horseradish fondue." She blotted watery eyes with her napkin and pointed to a bowl of shiitake mushrooms. "Everybody thinks—"

"I got it." He held up a hand. "Goes perfect with the mushrooms too." He laughed.

"Oh my gosh."

"Oh my gosh, what?"

"That's the first time I've heard you laugh."

The feeling of being exposed returned, and Pete looked down at the iPad, delving into a Google search for Royal Photography. In his peripheral vision, the tip of her fondue fork tapped against the side of her plate. He felt her stare.

"It's incredibly hard for you, isn't it?" she said.

"What's that? Being social?"

"No. To live your life."

And exposed turned into butt naked. Em's meal zeal slowed, her expression going from jovial to intense. He wasn't sure he wanted to be on the introspective end of her thoughts. The sloppier, open-book Em—brash, unapologetic, a whirl of energy—that, he could handle. No problem. This emotion made Pete feel off balance, particularly when he considered the opposite end of the spectrum. The potential for disaster. He went back to poking at the iPad.

"Okay, so the archives turned out to be a bust," she said. "Any luck with Royal Photography?" Em returned to slow but steady consumption of food, and the action put him at ease.

"Actually . . ." His eyes traveled a trail of Google misses and he looked back at her. "No. There's not one entry pertaining to Royal Photography."

"Oh, that's disappointing. I thought for sure we'd find our Nancy Drew clue."

Pete leaned back in his chair. "Seems the Case of the Mysterious Mystery Photos continues on. Or maybe it's hit a dead end."

Before he put back the iPad, Em asked to see it. She tapped the screen and turned the device on him, snapping his photo.

"What'd you do that for?"

"I was thinking, for all the photos you take, I bet there are hardly any of you." She looked at the image, blinking. "Oh my."

"How many floating lights?"

"How did you know . . ." The tone of her voice turned serious. "How many are there usually?"

"Two, four . . . sometimes more. Depends." Pete looked around the restaurant, the building obviously old. Floating around his photo were three orbs. Capturing his image opened a portal, and the hum of the dead began. "Mind if I . . . ?"

Em held out the device, and he took it, deleting the photo. To help silence the dead, Pete aimed for further distraction by taking Em's picture.

"Ugh. Why did you do that? I look a mess."

"Not my first impressions." He admired the result. *Bright . . . analytical . . . attractive.* Those words jumped to mind. *Impressions . . .* On that front, Pete had to admit he'd done a drastic one-eighty. He smiled at her, guessing the same could not be said about her impressions of him. Pete's focus still felt off, bothered by a drumbeat of otherworldly noises.

A waiter came by to clear their dishes as a second one rolled in with a cart. It brimmed with dessert fondues and foods, everything from sugar-dipped orange sections to marshmallows that came with mini chafing dishes for toasting. Em looked them over, and he laid the iPad on the table, excusing himself to the restroom. He needed a minute—to adjust to the oddly good time he was having and to banish the lingering dead. After the restroom, he stepped outside. Manhattan noise and traffic instantly quieted his mind. Pete inhaled sticky city air, then returned to the table, surprised—maybe a little disappointed—dessert fondues weren't piled six deep.

She shrugged at him. "My voracious appetite failed me. I can't eat another bite."

"You're sure?"

Em tapped fingers on the white tablecloth, her other arm tucked tight around her middle.

"Do you feel all right? No judgment, but with everything you ate . . . well, the water in Mexico might hold less potential for hazardous consumption."

She laughed. "It's not that. In fact, I was thinking I rarely pass on dessert. It's like I didn't get enough to eat in . . . never mind."

Pete saw something different in her mood. While his parents, even Grace and Dr. Kapoor, always showed concern, her troubled look appeared more personal. He wanted to ask again if she was all right, but it felt like overkill. Pete proceeded to pack the iPad back into the camera bag's interior sleeve.

"Could I see that for a sec again? I promise, no more pictures."

He shrugged, handing her the entire camera bag.

"I'm sure your search was thorough. I just wouldn't mind . . ."

"I don't blame you. *Don't let my past prevent your future,*" he said more quietly.

She flipped open the bag. He battled a sense of invasion but said nothing. Em had gone as far as to withdraw the iPad, but she wasn't looking at it. She continued to stare inside the bag. Absently, she went to place the device on the table. Pete had to reach across, grabbing it, before the iPad missed and hit the floor. "What?" he said.

"I don't see how—" Em dipped her hand into the bag again and came up with the postcard. "You said your mother was adamant about this card never bearing anything but a postmark."

"That's right. New York City, 1918. Until a few days ago. Until the message showed up at the bottom."

*"When I spent two weeks on this beach, I didn't dream of you then."*

"We talked about that, Em. How my mother swears the message wasn't there the entire time the ghost gift's been in her possession."

"I know. I remember." She held the card up with the postmarked side facing him. "What . . . what do you suppose she'd think now?"

Pete reached across the small span. He might have been distracted by the vibration elicited by her fingers on one corner of the postcard and his on the other. But random sensations were secondary as the homeless postcard, the one that'd been blank forever, now showed a return address: *"Hupp's Supper Club & Hotel, 61st Street and Lexington Avenue, New York City."*

# CHAPTER
# TWENTY-FIVE

It was after eleven by the time Pete saw Em to the door of her apartment building. "Do you want to come up, coffee, maybe?" she asked. "Caroline, she's probably home by now."

He assumed this was meant to inform him they wouldn't be alone. "I, um . . . I'm pretty tired." It was a lie. Pete was wired like he'd drunk a six-pack of Red Bull. But she was right to be cautious. There were too many unknowns—about himself and a girl whose future felt as if it rested gingerly in his hands. "Tomorrow," he said. "I'll see you first thing tomorrow. We'll go from there."

They lingered under the entry awning. "So you're all set with your hotel reservation?"

"Yeah. Sure. Hyatt, park side or something. A few blocks from here." He felt wildly conflicted. For someone who posed a threat—according to one telling prognostication—Pete felt protective, like he didn't want to stray too far. He scrubbed a hand around the back of his neck and forced a smile in her direction. "Just . . . just don't give up on me, not yet."

"I won't." She turned for the entrance.

"And make sure you lock your door."

She spun from the top step, her whipping hair, the motion, reminiscent. "Of course."

"Right." It sounded desperate. And it was, especially since she had to use a key to get into the Upper East Side building. "Good. That's good."

"Well, good night then."

"Em."

She stopped.

"When we were out on the sidewalk today, you said something to me. You said, 'Forever the hero.'"

"I didn't . . . I don't remember saying that."

"Yes you do. What does it mean?" Maybe Pete was only fishing for a compliment, a counterpoint to his grim past. "What do you know about me, other than a cryptic note you've been carrying around in a doll all these years?"

Her lips settled into a tight line. "I'm not like you, Pete. I don't see ghosts. I don't have a past life that I keep reliving."

"So you keep reminding me. Why do I get the feeling you're mostly trying to convince yourself of that?"

"Because you're the one with an incredible gift. I'm just a girl from Vegas. That's nothing special."

"Interesting. It's the first thing you've said that I totally disagree with."

She didn't smile at him but at the brick steps beneath her sandals.

"And there are other things we agree on, like the doll, the note, you . . . me. It all connects."

So did their gazes. Em was the serene object in an ever-moving city, maybe his ever-moving mind.

"'E.M.' The initials on the postcard. You realize that part too. Obviously, you realized it before me."

She clasped her fingers, looking as uncomfortable as he felt. "Lots of things in life aren't explainable."

"Like Stonehenge, the pyramids . . . why nine out of ten people are right-handed—"

"Let me guess, you not being one of them."

He only raised a brow.

"So we also might agree that there are greater phenomena than you in the universe."

"Maybe I'm even at the low end of the scale. We can keep going if you want. If that conversation would keep you from telling me what it is you're guarding like the whereabouts of D.B. Cooper." Pete was in full Levi mode now, the reporter determined to get his story. He thrust his hands into his pockets and squinted at a starry sky. "We can discuss the placebo effect or how migrating birds appear to have built-in GPS. Better yet"—he wagged a finger at her—"monarch butterflies. Did you know they winter in Mexico but their lifespan is only six months? So it's their offspring that return to North America. How do they know where to go? I'm sure I could come up with a dozen other examples. But none of that will alter this mysterious . . . *circumstance*. So if you know something . . ."

She came down two steps. "After Mary and the note . . . I don't want to be the person who causes you more burden. Clearly my existence, what I've shared, only complicates things that already . . ."

"Drive me a little mad?"

She looked back at her sandals.

"The facts aren't your fault, Em. If anything, I should apologize to you. I know what it's like to walk around with cryptic questions. I'm sorry you're tangled in this mess. But if you do know something else, have more to share . . ."

She crossed and uncrossed her arms. "Just understand, I don't have a wealth of life experiences. My insights, they're not on par with the Dalai Lama, probably not even a good life coach."

"Yet you seem to have a sharp focus on me, my life. What are you holding out on?"

"Nothing." But she spoke so fast it sounded like defensiveness. "Let me, um . . . let me back this up a step. My senior year at NYU, we did a thesis project in the prison system—hard-core stuff. I interviewed a dozen convicted murderers."

It was admittedly fascinating, the unexpected edges of Emerald Montague.

"I know. Why a thesis project on convicted killers and not child psychology?" She said this while wrapping her hands around her arms, hugging herself. "I guess when you have one uncle doing time for killing another, curiosity about that sort of mind is inbred."

"Still waiting to hear how I tie to your findings—a study of known killers."

"Every single one of those men insisted they didn't do it. I've met a charming sociopath or two. Several were so psychotic they couldn't tell right from wrong. All were determined to convince me they weren't such bad guys. Not one inmate said, 'Hey, I deserve this life sentence.'"

"Could be the reality of a long prison sentence skews their need to show remorse."

"Possibly. But my point isn't them, Pete. My point is you. In a short time, I've seen the burden you live with. I appreciate how responsible you feel for Esme's death, if only because it's what I didn't see from men convicted of similar crimes. Your guilt is so real. Your remorse remarkably evident—genuine."

It took his breath away, someone who didn't just believe him, but someone who acknowledged the pain, comprehended his culpability. It wasn't something Aubrey or Levi could ever quite grasp. It went beyond Grace's ability to cope or even a Jesuit priest's sage advice.

"We also know," she said, "that somehow I'm the keeper of pieces of your other life. So maybe that makes me the person who helps figure it all out. But what if just the opposite happens?" She was on the sidewalk now, looking up at him. "What if I only end up making this life worse?"

And burden tipped the opposite way. "I never thought about it. To be honest, before you, I never considered the possibility—another person who might be able to help me figure this whole thing out."

"Well, know that I am thinking about it. Regardless of what any note might mean for me. It's been on my mind since you walked into the bungalow."

Burden. It was something Pete understood. He had respect for hers. "Just let me say this: whatever the outcome, I'm ready to take the chance. I'm out of alternatives. I can't run anymore. Do you want to know . . ." He hesitated, but maybe full disclosure was the right move. "Do you know what I considered before I came to the city today? What I'd be doing right now if I hadn't come here to find you?"

She shook her head in the tiniest stroke.

"I'd be bloated and floating in the Long Island Sound."

"You were considering . . . you're not serious."

"Deadly. I don't want to live like this anymore. The exhaustion of my life is winning out." He shifted his stance. "I'm racing against that feeling, Em. I'm doing my damnedest to find a resolution. And you're right—I wasn't anticipating the complication of you. It changes things. So again, if you know something more, something that—"

Touch took the place of words. She reached up, her fingertips flitting over the scruff on Pete's jawline. He held perfectly still. Withdrawing her hand, she balled it into a small fist. "*Solve his troubles . . .*' Don't let go of the first part of that prediction. Maybe if I help resolve your past, I alter my future—at least according to one reliable source."

Pete guessed she was done communicating for the night. Whatever weighed on her mind, as much as he wanted to know, he didn't want to push for more. Turning fast, he walked away. As he neared the corner,

Pete wasn't sure if it was a ghostly whisper or Emerald Montague's voice, but he did hear the words, "God, I hope that much is right."

Restlessness was an understatement. Pete never even made it under the covers at the Hyatt hotel, lying atop the luxury linens, catching a few hours of sleep in fits and starts. He tried to put Em aside, which only brought him back around to the address that had mysteriously turned up on the postcard. He googled "Hupp's Supper Club, Manhattan, 1918," like he did with the name Esmerelda Moon. The search yielded nothing. He almost went to the address in the middle of the night, but Pete couldn't dismiss gut instinct that said he and Em needed to pursue the clue together.

By seven that morning, he'd showered, dressed, and recharged his camera equipment. Before leaving, he took another look at the postcard, tucked safe in his camera bag. He wanted to make certain the newly emerged return address was there. He ran his finger over cursive identical to the handwriting on the front. The card emanated considerable heat. Mindful of the power of a ghost gift, Pete put the card back in the bag's mesh pouch. Minutes later he was on city sidewalks, which had not yet turned sultry.

He walked the blocks to Em's apartment, if only to clear his head. At the entrance, Pete pressed the intercom buzzer. A voice that wasn't Em's croaked in reply: "Do you have any fucking idea what time it is?"

He looked at the leather-banded watch. Not good. He squinted at the box and the surly voice coming from it. "Sorry, uh, Caroline. It's Pete St John. Is, um . . . is Em awake yet?" He looked at his watch again. Maybe "get an early start" meant closer to ten. He felt completely stupid, his social cues more offline than usual.

Clearly, Caroline's finger remained on the button; Pete could hear every word.

"Sorry. I was changing." It was Em's voice, from the background, adding more softly, "Could you just buzz him in, tell him to come up?"

"Seriously, Em? Guests at the crack of dawn?"

"You have a bedroom with a door. Use it."

He was glad to hear Em stick up for herself, but at the same time Pete wanted to interrupt, say he'd come back in an hour or two. He found himself a voyeur in their roommate squabble.

"You look weirdly nice," Caroline said. "Not one coffee stain. Amazing." Pete knitted his brow at the remark, weaving it tighter as Caroline went on. "Geez, if he was that great of a date, why isn't he waking up here?"

"It wasn't a date," Em said. "And it's complicated."

"Already? A little advice, roomie. Don't be too much of a tease. From the looks of him, I doubt attracting women is an issue."

Pete cleared his throat. An awkward pause filled the air, intercom to apartment. Em's voice darted in, perturbed, obviously closer to the device. "Really, Caroline? You've had your finger on the button the entire time? Oh, for—would you just let him in?"

A few minutes later, Pete tapped lightly on the apartment door. Em inched it open, though the chain was on. She shut it and detached the chain before swinging the door wide. Neither said anything as Pete came inside, and awkward glances filled in for verbal greetings. She did look nice, wearing a brightly colored long skirt and a pink blouse that was an eclectic complement to her red hair. He'd been around the world enough. Only somebody with an innate sense of self could pull off the bold look. But on a breakfast bar stool, he saw a Starbucks apron, her macramé bag, and a cup of coffee with a pink lipstick smear. Caroline was also sitting in the living room, clearly on hand to eavesdrop.

"I'll be ready in a second. I got out as quick as I could."

He pointed to the apron. "You work at Starbucks?"

She was rummaging through the bag. "Guess you thought I was kidding about those four fab jobs, huh?" She rested her hands on the apron. "The four a.m. open shift sucks, but it's an extra two bucks an hour. Told the boss I had a dentist appointment this morning."

"You left early because of me? Why didn't you say something last night?"

She tapped her fingers on the macramé bag. "How much sleep did you get?"

"Not a lot."

"Me either. So don't worry about it. I was changing. Caroline grabbed the buzzer and . . ." She pointed in the direction of her roommate.

"Sorry I woke you," Pete offered.

"Caroline accepts your apology," she said in third person, slinking by the two of them. She plucked a bag of coffee off the counter. "Anyway, I'm up now." She held the coffee out to Em. "Did you want to put your barista skills to work?"

Em rolled her eyes. "You'll have to manage. We're leaving."

Moments later they were on the sidewalk, weaving through city blocks. Em chatted away, but it seemed she was trying to stay off topic. He knew that feeling, and Pete obliged, keeping conversation nondescript, asking what sort of professional work she'd done in New York. He recalled the script sitting on the steamer trunk.

"It's an off-off-Broadway new musical," she explained. "The audition is late this afternoon."

He asked if she shouldn't be rehearsing. Em insisted any more rehearsal would be excessive. Pete didn't know if he should believe her, but he couldn't think of any recourse and went along with it as they made their way down the avenues.

Cloud cover had thickened, and a block from their destination, heavy July air collapsed into a thunderstorm. They ran the remaining distance; soaked and panting, they stopped on the sidewalk. In front of them a narrow alleyway separated two buildings. Em pulled his hand, and the two ducked under the overhang of the building on the left. Rain continued—less intense, fatter drops. Em bumped her hand into Pete's. She pointed to a metal plate, not visible unless you happened to be standing under the overhang, looking low. It read: *Hupp 1918.* Pete sucked in a deep enough breath and nearly choked on the rain he inhaled. But their attention was diverted. A heavyset man with a key climbed the steps of the building next door. As he opened the door, Pete grabbed Em's hand and followed. There was a sign overhead: *Samsara.*

Pete and Em were tight on his heels; the man was surprised to find anyone behind him. "Sorry," he said. "We don't open for another three hours. Lunch crowd." He pointed to a dark room filled with even darker wood tables and panel-trimmed walls, the dim weather casting little light. But instead of throwing them curbside, like a New Yorker might, the man said, "'Course, if you just want to wait out the rain, I suppose that's fine."

In the silent room, Pete heard an instant distant clattering of dishes and clinking of glasses—voices, indiscernible but present. His gaze darted from corner to corner. Pete didn't anticipate vacant space but a bustle of people. His eyes assured him it was just the ghosts—perhaps none particularly associated to him.

It was Em who stepped forward. "The building next door, is it 1025?"

"No. This one is," Pete said before the man could answer.

"That's right," the barkeep said.

"Oh." Em looked at Pete and back at the man. "Could we ask you a few questions about it? Do you happen to know its history?"

The man had gone behind the bar and went about the business of moving glasses from a tray to a shelf. "Why do you want to know its history?"

Pete's mouth gaped; Em answered. "A thesis project on turn-of-the-century Manhattan architecture. This building, the one next door. They showed up on our research. We go to NYU." She retrieved an NYU student ID from her bag, waving it at him. "We're doing the project together." The man squinted at them and Em's ID. Fortunately, he didn't make an effort to look closely. If he had, he would have seen Em's *expired* NYU ID. He did look harder at Pete's camera bag. "My partner," Em said, "he's an amateur photographer, and—"

"What?" Pete said, not quite on board with her ruse.

"Since we're students," she said loudly, "he likes to photograph the architecture when we find what we're looking for."

"Right. Just a hobby." Pete patted the camera bag.

"So long as you're not from the city inspector's office. They're always coming up with a new fire code, some kind of plumbing that doesn't meet specs from the twenty-first century."

"We're not from the twenty-first century," Pete said.

Em elbowed him. "Inspector's office. He means we're not from the inspector's office. So do you know anything about the building, its history?"

"A little. I've worked here for almost twenty years. The trim work . . ." He pointed around the room. "It's solid mahogany. That and this bar." He slapped a hand against it. "They're the only original features left on the first floor. I believe Hupp was the last name of the original owners. This building belonged to them, and the one next door."

"Hupp?" Pete said.

"Yeah. Not Astor or Morgan name recognition. But the Hupp family owned a slice of New York real estate. Hotel business, upscale entertainment. They had money, influence until . . ." He squinted at a coffered ceiling. "Oh, probably around the Great Depression. Not really sure. This place used to be what they called a supper club—trendy in its time. That'd be pre–World War I, roaring twenties." He cocked his chins at a darker space, set to the rear. "There used to be a stage over that way. Tore it out years ago. Nowadays, we have open mic night." His thick finger moved toward a row of windows that faced the alley. "That's the kind of entertainment folks expect."

As he spoke, Pete was haunted by the impression of having been on this tour before.

"Don't know much more than that." He polished another glass and placed it on the bar wall. "Hey, if you two are doing a project on early-twentieth-century architecture, shouldn't you know the building's history?"

"We did," Em said quickly. "It's just helpful to hear someone else's take. In fact, we know that the floors above this one were once hotel rooms."

"Very sharp," Pete murmured, Em shooting him a glance.

"Can you tell us what became of them?"

"Are you sure you're not from the inspector's office?"

"Positive," Em said. "Why do you ask . . . again?"

"The building owner has been after a permit to reconfigure the old hotel rooms into condos. For decades, they've rented them out as supplement dorm space—medical students, a few law schools—but condos would be way more lucrative. From what I heard, the housing board has denied it twice."

"So the hotel rooms," Pete said. "They're still there? In their original state?"

"More or less. It's why it worked for dorms. I think the bathrooms were done over in the fifties. New students don't come in for a few weeks. Makes for nothing but a ghost town up there right now."

They traded a glance, and Em recovered first. "Would you mind if we took a look, maybe a photo or two? It's difficult to find architecture in its original condition. We'd love to get a feel for the elements. You know, the natural bow of the floors as time settled in, period woodwork, maybe a fireplace or two. There might even be copper plumbing!"

Pete's head ticked toward Em and the zeal with which she spoke—she had him believing that was their mission.

"Help yourselves," the manager said. "Nothing up there but stuffy old hotel rooms." With a bar rag in his hand, he pointed to a side staircase that appeared to rise and vanish into blackness.

# Act VI
# New York City
# Fall 1918

It seemed unlikely that being raped by your brother-in-law would become an insignificant memory. But that was Esmerelda's sharpest thought on a morning when rain pelted hard against the hotel. She'd forgotten the day, was unsure about the month. Thunder rumbled and she could feel the dampness in her bones. Her stomach growled. It'd been three, maybe four days since she'd eaten. Licorice was better fed with a steady supply of mice. Esmerelda could no longer calculate how long it'd been since her hotel room had become a prison cell, the window boarded up. Her brain was foggy, and with the sliver of sky gone, ordered thoughts had become an impossible task. She tried to stand but slumped back onto the chair, gathering Marigold in her lap. So much had changed and so much had gone wrong. But sitting there, Esmerelda was mindful of Oscar's warning. The chancy rolling of dice had proved to be snake eyes and then some.

A year ago, when she'd set things in motion, Esmerelda's lies and life had gone according to plan. Perhaps even better. She'd sung at the Palace from last fall and through the next three seasons. She'd sent a note or two to Oscar, making sure his commission had arrived in New Orleans. The only part Esmerelda had failed at was securing other living arrangements. She'd looked for a flat nearby, but even decent pay, less Oscar's commission, couldn't rent her one-room cellar housing—not in such an upscale section of Manhattan. She considered Phin's old neighborhood. But between the unrest of war and what was left in Hell's Kitchen, she wasn't keen on the idea.

Cora had come by ages ago. The first time was to ask if Licorice could stay on—the Elephant Hotel wouldn't allow pets. Esmerelda had taken the visit as a quiet cry for help. She offered Cora their old arrangement, tried to coax the girl into moving back to the hotel. Maybe if she'd been more convincing—less worried about Cora dragging her seedy life along—Esmerelda wouldn't be in such a spot now. Regardless of the lukewarm offer, Cora's dismissal had been immediate. "Once you get over the shock of it, it's not so bad. I have my own room. Keep more money than Oscar ever gave us."

Cora tucked fine strands of brown hair behind her ears. Oscar used to say her ears stuck out so far, a fellow could hide a whiskey flask back there. Her old roommate had gone on about her new line of work. "Although with so few younger men, it does leave a girl with nothing but old codgers, the kind who couldn't get water to freeze stiff in January, never mind their . . ." Esmerelda's eyes drew wide and Cora's thought trailed off.

When the spring of 1918 blew in, so did more alarming news from Europe. Battles dominated every headline, German U-boats sinking American ships and ground conflicts that bled farther into Western Europe with something called the Spring Offensive. There'd been talk on every street corner of bloody battles, men pointing to images and photographs in newspapers like the *Tribune*.

War seemed physically upon them when the city enforced blackouts and curfews. Esmerelda took it as precautionary when Benjamin insisted that the window of her room be boarded up. It was common practice up and down the avenue. "It's for your own safety, Esmerelda. New York's harbors would be first in an attack. Imagine how I'd feel if Germans made it ashore and their mustard gas or shelling reached your room."

The next most noteworthy change occurred when Benjamin was called to duty, though his father had managed to have him assigned to an office in Washington, DC. After this, for some time, Esmerelda had maintained a routine—performing at the Palace, though the upheaval of war dulled the crowds and the venue cut shows by half. No one's mind was on the frivolity of entertainment. Curfews made it a non-negotiable point.

In the always-dark room, lit by candles, Esmerelda wrote to Phin and he wrote back. Correspondence might arrive in a bundle, then none for weeks, sometimes more than a month. In reply, Esmerelda sent letters spritzed with gardenia mist. It was robust toilet water she and the boys had given to Cora on her last birthday. Esmerelda never wore it, though the heady scent had infused itself into everything she owned.

It was late that spring when Esmerelda looked through the writing desk, in need of more ink. She came across a postcard from Bayport, Long Island. It showed off the dock and gazebo where she and Phin had shared their picnic dinner. The beach where Phin had proposed. Oscar's friend, who'd owned the restaurant, had given her the card as a memento. She'd sent the postcard to Phin that day, writing in the small space at the bottom: "When I spent two weeks on this beach, I didn't dream of you then. E.M." She mailed it off, hoping he'd find it uplifting, romantic . . . pretty.

Love letters mounted. Among her favorites were two miniature paintings from Phin. The postcard she'd sent inspired him to paint similar images while on a short reprieve—a place he called Walberswick. It was on the River Blyth in England. The stack of mementos grew so thick Esmerelda eventually splurged on a handsome leather letter box. It was sturdy enough to hold the emotion that flowed through ink. Every letter from Phin began with "My Dear Esme, If Paris is France, You are the World . . ."

His experiences were terrifying and glorious. Over time, he'd written about different battles, one in particular—Belleau Wood. It appeared to affect him greatly, and Esmerelda could tell Phin was holding back ghastly details. His many letters left Esme proud and fearful, each one prompting a greater sense of longing. Back then, when she could claim her own freedom, if the worst were to happen, she'd only know because Phin's letters would stop. The war office wouldn't notify someone who was less than a wife.

Now, sitting there, Esmerelda had no idea if Phin was dead or alive. Was Phin thinking the same thing about her, wondering why he hadn't heard from her in months? She pushed the sad thoughts away, reverting to warmer memories of Phin's letters. Aside from Marigold, recollections of his words and handwriting provided Esmerelda's only source of comfort. Other letters had spoken of battlefield rigors that left her heart pounding. Curiously enough, it was one of Phin's first letters that had brought a smile to her face.

The letter had been mostly about Oscar. Phin asked Esmerelda to thank him for the saddle. She knew of the saddle but could not imagine how or why Oscar would have given it to Phin. The letter had gone on to explain that Phin found it waiting aboard the ship on which he'd sailed to Europe. He told her about a note from Oscar, which said, "This fine leather saw me through a Rough Rider battle. I've no use for it now. Our girl tells me it's you she wants. Make it back safe, else I'll have to track you down in Hell. Godspeed, boy."

Phin often wrote while he was waiting for the next battle plan. He talked about the small village of Aisne, war-torn like most of France. The few remaining farmers were grateful to the Americans, offering them straw beds since they had no food. He mentioned the Gagne family, and how the daughter, Maree, who was only fourteen, risked her life to carry messages between Phin's division of soldiers and officer camps miles away.

Phin had shared other glimpses of war, insisting that Hassan was the true hero. It all made clever sense then, why the army had recruited a Choctaw Indian from Oklahoma to New York and on to the war.

Hassan's native language was being used as code to thwart German attempts to steal information. Esmerelda thought it the one smart thing she could attribute to men in power, for those left to wage the bloodiness of war.

The letters mentioning Hassan and the daring French farm girl, Maree—reading them was the last time she recalled her heart beating with something other than fear. Not long after those letters, life came undone by way of a twisted spiral. Benjamin returned—a short leave from his Washington post. She knew this when he showed up unannounced in the audience of a Palace performance. She'd been wearing the white gown that night. With him seated in the front row, it crossed Esmerelda's mind that Benjamin appeared more aroused than usual by the sight of her.

Her ambivalent reaction turned to terror when she found him inside her supper club hotel room. The conversation had gone crooked from the start. He'd been seated at the table, Marigold discarded carelessly onto the floor. The letter box was open, Phin's letters strewn about like confetti, shredded to bits. Esmerelda was angry and she hotly confronted him. It'd been a spark that lit Benjamin's fury, which unleashed itself in that singular moment.

Benjamin told Esmerelda what he'd witnessed the year before from his new suite of rooms. He'd seen her kiss Phin in the alleyway. He insisted that he'd been devastated but kept hope it was nothing more than a girl giving a boy a sendoff—a warm memory to think of as he died on a battlefield. When Esmerelda had approached Benjamin about the Palace stage and remained at the hotel, his hope had renewed. He'd gone on, saying that at first he thought, like Ingrid, perhaps he only needed to give Esmerelda more time. "Like Ingrid?" she'd said. "The German girl you fancied? The one you sent back home to the soldier who loved her?"

"Well, isn't it lovely and convenient that no one questions a happy ending—or the disappearance of an enemy wench." He was seated at the table, and his dark gaze drew up and down her. "Not in this climate, nor on this side of the ocean." He'd gone on to throw the pieces of Phin's letters—which might as well have been Esmerelda's heart—into the air, pondering how he could have been so wrong about two different women.

"I tried, Esmerelda, for so long. To keep my affections in proper order, to wait like the gentleman my mother expected I should be." His rant escalated, Benjamin insisting that she'd done nothing but use him and his heart—just like Ingrid. "The girl cozied up to me only to keep herself stateside and employed. I swore I'd never be anyone fool's again." Benjamin paused, the moment at an impasse. Then his rage unhinged, starting with the mermaid painting. He'd slammed it against the hearth, tearing the canvas, before throwing it into the fire. Flames rose high, meeting with fresh fuel.

Benjamin had demanded to know what Esmerelda imagined his actions meant—his assistance, his attention, his benevolent gift of housing. His endless patience. "Why are women so obtuse? Tell me, Esmerelda. The keeper and the kept. The first time I thought it was a language barrier. But is the concept so difficult?"

He hadn't waited for an answer but took what he felt he was owed—forcibly and with greater zeal than Lowell. Initially, the act had only incensed Benjamin more. As his powerful, angry thrusts assaulted her body, he'd widened his eyes and said, "I see you did more than kiss the Hell's Kitchen pauper goodbye. Tell me, did fucking you make him feel like he had promise in life?" And in addition to raping her, this was the first time Benjamin struck Esmerelda. "No matter. It only goes to prove my point—what you are. A vaudeville whore who I should have never trusted."

After, his maniacal mood shifted again and he smiled, kissing her shoulder. Esmerelda gagged into a handkerchief, dabbing blood and tears from her cheek. "Not to worry," he'd said, touching her hair, dipping to meet her glassy gaze. "I'll make a distant memory of him—deader than the war has surely left him. With the fight nearly over, my father has seen to my reassignment, closer to home. I've seen to a lock on your door. The Palace will be informed that you're not well and must regretfully abandon your performances." He squeezed her bruised shoulder, and pain of every kind had snaked through Esmerelda, mind and body. "Forthcoming performances, my dear, will be a private New York affair."

# CHAPTER
# TWENTY-SIX

*New York City*
*Present Day*

Pete's heart moved faster than his feet up the hotel stairs. Em had taken the lead, pulling him by the hand. His head pounded. He couldn't untangle a thought. Expected nerves and anticipation, or was he walking into an ethereal apocalypse? When they reached the second-floor landing, he stopped. He couldn't shake the visual of heading up one more flight, turning left, opening the third door down, and finding Esme's ghost. Of course, the fact that he knew the precise route seemed to indicate that they were on to something. He stepped in front of Em. "This way."

From behind, she replied, "I know."

The rows of doors were identical, except one. It had two locks, though the door was slightly ajar. Pete gave it a push, and appropriately enough, it creaked. The vacant square footage was stifling. Em moved forward and he stayed near the door. His eyes watered. The room had the same effect as Em's doll—validation of a place he knew. Aside from a few scattered boxes, the room was empty. He knew the fireplace, the arch of brick, though the hearth had been sealed shut. He pointed. "The dresser was over there."

"So Esme, she—"

"Stood right in front of it. I see the whole thing in the mirror. Well, my action . . . reaction." Beneath their feet was hardwood, and the two looked down as if a brilliant bloodstain should surround their shoes. The floorboards were dull and scratched, but no more than the rest of the room. As the manager had noted, the bathroom was newer, or at least not circa 1919. Pete didn't go in.

But he did approach the fireplace. The rain had stopped. A blast of sunlight burned through dark clouds and into the window, past his shoulder. The morning sun met with the fireplace. He traced a faint outline on the wall with his fingertips.

"The painting," Em said. "You can see where the painting hung."

"The English hunting scene," he said with certainty. "The one with the fox running for its life." Pete pivoted toward the window, where the ceiling wasn't high and he could easily reach the top of the frame. "It's the same window."

"How do you know that?"

From the upper edge of the frame, he wiggled a small object free. "It's a shank-head nail, common in the early twentieth century. It held the other end of the clothesline."

"It held . . ." Her gaze rose from Pete's palm to his eyes. "That's, uh . . . that's amazing." She took a turn around the room. "Pete."

"Yeah."

"If we find tufts of black cat fur, know I'm out of here."

"I just realized something about you."

She spun around to face him, and he could see she was trying to hold her expression steady. "When you're nervous," he said, "you make jokes."

"Karma's yin to your yang?"

"It's been noted that my sober nature could use a counterweight."

"Lifelong habit for me. I make jokes if I'm uncomfortable, socially challenged."

"Interesting. Usually I say 'fuck this' and leave."

"I see." She continued to circle the room. "Right now, I'd probably slay it at open mic night downstairs."

"Why?" He stepped into her nervous path. "Tell me what you're afraid of, Em. What am I missing? What's here that's got you as spooked as me?"

The corners of her mouth turned down. "You'll be disappointed. It's more about me *not* being like you, not having any sort of extrasensory gift."

"We've established that. You don't speak to the dead. You haven't lived another life."

"No. But I think I may be the caretaker of one." She said it fast, like ripping off a Band-Aid. "Dreams," she said. "I've had endless dreams since I was little. They're all about one thing . . . a single time period. Dreams I vividly recall since . . . oh, since about the time Zeke gave me Mary."

"Dreams," Pete said. It was the go-to word people might use to describe his past life experiences, and he was leery of how easily one could be confused for the other.

"Back in East Marion, at the Rabbit Lane house, when I mentioned déjà vu, you were so quick to dismiss it—"

"I apologized. I shouldn't have been so insensitive . . . rude."

"It's okay. I can see that about you."

"More humor?"

She didn't say anything.

"Okay. So a fact. Still . . ."

Em squeezed shut her eyes. A tear seeped through and Pete brushed at it. He let the camera bag slide to the floor and pulled Emerald to him. He wasn't sure whose heart was beating harder. "Tell me, Em. If nothing else, maybe I can fix the parts that affect you. That'd be something." Pete sank into the notion. Actually, he reveled in it—the idea of fixing someone else's fucked-up life. Or in her case, the potential for one. He felt her arms tighten as Em whispered into his ear.

"My dreams, they're not like your repetitive, real visits. I understand what you've told me about that. My dreams, they're tiny pieces, brilliant flashes from another era. At least, that's the way I've come to think about them—like a mixed-up, torn-up storyboard sprinkled into my nights. There's no order. Sometimes there's a boy in them and sometimes they're beautiful." She clung tighter to him. "Sometimes he's the hero. Other parts are haunting . . . traumatic."

"I can definitely understand that."

"And it's not always about what I dream. The thing that bothers me most is what I feel when the dreams are over. When I wake up, it's as if—"

He stared down into her face. "It's as if all the emotion of what you dreamed belongs to you."

"Yes," she said, nodding hard. "I feel it—all the way to my bones."

"Different than, say, if you dreamed about showing up late to an exam or even had a disturbing dream about your family, friends."

"Very different. Like I'm not able to convince myself it wasn't real."

"Okay, so you've got my ear. I can relate."

"No. I don't think you can. Unlike your visits to another life, these dreams aren't about me." A flutter of laughter that wasn't terribly funny lilted from her. "Why do you think I majored in psychology? I wanted to figure out . . . *why me?* But it didn't help, or I was too afraid. So I end up talking to murderers, people who surely had to face worse things in their own dreams. I know . . ." The breath she pulled in bordered on hyperventilating. "I know it sounds crazy, doesn't it?"

Pete reached forward as if to touch her face, then didn't. "I'll let you know when you get to the baseline of the crazy meter. You're safe, believe me." Her bottled-up troubles continued to flow, Em swiping an arm across her snotty nose, tearstained cheeks. Pete wished it were 1919. Surely he'd have a handkerchief to offer her.

"So here's the rest. There's a girl in my dreams and she isn't me." She blinked at him, dabbing at a smudge of mascara. "It's . . . it's like being the caretaker of someone else's dreams, maybe their life."

"You're the eyes of the dream. Say it, Em. With everything you've learned since you walked into that bungalow. I saw you stare at the English saddle, look at the carousel horse. You know the beach in Bayport. You knew the truck in the barn too, didn't you?"

She nodded, her fist pressed tight to her pinched mouth. More tears spilled, the validation of haunting reveries.

"It's why you wanted to know if your uncle Zeke had any more specific message for you, isn't it? You were hoping—"

"He might give me a clue. If I should tell you about the dreams or if they really have everything to do with you." She brushed at another tear.

"He kind of has. Between Zeke and Brody, the timing of this trip home . . . what happened with my parents. It's taken the convergence of all of it to get me to here. But mostly, it's taken you."

"And I don't know if that's good or bad."

"Why? Tell me, about the dreams. Like this room we're in, you've seen it before?"

"Glimpses." She ran a hand through her thick hair. "A lot of the dreams occur outside, on a beach, in a giant, old-fashioned amusement park. When I was in high school, we covered a section on twentieth-century Americana. There were pictures of a place called—"

"Luna Park."

"Yes. Luna Park. Would you believe back in high school, when I saw the photos, I actually passed out. Hit my head right on the edge of Mrs. McKneely's desk."

Pete's eyes widened at the detail.

"Truthfully, it's the biggest reason I came to New York. I wanted an up-close look at the girl's dreams. Of course, Luna Park, the original one . . . it's been gone for decades." She shrugged. "I can only get so close to everything. To her."

"And whose dreams do you believe you've been taking care of, Em? Who do they belong to?"

"Esme," she said, as if making her own murderous confession. "I've known for certain since you showed me the photos of Esmerelda Moon."

"And have you ever—"

"Dreamed about what you relive? What happened in this room? No. But I wasn't entirely surprised when you showed me the photos of her bruised face. In some of the more disturbing dreams, I see flickers of it. It's so violent. There's so much anger. Those are the worst dreams."

"And whoever does this to her—"

"I don't know who he is."

"Why didn't you want to tell me this before now?"

"For a few reasons." In the stuffy room, filled with memories and dreams that so deeply affected them both, Em took a step back. "One, I wasn't sure if you'd believe me. Not because my claim was so grand, but because it's too small compared to yours."

"And the other reason?"

"Unlike those men I interviewed in prison, you admit to murder. You punish yourself for having killed Esmerelda Moon. I also can't say for certain it's only one man who hurts Esme. I've never seen a face." She looked at Pete's bruised hand. "Just his fist—her fear."

"So bring it full circle, Em. Say what it is you're thinking. You might not be able to pick Esmerelda Moon's killer out of a lineup, but there's still every chance it could be me."

# CHAPTER
# TWENTY-SEVEN

Em's schedule kept them from further tag-teaming history. At least that's what Pete told himself. But perhaps it was more about what she couldn't put together, and Em was right to be cautious. The two of them stood in the middle of a murder scene. Em now had a whole name for the girl in her dreams. She'd seen photos, proving this was not déjà vu. Everything she knew had been validated. So when present-day reality gave Em a way out, Pete didn't stand in her way.

"I have to go," she said, glancing at her phone. "I have a three-hour shift at the Y on the West Side."

"What do you do there?"

"Lifeguard. The under-twelve free swim."

"You're a lifeguard."

"Why do you say it like that, like you're surprised?"

"I'm not. In fact, I'm often impressed with a lifeguard's ability to save a life."

She left after giving him her cell phone number and the address of her late-afternoon audition.

Pete wasn't done absorbing a place so surreal and familiar. Compared to the memories racing through his mind, the space was disturbingly vacant.

The contrast was frustrating. Yet he stayed, even as sweat puddled down his back and the stale air bordered on suffocating. Eventually, Pete wrestled with the narrow window until it stuttered open. Its wood was so rotted the swell of humidity kept it raised. He sat on the sill and city noises flooded in. Aside from the dead rat in the alley below and a sliver of clearing sky above, the building across the way was the only view. A solid breeze billowed, so cool and at odds with the day, he thought July had given way to October. Pete breathed in fresh air but halted on his inhale. His hair wasn't blowing back, but forward. The rush of cool air came from inside the room. Startled and perched on the narrow edge, Pete lost his balance and grabbed on to the window frame. The decayed molding cracked and gave way. In a frantic second, he nearly plunged backward, out the open hole. A force hauled him forward. Pete tripped over his own feet, stumbling into the middle of the room. He blinked, keenly aware of the specter assist.

He looked to the barren corners. There was a presence and it felt demure. The specter was also vague, as if it'd expended its energy to rescue him from the fall. He couldn't imagine it was Esme. Hell, why wouldn't she have shoved him out the window and been done with it? "Talk about motive and opportunity," he said aloud.

Pete considered his uncle Brody, even Zeke Dublin. No. This specter was female, and he was forced to reconsider Esme. "So," he said, steadying a breath and his immediate fate. "You still don't want to talk. Fair enough. I get it, with everything that happened here, between us." He pointed to the window. "Sorry if I'm confused, but if you wanted an eye-for-an-eye, it seems like you passed on a golden opportunity." Then he muttered softly, "Of course, if you knock off the human, and your goal is torment . . . game over."

On those words, his camera bag moved. It slid inches across the hardwood, as if the antiquated building had tilted twenty degrees. Pete understood the energy required for a specter to move an object, even when drawing muscle off his extrasensory abilities. Physical demonstrations were rare. It also read as a sign. Whoever the specter, its aim was to bring a strong message. "Okay, so my camera bag has your attention. Photos?" he said, more to himself than the elusive ghost.

It'd always been his plan to photograph the room, and he retrieved the Canon 5D, changing out the lens like he was in a foxhole during a Fallujah bombing—steady but guarded. The 50 mm prime lens was better in tight spots or when semiautomatic gunfire rained down. This felt similar, just slightly scarier, and he concentrated on the business of being a photographer. In a fast rotation, Pete fired off a dozen shots, capturing the room in the round. Hurriedly, he reviewed the images. "Well, I suppose any other outcome would have been a letdown." In all the pictures, orbs were visible. They were faint in some shots—different hues, varying strength, but present in every frame. So obvious, in fact, if he were to turn photos like this in to Flagler, he'd tell Pete, "Don't give me crap like this—photoshop your shitty lighting errors before submitting, St John."

Looking between the last shot and the empty room, he realized the entity was gone. Pete didn't know whether to be disappointed or relieved. He felt alone. His memories had far greater meaning than a room where time had continued on for a hundred years. It felt like the Rabbit Lane bungalow—a structure filled with physical tally marks but no real answers.

Pete squatted next to the bag and changed the lens, putting the camera away. The postcard caught his eye. "You've got to be . . ." This morning, when he looked at the card, he recalled it facing picture-side out. The addressed side was now visible through the clear plastic pocket. Pete snatched it from the case, and his knees met with the floor. First, a message had mysteriously appeared on the front—old news now. Then yesterday, a return address had shown up on the back. It had delivered them to Hupp's Supper Club. And now the ghost gift appeared complete, bearing a recipient: *Phin Seaborn, 114th Division, American Expeditionary Forces, Aisne, France.*

It took Pete only a second to know what he needed to do next. Executing the thought took longer: fifteen minutes of googling and a half-hour cab ride across town, plus his press credentials, to access the best print archives of World War I available. An elderly woman led him to a temperature-controlled basement room at the *New York Times*. "We archive to whatever standard is available. But anything that old . . ." She pointed to narrow metal shelving, rows and rows. "Precomputer, pre-microfilm, it's preserved in its original format here. Library of Congress has microfilm, along with Recordak, but you seem kind of in a hurry. Like you'd rather not take a trip to DC."

"Uh, no. Not if I can help it." Pete gulped at the endless metal trays that looked like mini coroner slabs—stored and bygone. "I may be a while."

"You did note a specific time frame." She pointed to an isolated section. "We also adopted all the archived copies of the *New York Tribune* from that era. Seemed like the conscientious, custodial thing to do, print media being such an endangered species."

"The *Tribune*?"

"Yes. The paper actually trumped the *Times* back in the day. Let's see . . ." She squinted upward through round, black frames that contrasted with her white hair. "That would be 1866 to around the mid-1920s. Then it merged with the *Herald*."

"Thanks," Pete said, staving off the sense of being swamped by the past.

"Well, good luck. We close at six. Just let me know when you leave." She headed for the door. "The *Tribune* . . . ," she said. Pete looked at her from across the deep room. "You said World War I, right?" He nodded; she touched her fingertips to her head. "Took me a minute. We did have an editor years ago, photo-slash-history buff. He'd spend his lunch hours down here, fascinated with *Tribune* coverage of World War I. Photos in particular. Apparently, whatever photog they had embedded was way ahead of his time."

"Really? A photographer ahead of his time?" The camera bag on Pete's shoulder slid to the floor.

"Like I said, good luck." Her gaze trailed around the massive archives before she closed the door, keeping elements like humidity and modern-day technology at bay.

◆ ◆ ◆

For whatever the Hupp hotel room did not deliver, the archived *Tribune* pages did. Within an hour, Pete unearthed a long-ago past. His first inkling of Phineas Seaborn was not related to war but random society photos from a July 1917 edition of the *Tribune*. He recognized the rich paneling, the stage Samsara's manager had described. The people pictured meant nothing, set off no inner alarm—just a bunch of well-dressed patrons toasting champagne glasses, posing at tables filled with china dishes, cigars, and the air of money.

He continued to scour editions, trying not to go too fast or miss anything that might be a clue. A photograph from a March 1918 edition jumped out at Pete. It showed off a young man dressed in a tux, dimples so deep they struck him as dastardly as opposed to genuine. The photo credit didn't belong to Phineas Seaborn but to a Charles Carlisle. The caption read: *Benjamin Hupp, socialite and future heir, poses bravely, ready to embark on his duty to country. Hupp is to be stationed at a standby post in Washington, DC, awaiting further orders.*

For the longest time, Pete stared at the photo. He felt as if Benjamin Hupp glowered back, as if they'd stared at one another before. Pete's eyelids fluttered as he tried to summon where or when. It frustrated him so, to know specific moments from another life but never recall more than the parts he'd visited. From beneath his hand, the photo emanated heat—one small clue that there was a missing memory. It wasn't the blistering effect from the photograph of Esme, but hot enough. Pete shook his head at the winsome image of Hupp. He reeked of entitlement, looking like someone Pete probably wouldn't much like in this century or the last.

A story his mother once told him muscled its way into his thoughts. It was the grisly tale of how and why she'd ended up with the pockmarks and bites on her arm, the scar on her chin. It'd been a warning she'd reluctantly shared with her son. Evil. Her scars were left by the presence of evil. Looking at the deep-dimpled, fashionably savvy heir, a tingle crawled up Pete's back.

The woman who granted Pete access to the archives had said photo taking was prohibited. He assumed it was professional courtesy when they allowed Pete to hang on to his camera. Admittedly, the executive assistant knew of Pete's work, was familiar with photos the *Times* had run. Pete couldn't break the rules, at least not blatantly with the Canon 5D. Fortunately, that camera wasn't his only resource. While the room was surely monitored, Pete casually pulled out his iPhone, snapping photos under the guise of sending a text message. He was a lot of things, some shaky and unknown, perhaps traits as appalling as the ones Emerald Montague saw in her dreams. But he was also a heralded war correspondent, and Peter St John wasn't so easily deterred.

Neither was Phineas Seaborn, as the *Tribune* pages revealed. As Pete delved deeper into the archives, into the heart of the Great War, the photos and illustrations began to tell a macabre story. Pete's breath caught—again, he recognized his work. He found twenty, maybe thirty photos and sketches. All were of battlefields in France—bloody, gruesome, accurate, and defining of war. "Phineas Seaborn's war." Pete had been sitting on a metal stool. He stood and sat, repeating the motion. The antsy feeling was the same, the way he felt after a past life experience, the desire to climb out of his own skin. He forced himself to sit once more. His eyes darted between photos and illustrations.

He smelled blood and dirt, the rotting limbs of dying men, the stench of trench foot, the sight of tetanus—lockjawed faces, twisting muscle spasms, fever. Blood spouting from mouths and eyes. Even in his present-day war travels, he'd never seen anything like it, the volume of dead men gut-wrenching. The black-and-white images ran in color through his head because, really, these were his memories.

Pete closed his eyes. The English saddle and the black horse. The huge draft horse lay on its side, the left leg cannon bone protruding. In the animal's own blood, he'd marked its head with an X, between its right eye and ear. Then he held a pistol to it. He'd squeezed that trigger too. Pete's eyes teared—then and now—hearing the discharge of the weapon into the horse's massive skull, killing it instantly.

He blinked dry his damp eyes and snapped photos of his photos, the detailed illustrations. Beyond the similarity of artistic interpretation, he saw what Phin Seaborn had done. It was the same thing as Pete—he'd documented war, hoping to send a message of peace. "And so then what did you do?" he said to himself, posing the question to Phineas Seaborn. Pete did a quick Google search, but nothing about a Phineas Seaborn turned up.

Months after the Battle of Belleau Wood, the photos and illustrations stopped. The famed battle took place in June 1918, a fact Pete had known for years. The Seaborn photos and drawings last appeared in a December 1918 edition. That much made sense. Media from the era traveled by ship back to the States. Publication came weeks, if not months, after the fact. Yet this felt like something more than a war that had ended.

If it was not for Esme's murder, Pete might have thought Phineas Seaborn went down in the flames of glory on a battlefield. That he'd not only served his country but also recorded the devastation of war for the world to see. But Pete knew that wasn't Phin's fate. He knew it because his handwriting was on a strip of photos, showing off Esmerelda Moon's battered face. Photos taken in January of 1919. It was difficult to reconcile—the hard evidence of a war hero in front of him and the man who would shoot Esmerelda Moon. But Pete also understood how PTSD could ravage a mind, the hair trigger it could produce.

"Maybe it's exactly what happened. Maybe it all came to a head and he . . . *I* snapped in an Upper East Side hotel room."

Pete continued on, processing newspaper pages as fast as his mind's eye would allow. He panicked slightly, wondering if this hunt would end like the Rabbit Lane bungalow and hotel room and his other life—a dead end. He moved through years. Hope turned, like the delicate yellowed pages he touched, into a fragile thing.

With the last archived issue of the *Tribune*, May 30, 1925, an article and a photo caught Pete's eye. He studied the photo first: a solemn-faced bride, dark haired, so different looking from Esme in complexion, figure, and presence. The article next to it was titled: *American War Hero Lives Life in Europe*. Pete read, with bated interest, the long-awaited conclusion of the life he once lived:

> Phineas Seaborn, Great War hero, who fought in and recorded battles that amassed more than three hundred thousand American casualties, now lives a near-recluse life in a hut without electricity or running water on the banks of Walberswick, England. In addition to his eminent contributions as a fighter, photographer, and illustrative artist, Seaborn also made headlines for rejecting President Wilson's 1919 invitation to the White House to celebrate his Great War victories. Instead, after a brief stateside adjournment, civilian Seaborn returned to a post-war Europe in the spring of 1919.
>
> Over the years, Seaborn has refused requests for interviews or photos. It's believed that his abandonment of the United States is a protest

of the events he witnessed. In a related 1921 interview, conducted from the Choctaw reservation in Oklahoma, Native American spy Hassan Lightfoot referenced a friendship with the elusive Seaborn. However, Lightfoot's claims could not be corroborated, and it is reputed that the Indian spy, despite any purported war aid, embellished what was likely a brief encounter with the revered hero.

This article notes a recent surfacing of Seaborn. In the midst of a torrential downpour, a marriage ceremony took place between Mr. Seaborn and Miss Maree Gagne, of Aisne, France, this past week in Paris. The two met during Seaborn's term abroad, when Miss Gagne ferried messages between Allied forces. When approached by reporters, Seaborn was asked if he chose the French capital because of his wartime connections. Perhaps a testament to his personal ravages, with his new bride beside him, Seaborn replied, "I was once told Paris is France. I don't give a damn about the rest of the World anymore."

# CHAPTER
# TWENTY-EIGHT

The theater was black, and it made Pete think of the moments before the start of a movie. It also reminded him of the explanation he'd given Em, how he perceived messages from the dead. He thought it would be great if a reel could run right now; it might fill in his own remaining blanks. It was also cold as shit, like the bluffs overlooking Iceland's black sands. This was Pete's initial impression, having walked inside from the brightly lit, steamy street.

He was anxious to see Em, to share everything he'd learned. She'd told him auditions could take hours, and he wasn't sure he had that kind of patience left. Pete's eyes adjusted to the dim setting. Near the front of the theater, a row of seats contained a handful of people and a lamp. But apparently Em had done her waiting before Pete arrived. Her name was the next one called. He slipped into the last row and sat down.

The light changed as she came onto the stage, one gold beam shining down on her. She looked nervous. That couldn't be good. He shifted in his seat, concerned that she might break into a standup routine. A man in the closer row asked inaudible questions. From his back-row view, Pete couldn't make out Em's answers. She wrung her hands, smiling, then not smiling at the small group, whose job was clearly to judge.

Worry crept in like the cold had, a consuming and noticeable contrast. What if she was indisputably talentless? Sang like a bullfrog or read dialogue like her emotions were Siri generated. Pete fought the urge to propel forward, snatch her from imminent doom. Instead he inched to the edge of his seat until his knees dug into the next row.

Music from a piano filled the theater. Em let out a note. Then her voice went one way, the sound from the piano another. It all stopped abruptly. Em came to the edge of the stage. There was fast conversation between her and the piano player. She nodded, though her smile surpassed tense. "Come on, Em," he said. "You can do this. Keep it together."

The piano began again. He didn't know the song, but this time there were a few bars of introduction—a ballad. Pete's trepidation melted as her voice rose. Not only did she sing exquisitely, she sang in a voice scored to his soul—or so he knew the moment he heard it. In the icebox theater, a bead of sweat gathered on his upper lip. For the first time in his life, memories trickled in. Pete hadn't heard that voice in a hundred years.

The people in the up-close row did not appear to be drawn into the same mesmerized state. They simply offered Em a cursory thank-you, no compliment attached. Were they nuts? It was nothing short of astounding. He thought about expressing his opinion, but by the time Pete calmed, reentered the moment, Em was gone from the stage. Emotion took another hairpin turn, and he was consumed by the thought of her simply vanishing—like maybe Pete was just a bit player in one of her curious dreams. A floor-level side door opened. Em walked in a steady gait up the side aisle and toward the exit. He followed.

Crowds were thick on the sidewalk, the summer sun unrelenting, even past six o'clock. By the time Pete's eye caught hers, it wasn't apparent that he too had just exited the theater, and he kept this to himself. He touched her lightly on the arm. "How'd it go?"

"Oh, there you are. Good timing." The two skirted around crowds into the theater alcove. "It took forever. Fine." She shrugged. "You never know until they call—or don't."

"So you think you'll get the part?"

Laughter, which had begun to hit his ears with the need of a next breath, rose from her. "Probably not. Competition is beyond fierce. My résumé isn't that impressive."

"But you sang . . . I'm willing to bet you sang beautifully."

"Maybe. I had a little trouble with the key and accompanist at first. Nothing unusual there. But you know . . ."

He shook his head vaguely, stumped as to why the people inside hadn't chased her onto the sidewalk, thrusting a contract in her face.

"They'll want someone shorter or taller. Someone who doesn't stand out so much onstage." She shuffled a hand through her bright hair. "Someone who stands out more." She smiled at him. "Someone who's sleeping with the director."

"You'd never do anything like that." He spoke with feverish conviction and Em half smiled at him.

"No. I don't suppose I would. But it did work for Caroline. Got her a speaking part in *Chicago* last winter."

"Well, winters in Chicago, who needs that?"

She laughed. The sound nearly made Pete forget his afternoon until Em asked, "Tell me what you've been up to?"

◆  ◆  ◆

"Amazing," she murmured for the fifth or sixth time, scrolling through the archived photos he'd snapped on the sly. "Pete, finding these photos, the article about Phin . . ." Em sat cross-legged on the white leather sofa in her apartment. She leaned and picked up the postcard, which was on the glass-top coffee table. For the past hour, she'd been enthralled as Pete detailed his discoveries. "It's incredible." She examined the card again—message, return address, and now a recipient. "The new information on the postcard and what you learned about Phin *Seaborn*. He has a last name! He has an entire history. A hero, Pete. He was a hero."

He'd been captivated by her state of wonder. His mood, and he guessed his expression, darkened.

"What? Doesn't this put your mind at ease?"

"Not really," he said softly. "If anything, it further validates what I know."

"That's not possible—"

"Or just cleverly psychotic. Look at the timeline." She put the postcard back on the table, and Pete reached for his camera bag, plucking out the battered images of Esme. "That article was written six years after her death. Phin Seaborn came back to the States. The article assumes I . . . *he* ran away to Europe to escape the notoriety of being a war hero. But we know differently, don't we? Phin Seaborn fled to Europe to escape his crime—either literally or maybe the mental imprint of what he'd done. Which scenario makes more sense?"

She bit down on her lip, and Pete picked up his phone again, swishing past images. He flashed the phone at Em. "This is our hotel heir, Benjamin Hupp. The picture creeps me out. I don't know . . ." He shook his head. "Maybe Hupp was in cahoots with Seaborn, helped him get out of the country or something."

Em looked unconvinced.

"Okay, so that's total speculation with zero proof."

"Well, let's see if we can find some." She picked up her phone and searched the Hupp name. Her fair brow knotted. "Huh. There's not much, but it's all so old . . . wait. Here's an entry about a Winston Hupp. But it sounds like he could have been the father. According to this . . ." She scrolled past what looked like an old newspaper article. "Mostly it has to do with the Depression and money. Apparently, Winston Hupp went bankrupt." Em looked at Pete. "The barkeep told us that. It just says that the Hupps left New York in financial ruin, like many 'spoiled riches of the day.' It doesn't mention a son, but let me keep . . ." Em abandoned her search, wrapping her fingers around Pete's wrist and guiding his phone toward her, getting a better look at the picture on his screen. "Uh, Pete. Never mind the Internet, I can tell you something about Benjamin Hupp that's not speculation."

"What's that?"

"I've seen him—in my dreams."

"You've seen—"

The apartment door burst open and Caroline blew through.

"Wow," she said. "You're still here. Seems almost impossible."

Pete blinked, looking from his phone to the gust of air and disruption she brought. "And no one dropped a house on you today. Same conclusion."

As Pete said this, Em shot him a look. Caroline turned for the tiny kitchen, helping herself to the same bottled water as yesterday. He glanced at the two tap-filled water glasses on the table.

She carried the water in one hand, holding a black-covered notebook in the other, and came into the small living area. "I see you're also still on my sofa."

He looked at his watch and Em read his mind. "*Wicked* is dark on Mondays."

"So this is just a personal performance today."

Caroline smiled and something familiar prickled inside Pete. It was enough to shut him up. Her thin hair was pulled into a severe ponytail that highlighted her sad brown eyes.

Any visual was overrun by Caroline's mouth, going on about a television show pilot. "Here. Look at the script. It's perfect for you." She plunked down her water bottle which knocked into one water glass, spilling it onto the postcard.

Em grabbed the card from the coffee table flood, but it was too late. "Oh no! Oh, it's ruined!" She jumped up from the sofa and hurried to the kitchen, blotting the card with a dish towel. Seconds later she held it up, but the damage was done. Puddles of vintage ink swam together, the image and writing one murky blur. "Pete, I'm so sorry!"

Caroline squinted, her neck craning forward. "What was it?"

"A postcard," Pete said dully.

"Okay, so it's New York. I'll get you a dozen new ones tomorrow."

"It wasn't *any* postcard, Caroline. It was a vintage card from Long Island, from 1918." She continued to shake the ruined thing, as if drying it out might restore it.

"Fine. I'll have it fixed in a jiff. I'm sure there's another available on eBay."

"You can't replace it." Em's voice tensed. "You can't dial Daddy and have the collection's designer whip you up a fresh one! The card is irreplaceable. There isn't another one like it—anywhere."

"Don't be so dramatic, Emerald Ailish Montague. It's an old postcard. What could possibly be so special about it?"

"Are you honestly so self-centered that—"

"It's fine." Pete stood. Caroline had taken a defensive pose, and it probably wouldn't take more than another sentence for her to kick Em to the curb. "Really. It's not a big deal."

"How can you say that?" Em pressed.

"Because I think we learned everything we're going to from the postcard."

"Tracing your lineage?" Caroline said, fists planted into her tiny hips.

"Actually, you're not far off." He picked up his camera bag, passing by the puddle.

In one fast motion, Em stepped into the living room, throwing the dish towel at Caroline. "Mop it up." She grabbed Pete's hand and pulled him along until they were inside her bedroom, slamming the door. They were in complete darkness. "She just makes me so . . ." She knew every square inch, and a moment later, soft hues rose from a string of tiny globe lights. "Damn mad!" Em jutted forward, hitting "Play" on her iPod. Music rose. She still held tight to the waterlogged postcard. "I'm sorry. So sorry about the card."

"Seriously." Pete eased it from her grip, placing it on the makeshift book-stack table. "I wasn't making excuses when I said we got everything we needed from it."

"You don't know that."

"Yeah. I do." He swore he heard bells chime, but it was muddled in the iPod music. Oddly enough, what he also felt was calm. "My monsters don't live under the bed, Em. For sure there were clues on that ghost gift postcard. But the things that haunt me, they're not written in code or hidden there." He gestured to the card and muddied ink. "My answers aren't in old newspaper stories either. The thing I'm chasing, or running from, it lives in my mind . . ."

She moved closer. "Your soul."

"So far as I know." Instead of haunting emotions connected to Esme, for the first time since Pete was twelve, he felt that passion ebb. "I don't mind telling you, relocating all of those . . . *feelings*, it's not the worst idea." He closed his arms around Em; her head tilted up and his came forward until their foreheads bumped. "What is this music?"

"It's the score from the show I auditioned for—a new musical. The producers lifted the melodies from the vaudeville era, expired copyrights."

"Making it fair game."

Her head nodded softly against his. "It's kind of hypnotic after listening to it a few hundred times." They were swaying now, not really dancing, more like a subtle shift around the edge of time. "They've been auditioning girls for months. Rumor is they can't find anyone with the right authenticity." She inched back, her eyes fast on his.

"Em, I don't know a damn thing about Broadway auditions, but they're crazier than me if they don't see you as authentic."

Pete couldn't say that kissing Emerald Montague had been on his mind before that moment. But a few seconds later it was all he could think about, and Pete's mouth met hers in a way that said this wasn't their first kiss. She responded in kind, the two of them kissing until they were lying on the daybed. His mouth moved over her fair, freckled skin. The buttons on her blue cotton blouse were tiny, and they both laughed as Pete undid them, only straying slightly from suave. She was faster, tugging on his polo until it was over his head and on the floor.

While the bed was old and narrow, it was a perfect fit as long as she was beneath him. He kissed her hungrily, Pete making a smoother advance on her bra clasp than he had the blouse buttons. The garment fell away and his gaze met with her bare body. "You . . . you're so beautiful." In the dim light, Pete anticipated a subtle blush. But Em wasn't looking at him. She was focused on the ruddy, wide bruise on his shoulder.

Her fingertips came forward. "How . . . what happened to you?"

And reality crashed down onto the narrow bed, into the moment. Pete recoiled, their bodies parting. He shuffled hurriedly to the far end of the bed, crouched on his knees. She'd seen disturbing things in the past few days, but she hadn't seen this. "It . . ." Pete glanced at his own shoulder, still swollen. In another day or two, the red would turn a purplish black. In a few weeks there'd likely be another. Worse, there was no predicting how a night alone with her might end. "My last visit to my past life. The reentry slammed into a plaster wall."

She came forward, meeting his position. "Why didn't you say something? It must hurt like hell." Her hand came forward again. Pete jerked back.

"Don't. In fact, don't come any closer." He started to move off the bed. Em's fingers locked around his forearm. "I don't know what the fuck I was thinking. You can't do this. Not with a damn ghostly prediction all but screaming at you to stay away from me."

"Pete, I'm really clear on what that prognostication implied. I think I'm even more clear on necessary risks. The thing it might take to prevent any of it from coming to pass."

"This isn't smart. It will take 'complicated' to a whole new level. It's going—"

"You think it's going to put us in the same place as Phin and Esme. That history will repeat."

Her conclusion surprised him. Interesting. In the cycle of his life, so little did.

"Listen to what I'm telling you—that won't happen."

"It's wishful thinking."

"No. It isn't. You forget, I have my own insider information. Esme and Phin, they never have this moment. I've never seen a glimpse of it. Better still, I know how much she loves him and how much she wants him. There's a sad ache to her dreams, a hollowness. It's the loneliest part of Esme's world—and I promise you, Pete, it's not a part of this one."

He searched her eyes and the space around them. He looked toward the damn doll that brought more questions than answers. He only wanted to do what was best for Em. Pete squeezed his eyes shut. That was a lie. He wanted this more—for both of them. On this earthly plane, the impending moment couldn't feel more right.

Her fingers made contact with his chest, his unbruised shoulder. Desire was undeniable. He kissed her. Em's hands clasped around his face, and the note of expectation humming from her throat was hard to miss. In a life where Pete chose so little, he chose to trust her. The promise Em made about this being new history.

Time, which had always been a source of pain for Pete, became an exquisite span of pleasure. He'd never been so captivated by another human being, wanting to give as much as he got. Em was a tempting combination of desire and reticence, and as the physical moments traveled on, he thought of her. *Only her.* While Pete was unsure about giving in to passion, he couldn't deny the energy between them. And it seemed she was right—Pete had never wanted someone in this way. Not in this place or time.

Spoken words lapsed to unnecessary as communication turned intrinsic, the way Em touched all of him, the glide of her mouth over taut muscles and a body that had been through so much. A short while later, Pete understood his body and mind had never experienced this. Everything slipped into a beautiful rush of hues that Pete could see and feel and, damn—well, he felt like he could touch them. Trembling moments later, he searched for words, Pete's mind too overcome with present-day emotion to navigate the simplest prose. He trailed his fingers over Em's face. "If I said that was the most incredible thing ever, would it sound like a line?"

She appeared equally lost in the aftermath, her skin damp, pressed to his. She didn't answer right away, and Pete perceived it as an ambivalent pause. Maybe the fact that there also seemed to be no air in the room accounted for her breathless state. Or maybe her experience hadn't been like his. But then she smiled, fingers shaky as his, brushing along his unshaven face. "No. I think it sounds like the truth."

♦ ♦ ♦

Around one in the morning, Em ordered Chinese food, suggesting China Kitchen dumplings were the perfect post-sex sustenance. Pete happily went along with the idea of food. Act one in her bedroom had rolled smoothly into act two, and he was agreeably starving. But Pete refused to eat in her bedroom. He couldn't imagine the aura and sandalwood scents of her space drowned in dim sum and the rest of her order, which naturally included half the menu.

They agreed on the outdoors, devouring the Chinese food on the steps of her apartment, Pete shirtless, Em in a short floral bathrobe. Neither of them gave a damn what late-night passersby thought about their half-dressed state, sitting in a surround of cardboard containers and fortune cookies.

They crept back into the apartment, which was dark and quiet. Once inside her bedroom, they managed the narrow bed. Pete was too tall, but mercifully not too wide, and they made a nest of it. As she lay with her back to him, he got an up-close look at the tattoo he'd seen earlier. "That's unusual," he said, his fingertips gliding over a symbol he recognized, a cross with a looped top.

"You like it or don't?"

"I like the symbol on you. I've seen it in my travels—ankh."

"It stands for life," they said simultaneously.

Em laughed. "Well, I'm glad you approve."

"What made you get it, especially in a place where you can't really see it?" He kissed the edge of one shoulder, working his way down her back to the ancient Egyptian emblem. He swore it was warm under his lips.

Em twisted around, facing him. "You know, I'm not sure. It just seemed like the right spot." They settled deeper into the mattress, but Em popped back up. "Oh, the lights."

Faced with the prospect of sleep, Pete realized how distracted he'd been. "Em . . ." He kissed her shoulder again. "It would be better . . . smarter if I went back to the hotel. In the morn—"

"No." She rolled toward him in the tight spot. "You trusted me before—"

"Yes, but this is different." He glanced at his own shoulder. "You don't understand—"

She pressed her fingers to his lips. "I understand more than you think. Don't go by the past. Go by what you're truly feeling right now. If that's fear for my safety, fine. But if it's not . . ."

In the soft glow of light, the sure look on her face gave Pete confidence. He did feel different from any other night when the lights went out. The past did not echo in his head. Gingerly—protectively—he tucked an arm around her. It truly did feel like in the hours to come, Peter St John would be in control.

Em leaned over and shut off the string of globe lights. She yawned sleepily, her lack of trepidation marked. "You're going to sleep well, Pete."

He was already drifting, too exhausted, too tempted by rest to reply. A strong sense of belonging dominated his more relaxed mind, grounding Pete to a narrow bed in a tiny room in New York City. Only one distant reflective thought tagged along. Pete wondered if, despite the trauma of Esme, Phineas Seaborn had found the same peace that suddenly, miraculously appeared to be a part of his world.

He'd always despised January.

It was the month his parents had left him in the bitter-cold front hall of the Children's Aid Society. They gave their son away like the useless ash of a burn barrel.

January.

The month when a gang of ill-tempered, equally mistreated boys had locked him in a freezing, rat-filled outhouse.

January.

It'd been the month, a year ago, when Germans had taken advantage of disorganized British and Allied troops, shooting men like ducks in a Luna Park gallery, his division obliterated.

January. No, he'd never had much luck with the start of a new year.

Sitting on the deck of the battleship *Florida*, icy sleet hit Phin's face. He fought off the foreboding feel of the January into which he now sailed.

His mind wouldn't relent. He'd noticed this since the war had gone dead; he wasn't able to do much but relive the past. His brain couldn't navigate out of it, though for certain the war had ended. Seventeen months of blood-soaked battles, he supposed there might be an aftereffect. He shifted uncomfortably. Beneath a wet wool blanket, Phin ran his hand over an internal knot in his stomach, the shrapnel a souvenir from the Battle of Somme. He'd barely spoken on the voyage back to the States, though he did huddle tighter into the men beside him, trying to draw warmth.

His breath wafted like smoke on air, and Phin thought of two winters ago. How he and Hassan had nearly frozen to death in the butcher-shop shanty. *Hassan.* Phin had seen his friend briefly, not far outside Belleau Wood. Each was amazed to find the other alive, each gripped by the other's tale. They'd excelled in a war where both surely should have perished. Phin closed his eyes and tried to picture the brave Indian, but he could only see gore—the gruesome, never-ending battles, slaughtered men and horses.

Next to him on the ship was a tarp. Phin shifted the canvas covering to pet the sleek English saddle. Traveller, a steely draft horse, had taken a shell to his right flank, broken his cannon bone. Phin squeezed his eyes shut. For all the ravages of war, the memory of having put down his own horse was perhaps most excruciating. Phin had almost given up that day, and he closed his eyes again, imagining the person who'd kept him alive—Esme. His bearded chin shuddered.

Phin hadn't heard from her since before Armistice Day, when the war had stopped on paper. For another month, he and his last division hunted rogue Germans, who continued to fight regardless of peace. His final memory of war was putting his sword through the eye of a pinned enemy solider, one who screamed hysterically at him in German. Well, in such a moment, who wouldn't? After the fact, another German, who'd surrendered in English, told Phin that's what the dead soldier had been yelling: *"Ich gabe auf!" "I give up!"*

He shivered at his actions—how killing the enemy could so seamlessly turn into killing a man. His mind carried the weight of a thousand dead soldiers. He forced his thoughts back to Esme. When Phin's division was stationed in Aisne, he'd look anxiously for Maree, hoping she'd come with mail. The young farm girl, with her dark hair and shy smile, had been the timid sort, and Phin thought this was why she'd been so successful passing messages from division to division. When she brought personal mail, Maree would say in broken English, "Another love letter from Miss Moon, I think. Could I please see her photograph again?"

Phin would produce the now-dirt-stained, bent image—a copy of the photo he'd taken at Luna Park. Esme posed on a chaise, flowers in her arm, a coy smile on her lips. The girl he loved, the girl he hoped still waited for him. Maree would gasp as if he'd shown her heaven, saying, "She looks like an angel."

An angel that, perhaps, had fled from his war-ravaged, earth-bound self.

The horn from the ship blasted Phin from his worries, and to his left he could just make out the Statue of Liberty. The ship turned right, toward the harbor. As it docked, Phin rose and searched the crowds for Esme. Of course, she didn't know he was aboard this ship, and he tried to comfort himself with that.

He made his way through the hordes of gushing wives and sweethearts, a duffel bag over his shoulder and the heavy saddle on his arm. But as Phin moved toward the Upper East Side, he knew the weightiest burden was on his mind. He was covered in more sweat than sleet by the time he passed by Forty-Sixth and Seventh Avenues. Mercifully, he came upon the *Tribune*'s main office. Inside, he was surprised to find his name a known thing, clippings of the photos he'd taken, images he'd drawn pinned to nearly every wall. Phin was stunned.

Clive Baxter, one of the editors, moved faster than his printing presses. This was the same editor who'd been hesitant about giving Phin a shot at the ill Charlie Carlisle's beat. Now Clive approached Phin with reverence, shaking his hand enthusiastically and offering him a job on the spot. "Pick your beat, Seaborn. The *Tribune* would be honored to have you on board."

Phin was startled by the fuss and thanked the editor vaguely, asking if he could store the saddle for a time. Clive said he'd guard the saddle like gold, suggesting that Phin could pose on it. Perhaps they could commandeer a city police officer's horse, put Phin in uniform, and stage an entire scene for the war hero's homecoming. "What war hero?" Phin asked. Clive slapped him on the back, saying he was glad to see many battles had not ruffled Phin's witty humor.

Phin could not say how Clive Baxter recalled his name, never mind his humor, but he did accept the editor's hospitality. Phin glanced back as he left the newspaper office. Employees were gathered around the saddle like it contained secret plans for a German assault. The greeting and scene were a puzzlement. But maybe it would all work out. A job. Yes. If Esme had second thoughts, surely a job at the *Tribune* would sway her.

Phin approached the supper club, and his gut clenched harder than it had when riding into the Battle of Belleau Wood. More so than when he'd crawled on his belly through mortar fire in Saint-Mihiel, all to capture war through a lens. Foreboding came to fruition when he saw the club's boarded windows, the hotel clearly defunct. He looked around the street. Many of the surrounding buildings looked the same, but some were business as usual. He supposed this was how postwar America looked—sleepily rising from a snowy drift, as opposed to cities abroad, now cavities in the earth.

He crossed the street to where a tiny shoemaker's shop was located. An Italian called Papi worked there and lived above it with his wife. On evenings when Phin waited for Esme to finish her show, he'd chat with the old man, who sat out front, smoking cigarettes and sipping whiskey.

"Papi," Phin said, going into the shop. The old man turned from a grinding wheel. On sight, he dropped the boot he'd been repairing, hurrying around to greet Phin. Again, it seemed he'd transformed from ruffian to war hero. Phin quickly accepted the accolades and pressed the old man for information about the supper club.

"They closed it all months ago, the club and hotel. With blackouts and curfews, there were no customers to booze it up and be entertained." He smiled a toothless grin. "As it was, we've lived on bread and cheese, used candles at night. But things are settling down. Soon life will be the same. The club is not like shoes. It takes longer for people to need a party for no reason."

"The girl who lived there—Esme." Phin pointed as if the building were difficult to see. The old man's face was confused, wrinkle over wrinkle. "Esmerelda Moon," Phin said louder. "She sang at the supper club before moving on to the Palace."

"Yes . . . yes." Papi tapped grease-covered fingers to his head. "The pretty girl with the calla-lily hair."

Phin recalled the window boxes the shoemaker's wife kept out front. There were, indeed, peach-drenched lilies, the color of Esme's hair. "Her. Have you seen her?"

He frowned, shaking his head of thick white hair. "No. Not in months. I didn't know she'd moved on to the Palace." He laughed, gripping his hand around Phin's arm. "But if she did, this seems like a right thing—for a war hero to end up with a songstress who performs on New York's grandest stage."

"When was the last time you saw anybody at the supper club, coming or going?"

"Oh, a while now. Once it closed and they let all the help go . . . well, on occasion I see young Hupp. I think he comes to check the property."

"Hupp. He hasn't been gone like me, shipped overseas?"

"Heir to the Hupp fortune? Overseas?" He laughed. "For a savvy warrior, I see you still need to learn a thing or two about life. Young Hupp never left the country. I heard he was sent to our nation's capital, but even that was *corto*. He's been back in the city for months. Like I said—"

"Thank you, Papi." Phin sprinted from the shoemaker's shop, dodging heavy traffic. Motor vehicles had doubled since he'd been gone. Horns honked as a car swerved. The driver yelled obscenities, and Phin was glad to know "war hero" did not glow from him like a lighted sandwich board. At the front entrance to the supper club, he pulled hard at the handle, but the door was heavy and the lock solid.

Where was she? Why had Esme stopped writing? He'd resisted, but Phin had to entertain the obvious: she'd thrown him over for the sure life that Benjamin Hupp offered. Why the hell hadn't he insisted on a marriage before he left? A fifteen-minute city hall ceremony; that's all it would have taken. No. He'd been too proud—he refused to have Esme marry a pauper who'd likely die in a war.

Phin had almost gone to Oscar before he left. If he'd known the man had felt more than contempt for him, Phin might have. But he'd been of the mind that Oscar believed Esme could do better than a boy whose own parents didn't want him, street scruff who lived in a dirt-floor shanty on the poorer side of Hell's Kitchen.

Oscar. During last winter and before this one, Esme wrote about Oscar heading to New Orleans. That she'd been lonely and how much she was dreading another cold season. She heard talk of peace on the city streets and she hoped this was true. She hoped Phin would be back before spring. "I am, Esme. I am," he said like a prayer.

On the steps of the supper club, Phin tore through his duffel bag, coming up with a pile of letters bound by string, if not his heart. He broke the twine and riffled through, finding the last one, dated September 1918—she'd mentioned Oscar's plans for the coming winter but nothing firm. Oscar and his motor truck could be anywhere, with or without Esme. He fanned out the letters. A single postcard stuck out. In France, the postcard had made him smile again and again: in a trench during the Battle of Lys, and another, the Battle of the Selle, with Phin tucked under a tarp in the pouring rain of Hamel, where dead American soldiers were piled up not twenty feet away.

It'd taken three days for a wagon to arrive. The smell of the dead was so ripe and stomach turning that Phin held the postcard to his nose, the strong scent of gardenias surviving. He paused now, brushing his fingers over the tranquil bay scene, reading Esme's short note: *"When I spent two weeks on this beach, I didn't dream of you then. E.M."*

He remembered a different letter, one where Esme spoke of Cora. She hadn't gone with Oscar last winter; she was no longer rooming at the supper club's hotel. But Esme's explanation was vague, and Phin had had his suspicions about Cora. He stuffed the letter back in the duffel bag and took off toward Brooklyn.

In January, Coney Island was not the World. It was an amusement park of ghosts. The plaster forest of minarets that lined Luna Park was boarded up and abandoned, lifeless. It was strange to see the pounded dirt paths, where people walked elbow to elbow in June, so empty. Phin kept moving. Only one thing operated in Coney Island this time of year, and he aimed for the ornamental elephant on the horizon. He flipped up his collar against a blustery wind and stuffed his hands in his coat pockets. An occasional man scurried past, his hat pulled tight over his ears. If the men hurrying away hoped not to be seen, the Elephant Hotel announced their departure, the pink beast popping loudly against a gray winter sky.

Phin had been inside once. Old mates from his Hell's Kitchen squalor had insisted. They'd been tossed out almost upon entry—not enough money between them for one good whore. He'd been silently relieved. Pushing through the entrance now, Phin thought of the dirty louts—Archie, Ralph, Angus, and Floyd. Dead, every last one. Recollections of war and even its gutter rats walloped Phin's brain. So it caught him off guard when he saw Cora, her narrow face painted up enough to make her position obvious. Spying Phin, Cora leaped from the man's lap on which she sat and scurried toward a room veiled in beads. In a few strides, Phin caught up to her, grabbing her by the arm. "Long time no see, Cora."

She spun around and eyed him with new brazenness.

"I take it the war hasn't kept you from earning a living."

The manager was on them immediately, and Phin was quick to offer payment for an hour of her time. With cash in hand, the manager had no ear for Cora's objections, and Phin insisted they go to talk wherever it was she did her business. In a room just large enough for a bed covered in dirty sheets, Cora claimed no knowledge of Esmerelda's whereabouts. The two had grown distant, Cora said. She suggested that Phin be grateful not to find Esmerelda turning tricks in the room next door to hers. Phin had never struck a woman, and he came within an open-palm inch of Cora's face. The way she cowered stopped him. He apologized, staring at his trembling hand.

The exchange leveled and she became more forthcoming. It turned out that Cora, the juggler, had about the same amount of skill in the arts of the human flesh. Clientele had slipped in recent months. Last fall, Benjamin Hupp had offered her money to quit coming around the supper club, cease communication with Esme. She'd taken the cash and asked no questions. "I assumed Esmerelda came to her senses." She gave Phin a long once-over. "Surely she's agreed to marry Hupp. Do you find it that surprising?"

Beyond this confession and question, Cora insisted she knew nothing else. She did, however, have one piece of helpful news: last fall, Oscar had only gone as far as Atlantic City. All the venues closed in January and he'd just returned to New York. They'd avoided one another at the Elephant Hotel only a few nights before. Phin dashed for the exit, but not before hearing Cora's parting words hit his ears, "You're a fool, Phineas Seaborn. A girl would be worse than a ninny to turn down the likes of Hupp. If you feel what you claim, let Esmerelda go. Help a girl out of a hard life, not into one."

He'd reached the edge of Coney Island when Cora's warning gave him pause. Phin's icy-cold cheeks stung and so did the thought. He shook his head. *As if I should take advice from a girl who sleeps with her own bad choices . . .*

He hitched a wagon ride, heading toward the Flatlands of Brooklyn. Cora had told him about a rooming house on its edge; she guessed Oscar had gone there. *"Oh, he'd squat right back in those Flatlands if he could. If he and the boys wouldn't freeze their balls off. Oscar likes feeling as if he's the king of his kind, and that's hard to do in a rented room."*

After the wagon turned north, Phin had a few miles to walk, and he marched across unmarred earth. He brushed at his eyes. In this open space, he saw endless bodies and body parts. The stench of rot held firm to his nose—trench foot, gangrene, and dysentery. He closed his eyes, but it didn't stop the screams railing through his head, men crying out for their mothers and wives. Shell shock. He'd seen it plenty in soldiers, after battles. But Phin hadn't imagined it would follow a man back across an ocean. The visions walked with him, and he saw himself photographing shredded men, all certain to die at his feet.

Right after the Battle of Belleau Wood, his purpose in the army changed—or at least divided. A captain saw a drawing Phin had done of the bloody fight. A general, third in line to Pershing, was impressed to learn he could use a camera. Phin's second life in the war began. At the time, he thought this was a good thing. Now a well of guilt invaded—that he could do nothing but record brutality; that he'd survived it. That he'd caused a decent piece of it. Fate's only offering seemed to be a window of opportunity—capture the slaughter, pass along the warning: this should not happen again.

By the time Phin reached the boardinghouse, any justification for his actions fled faster than a deserter. He was a quivering mess. His legs were weak and he was having trouble keeping his thoughts in order. The boom of artillery fire reverberated in his head, the aftermath visuals of mustard gas crowded his sight lines.

Phin couldn't escape it, doubting himself. Had the compulsion to photograph war been about documentation or a sick desire to exploit? It didn't seem possible—not from this vantage point—how a person could perform such perverted tasks. Nothing lay before him now but a boardinghouse and empty field, but Phin could not settle himself in reality. Language eluded him. It was Oscar—smoking a cigar on the porch, wearing what looked like a trapper's haul—who made the first move.

"I see you took my advice. Good. You're not dead."

The march halted and Phin eyeballed Oscar, thinking that wasn't entirely true.

◆　◆　◆

Oscar explained to Phin that he'd returned to New York under the impression that Esmerelda was still playing the Palace. He hadn't heard from her since he left for Atlantic City. "There's nothing out of sorts there. Esmerelda knows I'm not the corresponding type. What's this about, boy?"

Phin's concern heightened after telling Oscar he hadn't heard from Esmerelda in months—too many months. "It's like she's vanished into thin air. I've been to the supper club. It's boarded up as if America still may come under attack."

Oscar urged Phin toward his truck. "One thing is for sure, we won't find her sitting on the outskirts of Brooklyn." He yelled up to a fire escape where Bill sat, smoking a cigarette. "Collect my bread and butter from the porch. I'll be back. And don't none of you be spending a dime on your cheap whiskey!"

Oscar's direction and the alarm in his voice told Phin a great deal. As the truck pulled away with the two men in it, Phin saw a stack of bills and coins on the porch table. He could only imagine the peril in Oscar's head that would cause him to leave his hard-earned cash.

On their way into Manhattan, they compared the little they knew. "I warned Esmerelda to think real hard before she took that Palace job," Oscar said.

"What does the Palace job matter?"

Oscar spat tobacco out the truck's open sliding door. "It was Hupp who got her the job." He spat again. "It was a bad scheme from the get-go, taking the billing and not telling you where it came from. Esmerelda thought herself crafty. And, I admit, when I was around last summer, it seemed to be working out for her. But now . . ."

"Hit that gas lever," Phin said, "or let me drive. I know this truck can go faster."

The drive into Manhattan felt longer than Phin's voyage across the ocean. When they arrived, the supper club looked as it did earlier—abandoned. But other signs of life stirred. More blackout shutters had been removed; people seemed to be going about their business. This included Hupp's second hotel, next door to the supper club. All its windows and doors were opened as if the place were being aired out.

Exiting the truck, Oscar and his heavy fur coat stepped in front of Phin, yanking on the supper club's door.

"Don't you think I tried that?" Phin said.

Oscar let go a few expletives and turned, looking up and down the avenue.

Phin mimicked the motion. "Do you think we should go find Hupp? As much as I hate to think . . . well, it could be Esme's made a different choice. One that doesn't have anything to do with you or me."

Oscar's street-side glance defaulted onto Phin.

"Esme," Phin said, "she's smart as she's beautiful. She's really never had any need for either of us."

"Don't be an idiot," Oscar snapped. "She needed me well enough in the moment. And it's you she wants in a more permanent way. I know Esmerelda Moon. Whatever's become of her . . ." His voice trailed off. Oscar stepped back and looked up at the rising stories. "This supper club is the only building still living under a war curfew."

Phin repeated the action, then looked up and down the avenue. Oscar was right.

"I always thought Hupp was a bit off his nut. Rich mates would call him eccentric, but this fellow . . ." He looked solemnly at Phin. "My roaming soul says he's downright mad."

"Mad? A spoiled ass for certain. What are you talking about, mad? Oscar, what do you believe happened to Esme?" And Phin realized that Esme leaving him for Benjamin Hupp was not a worst-case scenario. He stepped back again, looking once more at the well-secured building. "We're getting inside one way or another."

Phin flew around the alleyway with Oscar tight on his heels. He looked up to the room where Esmerelda had lived. Like all the other supper club windows, it was sealed off. The kitchen entrance was bolted too, tighter than the front door. "There's one more door," Oscar said. "They stocked the bar from the back."

The two raced to the rear of the alley, where a slim path separated the buildings. Phin turned and kicked at a corner brick, already loose from its mortar. Grabbing it, he beat on the lock like he'd pounded many a German's head. Oscar hissed at him to slow down. The invasion was over.

"Like hell," he said through gritted teeth, fiercely hitting the lock. "If she's in here, the invasion's only begun."

"Phin." The sound of Oscar saying his name seized Phin's attention, and he stopped. "Look here." Next to the door was a window, the only one without a shutter. Phin put the brick right through it, undoing the lock. It creaked against the cold but opened. The two men climbed through, Oscar barely fitting. The pair ran down a back hall and into the supper club's kitchen, where tiny shutter cracks left a stepping-stone path of light.

"This way," Phin said. In the main lobby, they were confronted by darkness. Oscar produced a silver lighter from his pocket and flicked it on. On a table near the base of the hotel steps was a lantern. Otherwise, the lobby was like Luna Park, a ghost town, complete with sheets covering the huge mahogany bar.

"The blackouts," Oscar said. "They've really done a job on places like this."

"The shoemaker said he and his wife lived like the old days most of the winter, with candles and such." He blinked into the glow of the lighter. "He also said the only person who's come by here is Benjamin Hupp."

By this time, Oscar had reached the lantern and lit it. More of the room illuminated. Chairs were turned upside down onto tables, and the red carpet showed a spotted path. The mark of yesteryear's heavy traffic. Phin followed it up the staircase. The tight twist of space smelled like the caves Germans had tunneled through, shuttling their armies to surprise attacks. Phin was amazed by the resistant thought, how it dominated his mind. *Esme . . . I only want to think of Esme . . .* Phin shored up his focus and took the next steps two at a time. Oscar came up from the rear, the two men slowing in the third-floor hall. Every door was shut. The lantern light was low, but Phin saw it straightaway. Esme's room had an extra lock. He dove at it with more aggression than he had any German opponent.

Oscar grabbed him. "Wait."

"Wait?" Phin looked at him wild-eyed. Then he lunged. Oscar's size impeded him. The huge man caught him from behind, his burly arm locked around Phin's throat.

"Listen to me, boy." His grip grew tighter. "If this is anything close to what we're thinking, we'll want to keep our wits about us. We'll need to stay a step ahead of Hupp. That's if we're all to survive. It's something I know a little about. From war. From life."

Phin was having none of it. He broke free and slammed into the door, screaming Esme's name. There was only the faint meow of a cat. He backed away, terrified that he'd lived through a war for the sake of ending up in hell. A human whimper rose from inside the room, and Oscar pressed his ear to the door. "Esmerelda, is there a key?" The response was inaudible.

"Fuck the key." Phin backed up. Oscar stopped him again, his sturdy frame taking the brunt of Phin's forward thrust.

"This isn't open warfare. It's a single enemy—one with a great deal more power than you." Oscar stood opposed, a solid object between Phin and the door. "If this is what Hupp's been up to, getting out from under him will require more brains than brawn."

"Brawn?" Phin said. "I should think it won't require anything but his presence, because I surely intend on killing him. I disemboweled Germans whose names I didn't know. I'll have no trouble ripping the throat from a man who's truly earned my hatred."

Oscar didn't argue this point, but he did reach above the door frame. "We're in luck." In his hand was a key. "Killing Hupp will be your choice. But if what's behind that door is more important, heed the advice of vaudeville riffraff. A shrewd sleight of hand may win you a better future." Oscar's calmness was a mystery to Phin. He far preferred to put his foot through the door but allowed Oscar to insert the key. The door opened with a woeful creak. Lighted nubs of wax flickered. Scents assaulted him, something akin to the squalor of his life. But what Phineas Seaborn and Oscar Bodette found inside, it nearly obliterated two men who, until then, had survived a world of evils.

# CHAPTER
# TWENTY-NINE

*New York City*
*Present Day*

That night, tucked close to Pete was a feeling he'd never experienced—
not in this life. And not in his last, like Em insisted. Lying in her bed,
Pete had just woken from a sound sleep. Em's bare back was pressed
warmly to his chest, her breath quietly rising and falling. Five in the
morning, or so said her clock. It glowed with enough light to outline
the swags of printed fabrics and the doll, which stared from a corner.
The ghostly, glass-eyed baby pinged at his heart, and Pete wanted to let
it go. For once, right here, right now was good. He tightened his arm
around Em. From a deep slumber, her fingers did the same in reply. Pete
blinked. His mind and body were sleepy enough. But it was sound that
intervened and intertwined.

Church bells.

They weren't Surrey's bells, the familiar chime of Our Lady of the
Redeemer. They didn't sound like the bells signaling prayer, the ones that
often coaxed him from a foreign land and into another life. But like all
chimes, these bells reflected atonement, beckoning to Pete. The single,

steady chime he heard now belonged to the Church of the Resurrection. It was the same bell that had tolled a hundred years before.

The spiral began, a whirlpool sucking Pete in and under. The battle of a riptide. The kind from which a lifeguard might not save him. He knew what was coming; he only wanted to go back, get out. Segueing was never less than a blistering entry into another atmosphere. Escape was futile. But this time, a wraithlike entity urged him forward. He felt himself fall faster, the way you might in a dream, landing not in his past nor his present, but somewhere in between. The place where ghosts lived.

*"Do it, kid. Put the pieces together . . ."*

Zeke Dublin, Em's uncle, he was there, the same presence Pete experienced in the Rabbit Lane bungalow. His mind, his logical thoughts, struggled for an exit, and he waited to be startled out of what surely was a twisted reverie. Then he was mesmerized, his attention rapt on a scene he knew well. A scene he usually participated in but now watched from afar. Pete was observing his other life.

*"Take it. Find a set. This is your brass ring. See the ride through and the carousel stops. It's Em's prognostication: 'Today you meet Phin. Solve his troubles.' Assure her future . . ."*

Instinct said to fight, not follow through. Hell, he'd found Em—he wanted to be with her, not Esme. More than anything, Pete wanted these to be the only facts that mattered. It wasn't to be. He needed to finish it. He turned away from the daybed where two bodies lay together. Pete stared into the hotel room. It was dark outside. The doll sat in her chair. The clothesline drooped from the window to the bedpost. The English hunting scene hung above the mantel. The fire burned, yet it was cold. But this time he could see everything. His point of view wasn't limited.

A young man stood where Pete normally did. He waited—for Esme to enter the room, for a gun to be aimed at her. His heart thumped. Pete heard her speak. She'd never spoken in such visitant scenes. She was only a silent victim. But he knew Esme's voice from his most recent visit home, from hearing Em sing.

"Doing it this way, Phin, it's the only choice," she said as if offstage, awaiting a cue.

Panicking seemed like a good idea. Pete was so attached to the scene, yet confused by this bizarre perspective.

"Oscar's right," the young man said. "It was a tough agreement to reach in my mind, but it's best this way."

The speech pattern was different, but the voice identical—like his handwriting. Pete knew his own voice. He peered into the dresser mirror and his own eyes looked back. The reflection blurred, like fun-house glass, the young man raising a revolver as if practicing his aim. He lowered the weapon and looked toward the window. "The light's come on across the way. I see him. It's time." And now, in this life, the bells of the Church of the Resurrection chimed.

Esme stepped from the bathroom, wearing the white gown with the sheer sleeves. And Pete understood how much he loved her. No. *He* didn't love her. The man opposite his reflection loved her.

She was so pale and fragile, as if a blast from a gun would be overkill. Bruises. He'd never seen the bruises through the sheer sleeves of the gown before. Bells chimed again. Pete dove violently from the reflection at the young man with his voice, his handwriting, his eyes. For the first time ever, Pete had a say, and he screamed, "No!"

The gun fired. Esme fell. He caught her—or the young man caught her. *They caught her* . . . Blood filled the front of the white dress. She slipped from his unsteady arms and hit the floor. Pete felt the panic of two men. Then one. He blinked at Esme's prone body. He turned to the window, its curtains pushed to the sides. A man stared back. Someone had witnessed the whole horrid scene. From the other side of the alley, the man threw open his window. He yelled at Pete—something his stunted viewpoint had never encountered.

Instinct said to follow moments so rehearsed he could perform them blindly. He scooped up Esme, the fallen swan. To his amazement, when he moved to the door, the whirlpool didn't churn the opposite way, dragging him back. Instead, Pete found himself in a hallway. He knew which way to go, guessing he still had to get rid of the body. With Esme in his arms, he hurried down a flight of stairs.

"I can walk."

He stopped so hard on the landing he nearly dropped her again. Her eyelids fluttered, though she looked as sickly as the starving children he'd seen in wars a hundred years apart. Her fingers were covered in red. So was the front of the dress. "You can put me down. We'll make it quicker to the truck if I walk. I can do it." She slipped from his arms and tugged on his hand.

"You . . . you're alive."

She smiled. "Isn't it the point of Oscar's theater blood, his death scene, to keep me that way? We need to hurry. He was right. A few sentences of submission from me and Benjamin was willing to bargain for open shutters. Luckily, the day is all we needed to play it out."

Pete couldn't speak; he could barely follow. They wound their way down the remaining stairs and through a darkened hotel. Doing so, he was acutely aware that Peter St John was the conscious being in control. They slipped out a rear door and down a narrow pathway. Bitter cold slapped at him, but it did nothing to alter this reality. On the side street of Hupp's hotel, Pete recognized the truck that idled. The city was silent, air so bitterly cold that church bells seemed to not chime but quiver. Pete's eyes bugged as a vivid Oscar Bodette, wearing a raccoon coat, approached.

"Move, boy! Are you going to help her into the truck? There are blankets in the back. Cover her up good. Like we talked about." He looked past Pete's shoulder. "Took you long enough to get down here. We don't have a second to spare."

Esme's hand, with blood running through its veins, continued to tug on Pete's.

"My shoes!" she said as he helped her aboard. "Oscar said to make certain he can see the dress and shoes."

A lantern hung in the truck, and he silently obeyed the directions. Pete made sure her feet and the white organza edge of the dress over-hung the truck's opening. She wriggled around, adjusting the blanket. Her frame was so thin, bones pressed to her skin. The dress had a low-cut back, and as Esme turned, he saw a raw-looking scar below her shoulder. "Esme, did . . . did he burn you?" Pete winced, unable to keep from lightly touching the mark.

She stiffened and didn't look at him. "It's like the other things we agreed not to speak of, Phin. Like your war." Then she did glance at him, her grief palpable. "He's left his share of reminders, at least I can't see that one."

Because it was Phin who'd been privy to the monstrous details, Pete could only imagine Hupp's abuse, and he imagined it was much like the horrors he'd seen in dicier travels. He said nothing else and adjusted the blanket as she lay down.

"I can hold my breath if I have to, but let's hope it's not for more than a minute. Oscar wagers that he'll behave like a wolf does toward rotted game—he won't want to sniff around ruined kill. Let's hope the sight of me and the dress is enough. Now go."

"Go? Go where?"

"Home, of course. It's fine now. We know it's safe. It's a good idea." Though her words aimed at encouraging, Esme's shaking fingers trav-eled her wet cheek and dabbed at her eyes. He thought to reach into his coat and produced a handkerchief. "Won't do us a bit of good if the corpse is crying."

She took the handkerchief, and he heard feigned bravery as she blotted her face. "You'd better go." But she'd clamped her small hands onto his lapels, and Pete's gaze caught on the wool of a military coat he recognized. She managed to pull him forward. He knew the kiss, so similar to the ones he shared hours before with Em. "Like you said, we'll get through this—all of it."

"Esme, wait. Tell me where home—"

A man shouted from a distance. Oscar leaned his head in the truck and hissed, "You're going to ruin it, boy." Pete didn't have a second to think, barely to move. He jumped from the back of the truck. "Run!" Oscar instructed. "I've staged a murder scene or two, but I can't say I ever needed one to stick after the curtain came down. Now get movin'!"

Pete took off, but he didn't go as far as Oscar and Esme intended—especially since he had no idea where to go. Instead, he hunched down behind a horse trough outside a shoemaker's shop and listened.

"You there! Mr. Bodette! I've just witnessed the most horrific thing. We need to summon the police at once!" Benjamin Hupp moved along, wearing a coat over pajamas, slippers on his feet. Pete's jaw slacked as he spied the man from the *Tribune* photo, the same one from the alleyway window.

"I know what you saw, Mr. Hupp." Oscar's voice was practiced, steady. "I also know what you've been up to, keeping Esmerelda Moon a prisoner these past months."

Hupp stopped cold on the icy street. "A prison—I don't know what you're talking about."

"Don't you? Phin Seaborn came back from the war. He found Esmerelda locked in your hotel. Then he came and found me. It was our plan to break her out of here tonight. It was Seaborn's plan to put a bullet in you."

Hupp startled, like a bullet might be inbound.

"But the war . . ." Oscar jerked his chin at the truck's open rear, about twenty feet away. "It's turned him into a rabid dog. Clearly he needs a head doctor, because when he went in for Esmerelda, he brought back her dead body." Oscar stepped aside, revealing a supine Esme, her shoes hanging over the edge, the white of the dress puddled around her ankles. "Seaborn couldn't live with what you did to her. But he was too much of a coward to take his own life, so he took hers." Oscar hesitated—a dramatic pause. "When it came to Esmerelda, seems the two of you shared a similar obsession."

"I'll not waste time arguing any of that, but I do know he shot her! I witnessed it!" He pushed against the frigid air, pacing toward the truck. "We need to alert the authorities!"

Oscar met him halfway. "Listen to me, Benjamin. You and I, we do a fair amount of business together. Despite the girl . . ." He glanced over his shoulder. "I'd like to keep it that way. Part of the reason I came with Seaborn tonight was to make certain he didn't kill you. But what the boy did end up doing, it shouldn't be ignored. All I'm sayin' is think your method through. You'll have questions to answer. You'll have to explain that room up there and what you did to that girl."

"I didn't do anything to her, and you can't prove a thing."

"That part I might not be too sure about. Seaborn got his hands on a camera. When he came to me with his plan, he showed me these." Oscar produced a strip of photos. The moon and streetlight were enough to illuminate photos of a battered Esme. Benjamin ran his fingers over his mouth, as if seeing something shocking for the first time. "The police will want to know how she ended up that way—your hotel, your lock. Your boarded up building."

He stared at the images, then confidence rode his voice. "And what's more believable, that I did that to Esmerelda Moon, or Seaborn did?"

"It'd be my story, if I were tellin' it," Oscar said. "And it's likely folks will give you the benefit of the doubt. But there'll be suspicion nonetheless. For what?" Oscar glanced back at the idling truck. "To tell a story about a girl you considered a possession, nothing but your personal uptown whore? Benjamin Hupp and kept women. Do you also want the authorities wondering about a German lass, one who I'd be willing to wager shows no record of passage home?"

Oscar ran a convincing con. It was all Pete could do to stay stationary. He also wanted his revenge against Hupp. Maybe this was what his other life had been about—unfulfilled revenge.

"Let me handle it." Oscar placed a steadying hand on Hupp's shoulder. "The boy dropped Esmerelda's body the second he came out of the alley. I'm lucky he didn't shoot me too. He's that daft." Even from the distance, Pete could see Hupp's reaction: surprise, maybe fear. "I'll catch up with Seaborn," Oscar said. "If I don't . . . well, gentlemen have a way of settling matters like this. A cushy cell. Is it really what you want for the man who killed Esmerelda Moon?"

Pete's eyes went wide at the threat. It surely sounded as if Oscar was prepared to throw him to Hupp's wolves.

Oscar's hand stayed gripped to Benjamin's shoulder, the young heir easing back and forth as if weighing the options. Bolt for Esme's body, run from the brewing scandal. He stepped back. "Perhaps I should consider the matter until morning. You may have a point, Mr. Bodette. There might not be a need for police interference. Lots of questions. I'm capable of dealing with Seaborn."

"That's what I thought." Oscar patted his shoulder, releasing it. "In fact, can I take solace in the fact that you won't let this go? Not as long as there's breath in your body—or Seaborn's?"

Under a spot of light, Benjamin Hupp smiled, deep dimples beaming. "Count on it, Mr. Bodette. For so many reasons, Seaborn's demise will be my mission." He looked once more at the truck. "I . . . I can't tell you what she meant to me. I should see her. Sit with her."

"No. You don't want to see her like that," Oscar said smoothly. "It's quite the mess. I'll arrange a nice little service for her. I know an undertaker that'll fix her up pretty. Maybe we can lay her out right in the supper club lobby."

Benjamin curled his fingers to a fist, drawing it to his mouth. "Oh, I do think that would be lovely. Yes . . . very fitting."

"I'll keep you apprised of the particulars."

Pete shook his head. How would Oscar deliver that not-so-minor detail?

"Would you?" Benjamin began to retreat. "I'll arrange for the flowers. Lots of flowers."

"I'm sure she'd like that." Oscar looked around an otherwise vacant street, tugging the fur collar to his chin. "Sun will be up soon. It wouldn't do for you to be seen in your nightclothes and bedroom shoes wandering the Upper East Side. The truck, it had best be gone come daylight."

"You're right." He turned and Oscar didn't move an inch. Benjamin pivoted back around. "Thank you, Mr. Bodette. For your wise counsel . . . and your discretion."

"My pleasure." Oscar nodded at him. "I look forward to resuming business when the spring circuit picks up."

His gaze bumped from the truck to Oscar. "Yes. I'm sure we will." Benjamin's sigh was visible, the pained look on his face more fierce than January air. He turned up the avenue, stepping heavily toward home.

Pete rose from behind the horse trough, ready to challenge the cryptic exchange. But he froze as Oscar made a sudden movement. Bells chimed loudly. Loud enough to mask gunfire as Oscar Bodette shot Benjamin Hupp in the back before calmly retucking a snub-nose revolver into the pocket of his raccoon coat.

# CHAPTER
# THIRTY

*New York City*
*Present Day*

There was no terrifying spiral back to Em's bedroom. Pete left his other life and all the violence behind. He woke, not with an outburst that would have put Em at risk, but more the unsettled sensation of a complex dream. The way most people did, he guessed. Slightly disoriented, flustered over what he witnessed, but not consumed by the guilt of having taken the life of the woman he loved. In fact, blinking into the dim light of Em's bedroom, the thing most apparent to Pete was that he no longer felt like a vessel.

The emotion of the romantic and tragic love he'd endured for more than half his life was absent. His gaze drifted back onto Em. There was only the light of the clock, but he could see it—the small tattoo on her back, the cross of hope indelibly etched where Esme bore a burn mark. He lay still for a time but grew restless, eventually slipping from the bed and room. Pete paused in the kitchen and scribbled a note before exiting the apartment. A half hour later, sitting on the building's steps, he heard the door open.

A set of toes appeared beside him—shocking pink, a shade that both complemented and contrasted with Em. "I saw your note. Just needed some air, huh?" She sat beside him, handing him a cup of coffee.

"I did. Thanks," he said. "For everything."

"It's only coffee."

She looked sleepy, her thick hair askew. She wore a T-shirt, a revival of *On a Clear Day You Can See Forever* stamped across the front, and striped pajama bottoms.

"Uh, you're not thanking me for . . ." She thumbed over her shoulder, toward the building, her bedroom.

Pete wrapped his arm around her shoulder. "No. Not that—though what you said, what we did, it might have tipped the scales. You're not going to believe where I went last night."

For the next hour, Pete recounted events. How he'd fallen asleep with his arm around Em, trusting in her promise that the night would be a peaceful one. How that alone was a fascinating and welcome thing. He went on to explain that tranquil sleep had given way to a different view of his past life, revealing the details of how he—or Phineas Seaborn—had not killed Esmerelda Moon but saved her life.

Pete repeated the last part for a second time; he needed to hear it again. "I'm not sure how to describe it, other than a phenomenon born out of shifts in psychic patterns, the present-day breakthroughs we made. You," he said, tugging her closer.

"That's incredible." Her hands gripped tighter around her mug. "I didn't want to believe you—Phin—would hurt Esmerelda Moon, no matter the circumstance."

"But you also didn't have any proof."

She leaned closer. "I think gut instinct was all I really needed."

They were quiet as this century's Manhattan came to life. The sidewalk grew crowded, people hurrying toward their day, oblivious to a man who felt as if an anchor had been lifted from around his neck. Beside him a redheaded beauty who'd cared for and carried a lifetime of dreams. Both of them absorbing how it had taken their combined burdens to reach a singular revelation.

"So what do you think happened after that?" she said.

Pete honestly hadn't gotten past the moment, the reprieve of being found innocent while waiting on death row. "I . . . I don't know."

"What do you think Oscar meant by Esme *going home*? To where? We know Phin married someone else, the French farm girl. That he lived his life in Walberswick, England. So why didn't they end up together?"

He looked hard at Em, only able to interpret so much—it wasn't as if a ghost whispered the story's end in his ear. "Good question. But I do know, from what I witnessed last night, the things Esme experienced at the hands of Benjamin Hupp were horrible." He sipped the coffee. "Phin . . ." Pete still wasn't used to applying any name but his own to Esme's other half. "For sure he suffered PTSD. Not something anyone would recognize back then. Not in a way he could be medically treated. It's a sad realization, especially—"

"Especially after everything you've gone through."

"I was going to say everything they went through. But I can't disagree. Maybe the damage was too great. Maybe they couldn't get past it, the things that happened to both of them."

"No way." Em shook her head in a feverish stroke. "I don't believe that. What you felt for her, what Phin felt for her, do you really think they gave up after all that, went their separate ways?"

"In your dreams, there's no hint, not a piece of Esme's past that goes beyond New York, her life here?"

"No." She shrugged. "I've never dreamt beyond that, or I don't think I have. The dreams are all vague snippets. Nothing is ever in any kind of order." Em tapped the knuckles of her hand against his knee. "It's so curious. To know what happened to Phin and not know what became of Esmerelda."

"It's like half an end—"

Their conversation was interrupted, Caroline's voice rising from behind. "Emerald, I need an answer. My dad's secretary is holding two seats on a red-eye. What do you want to do?"

Pete squinted up at Caroline, who stood with one hand on her hip, the other clenching a cell phone.

"You're crazy if you pass it up. It's a once-in-a-lifetime opportunity."

"Can we . . ." Em looked anxiously between Pete and Caroline. "Could we talk about this inside? I haven't decided yet."

Caroline heaved a stage-worthy sigh. "Well, pardon me for attempting to shock life into your career. Do let me know when you've reached a conclusion. I can't believe you'd hesitate—not because of some one-night stand!"

Pete aimed at a retort, but Caroline was barking into her phone as she went back inside. He smiled at Em, who didn't smile back. Of course, it could be that was her impression of last night. Well, maybe not a one-night stand, but a singular night meant for the one-time purpose of healing his long-suffering life. He went with a safer question. "What was that all about?" Traffic from the building grew heavier, and the two of them moved to the side of the awning.

"Passive-aggressive Caroline strikes again. A sitcom director in LA is looking for a fresh-faced redhead to play the ingenue. Caroline went ahead and sent along my bio, head shots, a few YouTube videos. Seems I'm on the short list for the part." She'd been holding his hand and let go, regripping the cup with both. "If I want it."

"So that's great." Pete stabbed at appropriate enthusiasm. "You should be excited. I mean, aside from an audition facilitated by Caroline, it's all good, right?"

She hesitated. "Yeah. Sure." Em stared toward the pavement, and then finally looked at him. "Of course. It's, um . . . it's great," she said, her voice hitting an uptick.

"An audition like that, it's got to be a big deal."

"A sitcom with a major network. Yes. Definitely, a huge deal. Like lucky-lottery-ticket huge." Yet her smile collapsed. "Caroline caught me off guard. She told me before I came out here. Before we . . . talked."

Pete continued to force a grin onto news he didn't particularly want to hear.

"It's very unexpected," she said. "That's all."

"But it's what you want, right? To make it in show business, here . . ." He hesitated. "On the opposite coast."

"Yes, it's what I want." She touched her fingertips to her forehead. "Absolutely. I got caught up in the craziness of the past few days. Distracted. That makes sense, right?"

Pete was determined *not* to interfere with forward motion—no matter what he was feeling. "It makes complete sense. Before the disruption of me and my madness, what is it you wanted most?"

She took a deep breath and pointed in the direction Caroline had gone. "This, of course. An acting career."

"So that can't change in a few days because of one night. That's not possible."

"Pete, you're seriously not the best person to advocate for things that aren't possible." She smiled, and he realized it was her attempt to make a joke. "Anyway . . ." Em took a step back. "I'm being ridiculous, and any prognostication has been stamped null and void. Your past won't affect my future in any way. You and Caroline are right. I didn't see a lot of things coming, most of all a red-eye to LA tonight."

# CHAPTER
# THIRTY-ONE

Pete pulled into the driveway on Homestead Road. He'd left New York abruptly, but not as abruptly as Em, who'd dashed out to one of her four jobs. Inside the apartment, she'd moved as fast as she spoke—a hummingbird of flurry—changing her clothes almost with one hand as she shoved his camera gear at him with the other.

"I don't suppose a part-time job matters, not if I'm heading to California on a red-eye. Finding another out-of-work actress to write your name on a Starbucks cup, that's a no-brainer, right? No one will ever notice I was here."

Pete had nodded at what sounded like nonsensical thoughts.

"But I guess that's just me," she'd gone on. "I feel responsible. I take things too seriously. I get attached." Em had pulled a sweater on, inside out, over a summer dress and sprinted from the apartment before he could add a thought.

The door closed and he said, "Bye. I guess." He felt Caroline's gaze, perched behind him like a stalking cat. He turned, debating saying "Have a nice life" or exiting without a word.

She'd been sitting on the white leather sofa, painting her toenails while talking on the phone. "Oh, I'm definitely ready for the LA scene."

She eyeballed Pete, her wide ears poking out through strands of fine hair. "For sure, Em and I are out of here."

And that had been his parting New York memory.

Pete continued to sit in the rental car and mentally organize the past forty-eight hours. They were going to be tough to explain to his parents. He looked at the house. "Maybe even harder to get them to listen." Would his mother even give him the chance? He felt his odds were better with Levi, but he saw that his father's car wasn't in the driveway. Before heading to the front door, Pete flipped open his camera bag. Inside were the ruined postcard and the photos on his camera—the ones he'd taken at Hupp's hotel. There were also the photos of Esmerelda Moon from the Rabbit Lane bungalow. He picked them up—all cool to his touch—running his fingertips over her face, the beautiful and the battered.

While Pete remained curious about what had become of Esmerelda, his thoughts defaulted to Em. She dominated, and this was a strange thing. Quickly as Em had stepped into his life, it seemed she was going to fly right out of it. He got out of the car, no longer pondering the fate of one woman, but two.

On the front porch, Pete knocked on the door, feeling like an unwanted salesman. Aubrey opened it, looking shocked, not terribly pleased to see him. It was the most bizarre feeling to have your mother come at you like she'd hit you with a shot of mace, run you right off her property if she could. "Mom, just hear me out. I have something important to tell you." The screen door stood between the two of them. "The first thing is thank you. Thank you for doing what you did, insisting that leaving was the answer. If you hadn't, I might not ever have hit the right bottom. Found the motivation to figure out what I *didn't* do to Esmerelda Moon."

This piqued her attention, and the front door remained ajar. She was skeptical but clearly anxious, and Aubrey told Pete to wait there. She called Levi, who was in the middle of recording the voiceover for his next *Ink on Air* segment. It took some time for him to arrive home from the Boston studio. In the meantime, Pete waited alone on the back deck. His mother wouldn't even come outside until Levi arrived.

Finally, his parents approached. Without a word, she placed a glass of ice water in front of Pete and the two of them sat. Pete couldn't decide who wore the more incredulous expression.

Step by step, Pete took them on a guided tour of his past life. Everything he'd physically unearthed, the factual news clippings about Phineas Seaborn: war hero, photographer, painter, someone whose very life could be documented.

"Phin . . . Seaborn," Aubrey said as if trying to apply a different name to her own son.

Pete went on to reveal Emerald Montague's dreams and the doll. He spoke of Zeke Dublin's unexpected role and one last prognostication. He paused, the words of the note coming out of his mouth in a wistful cadence. *"Emerald, today you meet Phin. Solve his troubles. Where Esme failed, you must succeed. Don't let his past prevent your future."*

"Pete?"

His distracted gaze drifted back to his parents, who'd said his name simultaneously. "Sorry . . . right." Softly, he dubbed Em the caretaker of dreams, a distant but vital wayfarer in the life of Esmerelda Moon.

After detailing more discoveries and conclusions, Pete arrived at the climax of his tale. "It was incredible and unnerving, from the moment I looked out from that dresser mirror and Phin looked back. Then it was like we were one person, seeing and doing the same things. I was stunned when I was allowed to step into the hall, when Esme opened her eyes and looked up at me. I don't have any words to describe what went through my head on that city street. Everything from Oscar being there—wearing the damn raccoon coat—to realizing he'd orchestrated the whole death scene. I didn't kill Esmerelda Moon, but Benjamin Hupp certainly would have. He would have hunted her down, and he absolutely would have murdered Phin."

"Wait," Levi said. Pete knew the tone. His dogged father/reporter would want to prove or deny every wild bit of the story his son had just told. Levi stood, hitting contacts on his phone. "Get me Louise in research, please." He walked to the far side of the deck, leaving Pete and Aubrey at the table.

His mother sank back in her chair. "Oscar Bodette shot him. Charley's Oscar? He killed this Benjamin . . ."

"Hupp," Pete supplied. He scrolled back on his phone to the dimpled, dashing image of Benjamin Hupp. "He looks like a player, even for his generation. Because we know the rest of Oscar's life, obviously he was never caught. But I'm not sorry if I don't feel like Oscar got away with murder. I think I'm only sorry Phin . . . *I* didn't get the chance to pull the trigger."

"Or maybe it was meant to be, Pete," Aubrey said. "Maybe Oscar thought Phineas Seaborn and Esmerelda Moon had endured enough life-and-death struggles."

"Could be. I guess it's safe to assume Charley never knew."

"Or she never spoke about it." His mother stared into the preserve. "I should give those old diaries of hers a closer look."

"Everything I've said, you do believe me, right?"

Aubrey answered with a sigh and a yes. The two spoke for several more minutes before Levi returned to the table.

"Thanks, Louise. Sure," he said. "A full vetting would be great, but that's excellent information to start. You're the best." He ended the call.

"What was all that?" Aubrey asked.

"Louise from research. She came up with some stunning basics on Benjamin Hupp."

"Did she? When Em googled him, she came up with nothing."

"*Em?*" Aubrey said.

"Yeah . . . Em. What?"

She smiled. "Nothing. Just the way you said it—familiar, relaxed . . . different for you."

"Anyway . . ." Pete huffed at her motherly observation. "Looking for information that old, what would you expect?"

"I'd expect I needed a research analyst with resources that exceed a simple search engine. Luckily," Levi said, poking at his phone, "I've got one at my fingertips." He read from his screen, glancing between mother and son. "This from a 1919 New York City police report: 'In the early-morning hours on January twenty-fifth, heir and socialite Benjamin Hupp was discovered shot to death in the middle of Lexington Avenue.' It goes on, but apparently his killer was never apprehended."

"That's amazing," Aubrey said.

"Why?" Levi took his seat. "Because the info came by way of human, documented facts instead of an otherworldly channel?"

Aubrey smiled and leaned forward, coming closer to Pete than she had since his arrival. "Okay, so I'm absorbing most of this. But why, Pete, why all the years of tormented reliving, the same scene again and again, if you . . . Phin," she said, trying the name on for the third or fourth time, "ultimately save Esme?"

Pete opened his mouth to answer, but it closed. He sank back into his own chair. "I don't know, Mom. I didn't say I had a resolution for everything, but at least I know now that I helped her. I didn't hurt her. That's huge."

"I agree," Levi said. "Aubrey, what is it you've said to me now and again, when stumped by the other side? 'I'm not that special.' You admit to not having all the answers. Can't the same thing be true for our son?"

Aubrey's gaze shifted between them. Pete lurched forward in his chair, snatching the word from his mother's mouth. "No." He pointed at her. "She's going to say no! I don't care what you say, Mom. You can't throw me out of this family. I'm not going. In fact, I may take a damn desk job in Boston or buy the house next door." He thrust a hand toward the Langford home, just past the fence line.

"Well, it's hard to argue with that sort of determination. And clearly it's been a world-rocking couple of days. I suppose all we can do is see where it takes . . ."

But her words petered out as Pete peered over the tall fence that separated the two properties. "Home," he said.

"That'd be here," Levi offered, a note of sarcasm evident.

"No. Last night. Oscar said Esme was going home. She said the same thing." He looked at his parents, thinking of hundred-year-old clues and what became of Esme. "Oh my God. It's not possible." Pete picked up his camera bag and scavenged through it.

"Pete, what are you looking for?" Aubrey said.

"Something Grace gave me before I left." He found an envelope at the bottom, wrinkled, nearly forgotten. "This." He tore into it, finding a few stapled sheets of paper, Town of Surrey letterhead. "Mom, have you ever looked into the history of our house? Do you know who owned it—say, a hundred years ago?"

"Not offhand. Compared to some homes . . . well, houses in Surrey date back to the early 1700s. I don't think of ours as that old."

"Maybe age isn't the point," Pete said. She and Levi peered at the pages, Pete running his finger along a list of names and dates. It started with the most recent, Levi's name being added to the deed a number of years ago.

"Rathbun," Levi said. "Odd name. Looks like they owned the house for a lot of years. Oh, I see how long, the sold date anyway."

Aubrey cleared her throat. "Yes. Those were the owners Owen and I bought the house from." She tapped her finger on the page, her expression softening. "I remember seeing the house the first time. It needed work, but it just kind of *spoke to me*." She looked into Pete's and Levi's faces. "Oh, come on. 'Spoke to me' like the average person says. You know, like an outfit you have to have, a piece of abstract art." She rolled her eyes at them. "Not everything has a psychic translation, guys.

Sometimes I do have a response to things not induced by the spiritual world."

"In my experience," Levi said, "that's a damn short list. If you think about it, I'm not even on it."

"Don't be ridiculous. We would have ended up together regardless of Missy Flannigan . . ." She hesitated. "Or your brother." She gave him a queer look. "Okay, so you're not the best example. Anyway, there was something about this house. I was so drawn to it."

"Mmm, and did your computer-brainiac ex-husband feel the same?" Levi asked.

"Actually, no," Aubrey said. "I had to convince Owen to buy it. In fact, he never even sold our Boston loft. I was the persistent one."

Pete flipped to the second page. "Look at this. Go back far enough and the records are handwritten photocopies. It notes here, 'Deed transferred to Lowell Slade, March 8, 1915, formerly of Penacook, New Hampshire.' Reads to me like he was gifted the house."

Levi turned the paper toward himself. "A gift. That's not an inheritance."

"Backward as it is," Aubrey said, "it might be indicative of the era. Men taking precedence over women. Property could very well have been something transferred from one man to another, and—"

"Property," Pete said, the word reverberating in his head. "Oscar said something about property." He looked at his mother. "So did Esme." He lightly closed his eyes, trying to will a conversation forward. But in the hours since last night, Esme had grown distant, if not vague—stars once bright as a moon, then all of it swallowed by a cloud-covered night.

"Property." Levi said this, and Pete felt the pages slip out from under his fingertips. When he opened his eyes, Pete and his parents were looking at the third page of the recording of deeds. "Elias Moon, he owned the house from 1896 to 1915." Blurred in the margin, Levi read the words. "Gifted to Lowell Slade upon his marriage to Hazel Moon."

"Home," Pete said. "That's what they meant. Here." Pete looked up at the lovingly maintained and modernized craftsman, but also a house full of history and secrets.

"Oh my God," Aubrey said, her fingers fluttering over her mouth. "It can't be."

It was Levi and his pragmatic logic that drew the mind-boggling conclusion. "It's not your mother who's exacerbated your visits to the past, Pete."

Pete looked across the backyard, his gaze traveling onto the vintage structure that had underscored his life. "The Long Island bungalow and a Manhattan scavenger hunt, they were clues. The answer was right here all along. It's this house."

"And every spirit connected to it," Aubrey said.

# CHAPTER
# THIRTY-TWO

Pete and his parents moved warily about for the next few hours. He supposed they were all trying to process information in their own way. It was a difficult trick, being as the house surrounded them. Pete ended up alone on the porch. Dusk was closing in as he swung passively on the swing, staring, not at the front yard, but at the house's siding. A wiry shadow rose, the image of a juddering, hunched-over reaper with a thousand moving fingers. The figure grew more intense on the pewter-colored clapboard. Pete stopped swinging, then he sighed, shaking his head. It was only the sun dipping behind the front yard's red maple, a spooky display of peek-a-boo light and stray clouds.

Humor subsided, and he sat a little longer, trying to untangle a lifetime of crossed ethereal wires. In the meantime, Levi called Louise again and Aubrey texted Grace. His parents put one strong-willed woman in touch with another, with both women combining their resources. A short time later, Pete sat up straighter, seeing Grace's blue Prius gliding into the driveway. She came up the front walk with a folder in her arm.

"Hello, Pete."

"Grace. Thank you for coming . . . for helping."

"No matter our past, you know I couldn't resist the idea of helping you resolve yours. Naturally, I was surprised to hear you were back. After the way you left . . ." She paused. "Well, when Aubrey told me the whole story, it's just amazing." Her gaze ticked along the frame of the now-suspect house. "By the way, that's some research guru Levi has working for him."

"I've heard him talk about Louise. Apparently her skills nearly fall into the sixth sense category. So the two of you were able to put something together?"

"I'd say so. I supplied her with what I knew and helped with additional Surrey info. Within an hour we managed to . . ." She sat in one of the vintage metal chairs. "Well, just wait until you see."

"Let me get my parents." But as Pete stood to retrieve them, Aubrey and Levi came outside, saying hello to Grace and thanking her for dropping everything and teaming up with Louise.

"Really," she said. "I didn't mind at all."

His mother sat in the empty chair. It was a slow sink, running her fingers through her hair and looking out into the yard.

"Mom, are you all right?"

"Yes. I think so."

"Aubrey?" Levi said.

"It's nothing." She glanced at Pete, then Levi. "Actually, physically, I feel better than I have in a good long while. But there's something . . ." She pressed her fingers to her forehead. "A presence has been batting at me since Pete arrived home. It's weak but adamant, like a bird fluttering its wings against glass." She shook her head. "I can't identify it. It's just . . . *there*." She glanced at the folder. "Grace, please go on."

"Like I was telling Pete, it was really all Louise. She's amazing!"

"She is," Levi said. "Louise is expert at tracing genealogy. She worked for Scotland Yard and headed one of those website ancestry services before ending up in my office. She wanted a narrower framework for her skill set."

"I see," Grace said with interest. She handed Levi the folder. "You look."

Grace stood and leaned against the porch rail, Levi taking her seat. Pete shifted to the far end of the swing for a better view. "Lowell Slade. It's his history," Aubrey said. "Oh my. This is remarkable."

"He was drafted into World War I. According to this, he died in the Battle of Amiens, August of 1918. I remember . . ." Pete stopped—his mouth, his brain. He realized he couldn't recall the battle with the clarity he might have a week ago.

"He was drafted," Grace said, "but according to Louise, records indicate he died of trench foot. She said it was quite unusual, not to get the disease, but to die from it. Men who did, it was widely believed they spent so much time hiding in trenches and foxholes their trench foot went untreated, going from gangrene to death." She glanced at the house. "Sorry to say it, but I don't think the house's former owner was anybody to brag about."

"What about Hazel Moon, Elias?" Aubrey asked.

"Was there any mention of Esme?" Pete said, aiming at the question that perplexed him most.

"We did find a record of her birth, which you'd already surmised— right here in Surrey. There was even a record of her high school graduation." Grace leaned forward and sifted beneath the papers to produce a photocopied image, which she handed to Pete. It was faintly warm to his touch. "She graduated in 1914 from Davis Thayer. That was Surrey's old high school." The facsimile photo depicted a small group of young men and women, all similarly dressed.

"Esme." Pete immediately pointed to a girl in the middle row. She wore a simple white dress, a giant bow at the back of her hair. Photos of her, while still an amazing sight, didn't deliver the wallop of emotion he'd felt over the years. It was melancholy, reverence—the feeling of having fallen out of love with someone. He looked back at the photo and at Grace. "There's no death record for her?"

She shook her head. "None that Louise or I could locate. The father, Elias, he died in 1918, a combination of alcoholism and flu."

"Of what?" Levi said.

"Remember, this was at the tail end of the great pandemic. Surrey actually kept a record of people who had the flu and lived, and those who died. It's what killed Esme's mother in 1914, prepandemic, and I guess a full determination couldn't be made on her father, so it lists both."

"And the sister?" Aubrey asked.

"Her records were the most complete. We found Hazel Slade listed as having had the flu in early 1919, but she doesn't die until 1968, when the house is sold to a family named—"

"Rathbun," Aubrey said.

"That's right." Grace shifted her shoulders. "So for as much as I've brought you intriguing information, I didn't figure out what everybody really wants to know—what happened to Esmerelda Moon." She glanced at Pete. "I guess I fell short again."

Levi and Aubrey traded a glance. They thanked Grace profusely, took the folder she brought, and disappeared from the porch into the house.

Grace flashed an uncomfortable smile at Pete. "I see my ability to clear a room is in good working order."

"No. It's not that." Pete stood. "They're just overwhelmed with everything they've learned today—including the fact that they might not have to give up a son."

"So what do you do now, just spend the night? See if anything goes *bump*?"

Pete knocked his knuckles against the clapboard siding. "You know, I feel fairly confident it won't. I might not have all the answers about Esme, but the biggest one has been resolved. The thing that's haunted me. And now, with so much history here, it explains a lot, right down to why my mother was drawn to it. As for the house, who knows how the energy residing here—not my mother—influenced my life. The incredible circumstances that brought me to it." He paused. "Or the house to me."

It was quiet, Pete standing a couple of feet from Grace. Only the rustle of the red maple scratched the air, a breeze picking up. "I'm sorry, Grace."

"For what?" she said, though a tear rested on the rim of her eye.

"For anything and everything I did that hurt you. For putting you in the line of fire that is . . . *was*," he said cautiously, "my life."

"I appreciate that. But don't blame yourself, Pete. Not for that." She arched a brow. "For being an occasional ass—yes, that one you can have." They both laughed. "I went willingly into Peter St John's past. I suppose I hoped if we got beyond your other life, you'd love me in this one." She looked sheepishly between the floor and him. "Let's just say point proven—perseverance doesn't always win the day."

"Yes, but—"

She held up a hand. "Be honest. Loving me that way, it wasn't something you were ever going to feel. With or without the complication of Esmerelda Moon. You can't be angry with someone for not feeling something they don't." The silence grew awkward. "I should get going. I'm actually not done for the day."

"Why's that?"

"I have to get my résumé together. Louise asked me for it. With any luck at all, I might be working for your father before the summer's out."

"My father?" Pete shoved his hands in his pockets. "Wow. Well, won't he be surprised."

"I sure was when Louise said she was looking for a new assistant. Maybe we both found something positive at the end of this long journey."

"For you, I absolutely hope so, Grace."

She left the porch, Pete watching until she got inside her car. A light rain started to fall, day giving way to night.

♦ ♦ ♦

No one said anything aloud, but come bedtime it was obvious what was on their collective minds. So much adrenaline pumped through Pete, he doubted he'd be able to close an eye. He looked at his laptop for a while and found himself perusing social media sites—something he never did. He'd almost forgotten he had a Facebook page; his last post was more than four years old.

Pete wanted to contact Em, and he thought this might be a way. Wherever she'd landed in LA, surely she was busy getting a foothold on her new life. Maybe she was rehearsing for the sitcom audition that very moment, and he didn't want to interrupt.

Pete finally found her on Facebook—at least he found an Emerald Ailish. He thought to search this moniker after it occurred to him that Grace went by Grace Maree, her first and middle names. But whether or not he'd found the right Emerald Ailish remained a mystery. Her privacy settings were clearly meant to keep stalkers at bay, maybe guys like him. He considered friending her, but stopped as his cursor hovered over the "Add Friend" icon. The request felt lame, obtuse. Stupid.

For him, last night had been worlds removed from a "friend request." He picked up his phone. He could leave a message. She'd call back. They could figure out what last night meant. Or what it could mean to a girl who'd hopped on a red-eye and relocated her life to the West Coast. A guy most likely bound for unsettled regions in the opposite hemisphere. *Right . . . that works out all the time . . .* Seconds later, it didn't matter. A recorded voice hit his ear, and he held the phone out in front of him. "The number you dialed is no longer in service."

He tried it again. Same result. Pete pushed his laptop and phone aside. He was halfway to his bedroom door, thinking his mother would have her mother's phone number. Problem solved. He stopped. Given the day, thundering into his parents' bedroom at . . . Pete glanced at the clock: 12:18. It wasn't his best idea. Pete went back to bed, where he did nothing but think about Emerald. For the first time in this life, a woman other than Esmerelda Moon ruled his drifting thoughts. And whether those thoughts were about the wisdom of keeping her at a distance or wanting to hold her close, the only images in Pete's head as sleep came were of Em.

"Pete!"

The timbre was manly and loud. He didn't know if it was minutes or hours later. He blinked from the midst of a rousing dream—a place he wanted to stay. Em was there. It was soft and sexy and it most definitely didn't include his father's voice, which was what he heard. Levi called out again.

He threw back the covers and shot into the hall. Their bedroom was dark, but the light was on in the hall bathroom. At the doorway, Pete hit the brakes. His mother sat balanced on the edge of the claw-foot tub, which was nearly filled. "What the—?"

"The running tub. It woke me up," Aubrey said, her fingers swishing through the water. "There was only about an inch of water. I've been sitting here for a while, watching it flow in."

"And you didn't think to shut it off?" Pete offered his father a squirrelly eyed look.

"I asked the same thing," Levi said.

She smiled at her husband and son. "You don't get it. Shame on both of you." But her voice was calm, her focus sublime. Aubrey swooshed her hand through water, which had reached an alarming level. "It's the sign of a fluid path."

From the corner of his eye, Pete noticed that the toilet seat was up. Always putting it down was one of a few regimented behaviors his father had instilled. Neither he nor Pete ever left a toilet seat up. "Mom, are you all right?"

"I admit it's been a while since a specter got my attention that way. Enough to make me race to . . ." She too glanced at the commode. It was old-school ghost habits, spirit-induced nausea. Pete was familiar with the pattern, but he knew his mother was far more susceptible.

"Who's here?" Pete asked. Levi folded his arms, shuffling his stance. He remained her champion, closely guarding Aubrey should a specter pose a threat.

"You don't know? How very interesting that it's me she's sought out in the end." Finally, she twisted both knobs, turning off the spigot. "Esme."

Pete was stunned. He had zero sense of any ghostly presence, never mind the one who'd loomed for so long in and around his life. "Esme?"

"Our earlier physical discoveries, they completed the pathway, brought her to a point of closure. There's so much history here for her." Aubrey looked around the confines of the bathroom, though clearly she meant the whole house. "Much of it is unpleasant. She actually doesn't like to be in the house. Yet she's so attached to your . . ." She fixated on her son, but Pete had the impression she was looking at a stranger. "Your soul, the one you share. The person you once were. From the time you were born, the energy circling you has amassed, bringing us to this."

"This?" he said.

"Well, this moment. Esme's ending, it's so tragic. I understand why she's ambivalent about being here, making herself known."

"You know what happened to Esme? Tell me, because—"

Aubrey held up a hand. "Slow down, Pete. You know how this works. I don't believe she's taking questions. Not even from you." She smiled and paused. "Thank you for that much," she said to the air. His mother focused on the tub's water, then looked at Pete. "Apparently, Esme felt a mediator was necessary. She says it's too painful, even now, being so close to you. It was something she learned last time you were together . . . here." They all looked to the cracked mirror, which hadn't yet been replaced. "She doesn't want to cause you any more pain, Pete— she never did."

"She never . . ."

"She swears she didn't trigger your visits to another life. She says she doesn't hold that sort of power over you—that it truly was uncanny circumstance." Aubrey looked from the water to her son. "The fate of ghosts. Her past, it felt so incomplete to her. She only ever wanted to make peace with it. The life she came so close to having. The things . . ." Aubrey stopped, and it was obvious to Pete what was happening. His mother was working hard to capture a precise message. "Things snatched away from Esme by war . . ." She tucked a piece of hair behind her ear. "By men."

"Benjamin Hupp," Pete said.

Aubrey tightened her brow. "The brother-in-law. He was the reason she left home in the first place, went to New York." She sat up taller and expelled a breath Pete and Levi could see, like it was twenty degrees in the bathroom. The chill of goose bumps rose on his mother's arms. "She doesn't want to talk about it." Her expression grew grave, her fingers moving lithely, as if channeling through the water. "What happened here, before Esme left home . . . it was awful. But she says if not for that tragedy, she would have never met Oscar." Aubrey hinted at a smile. "And never met Phin."

"But did Phin just leave her? Was it all too much—the things he went through in the war? What happened to Esme in New York?"

Aubrey didn't answer right away. A look of surprise overtook her as she came off the tub's edge, and not of her own volition, dropping to the floor. Both her arms plunged into the tub, water sloshing over the side. As her knees made hard contact, a gravelly sound rose from Aubrey's throat. Pete understood the discomfort; it was one thing to connect with the spirit world. It was another entirely when they took physical liberties. But it was clear that Esme felt she had her conduit, and she'd come prepared to make a point.

Levi was right there, not pulling Aubrey back, but making certain there was no further forward motion. "Nope. We're not doing that,

Esme," he said, putting the ghost on notice. "I'm calling a realtor in the morning. Let the next occupants deal."

"It's all right," Aubrey said. Her body relaxed and she easily raised her dripping arms. Cautiously, Levi stepped back. "And don't be ridiculous. How unfair would that be?"

"To the new owners?" Levi said.

"To the ghost," Aubrey replied. "Like it or not, I believe Esme has passed the torch, entrusted me as the last caretaker of her dreams."

Levi groused, handing her a towel.

"Would you please tell me? She must say something about Phin. Was she devastated when he left, went back to England, married someone else?"

"Sad," Aubrey said. "She was very sad. Not because Phin left her . . ." She drew a breath, the towel lowering to her lap. "Because she died." Aubrey pointed. "Right here in this tub."

"Holy—" Levi looked at Pete. "You said that both Oscar and Esmerelda insisted she was *going home*. We know the sister had the flu in 1919. She recovered."

Pete's hand raked through his hair, squeezing. "In New York, Esme was so weak, half-starved, beaten—emotionally, physically. It was the flu. She caught the damn flu from her sister. After everything she went through, Esme came home to die of influenza?"

"The same thing you and that Phineas Seaborn recovered from," Levi said.

Aubrey dipped her arm back into the vintage tub and pulled the plug. It began to empty, the three of them watching the tornado of water. "A doctor . . . the sister, they put Esme in the bath. They were trying to get her fever down." Aubrey blinked at her son. And in her eyes, Pete knew he saw Esme's tears. "Phin, he was here, shortly before she passed. The doll." Aubrey tilted her head. It was her own smile, someone else's pain. "Somehow Phin managed to bring her the doll." She closed her eyes. "My gosh, there were so many people in here. So much commotion. Then quiet. One man is speaking. He's a stranger; he's wearing black. I don't know him—neither did Esme."

"Last rites," Levi said.

Aubrey's expression turned vague. "Maybe. It's all so imprecise. She doesn't want me to pay attention to it. It's too painful. She says, *I felt myself slip from a life my fingertips had barely touched. After everything, all our damage, it was all right there. Then our World was gone . . .*" Aubrey looked at Pete. "She knows how much pain it caused you, but she wants to thank you for keeping her alive. Not letting that day be the end of her existence or her story. You did that for her, Pete, and she's so very grateful."

His eyes were wet too, watching the last of the water filter down the drain until it was clear that Aubrey was no longer communicating with Esme's spirit. She was gone. The house was quiet, nothing but three living beings taking up residence. They made their way from the bathroom back into the hall, where Aubrey and Levi returned to reverent, needful sleep.

Pete wasn't finished, not yet. He too needed closure. He went back to his bedroom and got his camera bag, not stopping until he'd crossed the deck and made his way to their backyard fire pit. The night air smelled of boyhood memories, the only sounds insects brought to life by darkness. The outdoor architecture bordered the nature preserve, the fire pit surrounded by comfy pillow-lined furniture, a stack of kindling. In the drawer of a side table were matches. Pete unzipped the camera bag and withdrew the photos of Esme, the ruined postcard. The moon glinted off an object. He knotted his brow. "How the . . . ?" From the bag, he also retrieved what was apparently his own ghost gift. "Okay . . . wow. I take this to mean we're all on the same page." In Pete's hand was a silver lighter, the initials O.B. engraved on the side.

Pete placed the photos of Esme, even the one Grace had discovered that day, and the postcard in the fire pit. In the preserve, he sensed the soul of a grifter nearby. "Thanks for the assist, Zeke. For hanging around for my mom. For me." As if in reply, a breeze kicked up and tall grass rustled. "But it's time. Time to let go of a whole other life." Pete flicked on the lighter. He made a point to watch, to burn all the photographs. To take a different path, letting memories turn to ash, Esmerelda and the moon vanishing behind clouds and the heavens until they no longer echoed.

# CHAPTER
# THIRTY-THREE

Pete woke to his buzzing phone. *Em.* He wrestled a tangle of sheets, coming up with the device. *Flagler.* Pete answered slowly, not even sitting up when his boss spoke in his usual "I need it yesterday" tone. He came right to his point: a group of Middle East dignitaries was gathering in New York City. Pete's assignment would be to photograph the UN meeting and follow as the pool photographer on the flight back to Dubai. Certainly a shift from assignments in days previous to this one.

Well, a great deal had changed in the past few days. Hadn't it? He finally sat up, clearing his throat and his head. "Yeah, Austin. I'm on it." He packed up his gear and said a fast goodbye to his parents, but not before asking about Nora Montague. Aubrey seemed curious but didn't press Pete about why he was asking. She also couldn't help. Nora and Ian Montague were sailing the Mediterranean with his mother. Nora would be out of touch for weeks. It was disappointing, but what could Pete do in the moment? He needed to be at the UN by noon.

As Pete left, at least he was able to assure his parents there was nothing to worry about, nothing upsetting—just work. His parents stood in the dining room alcove, a bottle of pure maple syrup in Levi's hand, his mother having set a table for three. She picked up the third plate and said, "Of course. Your job. Well, at least a hug goodbye."

"I'll call . . . see you soon." Pete said this with brand-new positivity, looking forward to following through.

While Pete felt a renewed sense of family, he could not say the same about his job. He drove toward Manhattan, figuring he'd ditch the rental car at JFK, working hard to reenergize his war correspondent photojournalist passion. Hell, the past few days would throw anybody off their game. He'd be back in the swing in no time.

A few hours later, the jump-start hadn't gotten the starter gun signal, with Pete stuck in dead-stop traffic on the Hudson Parkway. Idling, he scrolled through the e-mails on his phone, including the press packet and agenda Flagler had supplied. It would be an insanely busy week. After the UN summit, the entourage was scheduled for a Middle East meet and greet, six volatile countries in four days. Because Pete would serve as the official US pool photographer, he rated his own military escort. It was an important assignment with inherent risks.

A note of somberness took hold. Pete put down his phone and tapped his fingers against the steering wheel. He shifted in his seat and picked the phone up again, retrieving photos from two years ago. They were the last ones taken with his parents—Christmastime, in front of their tree, a place where it was hard to differentiate orbs from ornaments. Aubrey and Levi had been so glad to have him home, even if it had been for a few short days and a couple terrifying nights. Pete continued to stare at the phone, running his thumb over their faces. Why hadn't he taken a moment, snapped a damn selfie with them before taking off today? The car behind him honked. "Yeah, yeah, I'm going." He placed the phone in the console.

Traffic eased and he wove through Manhattan, moving toward the UN complex. He looked at his watch; at this rate, he'd arrive just in time to throw on the collared shirt that hung from a hanger in the back seat. The car felt stuffy. He held his hand over the air-conditioning, which was blowing hot air. "Hey, Uncle Brody, what gives? You promised me AC," he said lightly. Pete rolled down the window.

City smells and sounds filtered in, the subways venting, the collective vibrations of cultures, the indescribable vastness of human forms. Pete was attracted to the idea of photographing all of it. But the UN complex came into view, and he darted into a vacated parking spot. Still, Pete didn't bolt for his assignment. From his hot-car perspective, he looked at a city that wasn't so different from the one Phin and Esme had lived in a century ago.

For as much as New York melded, there remained a glaring division of classes. At the moment, it was best demonstrated by a homeless man asleep in a building alcove, covered by a cardboard sign. A well-dressed couple stood feet away. They fussed over a tiny dog in a . . . *doggy stroller?* The juxtaposition was too tempting. Pete hurried out of the car, but not before grabbing his phone and the Fuji X100F, a tiny camera perfect for taking photos from a stealthy vantage point. It worked well in unpredictable territory where the obviousness of a larger lens might get you killed. It would work well here. Pete shot from hip height without ever putting the lens to his eye, setting the shutter speed and letting the camera do the work, capturing the right mood, the astonishing diversity found in a two-foot span of the world's most well-known city.

The couple with the baby dog and Saks Fifth Avenue wardrobe moved on, and Pete realized something else: his usual distaste for New York was absent. Like it'd been erased. He didn't get back in the car but leaned against it. He looked at his phone, scrolling through photos again. There were the stolen images of Phin's work and Benjamin Hupp's photo. He should delete them too. But before he did, Pete realized there was a photo missing. Images from his iPad had also migrated over, including the one he'd taken of Em in the fondue restaurant. It wasn't there. There was just a burst of light on the screen, like maybe an orb had exploded. "How in the world . . . ?" He swished his finger back and forth. The photos on his phone went from the *New York Times* archived images to the last photo he'd taken in Mumbai—a friendly pose with Dr. Kapoor. Pete's heart started to race; so did his mind. He was confronted by a sudden and sharp realization.

Zeke Dublin had narrated his journey, offering guidance, if not clues from afar. He was a ghost known for grifter chicanery, even in death. Years ago, he'd fooled Pete's mother for weeks; she'd believed Zeke Dublin was alive. He was crafty—and he was also Emerald Montague's uncle. Pete looked back at his phone and the street view of New York—crowded, bustling, disinterested in him. "No. It's impossible." A bead of sweat prickled on his lip, and he swiped at it. "I'm going to call Em—as soon as I have the right number. Or figure out what happened to the one she had. Em's just on the West Coast. We'll get back to each other." Until that moment, Pete didn't realize how much he was counting on intention, the idea of seeing her again.

His phone was slick in his hand. He tapped her number again. The same "out of service" recording played. He looked at the street signs, then in the direction of the United Nations Plaza, flags from the world waving at him. Fuck it. He was done with the world. He pulled a twenty-dollar bill from his pocket and tucked it in the hand of the sleeping vagrant. Then Pete took off running, away from his job, toward Em's apartment. She might have gotten on a plane, but surely there'd be a trace of her left behind.

The distance was enough to have taken the car, but with the delegation arriving, Manhattan had turned into gridlock. On foot was fastest. He raced up the avenues. After blocks where he mumbled, "Excuse me" and "Sorry," stopping briefly to pick up packages he'd knocked from one woman's arms, Pete stuttered to a stop outside the Greek deli. He was heaving miserable breaths. His lungs ached, but the damn deli was there. The same one where Em bought him a bottle of water days ago.

Thoroughly winded, he still managed to run the final blocks. His strides petered out as her building came into view; he watched until a man was buzzed in. Then Pete was on his heels, helping himself to the otherwise locked entrance. Several people waited at the elevator. He took the stairs, two, maybe three at a time, his long legs spiraling up to the third floor. The apartment door was ajar. This startled him, and he stopped in the hall. "Okay. Enough craziness. Even if Em's not there, her stuff has to be." He pushed the door open. The tiny apartment was nearly empty, two men standing in the center, holding the white leather sofa. "Where is she?"

The men looked at each other and Pete. "Who?" one said.

"The girl who lived here. I know she went to LA, but do you have a contact number for her?"

"That witch?" the other mover said, and Pete widened his eyes. "You need to talk to Manny. He's in charge. She was here yesterday when we came by to take an inventory. Talk about an attitude." He laughed. "I asked Manny if she was flying her broom to the coast."

"No. Not her. Not Caroline." Pete aimed for her last name, realizing he didn't know it. Why the hell didn't he know it? "Her roommate. Emerald Montague." He pointed to the small door on the left.

"No roommate here. Miss Caroline's daddy hired us to haul her belongings to a warehouse on Orchard Street. Somethin' about subletters moving in right away." He stared at Pete, who was blocking the door. "If you don't mind, custom Italian leather. It's kinda heavy."

Pete shuffled to his right. "Sorry. Do . . . do you mind if I wait here a minute, catch my breath?"

The man shrugged, the weighty sofa his obvious priority. "We'll be back for the bedroom stuff. Don't steal nuthin'." They exited, and Pete moved farther into the tiny apartment. He hesitated, then rushed to Em's bedroom. Naturally, it was dark. He flipped the switch. Something between a groan and a gasp rolled up from his gut. Empty. It was completely empty. Like she'd never been there. *Never existed.* The narrow daybed and swags of vintage fabric, the books and the row of tiny potted plants, the sweet string of lights. He turned toward the closet. One wire hanger, not a piece of clothing or shoes. There was no doll, no message.

"It's not possible." This went beyond anything he could get his head around—tragedies he'd stood next to, otherworldly experiences that would boggle the mind of someone like Dr. Kapoor. The idea of ghosts. It was a fact many people flat-out shunned—something Pete might question if he didn't know them like he knew the alphabet.

But this, the idea that Emerald Montague had been nothing but a projection of his weirdly wired brain, a ghost product born out of his psychic abilities and a fertile imagination. The proven ability to access another life. It couldn't be. And yet, as Pete stood in what he swore was her bedroom, he braced for one more jolt to his weary mind. He poked at his phone, and it connected to home. "I may be lucky to find out my own parents aren't ghosts who haunt the house on Homestead Road." But a second later, he heard his mother's voice. "Mom?"

"Pete? Are you all right, did you make it to New York okay?"

"I . . . I need to ask you something." He sucked in a huge breath. "Do you think it's possible—"

"Pete. What are you doing here?"

He spun around. His brain scrambled to adjust, and after a few seconds, he reminded himself to breathe. "Uh, Mom. Can I call you back?" He hit "End" on his phone, missing the button the first time.

"Are you going to answer me?"

"You're real."

"What?"

He squeezed his eyes shut and opened them. Em stood at the edge of the small kitchen, tapping a key on the counter. "You're really here."

She looked at him as if a metaphysical reply escaped her.

"You had a red-eye to the West Coast. The sitcom audition. Caroline." Choppy words were all he could produce. His heart rate wouldn't allow for more, not without the risk of hyperventilating. Pete ruffled a hand through his hair. Given his sudden upset, he thought hyperventilating might make for a fairly weak showing.

"I didn't go. I got the part."

"In California?"

"No. The musical. The one I auditioned for the other day, when you were here. The producer called after you left yesterday."

"Did he?" Pete was breathless, amazed by the feelings that living in the present could produce. "That's fantastic. So you're staying . . . in New York?"

"Yes. Caroline was furious, naturally." She pointed to her empty bedroom. "She said if I didn't get my stuff out before hers today, I could pay the full rent starting tomorrow. Not exactly in my budget, even with a real acting job. Fortunately, I didn't have much to move, other than the bed and plants, my clothes. Lucy helped me. I'm staying with her for now. Six girls, one apartment."

"Six girls," he repeated. "One apartment."

She wriggled her brow. "Why? Do you have a lot of guy friends?"

"No," he said. "Not really."

She smiled crookedly. "The apartment will work for now. I can sit on the sofa whenever I want, if I can get a spot."

Pete thought he repeated himself, saying again that it was all great or how nice New York could be in the fall. But he wasn't sure. He was too taken, too busy with the sight of a redheaded actress who ate like a lumberjack and made endless jokes to hide her nerves. A girl who had the ability and heart to find answers that had eluded him for so long.

"So you still haven't said what you're doing here."

"I, um . . ." He pointed lamely in the compass direction of the UN. "I came back to tell you what happened last night." He held up his phone. "I must have gotten your number wrong. I got a recording that it wasn't in service."

"Did you . . . call?" She smiled wider. And Pete knew he'd never seen a smile like hers. "So you came all the way here to see me?" She too pointed at his phone. "Let me see."

Pete held out the device, clicking on her contact information.

"Nine. It's eight, nine at the end. Not nine, eight."

He nodded. "I'll fix it. I, uh . . . for sure." He tapped on his contacts and made the correction. Then he tapped on his photos. "The picture of you I took at the restaurant. It's gone."

"Oh, well, that one's my fault. When you went to the restroom, remember I was scrolling through the photos from the archives? I wasn't crazy about the picture of me, so I deleted it."

"Did you? I'll have to take another one."

"Give me a few weeks. The producer of the show wants new head shots. As soon as it's in my budget—"

"I'll take them for you."

"You'll . . . aren't you hopping a plane, heading back to your photojournalist life, somewhere chic, like Paris, France?"

"I've been to Paris."

"What about the rest of the World?"

"I hear that's right here—June through September."

She moved closer. "And after that?"

"After that . . . I don't know. But I have a strong feeling your future is safe . . . promising."

"Because your past is no longer a threat?"

His arms were around her now. "Because you succeeded where . . ." He couldn't say "where Esme failed." It was too disrespectful for a girl who never got the chance like one that stood before Pete right now. "You succeeded where the past failed me. Everything, from here forward, will be brand-new."

# EPILOGUE

*Three Months Later*
*Surrey, Massachusetts*

Aubrey threw back the covers and rolled onto her side. Levi sat up and reached for the down comforter, yanking it back over them. "A drive," she said. "We could take Pete and Em for a drive up to Maine. It's peak leaf season. They might like that."

Levi was on his back, staring at the ceiling. He turned his head, and she smiled at his handsome, sleepy face.

"Do you know how much traffic there'll be on 95 today? I'd rather take them to Disney World."

"Please, you didn't want to take Pete to Disney World when he was six."

"And if I recall, he really didn't want to go."

Aubrey propped herself up on an elbow. "He had his reasons. He hardly needed a live character breakfast after a night in his own head. But now—"

He grabbed her hand, an index finger pointing at him. "Now he's free and happy to visit anywhere he likes, theme parks included. I got it." Levi kissed her hand and let go, propping himself up on an elbow too. "You know, my lighter, happier son is not the only thing I'm grateful for these days. Promise me you're feeling as well as you say, that it's not just because you're happy for Pete."

"I can't give you a specific diagnosis, but I'd say a buildup of negative aura was a huge factor. Once Pete made peace with his past . . . with Esme . . ." She shrugged. "Between the medical world, the backstory to *Outlander*, maybe Wiccan lore, that's the best answer I can offer you. Spontaneous remission of the most ethereal kind. But as it is, I'm glad we had the cleansing just to even things out on the whole."

Levi fell onto his back. "Drawing a line," he said.

Aubrey got it. There were numerous things in Levi's life that he could not deny, things that wholly challenged his logical mind. But when she'd invited a prominent spiritualist over for a sage-smudging ritual . . . well, he'd played golf that day.

She heard a squeak, the telltale sound of Pete's bedroom door. "I think they're up! Do you think they're up? Is it too early to make breakfast? I don't want to spook her."

Levi laughed. "Aubrey, if we haven't spooked her so far . . ." Levi sat up, hearing a girlish giggle. Aubrey smiled. She had to admit, Em's personality complemented their son's somewhat serious nature. For the few times she'd seen them together, Aubrey thought Emerald was rather smitten with her son. This weekend was their first "couple" visit, and Aubrey was determined to keep it light and fun.

A short time later, they were all in the dining room, Aubrey and Levi seated at the table. She watched with fascination as Em coaxed Pete into the kitchen, insisting that they make breakfast since Aubrey had cooked dinner the night before. She and Levi traded curious glances as the clanking of pots and pans could be heard, and Em saying, "You seriously don't know where they keep the coffee . . . or flour . . . or napkins?"

"I know we have pure maple syrup somewhere. I've been away. I'm catching up."

And Aubrey beamed at this. They were all catching up. Pete had taken a leave from his PressCorp position. The Whitney Museum in

New York was putting together an exhibit of his work. Along with this, they'd offered him a healthy stipend to pursue street photography—something Pete loved. Something far less dangerous than endless journeys through treacherous terrain half a world away. While he might return to that work someday, he seemed content, for now, to stay in one place. He'd been home twice from his more convenient New York address. The visits had been uneventful and sweet. Adding to this, Aubrey had booked a getaway to New York. Em appeared truly flattered that Pete's parents would be at her opening-night performance.

When they all finally sat down to a breakfast of crepes—apparently an Em specialty—Aubrey asked what they'd like to do that day. A variety of ideas were passed around the table, Levi trying to tempt them into a round of golf, Pete saying that a hike in a nearby state park sounded fine to him. Aubrey asked Em if she'd ever seen the sights in Boston.

"Not since I was little, but I was wondering . . ." She hesitated, biting down on her lip. "Last night, I had a dream. I don't know if Pete's told you about my dreams." Aubrey and Levi admitted that he had, confiding how Em had been the caretaker of Esme's dreams. "I haven't dreamed about her since . . . well, since Pete resolved so much of what happened to her and Phin. But the dream I had last night . . . could you tell me . . ."

Her hesitation concerned Aubrey, and she wondered if newfound happiness might be a fragile thing. "Tell you what?"

"Is there a cemetery in Surrey? If there is, that's where I'd like to go."

"To the cemetery." Aubrey dropped her butter knife, which clanked against her plate. She aimed at a quick recovery, smiling wide. "The cemetery. Of course. Why didn't I think of that?"

♦ ♦ ♦

It was a quiet ride to Surrey's historic cemetery, the acreage connecting to Our Lady of the Redeemer's plots, making it one sprawling burial ground. Pete and Em held hands, walking in front of Aubrey and Levi. As with any hallowed place, it took Aubrey's practiced skill—and she assumed the same for her son—to keep a deluge of spirits at bay.

"You okay?" Levi said.

"Fine. I'd just love to know what we're doing here." Aubrey stopped, and so did everyone else. She hadn't been to the cemetery in some time. "This place is such a maze. I didn't realize we'd come in this way." Aubrey walked past a few graves to a well-cared-for plot, its marker carved with angels.

"Someone you knew?" Em asked, following.

"Missy Flannigan." Levi bent to straighten a potted mum. He stood, brushing dirt from his hands.

"It's, um . . . it's a long story," Aubrey said. "That's how Levi and I met, over the unremarkable life of Missy Flannigan."

"Really?" Em said. "Sounds like a curious tale. I'd love to hear it."

"Come on," Pete said, tugging Em by the hand. "I'll loan you the book."

Aubrey said a short prayer as the foursome moved deeper into the cemetery.

They came up on a curve, and Aubrey asked them to stop. "Em, you might want to see this plot." Again, she followed with Pete behind them.

"Oh, I knew he was here. Mum had told me."

"But it's not why you wanted to come here today," Aubrey said.

Em lowered herself to the ground, she and Aubrey huddling close to Zeke Dublin's grave. Aubrey had made certain the marker was bold and noteworthy, kind of like Zeke. Engraved at the top was the Celtic symbol for family. Em twisted a ring around her thumb, and Pete said, "It's the same engraving as on the inside of your grandfather's ring."

Em touched the headstone. "I'll come back, bring some flowers."

Levi had waited at a respectful distance. He may have forgiven what happened to his son because of Zeke Dublin, but Aubrey knew he'd never forget. "So your uncle, he's not the reason we're here?" Aubrey said.

Em pointed to a section where markers were white and smaller. A blank span of earth crested upward. At the top of a slow-rising hill were two huge pine trees. They made their way up, and Em said, "Last night, I dreamt about a wedding. Well, maybe more of a marriage. I also saw those two pine trees." She pointed. "Believe me, if we hadn't found them here, I might have told you I only came to visit my uncle's grave."

Glances passed between them, and Aubrey felt the nudge of a spirit. One with an ability to seize her attention, more so than the thousands of ordinary souls that surrounded them. Her breath quickened as they approached the trees, a majestic spot and peaceful if one was in need of a final resting place. A voice was so present Aubrey was surprised no one heard it but her.

*"It wasn't last rites. For a short time—minutes, really—it was every-thing I wanted."*

"Oh my God." Pete knelt by the stone of a simple white cross. Time and weather had taken a toll on the engraving, but it was legible.

Em smiled. "So my dream wasn't without a point."

Pete read the inscription aloud. "'Born May 30, 1898. Died January 31, 1919. Esmerelda Seaborn.'"

"It wasn't last rites." Aubrey's throat went tight, her eyes wet. "Phin married Esme just before she died. That's why there's no record of Esmerelda Moon's death."

"Makes even more sense now, Phin's return to England. He couldn't bear to stay in the same country after marrying her, after losing her that way." Pete's knees crunched into fallen leaves. He reverently brushed away nature's debris, more leaves and a few twigs.

Aubrey wondered how many years it'd been since a single soul had visited this grave. She took solace in the present, the things they'd healed from the past. Thanks to her gift and her son's, and even her father's, the dreams of a young woman, connected to them by way of a grifter's soul, were never truly forgotten. They stayed for a while, Pete and Em saying it would not be the last time they'd visit the grave of the girl who'd so poignantly affected his life.

When they walked away, Aubrey thought about that, how all spirits and earthbound beings connected. She understood what an amazing, wonderful thing it was to know of the next World and to be a part of this one—whether it was random carnie fairgrounds, long-ago Luna Park, or the sleepy town of Surrey. Aubrey considered the incredible life she'd led, the ghosts and gifts and people in it, and how this would be the story she wanted to tell.

*I think most authors have novel playlists. It is the background music we hope you hear when you read our stories. During the writing of this novel, my son was performing in Green Day's* American Idiot. *I found it fascinating how some of this contemporary soundtrack, along with other songs, perfectly complemented my yesteryear love story. These are the songs that belong to* Echo Moon—*at least in my head.*

*"Say You Won't Let Go"*
*"Dancing on My Own"*
*"Not Today"*
*"When We Were Young"*
*"21 Guns"*
*"Good Riddance"*
*"Whatsername"*

# ACKNOWLEDGMENTS

Editors make books go round, and few do it as well as editor Alison Dasho. I had the chance to spend time with Alison at last year's RITA Awards, and that was a thrill for this author. It has been my absolute pleasure to have her at the forefront of the entire Ghost Gifts trilogy, and as we detoured through *Unstrung*. Her enthusiasm and wonderful ideas truly enhanced each book. Much appreciation and thanks to the entire Montlake team. They are an exceptional group, and it's been my privilege to work with them.

A tremendous thank-you and sincere gratitude to developmental editor Charlotte Herscher. Once again, she perfectly interpreted my story, offered whip-smart editorial advice, and provided me with the chance to write a better book.

As always, thanks to literary agent Susan Ginsburg. I say it with every book, but I am just as elated to be a part of Writers House as I was with my first novel. Many thanks to Stacy Testa as well.

To Karin Gillespie, my favorite and only critique partner, who earned what I consider the most poignant spot in every author's novel— the dedication. Actually, she earned a dedication about four books back. Having brilliant eyes on a first draft is imperative, and she has been this person for me since *Ghost Gifts*. Her writing expertise and clever humor are a one-two punch that continues to inspire me.

Research often demands a true expert. Sometimes finding that person requires scads of phone calls and e-mails to people who probably think you're half-crazy. Then sometimes you get lucky and it's the friend of a friend who makes everything fall into place. Thank you to Noreen Burns for introducing me to her friend Lisa Schaefer, curator of the Coney Island Museum. Lisa was incredibly generous with her time and knowledge, answering my huge questions as well as the tedious ones. In addition to the facts, she truly helped me fine-tune the setting for many of the historical scenes.

Otherwise, research took me on a summer trip to NYC and a visit to the Tenement Museum. If you're ever in town, I highly recommend this insightful excursion into the past.

As with *Foretold*, my sister, Christine Lemp, provided wonderful assistance with World War I research, helping me narrow the focus of the Great War, carving out precisely what I needed for Phineas Seaborn.

This is usually the spot where I thank Steve Bennett, founder of AuthorBytes, for putting up with my writing schedule. He remains my part-time boss and a trusted friend. This time I get to thank him for his expertise as a photographer (SteveBennett.com) and his assistance in molding Pete's life and career as a photojournalist. The old saying is "Write what you know." I'd like to amend that to "Find someone who knows what you want to write about, and who can't lose your phone number."

Horses. What I know about steeds is as fine as a horse hair. Thank you to Emily Vermillion for supplying my horse sense. She was lovely to take the time, and I wish her fantastic success as a large-animal veterinarian. Emily's mother, aka my BFF Melisa Holmes, once again came to my aid with medical research as we consulted and speculated about early-twentieth-century medicine and how it might present in a twenty-first-century character.

Thank you to Lucy Gallagher and Penny De Groot, my Walberswick, England, guides. I very much hope to one day visit a place they so vividly painted for me. Much gratitude to the Wednesday night critique group and author Barbara Claypole White, an exceptional writer and confidante. Along with Barbara, thank you to authors Kerry Lonsdale, Rita Herron, Camille Di Maio, and Debbie Herbert. A huge thank-you to my enthusiastic readers and friends, many of whom take the time to shout about my books on social media. It really is difficult to express to them how much they help and how much I appreciate their kind words, heartfelt reviews, and continued support.

As I write this, I still live in the 130-year-old Rathbun house outside Boston. By now, I think, the ghosts have proven their worth when it comes to inspiration. But it's the living residents who deserve the big credit: Matt, Megan, Jamie, and Grant, who never make me feel like the very solitary and consuming act of book writing takes anything away from them.

# ABOUT THE AUTHOR

 Laura Spinella is the author of the Ghost Gifts trilogy—including *Echo Moon, Foretold*, and the #1 Kindle bestseller *Ghost Gifts*—as well as the highly acclaimed *Unstrung* and the award-winning novel *Beautiful Disaster*. She is a two-time RITA finalist who consistently receives reader and industry praise for her multifaceted characters, emotional complexity, and intriguing story lines.

Spinella lives with her family near Boston, where she can always be found writing her next novel. She enjoys hearing from readers and chatting with book clubs. Visit her at www.lauraspinella.net.